HARTFORD PUBLIC LIBRARY
ROPKINS BRANCH
1750 MAIN STREET
HARTFORD, CT 06120
(860) 695-7520

A Real LOVE

A NOVEL BY

PORSCHA STERLING

GET LIT WITH OUR LIT EREADING APP!

Download in the App Store or Google Play
Text **GETLIT** to **22828** to join our mailing list!

3 2520 11040 7102

© 2018 Porscha Sterling
Published by Leo Sullivan Presents

All rights reserved.
This is a work of fiction. Names, characters, businesses, places, events, and incidents
are either the products of the author's imagination or used in a fictitious manner. Any
resemblance to actual persons, living or dead, or actual events is purely coincidental.
Unauthorized reproduction, in any manner, is prohibited.

PROLOGUE

THE BEGINNING...

"*B*aby, roll the edges of those shorts up! You got nice legs so show them!" Mona commanded as she reached down and touched the ends of her own 'barely there' shorts.

It was the summer in HotLanta, and the parking lot of the Westgate Shopping Center off Campbellton Road was packed full of ballers sporting their nice clothes and their nice ass rides. The hood's elite were shining bright, with necks, ears, and wrists draped with jewels, rides sitting on flashy and expensive rims, and pockets full of stacks of cash wrapped by rubber bands.

No matter what she had to do, Mona was determined to get her one. Being beautiful came with its perks and being able to easily snag any man was one of them. Standing with a slim-thick build at five feet five and 125 pounds with cool butterscotch-brown skin, the most peculiar gray eyes, and long chocolate brown hair that had a soft curl when wet, she was a dream to look at, and not only did she know it, everyone who looked her way did too.

Baby also knew it. And though she loved her best friend, she couldn't help the fact that she'd grown tired of always feeling as if she played second runner up to her beauty. It wasn't that anyone ever *said* it or that she had a real reason to feel that way, but she just did—Mona

1

was the most outspoken of the two, and naturally, any attention given was usually focused on her.

Baby was also five feet five but was slightly thinner than her friend at 115 pounds, leaving her lacking in the chest and looking much younger than she was. She had thick and curly natural hair that she kept braided in a long ponytail, striking dark chocolate eyes that sat well against her amber-colored skin, and a regal look about her that made her peculiar to look at. She was beautiful in the most regular of ways, but it worked for her, and she didn't even know.

Even still, when it came to boys or men, after having their fill of staring at her and wondering what ethnic mixture she was composed of, their eyes would travel over to Mona where they'd stay captivated. Which was why while she seemed to have a new boyfriend before she could even get rid of her old one, Baby had yet to have her first boyfriend and was still a virgin—a fact that she would blush at when Mona teased her inexperience, but something she was actually prideful about.

"I'm not out here to be showing my legs," she remarked, pulling the hem of her shorts even lower. She hated that she hadn't had the nerve to tell Mona no when she had suggested them for her to wear.

"I'm only here because you made me come," she reminded with an indignant snort. "I'd rather be studying for the test that I—"

"Don't be such a nerd, Baby. I know you well enough to know that you don't need to study anymore, and you'll still get an A. Plus, this is only Saturday. You've got all of tomorrow to—Oh my God!"

As if stricken by fright, Mona gasped loudly and threw her hand to her chest with her eyes pinned on to something ahead of them. Baby turned and strained her neck to see what she was concentrating on, nearly giving in to her natural instinct of fight or flight. But when she looked, there was nothing to explain how Mona was acting.

"What?" she asked finally. When she brought her attention back to Mona, she could tell by the all-too-familiar light in her eyes that her reaction was not from fear but from lust.

Here we go again. She slightly sucked the skin off her teeth.

"The guy ahead! That's Memphis." Mona gushed as if that was all she needed to know in order to share in her excitement.

Giving in to her curiosity, Baby scanned the crowd of people situated around them but ended up even more confused. Who was Memphis? And why should she be excited by him?

"Memphis?" Baby repeated with her nose scrunched up into a confused frown. Mona eagerly wagged her head and gave her a pointed look. Baby finally followed Mona's eyes, and her focus settled on a tall figure standing not too far away from where they were gathered, looking like the odd couple; Mona, the smitten prom queen, and Baby, the displaced and clueless college girl.

"Yes!" Mona nearly squealed. "He runs the streets." Her eyes widened, and her brows wiggled, letting Baby know that she meant this in the figurative rather than literal sense.

"I mean… he *runs* this shit. Ain't nothing dirty being sold in and around here without him knowing and approving it. He's *that* dude. And he's sexy as hell!"

With that proclamation from Mona, Baby turned to look at the man once more to decide for herself whether that were true. Her eyes connected with his face, and she was able to fully scrutinize the object of Mona's thirst, and immediately, her attention was held hostage by his bold and obvious allure. He was well over six feet tall, with dark brown, almost black skin… about as black as the night. His hair was cut low, but he had a head full of waves that made perfect 360-degree swirls around his head. Although Baby knew nothing about labels—that was Mona's department—she knew that he was sporting only the most expensive threads, and he looked utterly and effortlessly breathtaking in them. In fact, he did seem to take Baby's breath away as it seemed she actually forgot to breathe while looking at him. *He was just that fly.*

"I'm going to go get a Coke," Mona announced all of a sudden, her eyes still glued to the man that had stolen the attention of nearly every woman in a three-mile radius. "Let's go."

Baby mired and dampened her lips as a brush of anxiety came upon her. Although she felt childish for her reaction, she would soon learn that it wasn't her fault—Memphis had that effect on everyone. Next to where Memphis stood with his crew, laughing and celebrating the good life, was the food truck that sold food and drinks. It was immediately obvious to Baby why Mona all of a sudden wanted a drink, being that she would have to sashay her wide hips right in front of Memphis to place her order. The only problem was, Baby was positive that she didn't have the nerve to do the same with even half as much elegance as she would have liked.

When it came to men, she lived up to her name. Instead of holding the confidence that a nineteen-year-old, almost full-grown woman should have, Baby retreated into herself when in the presence of men that she'd found the least bit attractive. But looking at Memphis had her questioning whether she'd ever really found anyone attractive before, because what she was feeling after looking at him was an emotion far different from what she'd felt from the little boys who attended college with her. They were boys but this—*this* was a grown ass man. Baby was caught up at first glance.

Licking her thin lips, she watched him as he spoke to one of the members of his rather large entourage, seemingly unaware of how utterly irresistible he was even while doing the simplest acts. He smiled at his friend, showing the dimples in his cheeks along with perfect white teeth, and Baby creamed within her pink lace panties. Mortified by her body's response, she squeezed her thighs together and shook her head at Mona.

"Um... no. While you do that, I'm going to go and get some cotton candy," Baby replied although she had no appetite for anything at all. Still, the lady selling cotton candy was in the opposite direction from where Memphis and his friends were, and she was positive that she had the nerve to at least do that. Maybe...

"Okay, fine. I'll meet you over there once I'm done."

Before Baby could even acknowledge her words, Mona had already turned and was walking in Memphis's direction, her shapely hips twisting seductively in the wind, earning more than a few stolen glances from every man she passed. Watching her, Baby suddenly wished that she had listened to Mona's urgings when she'd first told Baby to opt for the short Chanel romper she'd lent her. It was form-fitting and definitely showed off what little shape she had in ways that might grab attention, but Baby was always more low-key than flashy, and given the opportunity to show off her ass, she'd quickly decline. Mona, on the other hand, lived to show her beautiful body off to the world. After all, she worked hard to maintain it and considered it to be her most prized investment, which was the reason she spent more time in the gym than in class.

As Baby sauntered over to the cotton candy stand on the corner, she couldn't help but sneak a few lustful glances over at Memphis as he joked and spoke with his friends. They all seemed to relish being in his presence and Baby found herself craving that same privilege. Leaning on the hood of an iced-out Wraith like a boss, it was obvious that Memphis was paid but Baby wasn't interested in all of that. His pockets could have been filled with nothing but air, and she would still be just as caught up by him.

"Hi, sweetie, what would you like?"

"I would like the pink cotton candy, please," Baby replied, pressing her lips into a slight smile as she brought her attention to the woman working the stand. She fought her desire to turn back toward Memphis and his boys.

The dark-chocolate woman ahead of her smiled back, her gentle eyes softening as she stared at Baby. She probably regarded her as a child... definitely much younger than she was. True to her name, Baby had a baby face that often made people underestimate her age, something her mother told her she'd learn to appreciate once she got older. Unfortunately, older wasn't here yet, and Baby hated being seen as a child when she was, in all actuality, almost a woman.

Observing her nails, Baby waited as the woman got her order together, but the image of Memphis was still circling in her mind. She felt silly... Why was she spending so much energy thinking about a man she didn't even know? A man who wouldn't even give her the time of day, honestly. Memphis looked like he attracted grown women who had it all together—prestigious models with full careers, designer clothes, hi-rise apartments and fancy sports cars. Not little girls like her who had yet to go on their first date.

"Here you go, baby." The woman smiled, unknowingly calling Baby by her name. "Enjoy!"

Nodding, Baby reached over and grabbed the cotton candy, deciding to push Memphis from her thoughts, and immediately stuffed her mouth with a huge handful of the sugary treat. It was delicious, much better than she'd even imagined, and she wondered if Mona knew what she was missing out on, trying to nab the attention of a man when she could be with Baby, enjoying a mouthful of cotton candy instead.

"It any good?" A deep baritone suddenly boomed from behind her.

Her eyes brightened at the question, and Baby turned suddenly to let the person know that the cotton candy wasn't just good, it was to die for. But dying was exactly what she felt like doing when she saw who it was standing behind her, looking her right in the eyes, his beautiful browns piercing hers in the sexiest of ways. The way he looked at her was an addicting feeling, but she was certain that he didn't even know the effect he had. His ignorance of how on edge he had her feeling, only made her stomach butterfly even more.

"Yes," Baby mumbled through the glob of cotton candy in her mouth, instantly regretting it when a drop of drool slid down her bottom lip. She wiped it away quickly, feeling the sting of embarrassment in the pit of her stomach when Memphis chuckled at her expense.

"I can tell," he replied and then pulled his eyes from hers, looking at the woman behind them. He gave his order, saying it with an equal amount of pleasantry as well as authority, and Baby eyed him, mystified by this sort of man who operated with a level of confidence she'd never seen before.

For some reason, Baby felt cemented to the ground and couldn't move. It seemed like he hadn't quite dismissed her... as if he still had something to say. Or maybe she only wished that he did. It wasn't until the woman had handed him a small bag of Skittles and was counting out his change that Baby started to feel silly and told herself that she needed to walk away. She glanced quickly at him and then turned swiftly when she saw that he was already looking right at her.

"Hol' up," she heard Memphis say, and for a split second, she stalled, wondering if he was in fact speaking to her.

Baby had always thought that it was such a silly thing to have a crush on a man. It made women act in the strangest ways about the most trivial things. It made the smartest woman reduce herself to the dumbest airhead, and that's why Baby had never bothered around with boys for long enough to develop a real crush. She liked to have her mind clear and vowed she wouldn't be a silly little girl for anyone. But here she was feeling silly and probably looking silly too. And it was all because of *him.*

"You're talking to me?" Baby asked, eyes wide while pressing her finger into the center of her chest as she asked the question.

He nodded his head and popped a few Skittles in his mouth, smirking slightly at the wide-eyed look she was giving him. His eyes were centered on her face, instantly making her feel self-conscious about herself and regretful of the decision to purchase cotton candy. It made her feel like a child, and that's the last thing she wanted to feel like as she stood in the presence of this full-grown man.

Intrigued, Memphis couldn't help but smile as he looked at the young woman in front of him, somewhat amused by the way that she was reacting to him. Sure, she was trying to keep her cool, but his eyes were trained to pick up on even the subtlest signs when it came to people—a skill he'd honed to perfection over his tenure in the streets. Always aware of his surroundings, he'd seen Baby stealing glances in his direction for quite a while now because, unknown to Baby, he'd noticed her far before she'd sneaked her first glance.

"You from around here?" he asked, curling his brows into a slight frown as if he was scanning his own mind for the answer. "I haven't seen you around here before."

"I don't get out much," Baby blurted out, cutting her eyes away from the intensity of his stare so that she could muster a few coherent words. "I'm a student, and I kinda keep to myself."

Feeling nervous, she shifted her weight onto the balls of her feet before pushing forward to the front, teetering from back-to-front to offset her anxiety. Memphis's strong features softened, and a sly half-grin crossed his face as he watched her, admiring the childish way she tried to hide her uneasiness. It wasn't normal for him to be intrigued by chicks like this, but here he was, taking up her time and freely giving her his, something he didn't do very often. Time was money, and although Memphis wasn't short on money, he was always short on time, so he spent it wisely.

However, this young lady in front of him fascinated him for some reason. She had an innocence about her, and after spending the better half of the last hour looking at chicks who were desperate for his attention, prancing around barely dressed, shooting him seductive stares that let him know their pussy was up for grabs, it was some-what refreshing to see something so opposite. Maybe it was the way that she was stuffing her mouth full of cotton candy like the shit was going out of style, or maybe it was out of sheer boredom, but for whatever reason, he wanted to speak to her a little longer.

Memphis's boy Laz was the one who had come up with the idea to be out here anyways. It was the first day of summer, and this was what Atlanta niggas like Laz did on the first Saturday of summer: posted up in the parking lot with their fly ass rides in order to hook up with bad bitches. But Memphis had never been the type to sit anywhere for the sole purpose of getting a woman. Women came easy to him, even without using his money as bait. However, it was Laz's birthday, so at least for one day out of the year, whatever he asked for, Memphis gave him.

Baby turned slightly, as if she were preparing to walk away, and Memphis licked his lips before slowly finessing his perfectly cropped beard and deciding that he wasn't ready to let her go. Not yet.

"Why?" Memphis asked, pressing Baby for more information before she could get the chance to walk away. "Why do you keep to yourself?"

She turned to him, cocking her head to the side at his question. In his mind, Memphis cursed himself for not coming up with something better to say. He could see he was losing her... For once, he felt like his conversation wasn't enough to keep a woman, and that was new to him because, never before had he been short on some slick shit to say. But this one had him tongue-tied on how to approach her, which was frustrating but refreshing to him at the same time.

He waited, and Baby's eyes searched the fiery sky as she thought about her answer.

"Because... I'm just weird, I guess," she replied with a shrug and deep frown, repeating something that Mona told her repeatedly.

"Weird?" Memphis parroted, chuckling a little at her choice of words. "Nothing wrong with being weird... I can dig it."

Lifting her head up, Baby caught Memphis's eyes with hers, wondering if he'd just given her a compliment. He moistened his lips with his tongue, still smirking, and she took in a sharp breath before glancing away. She found his gaze too powerful to bear for prolonged lengths of time. She needed breaks to get herself together.

"Aye yo, Memphis!"

Without pulling his attention from Baby, Memphis lifted his index finger, signaling Laz to give him a minute. He wasn't ready to let Baby go just yet.

"Can I get ya name or it's a secret?" He smirked, and Baby shuddered slightly, overwhelmed by his swagger. Then her cheeks flushed, and she bit down hard on her bottom lip, mentally telling herself that she needed to get it together. How was she supposed to ever attract a grown man if she always carried herself like a child?

"Baby." Looking down, she kicked her foot at some imaginary object on the sidewalk. Anything to not meet his eyes. She couldn't deal with the flutters that erupted in the pit of her stomach whenever she looked at him.

"You callin' me baby already?" he joked with a smile, and Baby's eyes bugged as she looked up at him, for some reason feeling mortified. But she relaxed as soon as he caught her gaze, his half-smile and relaxed expression immediately putting her at ease. She giggled a little and shook her head as she began to correct him. He grinned even harder at the sound of her laughter, thinking that it sounded like a small bit of heaven on Earth.

"No... *my* name is Baby."

"Word?" He wrinkled his brows, frowning. His frown was just as sexy as his smile, and Baby wondered if he was capable of ever *not* looking sexy.

"Word," Baby confirmed, repeating his slang, something she instantly regretted with a deep frown of her own when she realized how lame she sounded. Memphis didn't seem to share the same thought. In fact, he thought it was cute the way that his presence seemed to cause her discomfort. It wasn't new to him—his presence caused everyone to be uncomfortable—but Baby had something about her that made their exchange feel a little different to him.

Not saying anything right away, Memphis paused and allowed his eyes to drop to look her over in detail, giving in to his sudden need to size her up. Baby tried to keep her composure while he scrutinized her, wondering if he liked what he saw and once again cursing herself for not letting Mona dress her.

"I have seven brothers and sisters... By the time my mama got to me, she said that she was tired of coming up with names and just called me Baby." She felt the need to explain in order to bridge the silence between them and get his attention back on her words and not her body. "She said that my name symbolized me being the last, and there would be no more after."

"How many of them seven are brothers?" Memphis asked, lifting one brow once he was done having his fill of her. She was a little on the thin side, but although he went for the more voluptuous types, he wasn't put off by that.

Feeling more at ease with the way the conversation was going, Baby answered quickly. "Four."

"So I got four niggas I'mma have to step to in order to take you out, huh?" Memphis cocked his head to the side with his question and noticed when Baby's eyes fluttered as she processed what he said. He deliberately tried to catch her off guard and succeeded.

"Babbbbyyyyy, are you ready to go? I need to get home and study."

Walking up behind Baby, Mona put her hand on Baby's shoulder and looked at her with her bottom lip pushed out in a pout. Baby cut her eyes at Mona, utterly confused about the words that she'd just heard leave her friend's lips. Since when did Mona *ever* care about studying? Thanks to her parents' connections and her own charm, Mona had cruised through her classes with minimal effort her entire life.

"Study?" Baby crinkled up her nose at Mona who had suddenly appeared by her side.

"Yes, you know we have that test coming up on Monday." Mona rolled her eyes and tilted her head to the side before finally resting her attention on Memphis's face as if seeing him for the first time.

"Oh! Am I interrupting something?" Mona inquired with wide eyes. "Who are you?"

Baby's frown deepened as she stared at Mona like she'd grown another head and wondering why she was playing dumb.

"I'm me," Memphis responded curtly but politely as he glanced at Mona quickly before putting his attention back on Baby, watching her with an intensity that said she was the only one he was trying to see.

Baby felt her cheeks get warm and started to fumble nervously with her hands. This wasn't the way things normally worked. Usually once Mona came around, Baby assumed her natural position as background and let Mona take the foreground. Baby could feel Mona's heated stare on her profile, and she swallowed hard, losing her words.

With Mona now standing squarely in front of him with her hands on her hips and her breasts pushed up and vying for attention, Memphis didn't seem at all fazed by her efforts. And truthfully, he wasn't. He was only hoping that the new chick who had just walked up would quickly dismiss herself so that he could continue his conversation with Baby.

Tongue in cheek, he looked at Baby, noticing the way that she seemed to retreat as soon as her friend walked up. It was obvious she wasn't used to the attention he was giving her, and he didn't want his interest in her to be taken in a negative way. He considered letting her go, but his selfish desire to get to know her won out over his want to put her at ease by ending their conversation.

"Aye, Baby, before I let you go, I wanna—"

11

"Oh, I *know* you," Mona interjected, stepping forward and slightly in front of Baby in an effort to pull Memphis's attention to her.

Much more experienced with grown men than her best friend, Mona knew from the few minutes she spent watching Memphis and Baby conversing that he seemed to be attracted to her childish, innocent ways, and she set her intentions on quickly breaking that up. Most of Mona's waking moments were spent readying herself to be the trophy on the arms of a baller, and Memphis was the most supreme of them all.

To be the lady on his arms brought about the type of status she'd always craved. It was well known that Memphis didn't mess with many women, and the ones that he did allow to earn his affections were all the baddest of the baddest. In Mona's mind, none was badder than her; she just hadn't had a chance to shoot her shot, but her time had finally arrived. And the fact that he had his sights on Baby at the moment was of no concern to her. Baby wasn't mature enough for a man like him, and Mona reasoned that she wouldn't know what to do with Memphis if she had the chance. Therefore, she felt no guilt about playing Baby to the right in order to get at him. In fact, she felt like she was saving Baby from the sting of embarrassment that was sure to come once Memphis discarded her like yesterday's trash for a real woman with real experience.

Memphis heard Mona and couldn't help but see her standing right in front of his face, but his eyes stayed on Baby, who was looking down at her sneakers, obviously uncomfortable. Licking his lips, he stepped a little to the side, ready to fully ignore Mona and continue his advances with Baby, but then she looked at him and shook her head slightly before taking a few steps back as if dismissing herself and offering Mona up instead. The back of Memphis's neck stung, and he rubbed at it, wondering if this was how it felt to be rejected by a woman. Really, he had no idea because he'd never experienced that type of rejection before.

Squinting his eyes at Baby, he bit the inside edge of his mouth and contemplated saying something more, but he could tell from looking at her that she'd shut down completely. Whatever was left of their conversation before her friend had stepped up was officially in the wind.

"You know me, huh?" He addressed Mona finally, thinking that speaking to her would at least keep Baby in his presence for a little longer. The sparkle in his eyes when he looked at Baby was gone as he peered at Mona. He knew her type and recognized her for what she was as soon as she'd walked up. There was no challenge involved. He knew he could put forth minimal effort and still get her.

"Who doesn't know about the *Murda Mob*?" Mona shamelessly flirted, cocking her head to the side. Memphis chuckled a little and cut his eyes to Baby.

"I guess a chick who is a student that keeps to herself," he said, baiting Baby for her attention by referencing what she'd told him about herself earlier. He saw her eyes flutter, proving that she'd heard him, but instead of catching his stare, she shifted uncomfortably before walking away.

Fuck, Memphis thought, knowing that whatever he thought would happen with Baby was over.

"Don't mind her," Mona said to him, nodding her head at Baby when she saw that his eyes were on her. "She doesn't know how to handle a man like you. Not like I do…"

Memphis's brows shot to the sky as he turned his attention on Mona, catching the sexual undertones in her words.

Although Baby intrigued him, she'd pretty much dismissed him, and this new chick was more in his comfort zone, similar to the women that he came into contact with on the daily. Not to mention, she had gone after him like she knew what she wanted, not letting the fact that he wasn't initially interested in her stop her from grabbing his attention.

Against his better judgment, Memphis decided to forfeit the challenge that Baby would pose for him and go for the sure thing. Pressing his lips together in a way that showcased the deep dimples in his cheeks that made women go crazy, he decided to take Mona's bait since she was offering it up so easily. Many of men had met their end by going for what was easy rather than challenging themselves to chase down what required a little more effort. And though Memphis had mastered many things in life, he was about to fall victim to the easiest trick in the book.

"Not like you, huh?" he mused, running a single finger over the light facial hair over his lip as he stared at Mona, slowly taking in her curves, not at all missing the kitty print between her thighs. "Why don't you tell me why you think you can handle a nigga like me."

Got him, Mona thought as she smiled, biting the corner of her bottom lip.

Now that she had his attention, she'd do anything to keep it at all costs. The infamous Memphis was as good as hers.

CHAPTER ONE

FIVE YEARS LATER

*B*aby never wanted to date a thug. She never planned for that to be her life. But when she met Semaj Daniels, something inside of her told her that he was the one for her. He said all the right things. Did the right things. He was someone she immediately fell for because he felt so familiar to her. And when Semaj asked her to be his wife, she said yes without a second thought. She spent her entire senior year of college, planning a wedding in between taking finals and preparing for her life as an elementary school teacher. Every girl daydreamed about the day they would marry the man of their dreams, and Baby was no different. She just hadn't thought that her moment would come so soon.

As she stood in front of the floor-length mirror in her bridal suite and looked at her reflection, tears came to her eyes. Never in life had she seen herself look so beautiful. On the outside, she appeared to be the perfect bride, the visual definition of a virtuous woman who was ready to marry her king, but on the inside, her gut was twisting up into knots.

"I can't get over how gorgeous you are," her mother said before planting a soft kiss on her cheeks, careful not to mess up her makeup. "You're a dream."

Baby smiled bashfully and then took a deep breath. When she looked up, she met her mother's eyes and saw them flicker with concern.

"Are you okay?" she asked, and Baby swallowed the small lump that had formed in her throat before forcing herself to nod. She didn't want to tell her mother that she was beginning to have second thoughts about this day.

Am I making a mistake? she wondered. Even though she felt like it was love, there was so much they hadn't discussed about their life together. Did she really know enough about him to marry him?

"Just nervous jitters. And I wish daddy was here." She admitted the last part quietly and then regretted it when she saw tears in the corners of her mother's eyes.

"I wish he was, too."

She kissed Baby's cheek once more just as Mona entered the room along with Baby's two older sisters.

"It's time!" Mona chirped with a huge smile on her face. "Are you ready to marry the man of your dreams?"

"He looks *really* good out there," Baby's sister Zarina added. "And the décor is beautiful. I don't know how much you all spent on this, but it's perfect, and I'm so happy for you."

"So am I," Gala, Baby's other sister and maid of honor, added. "You're ready to become a missus?"

Baby hesitated, and before she could respond to her sister's question, her wedding coordinator, Julie, was the next person to burst in the room with an anxious expression on her face.

"Okay! It's time to get going or we are going to be late. Everyone ready?"

Nodding her head, Baby took another deep breath. Her mother grabbed her hand and gave it a gentle squeeze. Though the embrace was appreciated, it did nothing to calm her nerves. Something wasn't right. She didn't know what, but she could feel it just as real as she felt the hand she was holding. There was no way she could go forth with this. She loved Semaj, but there was no way she could marry him.

God, please... get me out of this.

"Mona, can I speak to you for a second, alone?"

Julie whipped her neck around so fast that it was a wonder she didn't get whiplash.

"But Baby, we are—"

She put her hand up to silence her. "We will only be less than a minute."

Pursing her lips, Julie nodded and then pushed everyone out of the room before closing the door, leaving Baby alone with her other maid of honor.

"What's wrong, Baby?" Mona asked, frowning in Baby's face. "Tell me you aren't getting cold feet now."

Looking down, she fumbled with her fingers for a second before she was able to speak. How could she tell someone what she was thinking? That she wasn't sure she actually wanted to marry Semaj at all?

"I just… I'm getting a bad feeling about all of this. I feel like something is wrong. I don't know if I can—"

Before she was able to finish her sentence, the wail of multiple police sirens interrupted her. Furrowing her brow, she and Mona gave each other quizzical expressions before running to the nearest window when they realized that the sirens seemed to be coming from right outside.

"What in the world?" Mona whispered when they glanced out and saw that there were nearly six undercover cars outside. Armed officers jumped out of their vehicles and moved in on the church as if they were invited guests.

Baby's mouth went dry as she watched, frozen in place. Once she heard commotion coming from inside the chapel, she turned around and took off running out the door, eager to see what was going on.

"Baby, wait!" Mona yelled before following behind her, but she didn't listen.

Baby burst through the double doors of the chapel just in time to see a group of officers surround Semaj.

"We have a warrant for your arrest," one of them said to him, and Baby felt her legs go weak.

"What!" Semaj shouted. An officer reached for his arm, and he snatched away with narrowed eyes.

"If you resist, that's another charge," he was informed. "You are being placed under arrest for the possession of an illegal substance with the intent to sell, as well as tax evasion and fraud. You have the right to remain silent. Anything you say or do…"

"Oh God…" Mona whispered, bringing her hand to her chest. She turned to look at Baby, seeing the tears in her friend's eyes, and then wrapped her arms around her. Baby felt like she was living a nightmare. This couldn't be true… couldn't be happening to her on her wedding day.

"Baby… call my lawyer!" Semaj was yelling as the officers dragged him out of the chapel. "Don't worry about this shit. They ain't got nothing on me! I'll be back. I promise!"

She couldn't bring herself to speak, couldn't even move. By the time the police had taken Semaj out of the church, pushed him into the back of one of their cars and drove away, Baby was still standing in the same exact spot she'd been before he'd left. She was frozen in place, reliving the nightmare in her mind.

This can't be happening.

"Let's get her out of here," she heard her mother say. "Gala, Zarina, Rachel… help me get your sister."

She felt hands tugging at her body, but her mind was in another place. It seemed like a weight was placed on her shoulders, and her head felt heavy. The last thing she saw before she slipped into unconsciousness was what appeared to be a subtle smirk on Mona's face.

❦

"They said they got an anonymous tip… Someone that Semaj trusted told them that he had drugs in the house. They got a warrant to search his home and found enough bricks of coke and other things to lock him up for a very long time. If I'd been living with him, they probably would've gotten me too."

The weary look in Baby's eyes couldn't be seen from over the phone, and she was grateful for that. The past few months had been exceptionally hard on her, but she'd been doing her best to convince everyone around her that she was dealing with all the changes just fine.

"You should consider yourself lucky that this happened before you married him. I mean, I know the situation is fucked up regardless, but it could be a lot worse," Gala told her.

"I know," she hurriedly agreed. She'd thought about it about a million times since it happened, and she knew what her sister was saying was true.

"I just feel so guilty because, right before everything happened, I was thinking that I didn't want to marry him. I asked God to help me with a way out of it and then... he was arrested." Tears began to cloud her vision as she thought back to that day. "I didn't mean it. I was just scared..."

Not one to usually hold her tongue, Gala took a second to think about her words before she replied. "Baby, I need you to understand that you didn't cause him to be arrested. There is no reason for you to feel guilty. And there is no reason for you to stay with him if you really want to leave."

"I *don't* want to leave," she stubbornly affirmed to her sister. "I was just panicking and got cold feet. But I love Semaj, and if I could do it all again, I'd be his wife right now. I'm not leaving him."

With everything Semaj was going through, Baby had been reminded that he had no one on his side, and she felt a nagging feeling to be loyal to him, which Gala knew her sister was confusing for love. Semaj had no family that she'd ever met, and his friends were abandoning him for fear they would get sucked into his mess and meet the same fate. Once he was given his sentence, his fall from grace followed swiftly behind, and nearly everyone he knew turned their backs on him. One day he called her and told her that she was all he had, stating that he'd probably die if he'd lost her too. She made up her mind that there was no way she could leave him on his own.

"Baby, you don't owe him anything," Gala protested, not believing for a second that this was about love. She knew that her youngest sister was selfless to a fault and hated to see anyone she cared about unhappy. As soon as Baby introduced her to Semaj, Gala knew that he wasn't the one for her, and when she heard about the engagement, she knew her sister wasn't ready to be married. What she didn't understand was why Baby continued to deal with Semaj when anyone with eyes knew they shouldn't have been together. She was determined to not let her sister continue making that mistake.

"He's the one who got himself into this mess, and he's the one who should have to deal with it, not you. Especially not for the next fifteen years!"

"Gala... I have to go," Baby said and hung up the phone before her sister could object.

Swallowing hard, she bit down on her bottom lip to stop herself from crying. Her cab driver peeked at her through the rearview mirror as she fought off her emotions in silence while staring out the window. It was over three months to the day that Semaj had been arrested, and she had absolutely nothing to her name. He pled out to fifteen years in prison, and the FBI wasted no time moving in to confiscate everything, including the car that he'd bought for her and the home they'd planned on sharing. Since she'd given up her apartment before their scheduled wedding, she had been staying in his place. But now that it had been seized, she was homeless.

Thankfully, she had Mona who had been more than willing to lend a hand.

"DAMN, BABY! YOU GOT A LOT OF CLOTHES!" MONA GRUNTED AS SHE tugged at one of Baby's larger than normal suitcases and dragged it into the grand entrance of her home.

"I know." Baby sighed while attempting to pull another one of her suitcases in from behind her. "Semaj was always buying me clothes and jewelry. It's all I have left."

"That nigga should've been just handing you the money to buy your own shit. Then you could've stacked most of it for a rainy day.

You should never let a man make it so you gotta depend on his ass for everything."

Without a reply, Baby swallowed the lump in her throat and continued walking behind Mona into her home. She didn't want to admit that Semaj had always offered her money, but she rejected it, not wanting to take his hard-earned cash until she could call herself his wife. She used her financial aid to cover her apartment and little expenses she had, refusing to take anything from her fiancé other than the gifts that he often bought for her. The thought never occurred to her that she needed to take the money that he was offering and save it for a rainy day. She hadn't ever planned on having a rainy day, and now she was getting a lesson about finances that she never thought she'd learn.

As soon as Mona learned that Baby had nowhere to go, she made it known that she always had a place to stay with her. Before taking her up on her offer, Baby tried everything she could, even considered moving back in with her parents or one of her siblings. But when she landed a job in the city, moving that far away no longer was an option, and she was forced to stay with Mona until she got on her feet.

Not wanting to live with Mona had nothing to do with Mona because she'd enjoyed the few months that they'd shared an apartment in the past. And it also had nothing to do with having her own space, because Mona had a lot of it. Her home was more like an estate, enormous and just as grand as you'd expect from someone like Mona who demanded only the finest things. As many times that Baby had been to her house, there were still parts to it that she'd never seen.

When they were younger, Mona always swore that she would only be with a paid nigga who would give her the best of the best, and she'd done exactly that. She lived in the lap of luxury, and although she frequently flaunted her belongings and privileged lifestyle to anyone who would listen, Baby had always been happy for her, never envious.

"This here is your domain. I know you've been down here before, but we made some changes to prepare for your arrival. There is a small kitchen, washer and dryer, and everything down here. You can pretty much make it like your own apartment. There is only one room off limits."

Baby followed Mona into the basement, marveling at everything she laid her eyes on. A lot of remodeling had been done, making it look nothing like what it had before. She had her own luxury apartment.

"It's huge! I didn't realize how much space there was." Baby was in awe of the beautiful and luxurious details, noting that Mona hadn't spared any expense when it came to her home, even in the basement.

"You really didn't have to do all of this for me."

Waving her hand at her friend, Mona rolled her eyes. "Please, it's not a big deal. I've wanted to redo this space for years, but Memphis refused. As soon as I mentioned doing it for you, he gave me the word to spend as much money as I wanted to get it done right. So really... you did me a favor."

Baby giggled and then shrugged as if to say 'I guess so'.

"Anyways, let me give you a tour." Mona's lips curved into a smile.

Everything about Mona's home said 'exclusive'. It was almost as if she'd chosen every piece in her home to remind the normal person that she was anything but 'normal'. From the imported Italian furniture to the exquisite Persian rugs, nothing was common. Baby had no idea how she was going to feel comfortable sitting in front of the TV eating cereal, knowing her ass was propped up on something that cost more than her year's salary.

"This is the only room that you can't use. We wanted to keep it." Mona paused for a beat. "And by 'we', I really just mean Memphis," she clarified with a twirl of her eyes. "I wanted to use this space for an in-house hair salon, but my husband just *had* to have his lil' private space to 'clear his head' he says." Mona made sure to put extra emphasis on 'my husband' and the prideful emotions behind her words showed in her face.

It had been a hard task for Mona to secure her spot as Memphis's main woman, but after a year of refusing her on any level, he'd slipped up and had sex with her, and to her absolute delight, Mona ended up getting pregnant. As soon as Memphis got confirmation that the baby was his, he made things official with her so that he could take care of his family. He refused to leave her on her own to raise his seed just because he didn't care for her in any way.

Memphis was the type of man who vowed to do things the right way, so he decided to do what was best for his daughter and give her the family she deserved. It was no secret that he didn't love Mona like a man should love his wife, but as long as he continued giving her the lifestyle she'd always dreamed of, she had no complaints.

"I don't come down here often because Memphis likes to act like this space is top secret," she explained once they walked through the open door. "But he's out of town at the moment, so..."

As Mona continued rambling on about the room, Baby let her eyes walk around the inside, taking it all in with baited breath. Like the rest of the house, it was nothing short of remarkable, but it was obvious that it had been designed and decorated by Memphis himself. Taking a deep breath, Baby took in the scent, enjoying the strong cedar and musk smell as she scrutinized his domain.

In the center of the room sat a pool table, and on the far wall was a bar. Large leather sofas and recliners, expensive rugs and a card table decorated the main space. There was no television, however, on the wall hung huge speakers. The large space was designed for a boss. There was a beautiful bathroom with a jetted Jacuzzi tub that seemed big enough to take a few backstrokes in and a small room set up with two chairs, a grand table, and a magnificent chess board sitting in the center. Baby cut her eyes at it, frowning slightly. It was a delightful but unexpected surprise.

"He likes to sit in here and mellow out... listen to music, smoke weed and shit," Mona explained with a shrug, and she nodded her head. "I don't know why he even has that chess board down here because his ass never asks me to come down here and play with him."

"You know how to play chess?" Baby quipped, looking at Mona with surprise.

Snorting out a laugh, Mona rolled her eyes. "Girl, no. What I look like playing some nerd shit like that?"

Mona chuckled a little more as she walked away, and Baby fought the urge to remind her that she had been part of the chess team all through high school, something that she had actually been proud about. She still had trophies from her toughest wins.

"Make yourself at home." Mona then checked the Presidential Rolex watch on her wrist, admiring the way the light sparkled in the diamonds. "It's just us for a while. Memphis is out of town and won't be back until this weekend."

Baby frowned. "Where is Genie?"

Mona sighed before pushing her out of the room and then closing the door. "She's at the playground with her nurse. They should be back some time soon."

"I'll wait upstairs for them to come back so I can see her." Baby couldn't help but smile as she thought about Genie, Mona's daughter and her beautiful goddaughter.

Mona had a difficult delivery bringing Genie into the world, but baby girl was a fighter. At nearly four years old, she was still that. She'd been diagnosed with a rare form of cancer that affected her spine and paralyzed her from the waist down. Because of it, Genie couldn't walk and needed special care.

Being that Mona was much too busy to spend the majority of her day taking care of her daughter, she told Memphis that they needed to hire a private nurse, and he agreed. He did anything for his daughter, so Mona frequently used Genie to get her way. Once the nurse was hired, she barely spent any time at all with her daughter, leaving her either with the nurse or Ms. Donaldson, the woman who raised Memphis.

"Gotty!" Genie shrieked as soon as she wheeled into the house and saw Baby sitting in the living room waiting for her. 'Gotty' had initially started out as 'Gody', short for godmother, but when Genie first started to talk, she couldn't get it right and always said 'Gotty' instead. Eventually, the name stuck.

Jumping to her feet, Baby ran over and gave her goddaughter a huge kiss on the cheek. Genie's curls sprung to life as she giggled; her laughter was infectious and sounded like a chorus of angels. Genie was a gift from God.

"I didn't know you were coming here!" Genie exclaimed, sounding much older than her actual age. She was not only the most beautiful little girl that Baby had ever seen, but easily the smartest.

"Mommy didn't tell you that I was coming?" Baby asked, and Genie frowned before shaking her head. "Well, Gotty is going to be staying here for a little while, okay?"

"And Uncle Maj? Is he coming too?" Genie asked, referring to Semaj. Baby let out a deep breath and then sadly shook her head.

"No, Uncle Maj isn't coming."

"Okay," she replied, seeming sad for only a short amount of time before she smiled brightly once again. "Well, can we play a game?"

Seeing the excitement on Genie's face quickly transformed Baby's sadness into happiness. No matter what kind of day she was having, her goddaughter always made it better.

"Of course we can. I have nowhere to go, so we can play together all day."

CHAPTER TWO

Squinting through her Gucci shades, the first expensive thing that Baby had purchased for herself—a gift to herself on the day of her college graduation, she sighed and stepped out of Mona's fiery red Lamborghini Gallardo, thinking that she should have faked sick so she could have stayed in. One of Mona's most favorable pastimes, shopping, happened to be Baby's least favorite, but Mona couldn't possibly shop alone and always found a way to sucker Baby into joining her. In fact, throughout the years, Mona had been successful in conning Baby into a lot of places—clubs and parties as well as anywhere else she thought she'd meet a man who met her high standards.

"I thought you said we were going to lunch." Baby groaned, cutting her eyes at Mona who was smiling brightly, obviously satisfied with herself.

"We *are*, Baby," Mona stressed. "Lenox Mall has the best restaurants, and then we can walk off our food afterwards." Mona lifted her own shades and made a point of dropping her eyes down to Baby's midsection. "I have noticed you got a little extra cushion around the waist, and we can't have that. With Semaj locked up, you're on your own. You gotta keep your shit tight for the next nigga who comes around."

Baby curled up her nose at Mona's suggestion while shaking her head. "I'm not worried about the next nigga." She flashed her three-carat engagement ring in front of Mona's face. "I'm engaged, remember?"

A sympathetic look crossed Mona's face, and she pressed her thin lips together, thinking about how naïve Baby was. Fifteen years was a long ass time to be away. And it was much too long for anyone to be expected to wait on someone else. Had it been Mona, she wouldn't have even played with the idea of possibly waiting on Semaj to be released from prison. His ass knew the possibilities of what could happen to him when he made the dumb ass decision to hide his product in the same place where he laid his head—a rookie move to say the least. The second he received his sentence, Mona would have blown him a kiss goodbye, sold the engagement ring, and moved right on with her life.

"You just keep thinking that," Mona told her, before handing off her key to valet and refocusing her eyes on the stubborn expression on Baby's face. "There are a lot of niggas out here who wouldn't mind snatching up your young-looking ass. You ain't gon' be able to turn them all down. Shit gets lonely when the sun goes down and you're by yourself in that lonely ass bed."

Swallowing hard, Baby didn't respond. Mona had hit on one of the things that she'd often pondered to herself late at night, as she lay in the bed alone. She was conflicted because she knew Mona was right, but she also knew that she wasn't the type of woman to leave someone hanging when they needed her. She and Mona were well into their lunch at the Cheesecake Factory, and she was still thinking on the last bit of Mona's statement.

Shit gets lonely when the sun goes down.

Dunking a fry into her small container of ketchup, Baby looked at it while biting the inside corner of her mouth and pondering asking the question at the forefront of her mind.

"If Memphis got caught up and had to do time... would you wait on him?" She watched as Mona twirled her beautiful eyes upward, briefly contemplating her reply.

"I love Memphis but..." She paused and shrugged her shoulders slightly before spinning one of her long curls around her finger. "If he got locked up, I just feel like it would be unfair to ask me to do something his ass wouldn't do. What fine ass man would do a bid alongside a woman when he got a gang of thirsties throwing their coochie at him left and right? Just put money on my commissary and we even. That's how I see it."

Baby couldn't help but snort out a chuckle at the comical way in which Mona spoke. If nothing else, she was definitely honest, and she'd always been that way. She didn't mince her words and never left anyone wondering how she felt about anything.

Mona and Baby had met in high school, and being that the two were polar opposites, it was a wonder that they'd been able to become friends, much less maintain the friendship for over a decade. Mona was the only child of upper middle-class parents who doted on her, giving her everything that her heart desired, often sporting the latest styles and newest gear as soon as it came out, and Baby was the youngest in an overcrowded home full of children, which meant that nothing that was ever given to her was brand new.

But one thing that Baby had over Mona was love. While Mona's parents treated her more like a doll they dressed up in nice things and pulled out whenever it was time to show her off but ignored most of the time, Baby had grown up in a house with brothers and sisters who looked out for her—sometimes annoyingly so—and a mother who worked her hardest to give her children the things they needed. Where they were short on funds, they made up with love.

After being made to pair together on a class project one day, the two found themselves at Mona's house but were later dismissed by Mona's parents and ended up at Baby's house. Baby's family took to Mona instantly, pulling her in as if she were the ninth child, and from that moment on, Baby and Mona became best friends, and Baby's home became Mona's second home.

While Mona was unapologetically selfish, strong-willed, and

snappy at the mouth, Baby was kind-hearted, gentle, caring, and often sacrificed her own wants and needs for the sake of others. Throughout the years, it seemed like Mona's headstrong personality had worked out well for her, making it so that she'd always gotten exactly what she wanted. Baby, on the other hand, always seemed to find herself settling in order to protect or not disappoint others—this being the reason she'd never once considered not staying by Semaj's side throughout his entire sentence.

"I always thought that it was crazy you got with Semaj, anyways." Mona scrunched up her nose a little before poking a piece of lettuce from her salad into her mouth. "I always figured you'd end up with a nerd. No offense," she added with a genuine smile.

Baby was about to respond when her phone started to ring. She grabbed at it quickly, her heart racing at the thought that it was Semaj. He normally called her at night, but sometimes he was able to sneak in a call during the day, and Baby tried to always answer so that he wouldn't think she was planning to abandon him. But when she looked at the screen, she realized it wasn't Semaj calling at all.

"Hi, Mama," Baby answered, despite the lump in her throat. "I'm out eating lunch with Mona, so I can't really talk…"

"You can't really talk every time I call you, Baby. Is there a reason why you're avoiding me?"

Feeling the burn in her chest, Baby squeezed her eyes shut and forced herself to lie.

"I'm not avoiding you, Mama. I know we need to talk and we will. I'm just trying to get my life in order first. As soon as I do, I'll come home, I promise."

A pregnant pause followed before she heard her mother sigh. "Okay, Baby. I'm just concerned, and I want to hear from you. You're not talking to any of us, and it's a dangerous thing to go through traumatic events and to be alone."

It was a true statement, but Baby wasn't ready to deal with that yet. It was hard enough to tell her family what Semaj was going through. Forcing herself to go through a conversation of updates on his sentence and her current life predicament was too much for her at the moment. She'd only spoke to Gala about any of it, and even then, she hadn't said much. Once Baby ended the call, she saw Mona's judgmental eyes on her.

"If you gon' be dumb enough to stick with a nigga who is locked up, no reason to be all ashamed about it."

The venom in Mona's words made Baby's chest burn, but she only pressed her lips together and pushed around the food on her plate.

After eating, Mona set her sights on painting every inch of Lenox Mall with the bottom of her Ferragamo heels. One thing she did better than anything else was spend money, and with Memphis earning more money than a lil' bit while grinding out his days in the streets, Mona was able to spend her days indulging in her biggest addiction. Well… one of her biggest addictions. Being the lady on the highest paid hustler's arm and enjoying the power and prestige that came with it, was undoubtedly also one of her other addictions.

Atlanta was Memphis's city, and she was his woman, so no matter where she went, she received the star treatment and respect that his reputation granted. There weren't many places that she could go in Atlanta without running into someone who knew about Memphis or the infamous *Murda Mob*, and she enjoyed being treated like a local celebrity. Baby, on the other hand, felt like she would never quite get used to the scrutiny. Even now while walking next to Mona, she caught herself wondering if she had an undiscovered stain somewhere on her clothes, a booger in her nose, or a 'kick me' sign on her back—anything to explain the stares they got as they walked through the somewhat crowded mall.

"Is that girl over there staring at us?"

Baby shifted her attention once again to a woman a little ways off from where she stood, waiting as Mona eyed some jewelry in the window leading into the Cartier store. Her hands as well as Baby's were already full of her purchases, yet she couldn't help her hunger for the panther ring that was smothered with diamonds. It definitely cost a pretty penny, but it would make a beautiful addition to her jewelry collection.

"Everyone in this damn mall is staring at us." Mona dismissed her words with a wave of her hand. "C'mon... I wanna try on this ring."

"Yeah, but not the way she is. It's like she knows us or something. Look at her!"

Sucking her teeth at Baby's urgings, Mona finally turned to look in the direction of the woman she was talking about. As soon as she laid eyes on her, her eyes widened when she recognized her instantly as someone she wanted to keep tucked in her past. Forcing away the expression of shock and surprise from her face, Mona recovered quickly and shrugged.

"No idea who she is or why she's looking like that," she lied. "Anyways, let's get in this store."

Before following behind her, Baby couldn't help but cut her eyes back over to the woman who was still sneaking occasional glances her way, wondering if she knew her from somewhere. She was attractive, looked kinda young in the face, but her shapely body said that she was full-grown.

Maybe it's nothing, she told herself before joining Mona inside the jewelry store.

"Can I try on the ring in the window display?"

Baby watched the face of the pale-faced jewelry clerk as her eyes wandered back and forth between her and Mona, most likely sizing them up to determine whether they were worth her time or attention. When her focus dropped to the bags in their hands and the luxury brands decorating them, she managed to pull her thin lips into a wide smile and nodded her head.

"Yes... which one?"

"The panther," Mona replied, already studying another jewel.

"That one is $75,000," the woman quickly informed her without moving a muscle to get the ring. Cocking her head to the side, Mona went ghetto-style and smacked her lips, snaked her neck, and rolled her eyes. Baby's own eyes widened, sensing that shit was about to get real.

"Did I ask you how much the ring cost, or did I ask your ass to bring the shit here so I can try it on?"

Flustered and red in the cheeks, the woman scurried away with her keys jingling in her hands, silently reminding herself about how much she needed this job so that she could keep her composure.

Not one for confrontations, Baby shifted back and forth from foot-to-foot, anxious to leave. She smiled at another clerk inside the store, trying to ease the tension, but he only wrinkled his nose up at her before turning his back. Once the woman returned, holding the ring in her hand, she watched Mona snatch it up and slip it on her finger. Mona's lips spread into a wide grin as she looked at it, the diamonds in the ring twinkling in her gray eyes.

"I'll take it," she said nonchalantly as if she was talking about making a $7 purchase instead of $75,000. Baby's eyes nearly bugged out of her skull.

"You can put it on this card," she added, pushing one of Memphis's black cards in the clerk's direction.

Mona knew that she'd have hell to pay with Memphis later on. He'd been on her ass about saving money and cutting back on her spending ever since he got it in his head that he wanted to leave the streets alone. But in her mind, cutting back on spending was not an option for her, and leaving the streets was not an option for him. She planned on Memphis being a street nigga until the day he died and fully accepted that if he continued living out his life in the streets, it was a real possibility that it could be the streets that would one day claim his life. However, whenever Memphis brought that to her attention, she reasoned that he was too careful to get caught slipping and dismissed the subject.

"*Now*, we can leave," Mona said, admiring the ring on her finger.

The only thing that Baby could do was shake her head and smile, wondering how it must be to freely drop that much money on a single piece of jewelry. She had to admit that the ring was nice, though not her taste, but there was no way she could spend that much money on *anything* at one time... It didn't matter how much cash she had at her fingertips to play with.

THE NEXT MORNING, BABY WAS UP BEFORE THE SUN AND ON THE BUS, on her way to visit Semaj as part of her weekly ritual. He received visits every Saturday and Sunday, so she made it her business to be there regardless of how long the ride was. It cost her a total of sixteen hours to see Semaj, eight hours going and eight hours back, but she didn't mind it at all. She would simply bring along a book to enjoy for the long ride, but most times she would be so distracted by everything around her that she wouldn't get a chance to read more than a chapter.

"Girl, listen… all I know is that Dave ass better remember this shit I'm doin' for him once he gets out in three weeks. Shit gon' be different than it was when he left because I'm not dealin' with it no more! All them long neck ass females he was entertaining… tell me, where are they now? Heffas ain't nowhere to be found, but I'm the one running up the damn streets every week to see him and make sure he spends time with his son!"

Baby's eyes traveled from the face of the woman speaking and down to the small child beside her and found him staring right back at her with the most peculiar expression. Although his mama seemed to be sporting the flyest gear with her nails freshly done and her hair in a style that Baby wouldn't be caught dead with on her worst of days, the little boy was in a dingy spandex shorts set with a bulging soggy diaper. She peered at his severely ashy legs, wondering if his mother even owned a bottle of lotion, before her eyes went back to his face. The distant faraway expression in his eyes seemed to tell her that he'd seen and experienced much more than a child his age should.

Sitting beside Baby was a girl who looked like she was in her early teenage years. On her lap was a picture she was drawing. The words *"To: Daddy"* scribbled at the top almost brought tears to Baby's eyes. This was a bus full of people who had lost someone to the system but refused to let their loved one be forgotten. Crossing her arms in front of her, she hugged her body and took a deep breath, thinking about how this would be her life for the next fifteen years.

"Place everything in the container and walk through the metal detectors! One at a time!"

Used to the song and dance that she had to go through every week when she visited Semaj, Baby tossed her shoes and belt into the plastic bin after securing her cell phone and purse in the visitor lockers.

"Hey, Baby. It's nice to see you again."

She didn't even have to look up to know who it was speaking to her. Officer Reynolds worked the weekends, and he was in the same spot every time she came to visit Semaj. He was attractive with his genuine smile and caring eyes, but she never paid him too much attention, although it seemed at times that he was being more than a little flirtatious.

Walking through the metal detector, Baby gave Reynolds a small smile and a gentle nod before raising her arms so that he could use his wand to quickly search her body. Reynolds forced a straight face and tried to hide the satisfaction he was getting from being so close to her. He couldn't for the life of him understand why she continued to visit a low-life like Semaj, but he was glad she did.

Baby was beautiful to him; much too fine to be caught up in love with a man who would spend the better part of his life in prison while she sat on the outside waiting for him, letting all that good, sweet pussy go to waste. Reynolds couldn't help but think of it now as he traced the wand between her legs. Her perfume reminded him of warm peach cobbler, and he wondered sometimes if that was how her sex would taste...

"Semaj is a lucky man," she heard Reynolds whisper, his voice thick and raspy with longing. She brought her eyes to his face and confirmed his words with her own.

"Yes, he is," she replied firmly, crushing any explicit thoughts still lingering in Reynolds's mind.

Feeling sheepish, Reynolds ducked his head in response just as Baby's eyes connected with a familiar face walking behind him, leaving the visitation area. Looking at the shapely young woman with the long honey blonde weave trailing down her back, she ran through her recent memories, trying to remember where she'd first seen the face.

And then suddenly it hit her. It was the woman she'd seen the other day at the mall. As if being summoned by Baby's intense stare, the woman lifted her head and their eyes connected. It took only a second for the woman's eyes to flash with recognition before the fire they'd held when Baby had first seen her, returned.

Reynolds followed Baby's eyes and couldn't help but smirk to himself. Tucking his lips, he held in his thoughts, satisfied that it seemed like the truth would inevitably be brought to the light. He knew firsthand that Semaj wasn't worth shit and that Baby was wasting her time. The sooner she found that out, once Semaj broke her heart, the sooner he could make his move to be the shoulder she could cry on.

When Baby walked into the visitation room, she was delightfully surprised to see Semaj already waiting for her at one of the tables in the center. Usually there was a short delay while she waited for them to call him.

"You knew I was here?"

A bright smile crossed Baby's face as she stared at the man who she was promising her heart and loyalty to. Semaj was every bit of a thug, his upper body decorated with the most beautiful tattoos, each one perfectly engraved into his chocolate brown skin, giving him a dangerous edge that complemented his otherwise soft features.

With wavy hair, big almond-shaped brown eyes, and unbelievably long lashes, it was hard to believe that this man was responsible for the things that he'd done during his time on the streets. Unbeknownst to Baby, the same hands he held her with at night had sometimes been responsible for taking a life or two only hours before. Still, Semaj always cleaned up nice; even after the most egregious of crimes, he never looked like what he'd been involved in.

"Of course. I knew you were here," Semaj replied easily, his lips curling into a grin to match her smile. Standing up, he held his arms out to embrace her, and Baby couldn't help but notice that he'd lost a considerable amount of weight. Her brows arched at the sight of his slimmer figure. His muscular build still remained, but there was much less of him to love than before.

"How have you been, baby?" she asked as she hugged him, not

wanting to bring attention just yet to his physique. She figured she'd leave that for later after getting the pleasantries out of the way.

"I've been straight, you know." Semaj sat down and stroked his beard as he spoke, his eyes scanning the room behind her as he answered the question. She stared inside of his deep pools of brown, almost seeing the thoughts circulating through his mind.

"Tell me," she pressed, eager to be his peace. She wanted him to unwind his worries onto her, placing them on her shoulders instead of holding them on his. That was the least she could do.

With a sigh, he leaned forward, pressing his elbows into the table-top, and ran his hands over the top of his head in obvious distress.

"Ain't nothing to worry your pretty little head about, mama." When he lifted his head again, his smile had been renewed. "Just some grown man shit that I'm handling. But how you been? You all moved in with Mona?"

Nodding her head, Baby's brows were still furrowed, but she urged herself to do as Semaj wished and move on to the next topic.

"Yeah, I still have a lot of unpacking to do, but everything is fine so far. I pretty much have my own apartment in the basement." Twirling her eyes to the ceiling, Baby giggled a bit before she continued to speak. "And you already know Mona's entire house is laid to perfection. So I'm settling in well."

Semaj observed her for a minute, and he sucked in his lips as thoughts ran through his mind. He knew Mona well... much better than even Baby knew. He definitely wasn't thrilled at all with the fact that his fiancée was now living with her.

Mona was the type of chick that people referred to as being 'hot in the ass'. The club was her regular stomping grounds, and although Baby never was the type to find her Friday night comfort within the walls of the hottest clubs, Semaj knew that living with Mona meant that she would be there more often than he felt comfortable with. Still... what could he say? With him in here and her out there, how long could he really depend on Baby to wait on him?

"Oh yeah?" was all he said, squashing the urge to make her promise her faithfulness to him while they were apart.

Although Baby walked around with her head in the clouds, Semaj was no fool, and he knew that one day these visits would come less frequently until the day that they'd come no more. Baby was fine as hell to him, easily the sexiest woman on Earth in his mind. There was no way that he could compete with the niggas on the outside who saw in her what he did. So, until then, he'd just enjoy his time with her and treat it exactly like what it was: a gift.

Leaning back in his seat, Semaj closed his eyes and put his hands behind his head, for Baby's sake, appearing much more relaxed than he felt.

"Tell me what else been good. Let ya nigga know what you been up to."

Smiling hard, Baby bent her head to scrutinize her manicure as flutters erupted in the pit of her stomach. This wasn't the ideal situation, and their love wasn't perfect, but whose was? So she moistened her lips with her tongue, breathed out a breath, and then did just as Semaj asked, filling his head with all of the good things that it pleased him to hear.

CHAPTER THREE

Mona: *I love and miss you.*

Memphis looked down at the text message, reading it quickly before typing in his reply.

Memphis: *I'll be home tonight.*
    Mona: *Ok... I'm going out so you may beat me home. See you soon, baby.*

The back of his neck prickled with his irritation. One thing about Mona, she always stayed in the damn streets no matter how much Memphis wanted her to keep her ass home. Still, he couldn't complain because she'd been this way since the day he met her. She always made it clear that she loved having a good time and being the center of attention so that she could flaunt all of her nice things.

Placing the phone in his back pocket, Memphis ran his hand over the top of his head, pressing down his smooth waves, and returned his attention on the man in front of him who was popping his jaws, desperately trying to say something that would save his life. It wasn't his style to let a nigga beg this long for anything, and he wasn't sure why he was entertaining it now, but it was time to put it all to an end.

"… I mean, I ain't know that nigga was part of the *Murda Mob*, yo! If I hada known, then I wouldn't have planned that hit on his ass. You *know* me, Memphis. You *know* I wouldn't touch one of y'all niggas. I put that shit on God!"

"I know that, huh?" Memphis replied, only half paying attention as he glanced at Laz, signaling that his patience had just run out. Catching the words behind his eyes, Laz nodded in return and pulled his piece out, simultaneously cocking it.

Zip, zip!

Two silenced bullets pierced the man's body, one in the skull and the other in the chest, killing him instantly. His lifeless body slumped over in the chair he'd been tied to as blood oozed from the two holes in his body. The dead man then released his urine, darkening the front of his jeans. It was the body's automatic response to let go of everything once the spirit left.

"'Bout damn time you let me bust on his bitch ass. Thought you was thinkin' 'bout turning over a new leaf for that nigga." Laz chuckled, joking with Memphis, even though he knew it wasn't true. Never had the *Murda Mob* boss shown anyone mercy, because he felt that it was a weakness. He hadn't taken over his throne by being weak or by handing out second chances, and he didn't plan on ever doing so.

With a light snort, Memphis flicked the bridge of his nose with his thumb as he shook his head.

"You know I ain't the type to leave loose ends," he replied nonchalantly.

He felt his phone vibrating in his pocket but ignored it, not wanting to get involved in some personal shit when his mind was supposed to be on business. More than likely it was Mona. She was always happiest when he was in the streets. There was something about the thug in him that excited her. Maybe it was the thrill of the lifestyle. Memphis had long ago grown beyond the allure that this kind of life used to give him. He'd been stacking his bread in the streets with full knowledge that he wasn't the type of nigga to be in them for long.

Once he reached the height of his empire, there was nowhere else left to go but down, and he wasn't going out like that. He'd seen plenty street niggas he admired wind up either dead or in prison, and that wasn't the route that he had planned for himself. On the other end was Laz, who pledged his life to the streets and was more than capable of taking over once Memphis made his exit so that he could start on this family shit he had planned. Being a single child, he wanted to have a large family. His dream was always to have a house full of kids.

The only problem was getting Mona to see it the way he did. For some reason, she'd made her goal in life to be the wife of a thug as if she considered it something to brag about. Memphis didn't understand it; the flashy, dangerous lifestyle of a hustler was addicting to some, but it had never been to him. Taking to the streets at an early age had been a choice he made for the sake of survival and nothing else. It was something niggas who grew up the way he did *had* to do. He didn't glorify it. In his mind, he celebrated simple shit—like coming home to his family without worrying about the day he may not be able to make it home— 'green' shit that niggas in his hood never dared to think on because they considered it that unattainable.

Sometimes Memphis couldn't even see that life for himself. Picture a cat like him coming home to a wife and three kids, picket fence, and a dog in the front yard. Thinking about it made him chuckle sometimes, but he couldn't help but feel that it was the inevitable next step. He just couldn't see how he'd do that with Mona. It was hard enough getting her to even be a mother to Genie. She seemed more concerned with making appearances in the clubs than sitting down and being a wife and mother. In fact, the thought of settling down and having more children seemed to disgust her, and she often mentioned how there was no way she was messing up her beautiful body just to pop out more snotty-nose kids.

For an entire year, Mona chased Memphis down before he even decided to give her the time of day, and the only reason he even dealt with her on any level was because he had been waiting for Baby to pop up again. After an entire year of waiting, Baby never showed, and Mona eventually told him that she was dealing with someone else, which pissed him off in ways that he'd never expected. In anger, he finally broke Mona off with a little bit of what she wanted but instantly regretted it and vowed to never go there with her again. Unfortunately, she became pregnant, and he was stuck with her for life.

Even still, he never treated her less than her worth. A lot of niggas did a lot of things, but one thing that he prided himself on was the fact that he never lied to a woman or mistreated her. Although his own mother wasn't worth shit, he'd been raised by someone who taught him to respect women, and he did. He could never bring himself to dog chicks out the way that other niggas did.

His phone vibrated again, and this time, he stopped to pull it out and read the text Mona had sent.

Mona: *I forgot to remind you... Baby moved in last week. She's in the basement.*

Massaging his facial hair, he tried to ignore the stirring feeling in his chest when he thought about Baby. He'd seen her a few times since he and Mona were married, but out of respect for his wife and daughter, he never made a move or treated her as anything other than a friend. Still, he knew that she was the one that he really wanted and that Mona was only the one he'd settled with. Ignoring his feelings for her was easy when it was only for a few minutes at a time, but now she would be living in his house. This was a test he wasn't sure that he was prepared to take.

"Aye... you think you can handle the rest of this shit on your own?" he asked Laz, knowing fully well that he could. Runs like this, Memphis wasn't even supposed to be with him on, but with Mona continuously pushing him out in the streets, he was beginning to accompany Laz more often than not.

"You already know I can handle this lil' shit down here, nigga," Laz replied as he sent off a text to the part of their crew in charge of cleaning up the bloody mess he'd just made. After hitting send, he ran his fingers through his long locs and focused his eyes on Memphis, noticing the distant look in his eyes as he held his own cell phone.

"What, you got problems at home with wifey?" he asked playfully, fully aware that female problems were the last thing that Memphis dealt with. In all the time he'd known him, Memphis had never been involved in any drama with a woman—something Laz was very familiar with. Any given day, he was involved in some shit that his dick had walked him into. Women were an addiction to him, and he had no thoughts about getting help for it.

"Naw," was all Memphis said before placing his phone back in his pocket without replying to Mona. "I'll catch up with yo' ass when you get back in town."

Before Laz could reply, Memphis turned to leave, his mind on things better left alone.

TWIRLING ONE OF HER LONG, CURLY, DIRTY-BLONDE STRANDS AROUND her finger, Mona sipped champagne and bobbed her head gently to the music. Adorned in a dress, shoes, and jewelry that easily cost as much as a mortgage, Mona loved the attention she was being given as she sat in the V.I.P. at Memphis's club, *Views*. She was enjoying all the special treatment that a local celebrity like her deserved. The entire atmosphere in the club changed once people saw that Memphis's woman had arrived. *Views* was not only his club; it was the primary party spot for the *Murda Mob*, so everyone was on their best behavior the moment she entered the doors, treating her like the royalty she was.

Being there, Mona didn't have to lift a hand to do anything, and every nigga in the building who claimed to be part of the *Murda Mob*, saw to that. It delighted her to see the jealous stares that came from women when they saw their men run to the V.I.P. to make sure that she was being cared for in the way she deserved. Once she became Memphis's wife, it became the law of the streets that, in his absence, every nigga on his team was responsible for making sure she was good. They were expected to give their own life to protect hers, and they took that shit to heart.

This is the muthafuckin' life! Mona gushed in her mind as she looked out at the crowd, feeling like a queen sitting on her throne.

It was a powerful thing being in her position. This was the lifestyle that she'd always wanted, and now that she had it, the last thing she wanted to do was let it go. She knew that Memphis was experiencing some kind of midlife crisis or something, constantly nagging her about settling down and giving him more babies, but that was the furthest thing from her mind. She was in her early twenties, and having more kids was not on her radar. She'd given him Genie, so that should have been enough. And with all the problems their daughter had, who in their right mind would want to risk having another child? Every time he mentioned it, she looked at him like he was crazy. But Memphis didn't see a thing wrong with his little girl, and that was the difference between the two of them.

To Mona's side, her girl Bambi snapped her fingers in the air and worked her curvaceous body to the music while singing the song loudly as if she was the headliner at the club that night.

"Bitch, you gon' calm down so I can hear the song, or do I need to tell them to put your ass on the stage?"

Curling up her nose, Bambi playfully pushed Mona on her shoulders and rolled her eyes. "You know this is my song. Why you gotta be hatin' all the damn time, Mo?"

Without reminding Bambi that she had *nothing* for her to hate on, Mona took another sip from her drink before placing it down and looking out at the crowd below. She was a queen looking down at her kingdom.

"Can I get you anything else, Mrs. Luciano?" a server asked, stepping into Mona's line of vision. With a nod of her head and a slight wave of her hand, she dismissed her like she was trash. Biting back a giggle, Bambi turned and looked at Mona with her lips twisted up to the side.

"Mrs. Luciano, huh? Must be nice being the wife of the most sought-after nigga in the city. All these bitches out here want what you got."

"Can't no bitch out here compete. And Memphis has already let them know." Mona cocked her head to the side and brought her left hand up, wiggling her ring finger to show off the seven-carat diamond that her husband had placed there when he asked her to be his wife.

"So you tellin' me that Memphis don't have no little side bitches hiding out in the cut?"

Mona rolled her eyes. "Memphis wouldn't cheat if he was getting paid to do it. It's just not in him. He takes this marriage shit serious. Once I had Genie, it was a wrap for any bitch who thought she could get what I got."

"Girl, you know I'm just hatin' because Laz's ass ain't asked me shit yet. I been holding that nigga down for nine years, and he hasn't even mentioned marriage," Bambi admitted, the corners of her lips turning down in a sad pout.

"Is that why you singing all these sad ass songs to the top of yo' lungs?" Mona joked at her expense but poked her lightly in the side to ease the sting of the reality of her question. "You just need to put your time in. He's doing stupid shit, but stay with him, and at some point, he'll see that through it all, you're the only one who has ever held him down."

"That's what you did with Memphis?"

Mona nodded her head without looking at Bambi. If she were honest and told her everything that she'd done in order to lock Memphis down, Bambi would never look at her the same. The path that led her into Memphis's arms was paved with lies and deceit, but she hoped that her sins would never come to the light. Although she didn't live the street life, her hands were just as dirty as the ones who did. From the time she laid eyes on him that day on Campbellton Road, she made a promise to herself that she would find a way to make Memphis hers, no matter what she had to do. Here it was years later, and she'd managed to get it done.

"When I first spoke to Memphis, he was in another bitch's face," Mona began, careful to leave out that the other 'bitch' had actually been her best friend, Baby. "I knew that she'd caught his interest, but I also knew that he belonged to me. So, I made my move to claim him as mine, and I've been doing it every day since. You've got to realize that when you're dating a powerful man, you have to be a powerful woman in order to keep him. Laz is used to making his own decisions, so you have to work behind the scenes to make him feel like it's his choice to make things official with you when, in reality, you're pulling all the strings."

Nodding her head, Bambi let her words marinate. At only twenty-five-years-old, Bambi was in her prime. Given her nickname because of her beautiful doe-like hazel eyes, Bambi was beautiful in every way. In fact, she was so stunning that initially Mona had felt intimidated by her and refused her friendship until she realized that Bambi didn't even seem to know how gorgeous she was. She offered her companionship without pretense, sincerely wanting to get close to her because she felt that Mona would understand her life in ways that others didn't. After all, both of them were the girlfriends to the two leaders of the *Murda Mob*, a position of prestige but also a place of loneliness, because being attached to two street goons meant that you never knew whom to trust.

While Mona loved the life because of what it gave to her, Bambi wanted nothing but to be with Laz. She fell in love with him when she was only in the tenth grade, even though he was fully-grown at twenty-three years of age. Ignoring all the warnings she was given about who he was and what he did, Bambi became his girl as soon as he asked without giving it a second thought. Immediately, he changed her from a girl to a woman, and she'd been by his side ever since, no matter what pain loving him caused.

"Didn't your friend move in with you this week? Why isn't she here with us?"

Mona eyed her curiously, somewhat put off about the fact that she had mentioned Baby right after she'd indirectly brought her up.

"I asked if she wanted to come out, but she said no. I left her with Genie, watching movies and shit, but I know the real deal of why she stayed. She'd rather sit up and wait for that nigga's locked up ass to call her."

Pressing her lips together, Mona rolled her eyes and then shook her head. She couldn't understand Baby wanting to sit at home by herself and wait by the phone for a man who couldn't do a damn thing for her.

Bambi couldn't help but laugh at the look on her face. "Don't act like that. She's in love."

"Love is overrated sometimes," was Mona's response.

At that very moment, the screen on her phone lit up. Without picking it up, she peered down at the screen and read the text.

Memphis: Just pulled up. Where are you?

"Hubby's home!" Bambi exclaimed with far more enthusiasm than Mona was showing herself.

"Damn, yo' ass is nosy." Grabbing the phone, she typed up a reply and hit send, letting Memphis know that she would be home soon.

"I didn't mean to look! But I guess it's time to go, huh?" Before waiting for her to answer, Bambi began collecting her things, knowing that if it had been Laz hitting her up saying that he was home, she'd already be halfway out the door.

"Not yet. Shit, we just got here!"

Bambi's brows bunched together on her forehead before she half-turned, bringing her full attention to Mona who was snapping her fingers and twerking her hips in her white leather chair. She didn't appear to have a single worry about her man while she was shaking her ass.

"You sure? He's been gone a whole week, and you straight with him coming home to an empty house?" Thinking for a second, Bambi then added, "Well, it's not empty, I guess, if your homegirl is there."

Catching the dark undertone in her added remark, Mona cut her eyes in her direction and then rolled them hard. Yes, Memphis had been interested in Baby when he'd first saw her, and yes, Mona had to resort to some shady tactics in order to push that interest from Baby to her, but it had been years since then. No matter how stupid it was, Baby's heart and soul was wrapped around Semaj, and Mona made sure that Memphis's attention stayed on her. And even if that wasn't the case, Baby didn't have the nerve to do anything against her naturally peaceful and easygoing nature. It wasn't like her to hurt anyone, so there was no need for Mona to worry. And there definitely was no reason for her to end her night early when the fun was just getting started.

"Mrs. Luciano, we would like for you to enjoy this premium bottle… on the house." A beautiful brown-eyed waitress set a bottle of Moet on the table between Mona and Bambi before pouring them each a glass. Mona cut her eyes to Bambi and smiled before grabbing her glass and sipping the champagne.

These were the perks that came along with being married to hood royalty. No matter what, Mona could never give this life up. It was the next closest thing to being a celebrity, and she was addicted to the lifestyle. There was something about power that changed the people privileged enough to have it, and she was a testament of that. She didn't get why Memphis didn't enjoy it as much as she did, but as long as he allowed her to do her thing whenever she wanted it, she would have absolutely no complaints.

CHAPTER FOUR

*A*fter putting Genie to bed, Baby had just gotten fully relaxed in the tub when she heard her phone ringing from the bedroom. She snatched her eyes open and jumped up, grabbing a towel to cover her soaking wet body. Normally she would have let it ring, figuring that she could get back to whoever was calling her once she'd finished her bath. But these days, a missed call could mean a missed opportunity to speak to Semaj, and she couldn't have that.

It was hard dealing with the loneliness of being alone, and it was even harder wrapping her mind around the fact that she wouldn't be able to live with her fiancé for another fifteen years, but she took everything a day at a time. She urged herself to look forward to his calls and use them to push her through each lonely night.

With the towel pulled around her body, she ran to the bedroom and grabbed the phone, answering as soon as she saw the call was coming from a blocked number.

"Yes!" she yelled out, hoping that she'd answered in time.

"You've received a collect call from..."

Closing her eyes, Baby thanked God that she hadn't missed it, pressed '1' to accept the charges, and waited for Semaj's voice to grace her line.

"Aye, mama, what's up?"

The sound of his voice reminded her about how much she missed him, and she sighed out her sorrows with a heavy breath before replying.

"Nothing much. I'm good," Baby replied, careful not to ask him how he was doing. He was doing his time, and she never wanted to bring light to his harsh reality during their conversations.

"Was taking a bath when you called. I'm trying to get my mind right before my first day of work tomorrow." She ended her statement with a chuckle and awkward shrug. It seemed odd to engage in small talk in the midst of their current circumstances.

"Mmm... so what you tellin' me is you ain't got shit on?" Semaj asked.

Slipping into some sexual shit wasn't the primary reason for his call, but once Baby mentioned being in the tub, it was hard for him to get the image of her naked body out of his mind. Closing his eyes, he licked his lips as he waited for her response. Knowing her man, Baby could hear the smile in his voice, and she couldn't help but return it with one of her own.

"Just a towel."

"Damn, so that body still wet, huh? How Ms. Lady doing right now?"

Baby felt her cheeks get warm as Semaj referred to her lady lips down below. She definitely wasn't the virgin that she'd been when they first met, but the course of the conversation was making her feel as though she was.

"She's... doing okay," Baby replied slowly, feeling somewhat silly.

"Oh yeah? Well, this what I want you to do. Reach down and... with... fingers... I—"

Frowning, Baby pressed the phone even closer to her ear, desperately trying to make out what he was saying.

"Hello? Semaj?"

Baby pulled the phone away and looked at the screen, noting that she had no bars at the top. Her signal wasn't good, and if she didn't fix it and fix it fast, the call would drop.

"Semaj, if you can hear me, hold on! My reception is bad!"

With the phone balancing in one hand and the towel in the other, Baby placed it on speaker and ran out of the room and up the stairs, happy that she was alone other than Genie who was asleep. Hopefully, she would have a better signal on the main floor.

"Hello? Semaj? Can you hear me?"

Anybody looking through the windows would have thought her to be a crazy person, as she ran about through the house with one hand holding her towel up and the other holding her cell phone in the air. She was frantic to save the call, knowing that if it ended, there was a possibility that he wouldn't be able to call her right back.

Just seconds out from walking through the front door, Memphis stood silently at the entrance of his home as a myriad of emotions surged through his body. While clenching and unclenching his jaw, he stared as a crazed Baby ran around his house, desperate for something he had yet to figure out. It had been at least a year from the day that he'd last seen her, but she looked exactly the same—dressed in far less clothing, but almost an exact replica of how he remembered her.

Watching her, he suddenly felt like he was being allowed to see something forbidden and knew that he should look away or alert her to his presence, but for some reason, he waited. She didn't even know how she had him spellbound.

"Yeah… yeah, I hear you, lil' mama," Baby finally heard Semaj say, and she finally relaxed, breathing out a sigh of relief that she hadn't lost him.

"Good. I thought the call was going to drop."

Baby sat down on the arm of one of the beautiful white suede recliners before remembering that it cost more than her whole life. She then stood quickly and cursed herself when she noticed a damp spot under where she'd planted her ass. Peeling a part of the towel away from her skin, she wiped ferociously at it, praying that it didn't leave a stain. As she worked, the bath towel rose up further, exposing a nice chunk of her upper thigh. Memphis felt his chest get tight, but he still couldn't bring himself to turn away.

"Naw, I'm still here. We gon' get back to that other shit I was talkin' 'bout a little later on. But tell me, how you been holdin' up?"

Before she could answer, tears came to her eyes. She wanted to tell Semaj the truth—inwardly, she was a mess. Each day, it was all she could do to simply keep it together and focus on going on with her life. She missed him being there more than she'd been prepared for… but she couldn't tell him that. There was nothing he could do about the situation, and she didn't want to make him feel guilty or hopeless about things he couldn't change.

"I'm good. Like I said, I start work tomorrow and—"

"You miss me? Still love me?" he asked, cutting in suddenly. She pressed her lips into a straight line and wiped away a tear from her eye.

Something about hearing Semaj's question and seeing Baby's reaction bothered Memphis in a way that he couldn't quite explain. It was a mild irritation, so subtle that he wasn't even fully aware of it and simply pulled his eyes away from her, scratching at his chin in order to ease his sudden agitation. He realized that he'd become too comfortable staring at her and all of a sudden felt the urge to put distance between them as quickly as he could.

"Yes, I—"

Before she could get her sentence out, Memphis moved slightly, catching her completely off guard. Eyes bulging from surprise, she lifted her head, and her heart skipped a beat when she finally noticed him standing across from her.

"I—I—uh…"

"Huh?" she heard Semaj ask over the phone that she now held in a death grip. "What's the matter?"

Baby couldn't speak right away because her mouth had gone dry. Memphis, on the other hand, seemed entirely composed as he stood stoically, cradling her stare in his. The doe-eyed look of shock, surprise, and shame brought back to his mind memories of the first time he'd met her. Plenty of times he had thought of that day, wishing that it had gone differently than it had. But those were lost moments, and he told himself he was content with that and moved on.

"Memphis, I'm sorry, I—"

Before she could even get the rest of sentence out, Memphis turned and walked back out the front door, closing it behind him. Her brows bunched. She hadn't seen Memphis in a while, but he'd never been so rude.

"Hellloooo? Baby, you there? The fuck goin' on over there?"

"I'm here… Sorry about that, Semaj," she apologized before swallowing hard in an attempt to dislodge the lump in her throat. Her mind was jumbled, but she closed her eyes and tried to focus on her conversation enough to at least make him satisfied that everything was fine.

She knew at some point that she'd have to come in contact with Memphis—he lived here after all—but she wasn't expecting it to be so soon after Mona mentioned that he was out of town. His presence caught her by surprise, and then there was the fact that she'd been standing in front of him wearing nothing but a towel. How long had he been there watching her? The thoughts running through her mind were too much to deal with at the moment, but she knew she had to push them out for now so she could tend to Semaj.

Cutting her eyes to the space that Memphis had been standing and cautiously pulling the towel tighter around her thin frame, she forced a smile on her face and continued her conversation with Semaj, easily coming up with an excuse to put his mind to rest about what had taken her words earlier. The last thing she wanted to talk to him about was Memphis.

She never expected Mona to get a man like Memphis to be with her, but she had, and Baby swallowed her pride and attempted to move on, which was how she met Semaj in the first place. Once Memphis and Mona started really kicking it, Baby kept her distance when she knew that he was around, and he began to take up less space in her mind as time passed.

But now circumstances had brought them together once again.

HANGING A LEFT OUT OF HIS DRIVEWAY, MEMPHIS RAN HIS HAND OVER his deep waves and sighed out his frustrations. The air around him seemed peculiarly frigid, like a morbid warning of dark times to come. His intuition told him that nothing good was going to come of Baby living in his house. He knew it was wrong to leave in the middle of her speaking, but he didn't trust himself enough to have a conversation with her while she wasn't fully clothed.

"Fuck."

Grabbing his cell phone, he pressed on a name and waited impatiently while the line seemed to ring endlessly.

"Hello?"

"Mo, where da hell you at?" he gritted a little rougher than he'd intended.

It was nothing new for him to come home and realize that Mona was gone, but running into Baby, who was home on a Friday night, on the phone with a nigga who was doing major time, had him feeling some kind of way about not having the attention of his own wife. Was it too much to ask that when he got home from being in the streets, he could come back to a woman who was happy to see him?

"I'm out with Bambi! Damn, what's wrong with you now, Memphis?"

"What's wrong with me?" he started and then pushed out a breath of hot air, forcing himself to calm down. Pulling to the side of the road, he placed his car in park and ran a hand over his head before replying to Mona. His tension showed as he spoke to her through clenched teeth.

"Just let me know when you gettin' home, Mo. Ya girl in the crib, and I don't wanna make her uncomfortable by bein' there without havin' you around."

"You talking about Baby?" Mona asked, frowning from the other side of the line.

"You got another fuckin' friend stayin' at my crib that I don't know about?" Memphis shot back with a calm but icy tone, to which Mona rolled her eyes.

"She's fine with you being there. Hell, she knows you live there; where else would you be?"

When he didn't reply right away, Mona sighed into the phone and glanced at Bambi who had just finished rolling up a blunt. It was laced with Molly, and Mona was so ready for the turn up that came along with it. The last thing she wanted was to be listening to Memphis whining on the phone for her to come home. She wasn't about to stop what she had going on to cater to his needs, so he needed to man up.

"Look... I'll call her and talk to her. Everything will be fine, and I'll be home soon."

Without waiting for his reply, Mona hung up the phone and dialed Baby's line. She held on, but the call went to voicemail. Before she could leave a message, her phone beeped, letting her know a text was coming through.

Baby: I'm on the phone with Semaj. Sorry.

Fighting the urge to roll her eyes, Mona replied quickly, her long blood red stiletto nails gliding easily across the screen.

Mona: Memphis is on the way home and he's trippin about me not being there and leaving him alone with you. Just stay in the basement until I get back.

BABY'S LIPS PARTED SLIGHTLY AS SHE READ MONA'S MESSAGE. READING it a second time, she tried to ignore the fiery sting of anger that was running along her spine. She knew that she was wrong for walking around with nothing but a towel on, however, it wasn't something that she'd done deliberately to be disrespectful, and she definitely wasn't coming on to Mona's husband. For him to make it seem like he couldn't be alone in the house with her there didn't sit well with her. Did he think that she had done it on purpose? It hadn't even been a whole week, and she was already finding herself involved in the first bit of drama.

Biting down hard on her bottom lip, Baby quickly pecked out a reply, promising herself that she wouldn't allow Memphis to come between her relationship with her best friend. No matter the history of how they all came to know each other, the fact was that Memphis was Mona's, and she was Semaj's. Regardless of what he seemed to think about her, Baby wanted them both to know that she was in no way harboring any feelings for Memphis other than whatever came from him being married to her best friend.

> **Baby:** *Don't worry. I'll stay in the basement unless you're home. Promise.*
> **Mona:** *Thanks... And sorry about this shit. He's just trippin.*

Baby read her reply and then rolled her eyes before sighing heavily. She finished her conversation with Semaj, careful to listen out for anyone pulling into the yard, but no one came. By the time Memphis did make it back, she was in bed, fast asleep, and Mona was still not home.

CHAPTER FIVE

On her official first day of work, Baby woke up before anyone else to start getting herself together. With her nerves on edge, she crept up the basement stairs and into the kitchen to make a cup of coffee and prayed that it would get her right.

"Good morning to you."

She jumped high enough to qualify as a pole jumper in the Olympics. Once she overcame her shock, she saw Memphis sitting at the table with his hands wrapped around a mug. It was impossible not to see the way his muscular physique bulged from out of his simple white tee, nearly demanding her attention.

"Good morning," Baby replied with her eyes low. "I didn't see you there."

"At least this time you're fully clothed," he remarked, his tone almost reprimanding. Her neck snapped up, and she stared into him with fire in her eyes, ready to read him from A to Z. She was humble, gentle, and kind, but a pushover she was not.

"First of all, I—"

"Save it," Memphis said, raising his hand as he cut her off. "I'm not interested."

Baby's nose flared along with her rage. Who did he think he was talking to? Disrespect was not something she tolerated, and even though Memphis was probably used to talking to everyone he met any kind of way that he wished, she wasn't scared to put him in his place. However, the fact that she was living in his home made her fight to control her tongue.

She turned to grab a mug and make a cup of coffee as Memphis cut his eye at her, taking the opportunity to watch her movements. There was no mistaking it; he could tell she was boiling hot and most likely cursing his existence in her mind, but she kept her cool.

"How are you gettin' to work?" he asked before standing to toss his cup of coffee down the drain. Pouring it was a habit, but he never drank it. He hated coffee but sitting alone at the table each morning with a full cup had become one of his daily rituals.

"I figured I'd take the bus," Baby replied with a shrug. She would have been perfectly fine without the small talk but didn't want to be rude. Unlike Memphis.

She brushed past him at the same moment that he turned away from the sink. The suddenness of his movements threw off her balance, and she nearly stumbled. Reaching out, Memphis steadied her by placing his hands lightly around her waist. The subtle touch alarmed Baby enough to make her jerk, but she recovered quickly and forced out a giggle.

"Sorry about that…" she apologized, but then realized that Memphis hadn't yet pulled away. With a curled brow, she turned to him, and once her eyes connected with his, a surge of energy shot up her spine. She waited for him to say something, but he simply snatched his hands back and frowned.

"Keep your apology," he muttered without looking in her face. Stuffing his hands in his pockets, he stalked away, careful to make sure that not a single hair on his body came anywhere near hers. Her skin prickled at his body language; it was like her presence bothered him.

"Is there something wrong?" Baby couldn't help asking. She watched Memphis clench his jaw before he turned around and pierced his eyes through hers. His expression was tight… unreadable. She was usually good at picking up emotions, but he was blank.

Memphis knew that Baby was confused by his reactions toward her, but he wasn't sure how to fix it. Just before she'd walked into the kitchen, he had been at the table telling himself that it was possible to have a regular conversation with her and control his desire, but as soon as he laid eyes on her, tiptoeing through the kitchen on her pretty toes, he lost it. And then when he touched her waist... the feel of her body on his fingertips felt so familiar to him. *Too* familiar... as if they'd been lovers in another life. He couldn't trust himself around her, so he had to push her away.

Yawning, Mona waltzed into the kitchen before Memphis had a chance to respond to Baby's question, and he counted it as his saving grace. He wasn't sure how long he could keep his charade up, but at least Mona's presence saved him from a conversation he wasn't sure how to have.

"Why are y'all up so early?" Seeing Memphis sitting at the table, she walked over, placed her hands on his knees, and leaned in for a kiss. With a raised brow, he sat still as she pressed her lips against his. This wasn't their normal... they weren't the 'kiss and cuddle' type of couple, so it was obvious Mona was putting on for her audience.

"I have to go to work. It's my first day," she informed Mona, who turned up her nose at the mention of 'work'. She thanked her lucky stars each day that she was with a man rich enough to provide everything she could ever dream of. If she never wanted to, she didn't have to work a day in her life.

"Well, I have stuff to do," Mona replied, thinking of her weekly hair and nail appointment. "But Memphis can probably give you a ride."

"No, I can't." Memphis countered so quickly that both Mona and Baby fell silent for a few beats. Mona was the first to speak.

"What do you mean?" she asked, the corner of her lip pulled up into an awkward half-smile. "You're going to see your mama, right? The elementary school is on the way."

Shaking his head, Memphis stood. "Change of plans," was all he said before making a quick exit, leaving the two women alone in the tension he'd created.

"I'm sorry," Mona apologized on his behalf. "He's never said anything to me, but maybe he doesn't like you all that much. Crazy, huh?"

Without replying, Baby sipped from her coffee and tried to ignore the way her ears burned. She didn't think Mona meant anything bad by pointing it out, because it seemed obvious by his actions. She didn't know why, but it was clear that Memphis didn't want her there.

"Do you have your lesson plans completed?"

Smiling, Baby nodded her head and opened her notebook to pull out the detailed schedule she made for the year so that her new boss could see them. With a straight face, Principal Fletcher leaned over her desk to peer at the papers that she placed in front of her. She was most impressed by the way that Baby seemed to be on top of everything, but she was careful not to show it right away, a strong believer that her employees needed to prove themselves before she offered up any praise. However, it seemed that Baby was ready to do just that.

"Splendid," Principal Fletcher replied as she read through what Baby had planned for her classroom.

Regardless of the sudden turn of events in her life, Baby took her job as an elementary school teacher seriously. In fact, she dove head-first into work as a way of forgetting about her personal life.

"Well, I guess all that is left is for me to show you to your classroom."

That being said, she stood, and Baby followed behind her, biting on the inside of her cheek to keep herself from crying out with excitement. Nothing brought her more joy than spending her days teaching children, and she could hardly wait to start decorating her classroom exactly how she planned.

Although her siblings all had taken the route of getting highly decorated careers in the corporate world, becoming lawyers, doctors, and business professionals, Baby couldn't see herself doing anything that didn't involve working with children. She knew that this type of life meant that she would work twice as hard and be paid much less, but she'd never been the type of woman to need much, so she could deal with it.

"Wow," was all Baby could say once Principal Fletcher opened the doors to her classroom and then stepped back so that she would be the first to enter.

Pushing her thick bifocals further up on her thin, bird-beaked nose, Principal Fletcher let out an apologetic shrug as they both scanned the room.

"Well, it's a little small... and a little plain, but we all have to work our way up from the bottom."

In awe, Baby shook her head as she circled around the room inspecting every detail. "No... it's beautiful."

That brought a smile to Maria Fletcher's lips. It was rare that she was able to witness the pleasure that came from teaching. Spending years in the business had robbed her of her own joy, but she hoped that Baby would always feel this way, even though she suspected she most likely wouldn't. New teachers always came in with the same blissful look in their eyes that Baby had in hers, but after a few years, the reality of what they'd signed up for would settle in, and they'd realize that the difference they wanted to make in the lives of children was often shut down by politics, a meager budget, or uninvolved and uninterested parents.

"I can't wait to put up all my stuff. My goddaughter helped me make some things for the wall." Baby walked over to her desk and sat down in the chair, feeling it out for comfort before deciding that it fit her perfectly. With a shake of her head, Maria chuckled and walked back toward the door.

"Well, I'll leave you to it," she stated before making her exit and closing it behind her.

Not wasting a single second, Baby grabbed her cell phone and started taking pictures of the room to help her later on that evening when she started planning out how she would arrange all of her items in the room. But once she was done, she was hit with a wave of sadness. This was exactly the thing that she would normally call and tell Semaj about.

Although Mona was her best friend, there was no way that she would understand her feelings about her new job. Mainly because one thing that Mona vowed was that she would never work a day of her life. She had Gucci taste with a Payless work ethic and was unapologetic about it. From the beginning, her goal was always to live the life of a kept woman, and no matter how much she tried to pretend she understood, Baby could see that Mona was unable to really comprehend how it felt to have a career. Mona's only reason for going to college was to find a man, so once she latched onto Memphis, she dropped out and never looked back.

Even still, Baby was too excited to hold in her good news and found herself dialing Mona's number anyways.

"Hello?"

Frowning, Baby pulled the phone away from her face to make sure that she'd called the right number before pushing it back to her ear after realizing she had.

"Um... hello? Is this Mona's phone?"

There was a snicker before a response. "It is, but she's taking a shower."

The silence felt thick. Not only was Memphis's expressions unreadable, but his tone was as well. She couldn't pick up on his mood, and it was throwing her off. Baby's eyes darted over her classroom for a few seconds before she found her voice again.

"Um, I was... I just saw my classroom. I was excited, and I wanted to tell her about it."

"Word?" Memphis said, and she stalled, unsure of how she was supposed to respond at first. It reminded her of the first time they met, and warm tingles filled her as she was hit with nostalgia.

"Uh... yeah."

He paused, and she held her breath as she waited for his response. A normal conversation had never put her on edge like this before.

"Yo, I want you to know I think it's mad dope what you doin'.

Takes a special person to decide to work with somebody's bad ass kids."

A warm feeling started from the top of her head and spread throughout her entire body. Smiling hard, all Baby could do was mutter out a quick 'thanks'. He seemed so genuinely proud of her, even though she felt that her small accomplishments were nothing compared to his.

Scratching at his beard, Memphis lifted his eyes when he heard the water in the master bathroom come to a halt. Mona was on her way out, and as much as he wanted to continue his conversation with Baby, his time had run out.

That's for the best, he reminded himself.

"You still wanna talk to Mo? She's on her way out."

"No, I'll just call her later on," she replied, her voice much quieter than it had been before.

Memphis squeezed his eyes tight and ran his hand over his face, agitated about what was about to come out of his mouth.

"I think I owe you dinner—we… we owe you dinner," he quickly corrected himself. "A congratulatory dinner to celebrate your new job. I know you'll make a great teacher, Baby."

For a second, Baby seemed to forget that he was calling her by her name and not using a term of endearment. Still, the explosion that the word set off in her chest wasn't any less.

"Thank you," she forced out beyond the lump in her throat. "Being that I'm only working with a teacher's salary, meaning I'm broke as hell, I'm happy to take you up on that dinner offer."

Brows shooting upwards, Memphis couldn't help his surprise before he began to laugh. Being constantly surrounded by niggas who had more than a little change to spend on nonsense, along with Mona who ran through his bank account like Usain Bolt, he had forgotten how it felt to be around someone who was appreciative of the little things. It was refreshing to say the least.

"Aye, I'll see you when you get in, if I'm still around," he said, knowing damn well he would make sure to still be around. "But congrats again, a'ight?"

"Okay," was Baby's final word. She hung up the line at the exact moment that Mona opened the bathroom door and walked out. Seeing the slight smirk on Memphis's face, that she had definitely not put there, immediately piqued her curiosity.

"Who was that on the phone?" Then her eyes darted to his hand. "Wait... you answered *my* phone?"

Memphis put his hand up to stop the attitude he knew was coming before she got it started. "Yo, chill. That was just Baby. I answered to make sure she wasn't in no trouble or shit like that."

Sighing deeply, Mona rolled her eyes before sitting down to apply her body cream. "Baby is a grown ass woman. If she's having an emergency, I'm sure she could handle it on her own just fine until I got out the shower."

"Wasn't no emergency. She called to tell you that she just saw her classroom for the first time."

Turning to Memphis, Mona hit him with a blank stare.

"And?" She lifted her hands, palms-up.

Irritation burned in his chest. "And she was excited to tell you. It's her first gig, and you're her best friend, Mo."

Rolling her eyes once again, Mona continued moisturizing her body. "I don't see what's to be excited about. She's making pennies to deal with somebody's raggedy ass kids all day. Whoop-de-doo."

"Whoop-de-doo? She's your friend, Mo. The least you could do is pretend to be happy for her. Bein' a teacher ain't nothing to look down at. If it wasn't for havin' one who gave a shit about me, I wouldn't have made it this far."

It was true, and Mona was well-versed in the story of Memphis's upbringing and how, after being born to parents who failed him, his teacher, Ms. Donaldson, pretty much took him in and made sure that he was cared for. She couldn't officially take him from his parents' home since his mother refused to let him go and lose out on the check she was getting for him, but he spent the majority of his time at Cleo Donaldson's house, and she raised him like her son. Mona didn't care for Cleo at all, and the feeling was mutual because Cleo couldn't stand her either, but she dealt with the woman for Memphis's sake.

Mona didn't give a damn about the fact that she might have offended Memphis because of how he felt about teachers, but it did concern her that he was so into taking up for Baby. For only this reason, she decided to back down.

"Memphis, I'm sorry, baby," Mona apologized, fidgeting with her fingers as she walked to him. "I wasn't thinking about you. I just—"

"That's the problem we keep havin'," Memphis began with a clipped tone that showed his frustration. "You never think of anyone outside of yourself. You think I wouldn't notice this?"

Opening his hand, Memphis revealed the panther diamond ring that he'd been holding inside of his clenched fist. Anyone with eyes knew it cost a grip, and it was a direct violation of his request for Mona to curb her spending habit. As soon as her eyes landed on the ring, Mona withdrew a little from him, dropping her jaw. Her eyes scanned the room as she fumbled for a reply.

"I—I just... well, it's not like we can't afford it!" she snapped after failing to come up with an adequate response. "Why would you give me all these cards if you don't want me to use them?"

Without saying a word, Memphis positioned his steely gaze on her face, stuffed the ring in his pocket, and then held out his empty palm as Mona stared at it in sheer horror. The kind of horror felt by those who had never worked a day in their life but was ready to crumble into a stupor at the thought of losing their black card.

"W—what's that for?" She squinted at his hand and then at him. "You want me to give them back?"

Memphis said nothing, and Mona's eyes bugged further out of her skull. They had their issues, and anyone could see they weren't the typical loving couple. Mona had gotten used to the fact that she was married to someone who tolerated her rather than loved her and always fell back on her love for nice things to make her feel better about it. But now Memphis was trying to even take that away and leave her with nothing.

"Fine!" she spat and then grabbed her wallet. Slipping the black card from out of it, she tossed it angrily into Memphis's open hand, but he still didn't move a muscle.

"What? You can't want *all* of them?"

Still nothing from him, and Mona's fury quickly grew from a flicker to a roaring flame. With her gray eyes hot enough to melt ice in the winter, she opened her wallet then snatched out every single card that Memphis had ever given to her and threw them all across their bed.

Memphis was immune to her temper tantrum because, over the years, he'd gotten used to her antics and simply waited for her to finish with the dramatics before grabbing the cards and pushing them into his back pocket. He then walked over to the safe that was hidden behind a picture of Genie inside their closet, keyed in the code and pulled out a few stacks, thumbing quickly through them before closing it back. Returning to her, he slapped the stacks of cash on top of the dresser, with a resounding thump, and then turned to her. Mona was enraged as she glared at him. She was not some bimbo playing the role of his sidepiece. She was his wife, and she refused to be treated like a child who couldn't be trusted.

"I'll give you more next week. But when this runs out… it's out," he explained to her, laying down the law without leaving room for rebuttal.

"So that's how you wanna play this?" Mona shot back as if it were a challenge. "You're making the decisions about *our* future without caring whether I agree or not? I have to be on a budget and live a regular ass life just because you suddenly decided that you wanna get out the streets and play it straight? What? Is there some new street nigga 'round here who got you shook or something?"

Brushing the bridge of his nose with his thumb, Memphis felt his temper rising and knew that Mona was dancing dangerously close to a line that she knew better than to cross. If you couldn't keep your own woman in check, your word didn't mean shit in the streets. That was the code he lived by, and she was aware of it but needed a reminder. Walking back to the dresser, Memphis snatched up the stacks of cash and stuffed them in his pocket.

"You know what? Fuck all this. Just get your shit and get the fuck out." He said the words so calmly that Mona wasn't sure she'd actually heard him right. Her eyelids fluttered as she fought to make sense of his demand.

"Wh—what did you say?"

His eyes flared, and he launched his glare at her like missiles. "Ain't no muthafuckin' repeat. You heard what da fuck I said."

Astonished, Mona's mouth dropped wide open. The room was so quiet that you could probably hear a mouse pissing on a wet blade of grass somewhere outside. Never before had she seen Memphis as furious as he was now, but never before had she mocked his status in the streets or his manhood.

"What about Genie? You can't just kick me out like—"

A harsh chuckle escaped through his lips. "You mean your daughter? The one I barely even see you with? I'm sure she'll be fine. Long as the nurse here, right?"

Her cheeks burned. Although she had to agree that what he was saying was true, he'd never opened his mouth to talk down on her as a mother. She knew that he had his judgments about how much she avoided dealing with Genie, but he'd never once said a thing.

"I—Memphis… baby, I'm sorry!" Mona panicked; her eyes darted around while she tried to think of a way to earn his forgiveness. After what he'd said about Genie, there was no doubt in her mind that he would actually put her out onto the streets. If nothing else, Memphis was definitely a man of his word.

"I was so upset, and I…" Her words trailed off into the thick air surrounding them.

Unable to think of anything she could do to ease the tension in the room and eager to save her own hide, Mona fell back on the one thing she knew she was good at and the only thing that Memphis ever seemed to need from her: her sex. Dropping to her knees, she scrambled toward him and grabbed at his jeans.

With an indignant snort, he took a step back and swatted at her hands. But she was desperate to right her wrongs and remained diligent until she'd managed to snatch open his jeans and release his flaccid pole. Even completely soft, he was working with a monster. He watched her illustrate her subservience and eagerness to please by taking him within her jaws and sucking hungrily, steadily forcing him down her throat. Within no time, he was elongated to his full length and thick as a fist as she continued her masterful work, spitting and gagging while pleasing him.

"Where is Genie?" he asked, his tone coarse with lust.

"At the park," Mona replied and darted her eyes to the clock beside her. "Should be back in about thirty minutes." She sucked him back in, pushing him deep down her throat, and he relaxed, closing his eyes as she brought him pleasure.

After having his fill, Memphis nudged her away and she fell back on her naked butt, looking up at him with eyes full of pain and hurt. Without saying a word, he bent down and scooped her up into his arms, wrapping her legs around his waist. She kissed his jawline, her attempt at romanticizing the moment, but he pulled away. This was not about love... For him, it was just necessity. He placed her back against the wall and began to impale her sharply, filling her completely. It had been so long since the last time he'd touched her, and Mona was reminded of that when she felt her walls begin to stretch. She crooned to the high heavens, singing a song that Memphis was dictating into her with each thrust. Like a hungry animal, he grabbed at her pendulous breasts and sucked them into his mouth, teasing her hardened nipple with the tip of his tongue before sucking feverishly to make her gush.

"Ahhhhh..." Mona could feel her succulent juices running down from her honeypot, and she tossed her head back as she enjoyed her impending climax.

Something told her that he never meant to make her cum, but his dick was so good to her that she did every time. With each stroke, Memphis was skillfully hitting her g-spot and she was about to explode. And from the way that he was spreading her thighs and sending long, harsh jabs straight to her center, she knew that he wasn't far behind.

They came together, and it was like electricity shooting from

Mona's middle straight up to her brain, a cataclysmic overload of pleasure that she could barely comprehend. She felt her body go limp in his arms, but he supported her without waver, carrying her to the bed where he carefully lay her on top of their sheets. He watched the peaceful look on Mona's face as she rolled over and clutched the pillow under her head.

Before long, Memphis knew that she'd be fast asleep. A part of him wished that she had left and he could be through with her, but he knew how much Genie loved her mother. He never wanted to destroy his baby girl by ripping her family apart, unless he couldn't help it.

Directly below where he stood staring at the woman he was forced to be with, the woman he desired had just walked into the front door. After arriving home and catching more than an earful of Mona's loud erotic testament to their lovemaking, Baby was frozen in place. She'd caught only the tail end of their passionate moment, but it was still enough for her to long for the days when a man had made her feel that way.

With her head down and her shoulders hunched over, Baby scurried through the large house as quickly as she could, not stopping until she closed the basement door behind her. It wouldn't be quite the same, but luckily, she had a battery-operated tool for moments exactly like this.

CHAPTER SIX

"I can't believe I'm letting you convince me to go out with you. And on a school night at that! I still have to be at work in the morning and—"

Completely uninterested in her excuses, Mona waved Baby's worries away with a flick of her wrist and continued zipping up her knee-high stiletto boots. All she was getting from Baby were constant protests, but she wasn't paying them the slightest attention. She was focused on getting out of the house, and if Baby tagged along, it meant Memphis wouldn't be on her ass about going out yet again. Plus, she felt it might do some good for Baby to go out and party. Outside of playing with Genie, she spent all her time moping around, clutching her phone and waiting for Semaj's calls. Mona wasn't taking no for an answer and was determined to have a night of dancing, drinking, and fun with her best friend.

"Girl, relax," Mona said. "We won't be out all that long. One of Memphis's homeboys is throwing his birthday party at the club tonight, and everyone who is anybody is going to be there. I definitely have to make an appearance."

Cocking her head to the side, Baby watched as she applied cherry lipstick to her full lips, wondering why Mona felt she needed to make an appearance if it was Memphis's friend's birthday.

"Well, if Memphis is going, why do I have to go with you?"

Snorting, Mona rolled her eyes yet again. "Because Memphis *isn't* going. He stopped going to these parties a while ago... around the same time that he got it into his head that he wanted to pull out of the street life. The only time he steps out is if it's for a top member of his crew."

Baby wrinkled her nose when she saw the disdain on her face. "Shouldn't you want him to pull out of that life, too? I mean... look at what happened to Semaj."

Mona put the finishing touches on her lipstick before raking her eyes at Baby and giving her an arrogant look.

"Baby, I hope you don't take this the wrong way, but Memphis is not Semaj. He wouldn't make those same stupid mistakes." Baby's cheeks burned red, but Mona continued. "Memphis has the potential to take over the entire east coast if he wanted to. To step out at the height of his empire is a stupid move. Even Jay-Z had to come back after retiring at the height of his career... It's foolish to leave all that money on the table and just walk away. Everybody knows that."

Baby couldn't disagree more, but she decided to let the topic go. Although she didn't know as much as Mona about Memphis and who he was on a personal level, she would have to be blind to not see that he was intelligent in ways that went far above his gangsta ways. At the very core, he operated like a businessman and made decisions in the streets the same way that a CEO of a Fortune 500 company did. It didn't matter what business he was over, he would prevail like a boss in every way.

Walking out of Mona's room, Baby stepped into the kitchen to raid the liquor cabinet for something to calm her nerves so that she could have fun and relax, even though being at a club was out of her element. Opening the cabinet, she pushed through the drinks until she saw something that was a little more sweet than sour, and poured herself a shot.

"Getting your pregame together, huh?" a voice said from behind, nearly making her choke as she tossed back her drink.

Turning around, her eyes connected with Memphis who was standing at the large island in the middle of the kitchen. With a knowing look on his face, he watched her. She was a vision of perfection in his eyes, but it would be his secret.

"I guess Mona's draggin' you out the house with her tonight," he added, and Baby nodded her head before wiping her mouth with her forearm.

"Clubs aren't really my thing, but I guess it wouldn't hurt to dress up and have a good time," she replied with a shrug.

Her mention of 'dressing up' made him lower his head to fully take in what she was wearing. He couldn't deny that she looked amazing. Wearing only a simple, short all white dress, cinched at the waist by a Hermes belt and paired with camel-colored boots, she was breathtaking and had no idea of the effect she had on him.

"You look really nice," Memphis complimented with a nod as he spoke. "I like your style: simple, low-key, but still fresh as fuck."

Baby blushed at his choice of words but appreciated them. She'd felt self-conscious about what she'd chosen to wear once she saw Mona's outfit which looked like she'd snatched it straight off the runway during Fashion Week. It couldn't possibly have cost anything less than a couple thousand dollars in total.

"I'm not all that much into fashion and labels, but I do my best," Baby replied with a slight shrug. Memphis watched her body language, noticing how much she valued his praise even though she never struck him as less than confident. He'd long ago stopped giving Mona compliments when he realized that they were expected instead of cherished.

"Your best is more than enough," Memphis found himself saying, and Baby's entire body went warm.

They stood in silence for more than a few minutes, his eyes on Baby and her eyes on her feet. She teetered a little, her way of trying to suppress the emotions stirring inside of her... emotions that she knew she couldn't allow herself to feel. But how do you tell the butterflies in your stomach to go away when you didn't make them come? She was at the mercy of her body's automatic response to Memphis and at a loss on how to deal with it.

"Daddy, I'm ready!" Genie called from the other room, breaking the silence. A second later, she'd wheeled into the kitchen wearing a big grin on her face. Baby took the opportunity to break away from Memphis and walked over to plant a kiss on her forehead.

"Ohh, Gotty, you look pretty!" she squealed, and Baby turned around to model off her outfit.

"I'm glad you like it."

"You look like a princess," she added. "Doesn't she, Daddy?"

Blushing, Baby turned to Memphis but shook her head to let him know that he didn't have to respond.

"She's beautiful," he said, looking her right in her eyes with a straight face. The intensity in his pupils sent chills up her spine.

"Stunning," he continued. "And a princess is a'ight, but she looks like a queen."

Giggling, Genie began to clap in agreement, and Baby took a deep breath to still the butterflies swarming in her belly.

"Daddy, make sure you get the honeybuns, and don't forget the extra butter on the popcorn," Genie requested of her father who turned to her and bowed deeply.

"Your wish is my command."

"That's *my* line, Daddy!" she squealed in laughter. "I'm the genie, not you!"

"But I'm the Daddy, so it's my job to give you everything you ask for. I'll be in there in a minute, okay?" Satisfied with his answer, Genie nodded and rolled away, but not before blowing her godmother a kiss.

"I'm a little late for daddy-daughter movie night," Memphis said with a wink.

Baby eyed him from behind with complete admiration as he opened the cabinet and started pulling out chips, cookies, and all kinds of other snacks. Watching him, she felt a familiar feeling stirring in her the pit of her stomach, but she knew it was taboo to give into it. She dampened her lips and forced herself to glance away.

"Okay, I'm almost ready to go," Mona's voice rang out from somewhere down the hall.

Looking down at her wrist as she struggled to clasp a diamond bracelet, Mona entered the room, and Baby had never been so thankful for her presence in all her life. Her emotions were walking dangerously close to a line that shouldn't ever be crossed.

An expert at reading the people around him, Memphis could see Baby's relief once Mona entered the room and wondered if he'd done anything to make her uncomfortable. He could barely control himself when Baby was around. She was gorgeous to him... just as gorgeous as she'd been the day that he'd first laid eyes on her.

The fact that she was standing in his kitchen with a short ass dress on and her thick, smooth thighs on display already felt like the most wicked form of temptation. She had his nature rising, and she wasn't even trying. Being the type of man that was disciplined when it came to all things, it frustrated him that he couldn't pull back when it came to her.

"You look beautiful," Baby said as she took in Mona's complete ensemble. "I love what you did with your hair."

"Would you have expected anything less from me?" Mona replied in her typical way, spinning around to give Baby a better look. "I'm going to grab my clutch really quick, and then we can leave."

Almost as fast as she had come, Mona was gone again, leaving Memphis and Baby enveloped in the same awkward silence they'd be in before she'd made her entrance. Being that Baby's mouth seemed glued shut, Memphis was the first to speak.

"That tattoo is new." He pointed to the base of her neck when he saw the puzzled look on Baby's face.

"Oh, yeah..." Smiling hard, she nodded, realizing that he was referring to the baby elephant tattoo behind her neck. "It's not all that new. I've had it for about a year."

"I knew I didn't remember it. Definitely didn't have it when I first saw you. You was all innocent and shit then... now you tatted up. I guess you're a bad girl now." The teasing smile on his lips filled her stomach with butterflies. She grinned at the playful expression on his face.

"Innocent? So you think you know me, huh?"

"I know enough," Memphis said, crossing his arms in front of his chest. "When I first met you, I knew you wasn't the type of chick to get a kick out of entertaining these empty-head ass niggas out here. I picked up on that even with them little ass shorts you had on. You wasn't the type of chick that was for everybody."

"But that's what you married though."

The words flew out of Baby's mouth before she realized exactly what she was saying. Her mouth dropped open, and she immediately felt the need to apologize.

"I can't believe I said that," she whispered to herself, but Memphis still heard it.

"Never apologize for telling me how you feel," he told her, even though he could still feel the burn of her words in his chest. It was true. He'd married the exact kind of woman he couldn't stand.

"Even if you think it's fucked up to say it. If it's what you feel, I wanna hear it."

Before Baby could reply, the sound of Mona's heels against the tile floor announced her arrival, and before long, she entered the kitchen, texting on her phone while holding her gold Chanel clutch in her hand.

"Ready?" she asked without raising her head, and Baby nodded, her cheeks growing warm as she thought about what she'd just said about her friend.

Though true, it seemed like betrayal to mention it to Memphis the way that she had. Mona had always been thirsty for male attention; it wasn't like it was a lie. Still, she'd said the words with the intention of throwing them in Memphis's face like a diss, subtly reprimanding him for the choice he'd made. Until that moment, she hadn't even admitted to herself what her true feelings were about how he'd picked Mona over her. She'd simply pushed him from her mind and considered him off limits. The fact that she hadn't seen him much since made it easier to pretend that he didn't exist. Being in the position where she was forced to be in his presence and reminded of him each day was making it impossible to forget and ignore how she felt about him.

"I'm ready," Baby replied, realizing that Mona couldn't hear her nodding.

Without looking back at Memphis, who was openly admiring her without shame, Baby grabbed her own clutch and cell phone from the kitchen counter then waltzed by him. He took a deep breath as she passed and found himself spellbound by the scent of her perfume. She was pleasing to three of his five senses. He already knew she looked, sounded, and smelled good. All that was left now was touch and taste.

"I'll be back late, so don't bother waiting up," Mona said, and Memphis glanced at her for the first time since she'd entered the room.

"You gon' kiss your daughter goodbye?"

"Of course I am," Mona shot back although speaking to Genie before she left hadn't even been on her mind. She doubled back to Memphis before leaving.

Staring into his face, Mona puckered her lips for a kiss, and he mired as he battled the thoughts in his head. Behind him, Baby had been watching while waiting for Mona, but an uneasy feeling settled on her, and she left to tell her goddaughter goodnight.

"I wish you could stay and have fun with me and daddy," Genie said as Baby kissed her on her cheek.

"I wish I could stay with you too, but mommy wants me to go out with her tonight."

A frown fell upon the young child's face. "Mommy is always going out." She paused for a few seconds, and Baby could see her thinking about something. Suddenly, her eyes clouded with tears.

"Do you think she loves me?" The question broke Baby's heart, and she found her own eyes filling with tears.

"Of course she does, Genie. There is nothing about you *not* to love. You're beautiful, you're smart, and you're the most amazing person I've ever met. I love you more than life itself, and I know your mommy does, too. Don't ever doubt that."

A small smile came up on her lips, and Baby kissed her once more on the forehead before telling her goodnight and walking out the front door to meet Mona in the car. She took a deep breath and let it out slowly. In only a few seconds, her mind went back to Memphis and the way she'd been feeling with him in the kitchen.

God, please help me. This is wrong.

She felt it and she knew it. Never in her life had she thought she would be in the position that she was finding herself in. Maybe it was the loneliness of being without Semaj. But even as the thought crossed her mind, she knew it was a lie. What she was feeling wasn't new. They were emotions that she'd buried long ago, and they were only coming to the surface once again.

"We are going to have *so* much fun!" Mona gushed as soon as she jumped in the driver's seat of her luxury ride and started the engine.

Baby wasn't convinced, but she forced a smile on her lips and simply nodded her head. Even though she would rather have stayed in, being at the club and away from Memphis would do her some good. She was beginning to think that she had made a huge mistake by moving into his home in the first place.

MONA COULDN'T BE ANYONE ELSE BUT THE WOMAN SHE WAS BORN TO be, and she was unapologetic about that fact. Although Memphis always voiced how much he hated that she just had to be at every party that was popping, she never let his opinion stop her from going. At the end of the day, he made decisions to do what made him happy, even though she didn't always agree, so why shouldn't she do the same?

As soon as Mona took off her coat and tossed it to the hostess of the club, she was snapping her fingers and working her neck to the music. This was her comfort zone. Memphis didn't get it because he liked to live life in the low-key lane, but there was nothing low-key about Mona. She was fabulous, and she was born to live that way.

"Oh shit! The first lady of the *Murda Mob* has entered the building! Everybody, throw your sets up and represent!"

Smiling, Mona rolled her eyes at the announcement, making it seem like she didn't appreciate being called out before turning to Baby who was standing a few steps behind her, comfortable outside of the spotlight.

"It's lit as fuck in here! The crowd is thick!"

Thick wasn't the word. The club was stacked to max capacity, making Baby wonder how they were going to squeeze their way through. Fortunately, this wasn't something she had to think on for too long, because with every step that she and Mona took, the crowd parted like the Red Sea for them to make their way through.

It's like being royalty, Baby thought as she walked behind Mona who led the way like a queen maneuvering through her loyal subjects.

"Is this how it is every time you go out?" Baby asked with a slight frown once they were situated in V.I.P. Mona nodded her head and cut her eyes at Baby, making a face that screamed 'duh!'.

"This is Memphis's city, and this is the treatment that comes along with being the first lady of the streets."

Retreating into her thoughts, Baby cast her eyes over the crowd and noticed that more than a couple eyes were staring back at her. Thankfully, she had taken a shot to ease her nerves because there was no way that she would be able to find comfort while being on display had she been absolutely sober. Mona noticed that she was not the center of attention, and it automatically ruined her mood.

Glancing at Baby, she sized her up quickly, wondering whether or not she'd been right about what she'd picked for her to wear. Although she had selected something that she knew Baby would look decent in, she'd been careful to make sure that it couldn't touch how she looked in her fit. Even so, it seemed that the lion's share of attention was going to her friend, and Mona was not having that.

"Would you like something to sip on?" a waitress asked once she approached them. Mona smiled evilly as she looked at the red-colored wine, thinking that she'd shown up at the perfect time.

"Yes," she replied, grabbing a glass flute. She put it to her lips as Baby's eyes scanned around the thick club giving Mona the opportunity she needed.

"Oops! Oh my God, I'm so sorry!" She apologized after faking a 'slip' that ended up with the front of Baby's dress being doused with nearly half of the wine that was in her glass. "Let me help you. Can we get some napkins?"

She looked at the waitress who was still standing there and had witnessed the entire accident, which was apparent by the sour look on her face. Mona didn't give a damn if she'd seen what happened or not; the woman knew better than to say a word about it.

"Sure, I'll bring them up to the V.I.P.," was her tense reply before she walked away.

"Don't worry about it," Baby said, stopping her. "I'll just go to the restroom and clean up."

"I'm so sorry about that. Damn, I ruined your entire outfit."

"It's no big deal," Baby replied as she wiped at the liquid. She hadn't really wanted to be at the club anyways and wasn't planning on talking to anyone, so this was no disaster for her.

"Damn, shorty, you lookin' good as hell. You need help with that spill?" a man asked, his eyes on Baby as he stepped up in front of her and Mona. "Aye, Mo, you wanna introduce me to your friend?"

"Craig, she's not available, so move the fuck on," Mona replied with a frustrated swat of her hand that told him to leave. Even with the stain, Baby was still collecting the attention that should have been going to her. She vowed that this would be the last time she invited her out again unless she was dressed like a nun.

ACROSS FROM WHERE BABY AND MONA STOOD, A STREET NIGGA BY THE name of Sly stood watching the both of them with an intense look in his eyes. A knowing smirk rose up on his lips as he watched their exchange.

"That's her right there?" he asked one of his men standing by his side. "That's the one you heard about?"

"Yeah, that's her... Memphis's wife."

This is going to be easier than I thought.

The last couple months since he'd been let out of prison had been difficult for Sly, but things were looking up. He'd had a major setback when he was released and found out that he was without a connect. His luck took another turn for the worse when Memphis had refused to meet with him to discuss putting him on, but he had a feeling that things were about to change.

"What you thinkin' 'bout right now, nigga? I see the wheels in your head turning," his boy Rome asked with a grin on his face. "I hope you ain't tryin' to holla at ole girl. One of my niggas said he might be able to get us in to meet with Memphis. You don't wanna fuck that up."

Sly heard him, but he had a feeling that things with Memphis may not turn out the way he wanted them to, which meant that he had to think ahead.

"I'm thinkin' of a backup plan," he replied and watched as Baby walked toward them still wiping at the stain on her dress. He moved, positioning himself so that she had to pass right in front of him.

"Hey," he whispered almost directly in her ear before grabbing her lightly on the arm. "Let me holla at you for a second, beautiful."

Frowning, Baby pulled her arm away before lifting her head to meet his eyes. "No, that's okay. I'm fine."

"I know you're fine. That I can see for myself." He smirked, biting down on his bottom lip as he slowly looked over her body.

Baby snorted at his lame line and was about to move past him when he blocked her way. One glance up at V.I.P., and he saw that Mona's eyes were on them, watching with a jealous glare as he tried to shoot his shot at Baby. He had to stop himself from chuckling at the success of his carefully laid plan.

"I can't get a few minutes of your time?"

"No," she shot back, not rudely but as a matter of fact. "I'm not really in the mood to meet anyone new." She lifted her hand and showed off the ring on her finger. "I'm engaged."

"What that mean? You can't have friends?"

"I already have all the friends I need. Now can you move so I can take care of this?" Baby pointed at the stain on her dress and Sly paused, admitting to himself that he kind of liked the fact that she was not at all interested in him in the least. As a man, he liked the thrill of the chase, and Baby was proving to be the type that would definitely give him a run for his money, but she wasn't his target. He glanced up to see if Mona was still watching and was delighted to see that not only was all of her attention still on them, but she had left her seat and was heading their way.

"I'll move when you give me your number," he countered, and Baby scoffed.

"That's not going to happen. I'm not interested."

Feeling the sting of her rejection, Sly looked her over and once again reminded himself that Baby was just a means to an end. He was intrigued by her and would have jumped at the chance to fight to gain her affection, but he would have to think about all that much later.

"Listen, all I want is—"

"She *said* she's not interested," Mona quipped, coming up behind Baby. She narrowed her eyes at Sly before turning to her friend.

"I saw that you were being bothered, and figured I'd come help."

Although Baby ate up the lie that Mona was feeding her, Sly recognized it for the game it was. He'd seen many women like Mona before. She was the type who viewed her friends as competition and couldn't stand to see them get the attention that she felt only she deserved.

"Aye, I was only trying to holla at shorty, that's all," Sly explained with a shrug. "A nigga like me just wanna find something young and fine to spend my money on."

Just as he'd suspected, his last sentence sent a spark through Mona's eyes.

Bingo.

He could read her like a book. She was the typical gold-digger. How in the world a nigga like Memphis got caught up with a chick like this, was beyond him. The nigga had gotten caught slipping in the worst of ways. Sly knew that chicks like Mona were poison in the game and the downfall of a lot of street niggas because their loyalty was only to themselves.

"Well, she's not interested," Mona repeated, but although her mouth was no longer moving, the rest of her statement was all in her eyes. *But I am.*

"I get it," Sly replied, looking at Mona in a way that let her know he'd picked up on the words she hadn't said. While running his tongue over the inside of his bottom lip, he let his eyes run down her body lustfully and watched the slowness of her breaths as she watched him. He undressed her expertly with just a single look. Once he connected back with her eyes, he knew then that he had her right where he wanted her.

Without saying a word, she turned and walked with Baby into the restroom and he watched them as they left. Before disappearing around the corner, Mona cut her eyes to him one last time, and he cradled her stare with intensity, letting her know that he was looking at the woman he needed in his life. She smirked slightly before disappearing out of his sight, but he knew she'd be back.

❧

"HERE YOU GO," A WAITRESS SAID AS SHE PASSED BY BABY AND PLACED A bottle of Moet on the small table between them. With her eyes pinned on Mona, she said, "This bottle is courtesy of the gentleman over there."

She nudged her head in a direction that Mona's eyes followed until they settled on a large, muscular figure in the far-right corner of the club. It was the man that had been trying to speak to Baby earlier. Mona squinted to get a better look and watched as he raised his hand to his forehead in salute. His swag was impeccable as he sat in the middle of a group of men, none of them quite as fly as he, wearing an all-white ensemble that reminded Mona of something she'd admired on the Givenchy runway.

"Who did he say for you to send this to?" Mona asked the waitress. "Me or her?"

"You."

A grin spread across Mona's face, but just as soon as it arrived, it was gone as she feigned a look of disgust.

"So he was only talking to you to try to get to me. Nigga's ain't shit," she spat. She didn't know how true her statement was. Sly *had* only talked to Baby to get at Mona but not in the way that she thought.

"I don't really care anyways," Baby replied with a shrug. "He's not my type."

"Oh right. I forgot you prefer felons."

Baby's cheeks flamed at Mona's words, but she fought to not show in her face that she was hurt by Mona's words. She knew that her friend always said what was on her mind, and through the years, she'd learned to not be bothered by it. But sometimes her opinion still stung.

Much later, after the bottle of Moet was long gone, Mona still couldn't pull her eyes away from the man who had purchased it for her. Her eyes settled once again on him, and she watched with an unwavering stare as he interacted with his counterparts. It was obvious to anyone watching him that he was the natural leader of the crew. The others revered him in a way that was observed rather than heard, their behavior and body language showing that they regarded him for the boss that he seemed to be.

Sly knew he was being watched, so he made sure to put on extra hard for Mona, using every opportunity to pull out the wad of cash in his pocket and flash his wealth. What little bit of wealth he had anyways. Truth be told, what he had in his pocket was pretty much all he had left of his past fortune that had dwindled away to nearly nothing since he'd been in prison. When he pulled out his knot and pretended to count through the big face hundreds, Mona could no longer stay in her seat. She just had to see what this new paid nigga was all about.

"I'll be back," Mona muttered and dashed away before Baby had a chance to ask her where she was headed.

With her eyes pinned on the subject of her jumbled thoughts, Mona scurried away, eager to know who he was. No one she'd ever seen had commanded so much awe and admiration by his mere presence. No one other than Memphis, that is, but he didn't seem to flourish in it like this new man did. Just as Mona had nearly made it over to him, the man lifted his eyes and found hers as if he'd known the entire time that she was heading his way. With a subtle toss of her head, she silently requested him to follow her as she hugged a left and made a beeline down the back hall of the club that led to the restroom. Standing in the center of the hall, Mona waited until she saw him round the corner, before she keyed in a code and walked through the door and into the room where they stored their alcohol products.

"You sent me that bottle... Why?" Mona asked as soon as he entered the small room, wasting no time before getting to the question that had been lingering in her mind. "I thought you liked my friend."

She swallowed hard, struggling to keep her composure as she got an up-close look at him.

Damn, she thought as she scrutinized his features.

He was even sexier than she'd initially thought. With large, almond-shaped eyes that seemed to say a hundred words before his lips had the chance to utter one, the way he looked at her had her clenching her lady lips below extra tight. His hair was cut low to perfection with waves flowing in 360-degree swirls around his head. His goatee was slightly thicker and provided a nice frame around his thick, juicy lips, which held a subtle pout, making Mona wonder how it would be to suck on them to her heart's content.

"That was before I saw you. I ain't trying to diss yo' girl, but shorty can't hold a candle to you," he replied smoothly, and Mona's grin spread across her lips like the Cheshire cat. He was definitely speaking her language, and she was too selfish and caught up in herself to even recognize it for the game it was.

"You know who I am, don't you? I'm sure you do," she declared cockily. Without batting an eye, the man nodded his head sharply.

"I heard a little something, but I'm not the type of nigga who dwells on the past, because I'm too busy planning for the future." With that, he grabbed her hand from by her side and lifted it to his lips, pressing them gently against her skin. Mona sucked in a breath and tried to mask the way he was making her feel, but he picked up on it anyways. He was playing her like a fiddle, but she craved the attention of a boss too much to even realize it.

"They call me Sly."

Cocking her head to the side, Mona let her eyes smile while her lips did the talking.

"*They* call you Sly? Well, what do you want me to call you?"

"Your man," he replied as if the words had been waiting on the tip of his tongue.

His brazen confidence made her laugh. It had been a while since any man had flirted with her in this way. Being that it was well known whom she belonged to, no other man had the nerve to step to her in this way for fear of Memphis.

"I think I prefer to stick with calling you Sly for now."

Mona called herself playing hard to get, but Sly knew better. They called him Sly for a reason; he was just as smart as he was arrogant and cocky. There wasn't a single doubt in his mind that he could fuck Mona tonight if he played his cards right. In all of his twenty-eight years of being on God's green Earth, he'd never met a woman who could resist his southern charm, good looks, and confident swagger. His quick assessment of Mona told him that she was no different from any broad he'd had the pleasure of charming the panties off before.

"Let me get that for a minute," Sly told her before slipping her cell phone out of her hand. He keyed in his number, pressed the call button, and then handed it back.

Pursing her lips, she rolled her eyes at the way he'd gotten her number without asking.

"Very smooth." Her voice was dripping with sarcasm.

"Yo, you got a slick ass mouth," Sly told her with a charming smile. This shit was too easy for him, and he wasn't the least bit interested in her, but since his life depended on it, he played his part like a seasoned actor.

"I'll be calling you."

With that final proclamation, Sly bent down and kissed her gently against her lips, succeeding in stealing every breath from her body, before turning around and walking out the door. His exit was as smooth as his entrance had been, and as soon as he left her, Mona found herself missing him.

"Damn," she uttered, bringing her fingertips to her lips. It was almost like she'd imagined their interaction, but she could still feel the way his lips felt against hers. The quick embrace had been so soft but so commanding. He kissed her how a man was supposed to kiss a woman. The way a man kissed a woman who *belonged* to him. The way a man kissed a woman he *desired*. It hurt Mona to admit, but it had been a long time since she'd been kissed like that. And she knew for sure that Memphis had *never* kissed her in quite that way.

After taking a few minutes to get herself together, Mona walked out of the room and headed back to rejoin Baby in the V.I.P. She felt the heat of Sly's stare on her back, but she kept her eyes forward and battled the desire to glance his way.

"Everything okay?" Baby asked Mona once she sat down in her seat next to her. She'd noticed that Mona had been followed down the hall and also noticed that as soon as he emerged, Mona soon appeared after him.

"Yes," Mona replied. "He just tried to get me to pay him some attention, but I wasn't feeling that shit. I especially wasn't about to pay him any attention when he dissed you. He told me that he was interested in you until he saw me and knew I was the real prize. What kind of shit is that to say?"

Baby frowned. "Wow…"

"I know!" Mona gushed, knowing that she'd probably hurt Baby's feelings, but she had to put her in her place. In Atlanta, Mona was the head bitch, and just like everyone else, Baby had to understand that.

Throughout the night, Mona tried her best to have a good time while dancing, having girl talk with Baby, and sipping drinks, but she couldn't brush away her curiosity about the man who called himself Sly. She tried her best to appear that she wasn't looking as he fraternized with his homeboys and even swallowed down the bitter taste of her jealousy when she saw him pull a beautiful woman onto his lap.

You want me to tell her to fuck off? He'd texted her as the woman grinded on his lap.

Yes, was Mona's reply, and he wasted no time pulling the woman up and dismissing her. It was his subtle way of letting her know that couldn't no bitch come close to her, and Mona ate it up like a gourmet meal.

By the time she left, he knew their brief encounter had her mind hostage just as he'd planned. He'd carried out his plot so well that even when Mona got into the bed that night and pulled the covers over her body, the last person on her mind was not the man who was supposed to be lying in the bed by her side.

The last person on her mind was Sly.

꜊

UNABLE TO SLEEP, BABY WAS LYING IN HER BED STARING AT THE CEILING as Sade sung in the background about how love was stronger than pride, thinking about the day she met Semaj.

She'd been on her way to class when she got a text from Mona asking if she could skip her next class because there was something huge that she had to tell her. Baby wasn't the type to skip class and hated even considering it but did it anyways since Mona insisted. But as soon as she heard what the 'something huge' was that Mona just had to share, she regretted it.

"Look!" Mona gushed, waving her hand in the air while making sure to give an extra wiggle to her ring finger. "Memphis popped the question, and I said YES! Isn't my ring gorgeous?"

It felt like the hardest thing she'd ever attempted for Baby, to keep a neutral face and fake her happiness for her best friend.

"Yes, it's... amazing!" she pushed out with a tongue that felt as heavy as a ton of bricks.

Baby smiled and tried to swallow down the lump in her throat, while Mona continued chatting away excitedly over the details of his proposal, but the lump only seemed to grow. Ever since the first time she'd laid eyes on Memphis, she couldn't get him out of her mind. However, she kept her distance because Mona was clear about wanting him, and Baby never wanted

86

a man to come between them. Even with that, it still felt like she died a little every time Mona mentioned how she'd seen him or gone out with him... and it definitely killed her to hear the details of when they'd made love. But now, she had to endure this? He was marrying *Mona?*

"And that's not just it..." Mona started, her lips spreading into a wide grin as she hesitated for dramatic effect. "I'm pregnant!"

She was crushed. She'd fought through Mona's tales of their whirlwind romance, telling herself that at some point he'd moved on because he couldn't really like her... couldn't possibly. But now there was no avoiding it. They were engaged and having a baby. The man she'd crushed on, nearly obsessively, since the moment she saw him, was going to marry her best friend. It felt like God's cruelest joke.

Her heart was beneath her feet as she walked home with her head hanging nearly between her shoulders. The piercing pain going through her heart didn't lessen any since she'd first heard Mona's good news.

"Aye, ma, why you lookin' so down?"

Normally, Baby would've ignored him, but she was feeling so low, any bit of kindness was welcomed. Looking up, she was greeted by a gentle smile and kind eyes. Upon further scrutiny, she noticed the tattoos on his arms and his street swag. Although he was dressed neatly in a pair of dress pants and a lightweight, long-sleeved sweater with the sleeves pulled up to his elbows, it was obvious that he wasn't the typical businessman.

"I just had a pretty disappointing day," Baby shared, not sure exactly why she was opening up. "I can't wait to get home."

She started walking and stopped when she saw a woman pushing a cotton candy stand coming right toward them. It was an instant reminder of everything she was trying to forget. The day she'd met Memphis would always be one she'd regret. Why hadn't she been more fearless? More bold? If she had, she'd be with him now... not Mona.

"You want some?"

"Huh?" Baby batted her eyes as her mind returned to the present. "Some what?"

"Cotton candy," Semaj had said, nudging his head toward the woman approaching them. "I don't know what happened, but I'd like to make your day better, if you allow me."

For the first time, Baby took a really good look at him. He wasn't her normal type, but losing her crush such a short time before had her wanting to cling on to anything similar to him that showed her interest. And Semaj, with his street swag and charming demeanor, seemed like he could be a good distraction to keep her mind off Memphis.

"Sure..." Baby said slowly, feeling the edges of her lips curl into a slow smile. "We can do that."

And that was the beginning of their story. After a while, Baby programmed her mind to forget that Semaj was who she settled for and not who she'd really wanted...

"You mind if I close your door?"

Baby jerked to attention the second Memphis's voice entered her consciousness. She'd been so deep in her thoughts that she hadn't even heard him walk down the stairs.

"Um, yeah..." she told him.

She waited, but he lingered a few moments longer. He lifted his eyes to meet hers, and there was a gentleness there that sent shivers down her spine. But in the next instance, he pushed all the emotion from his eyes, replacing them with a blank stare. She frowned, wondering what had happened to change his mood so swiftly.

"Did I do something wrong?"

"Naw," he replied. The friendly charm from earlier was gone. It was like she was a stranger.

"Are you sure?" she pressed, squinting. "Because I get the feeling that I've done something that I have no idea about."

She *had* done something that she didn't know about. Baby didn't even know how much she tempted him just by being around. He had to force himself to be indifferent with her because anything else required interaction. The more he interacted with her, the more he desired her. He couldn't put himself in a position that would cause him to slip.

"Whatever you feel is on you. I already answered you, so just drop it."

He disappeared after slamming the door closed, and her jaw dropped.

"Oh, *no*, that nigga didn't!" The hood in her came spilling right out.

Standing, Baby nearly wore a hole in the floor as she paced back and forth, fuming. She didn't need Memphis to like her, but at the very least, he could treat her with some respect. He was sending mixed signals... Sometimes he was hot and others, cold. She refused to keep dealing with his crazy ass. Once she got a few checks saved, she was determined to drop a deposit on a new place so she could move the hell out. There was no way she'd continue feeling like his burden.

Swinging the bedroom door open, Baby stomped out into the hall and followed it around until she was standing right in front of Memphis's private room. She knocked hard on the door and then waited with her arms folded at her chest for it to open.

The moment it did, Memphis appeared, and her stomach twisted in knots, despite her anger. Silent, he looked at her through hooded, slightly red eyes and waited for her to speak.

"Look, I didn't want to say anything because I thought it would make things awkward, but they already are, so I'm just going to get this off my chest," she began, growing angrier as she spoke. "I don't know why you feel uncomfortable by me, but I'm not checking for you... like, at all! I have a man, remember?" She wiggled the diamond ring on her finger in his face, and he gave it a blank stare. "So there is no need to be so rude, and there is definitely no need for you to relay your messages to me through Mona. If you feel uncomfortable by my presence, you can tell me yourself!"

Her eyes were sharp like daggers. He was able to hold his composure despite being shocked at her talking to him in this way. Never had he seen this side of her, but he liked it. She ignited his desire, and the fact that he'd spent the last hour drinking while he thought about her had his defenses down. But the liquor also made him even more frustrated about being forced to control himself around her when he didn't want to. So he matched her energy and reacted with the same aggression. With his eyes narrowed, he leaned into her, so close that it caught her off guard.

"Yo, check this," he began, falling easily into his street slang. "I don't know what kinda nigga you take me for, but I'm not afraid of you. And I don't give a fuck about your man." He added the last part under his breath, making Baby unsure about whether she'd actually heard it or not.

"I didn't say you were afraid of me," she countered while struggling to keep her attitude in place. Their closeness was throwing her off, but she refused to back down.

"What you sayin' then?" He asked the question without bite, but the way he seemed to hover over her was intimidating.

"I—I'm saying that..." She took a deep breath to stop from stumbling over her words. "If you don't like me or something, that's fine. But I am not going to put up with disrespect."

There was silence, but Memphis's eyes never left hers, and she refused to look away and appear weak. She had courage, a trait he admired in her. Not many could stand toe-to-toe with him and go hard without backing down eventually. He watched her as she took even, controlled breaths with her chin jutted stubbornly upward, and he gave up. He couldn't even pretend to stay angry at her.

Memphis licked his lips as he prepared to speak, and she began to ache between her thighs. Her face heated, and she shamefully ducked out of his gaze, feeling as though she'd made a mistake by being there in the first place. Rude Memphis was easy to resist, but the soft look he now held in his eyes had her feeling a way that she knew was wrong.

"So you been holdin' that shit in for a whole hour. Baby, the pretty savage." He added the last part with a bit of a chuckle. "Never knew your mouth was so reckless."

"It had to come out," she admitted with a shrug. "I have too much on my mind."

"So do I."

His words lingered in the air as he leaned slightly into her. He was about to ask her something that he knew would lead to nothing but trouble, but he couldn't stop it from happening. His resolve was sitting at the bottom of the last glass of Louis VIII that he'd tossed down his throat.

"Aye, how about you come in here and chill for a minute? I could use good company."

Baby mired and crooked her brow. "I don't think that would be appropriate."

"Why not?" he asked with a shrug. "We're friends... or at least I thought we were. You don't know how to be friendly?"

She almost laughed at the audacity of him to ask something like that when he'd been the one tramping around, giving her the cold shoulder.

"Of course I do. Can you be friendly?" she posed and regretted it when she saw the flicker of emotion pass through his eyes.

"I can be whatever you want me to be," he replied with pure honesty, even though he knew it was wrong. But a drunk man told no lies, and he was no exception.

Alarms sounded off in Baby's head, but she ignored each one. Memphis took a step back to welcome her into his place and offered her a drink, which she eagerly accepted. Her nerves were on edge, a sign that she should leave, but she stayed. They listened to music and talked for what felt like hours about the random happenings of her normal and basic life, but Memphis listened so attentively... as if she were telling him the best things he'd ever heard.

At one point in the conversation, there was a long pause, and Baby looked down at the glass in her hands, seeing that it was only half empty. She took a sip, and when she raised her head, she saw that Memphis was watching her. But not in the way that a man did his friend... There was so much more than that hidden behind his eyes.

"I wanted to tell you that I'm sorry... about what happened to you on your wedding day. You didn't deserve no shit like that," he told her with his brows furrowed, as if he were battling his thoughts. "If it were me marrying you..." He paused, and Baby felt the fine hairs on her arm raising on end. "...I would never have put you in that position. Any low-level hustler knows that you never shit where you eat."

Baby was well aware that Semaj hadn't even been half the man that Memphis was when it came to the streets. He made a good amount in the underground game, but Memphis was legendary. Semaj was a mediocre hustler at best, and Memphis was subtly reminding her of that.

"What made you get with dude anyways?" he asked out of sheer curiosity.

Because some small part of him reminded me of you, her mind immediately answered, but she knew she could never say it aloud. Especially not to him. She felt uneasy about his question, so she fell back on her slick-tongue to push away the awkward feeling coming upon her.

"They say 'bad boys do it better,'" she eased out with a coy smile.

His eyes widened slightly and then he recovered with a snicker. "You always follow the word of random muthafuckas?"

"You always butt into the business of random muthafuckas?" she shot back with a fiery twinkle in her eyes. He half-smirked, and she realized that he never fully smiled.

"You're no random muthafucka." His voice dropped a bit. "With your slick talkin' ass."

They locked eyes, and neither of them could speak a word. Her energy captured him, and her smile tugged at his cold heart. He felt the need to speak again... to say something clever, something else to make her laugh, but he was at a loss for anything appropriate to say. His every thought was of how beautiful she was, how good she smelled, and how soft her skin looked, but it would have been wrong to speak those thoughts aloud. In fact, it was wrong to even think them.

"Bad boys will fuck up your life," he told her, and it was all true. And he wasn't even talking about Semaj... He was referring to himself. She thought that Semaj had ruined her life, but it was nothing like what he would do if he pursued her the way he wanted to. Not only that, but he wasn't so sure she'd go for it anyways. He didn't peg Baby as the type to betray her best friend for a man, and if she was, that meant that she wasn't the woman he thought she was. And what kind of man did that make him if he cheated on his wife with her best friend?

The type of man who is in love with a woman he can't have.

His heart spoke the truth before his mind could even come up with a lie. It was true. He did love Baby, and during the couple times he'd seen her over the years, his affections had grown, but he was married to Mona. The two of them could never be together.

"Isn't it time for you to get to bed? You got a long day of yellin' at bad ass kids ahead of you." He forced a small chuckle even though his mind and his heart were at war. He didn't want Baby to go, but he also knew it was the right thing to do.

"You're right." Baby agreed and stood. She reached out to hand him her glass, and his fingers grazed hers when he grabbed it. The connection was electric.

Memphis withdrew from her and eyed the leftover alcohol in her glass before tossing it back without thought. When his lips touched her glass, he found himself thinking that it was the closest they would ever get to hers. And it was a sad fuckin' thought.

"Goodnight," he told her without looking up.

Looking at him, she knew that something was weighing heavily on his mind, but she also knew it wasn't her place to inquire. He was not her man, and it was not her job to ease his mind.

"Goodnight," she said and then turned to leave.

Baby walked away with her head straight and fought the urge to turn around and get one last look at the man she could never have. Memphis didn't even try to fight it. He couldn't stop staring. If he couldn't touch, at the very least, he should be able to do that. His passion pumped through his veins as he watched her until she disappeared from his sight. She closed the door and his heart dropped... or maybe it had followed after her. Either way, he knew that he'd felt whole in her presence, but in her absence, he was now incomplete.

CHAPTER SEVEN

"**G**ot somewhere you gotta be?" Laz asked, noticing the calculated way that Memphis had glanced at the face of his watch. "You know you free to do what you gotta do. I'm on top of shit. Got everything handled just like you need me to."

Nodding his head, Memphis didn't verbally reply, although there was a lot that he knew needed to be said. True, Laz was living up to his expectations and more by easily falling into his place and taking over the game, but there was one thing that Laz hadn't learned, and it was something that couldn't be taught. Memphis had the intuition of a street king, and that was part of what made him as successful as he was. He could sense danger lurking around the corner long before he'd even stepped out onto the street. Like a masterful chess player, he was always many moves ahead of his opponent, and his senses were telling him that something was brewing.

"You still ain't heard from Johnny?" Memphis asked, and Laz shook his head. "Hit 'em up again."

"You know somethin' I don't?"

Memphis heard but didn't acknowledge Laz's question and waited for him to do as requested. Seconds later, Laz had called Johnny's phone and was greeted by a voicemail message saying that his inbox was full.

"No answer."

"Send somebody out there," Memphis ordered without hesitation.

Laz didn't understand what the urgency was with getting in touch with Johnny, but he dialed a number in his cell phone to do as ordered. Johnny was one of those types who was good at one thing but terrible at everything else. The one thing he was good at was the one thing that kept him on their team: he was a skilled negotiator. Johnny could talk a starved cat off the back of a fish truck. In Memphis's line of work, where he was always cutting deals for product, weapons, or working alliances in order to expand his territory, having another smooth-talker on the team was an asset.

"Got Taraj on it," Laz said, and Memphis replied with only a curt nod before standing.

"I gotta handle something. Hit me back as soon as you hear from him."

"You goin' to Dino's lil' shindig later?" Laz asked, and Memphis nodded his head.

"Yeah, I might swing through at some point."

"Good, because you know that D.C. nigga who wanted to meet up with us a while back? He gon' be there. I think you should holla at him."

"I already said I don't want nothing to do with dude," was Memphis's reply. "He's a fuckin' rat, and I can see that shit from a mile away. He was caught with ten bricks and only served three years Fed time, while all his homies got locked up right after he cut his deal. I don't want nothing to do with that shit."

"Word?" Laz's brows raised to his hairline. "Shit, I ain't know dude was greasy like that. Fake ass thug."

"I keep sayin' you can't trust these off-brand muthafuckas."

Memphis checked his watch one more time before saluting Laz and turning to leave out of the meeting area in his club. He had about thirty minutes to spare before he was supposed to be at dinner with Mona and

Baby to celebrate her new job. Memphis knew what it felt like to feel like you didn't have anyone to celebrate your wins, and he didn't want Baby to feel that way. He cared about that, even if Mona did not. Real talk, Mona wanted to talk a lot of shit about him demanding they have the dinner, but she knew better than to say it aloud and kept it in her mind.

"Mr. Luciano! We have your table reserved and ready for you," the hostess greeted Memphis as soon as he walked into the restaurant. As usual for a Saturday night, the place was packed to max capacity.

"Thank you," Memphis said politely to the hostess, causing the young girl to grin.

His charm and well-mannered disposition were always present, unless otherwise was warranted, but he found that people usually didn't expect it. Men of his stature usually walked around with an arrogant and cocky flare that made everyone around feel beneath them. In Memphis's line of business, he found it more rewarding to have the type of charisma that made people fall over their own feet to please or demonstrate their loyalty to him.

Memphis was halfway through his second Hennessy and coke when something beautiful near the front of the restaurant caught his eye. He pensively ran his hand over his mouth as he watched Baby converse with the hostess, her expression animated and bright as she spoke. She was casually dressed in a simple black form-fitting dress, something more Target than vogue, but Memphis didn't see it as any less than the threads that would adorn the body of a runway model. And she wore it with the exact same regal flair and confidence in her eyes.

She approached Memphis, and he stood, holding out his hand to greet her, but she surprised him by instead pulling him into a hug. He inhaled the sweet scent of her perfume and thought that he'd never in life gotten aroused from a woman's fragrance. But here he was, his man's below on brick from the combination of her perfume and simple embrace.

"I've never been here before," Baby said enthused, her bright eyes glancing around the restaurant as she took her seat. "It's so nice inside."

Memphis smirked. *Who in Atlanta hasn't been here?* he thought to himself, but he adored the graciousness in her expression. He'd taken Mona here so many times that it didn't even impress her anymore. She treated it with about the same excitement as she would if he'd taken her to McDonalds for a date.

"Mona should be on the way," Memphis offered, pushing Baby's seat in for her before walking over to his own.

"How long have you been here?" she asked.

"About thirty minutes," he replied with an easy shrug.

"You were early."

"I'm always early." He made the statement with all seriousness, as if it were a personal commandment.

She couldn't resist noticing how attractive Memphis was in his suit that fit like it had been poured over his body. It was obviously custom-made. It was refreshing to see a man be able to shed the street clothes for something more grownup... a classically sexy look that she'd never seen anyone pull off as effortlessly as Memphis was doing right then. Semaj was against suits, no matter the occasion. He told her that their wedding day would be the first and last time she'd see him in one.

And for the next fifteen years, all he'll wear is that orange jumpsuit. She shook her head slightly to rid herself of the thought.

"Can I take your drink order?" the waitress said to Baby, but Memphis cut in quickly.

"Bring us the most expensive glass of wine y'all got back there," he requested, and the waitress smiled deeply before nodding her head and walking away. "This is a celebration, right?" he said after noticing the surprised look on Baby's face.

"Thank you... You didn't have to do that though. I'm just happy to be here," she replied honestly. She ducked her head down to look at the menu, and Memphis took the opportunity to watch her, for some reason, fascinated by the subtle excitement in her eyes as she perused the different options.

"How are things? You gettin' adjusted okay?" Memphis found himself asking, eager to hear her speak. He loved the way she

97

scrunched up her face when she was thinking hard about her answer to his questions. She was so careful about not offending anyone... so thoughtful and kind. He loved that about her.

"I'm..." Baby lifted her head and thought to herself for a moment before answering his question. "I think I'm doing okay. It's hard... I mean, I'm thankful for you and Mona letting me stay, but it's definitely tough to one day know where you're going in your life and then have it all taken from you in seconds. I thought I would be married and happy by now."

There was a sharp pain through Baby's chest that stopped her from continuing on. She blinked a few times when she felt tears surfacing in her eyes. Her loneliness made her emotional. It was embarrassing to her for Memphis to see her that way. He hated it as well. It wasn't his intention to bring up Semaj, but he tried to remind himself that he could only be her friend and pushed himself to be a good one.

"What you feel makes sense. And it's going to take time to get used to not being around someone you were with for five years."

Baby shook her head. "No, we weren't together that long. We got together the day Mona told me y'all were engaged, but Semaj was my first boyfriend... the only relationship I've been in, so it's still hard."

Memphis's brows bunched together. "Your *first* boyfriend? Wasn't you datin' some nigga when you and Mona slid by my boy's party that one night right after we first met?"

It took a minute for Baby to remember the night Memphis was referring to, but when she did, she shook her head once more.

"No... I didn't have a boyfriend. Why would you think that?"

Pressing his lips together, Memphis didn't answer because it had suddenly become clear to him what had actually happened that night. Mona was the one who told him that Baby was dating someone once she saw that his attention had been on Baby and not her. She'd offered him the lie under the guise that she was trying to help him save face from being rejected. It was obvious now that she'd played him, and lucky for Mona, everything had gone according to her plan.

"No reason," was his simple answer. "I guess I was mistaken."

His brows were pulled tight, and Baby could tell by the stone expression on his face that something was bothering him. She watched as he drained the rest of his brown liquor, looking away from her but definitely brooding over something that was heavy on his mind.

"I hope you weren't thinking that I was being rude that night," Baby began, fishing for a reason for his sudden change in temperament. "It's just... Mona had made it clear that she was crushing on you and kept saying that you were her soulmate. She's my best friend so..." She paused and shrugged, letting the rest of her sentence hang in the air. "I guess everything worked out how it should because now you and Mona are married with a beautiful family. She was right after all."

Memphis decided not to answer, his mind still bothered by the fact that he now knew Mona had been manipulating their story to her benefit from the very beginning. It was after that night that he'd finally given Mona some play because he'd given up on running after Baby. He couldn't help wondering how that night would have gone if Mona hadn't been working both ends, pulling their strings. Would it be Baby wearing his ring today?

Never one to waste time on things that couldn't be changed, Memphis pushed the thoughts away of what could have been and dropped his attention to the face of the watch on his wrist. It was nearly a half hour after the time they had all agreed to meet for dinner, and Mona still hadn't shown up.

The waitress returned with the bottle of wine that Memphis had ordered and poured each of them a glass. Baby eyed it with apprehension before grabbing the glass to take a sip. She wasn't a drinker, but the atmosphere around them had suddenly grown tense, and it would be nice to have something to help ease the pressure. Three glasses later, she was still sipping, Mona still hadn't arrived, and she was having the best conversation she'd had in a while.

"What I don't get is why people find it so crazy that I'm deciding to wait on Semaj," she vented to Memphis who was all ears, not too enthused that she was speaking on another nigga but grateful for the chance to kick it with her nonetheless.

"I mean... if you love someone, isn't that what you're supposed to do? Aren't you supposed to be there for them through the ups and downs?" she continued to question, giving him a pointed look that said she only expected him to agree with something she felt was so obvious. But unlike her, Memphis wasn't that naïve about life.

"That's just not the type of shit people do," Memphis replied with a light chuckle.

Frowning, Baby couldn't help but ask the question at the forefront of her mind. "You wouldn't want Mona to wait on you?"

"You think Mona would wait on me?" he shot back so quickly that Baby wondered if he'd been waiting for the opportunity to pose the question.

No, she wouldn't wait, she thought to herself, remembering their talk from the other day. But she didn't want to tell him that.

"I don't hold any fantasies about the woman I'm with," Memphis said, freeing her from finding a response. "I know she wouldn't wait, and I don't expect her to."

"And you're fine with that?" Baby blurted out before she had a chance to stop herself. She wished she could take the question back, but it was too late. It was out there, hanging in the space between them, so she could only wait to see if Memphis would answer.

"There is a limit to loyalty. Everyone has a limit... Some just take more shit than others before they reach their breaking point. I can't fault her for that." Feeling the liquor loosening his lips to the point that he found himself more willing to say things he would have normally left in his head, Memphis continued. "What I know about you is that you're one of the most loyal people I've gotten the chance to meet. But I also know that you're beautiful, and there are niggas out here who would break their fuckin' legs, jumpin' at the opportunity to be with you. How long you think it'll be before you give in to one of these knucklehead muthafuckas out here?"

He said it with a hint of humor, but the intensity in his eyes made Baby's face go warm. Memphis's trained eyes noted the slight tinge of red in her cheeks and felt himself nearly about to succumb to the desire to reach out and run his finger along the side of her face to ease her mind.

Fuck, I'm trippin', he thought to himself, shaking his head as he fought to regain his composure. The hell was going through his mind? Baby was Mona's friend, and regardless to how much he wanted her —*still* wanted her after all these years, he had to find a way to control himself. He had to do that for Genie's sake if nothing else. She was dealing with enough already. Seeing her family split apart would destroy her.

"I need to call my fuckin' wife to see where the hell she is," he muttered, suddenly annoyed at himself as well as Mona for the situation he was finding himself in.

Baby noticed the way that Memphis's brows knotted up as he pecked on his phone to check on Mona and was, once again, curious about his sudden change in mood. She couldn't lie and say that she wouldn't be happy for the moment Mona joined them either, because the wine had her feeling things that she shouldn't be. With every sip, it was becoming increasingly hard for her to remind herself that Memphis was Mona's husband and therefore off-limits in reality and also in her thoughts.

"I'll be back," Memphis told her before getting up to walk away and handle his call. He knew Mona well enough to expect that it wouldn't be a good one and didn't want to be overheard.

EYES CLOSED, SOAKING IN A JETTED, JACUZZI TUB OVERFLOWING WITH lavender-scented bubbles, Mona felt absolutely no guilt for bailing on Baby's dinner. Later that night, Memphis was taking her to one of his men's engagement party, so she had to get ready so that she could step in there like the first lady of the streets she was. There would be hell to pay later with Memphis, but she already had an excuse in mind to get him off her case. The last thing she wanted to do was sit through three courses and pretend to be happy about Baby's mediocre accomplishments. Besides, Memphis was more than capable of decent conversation in her absence.

When Mona's phone rang, she rolled her eyes sharply because she knew exactly who it was and had been expecting the call. Even so, having it arrive when she was at the height of peaceful relaxation still annoyed her.

"Hello?"

"Mo, where da fuck are you?"

"Damn, well 'hi' to you, too, *my love.*"

"Yo, chill with that fake shit," he shot back with a pinched tone, and Mona sighed, knowing that he was not in the mood for her games.

"I'm home, getting ready for Dino and Jade's party. You didn't get my text from earlier?" She waited for Memphis to respond, knowing damn well he didn't get a text that she'd never sent.

"No, I ain't get no fuckin' text. Don't start this dumb shit with me, Mo. You know you're supposed to be here for Baby's dinner. She's your best friend. How the fuck you think she feels about you skipping out on it?"

"Baby will understand," Mona argued, feeling herself getting heated even though she knew this conversation was coming when she answered the phone. Best friend or not, Memphis should have known better than to take up for another bitch.

"And I already bought her a really nice gift to make up for not being there."

"That's fucked up. Even for you." Memphis couldn't believe the level of selfishness Mona was on. He knew that she had a tendency to be that way, but he couldn't see her doing it to her best friend. There was a loyalty that came with friendship, and it made you do things you didn't always want but decided to for the sake of friendship. Obviously, Mona didn't think that way.

"Look... why don't you bring her to Dino's party? She might meet someone there to get her mind off Semaj so she can move on. It'll be fun. Trust me."

Memphis listened to Mona's words, immediately getting irritated at the thought of Baby finding someone to chill with who was part of his crew. Turning, he glanced back and saw her sitting at the table, happily sipping wine while bobbing her head gently to the music.

"Naw, street niggas will ruin her."

"Ruin her?" Mona queried. "So you're saying that being with you ruined me?"

"That statement doesn't relate to you. It's like comparing an apple to shit."

"Aw, thank you, baby," she cooed, totally missing the undercover shade. Her narcissism made it impossible for her to see that he hadn't been referring to her as the apple, just as he'd suspected.

"If she wants to go, we'll swing through," he continued. "You bringing Genie with you? There will be kids there and it might be good for her to get out the house."

Mona nearly had to bite her tongue to stop from sucking her teeth. "No, I don't think so. It'll be too much getting her chair up to V.I.P. and all. She'll be fine here. I'll just pay Trina to come by and stay with her."

Memphis's brows shot to the sky. "Trina's not there now?"

"No!" Mona smiled at being given the perfect opportunity to slide in the lie she knew would get Memphis off her case. "I thought about what you said the other day and let Trina off early today so Genie and I could spend some time together. We had so much fun that she was exhausted and fell asleep."

What she neglected to tell Memphis was that Genie was only sleeping after Mona had given her a healthy dose of Benadryl. She'd barely spent five minutes with her daughter before drugging her so that she could tend to her own interests.

"That's what's up. It's nice that you took out time to chill with her," he heard himself saying, not believing he was letting Mona off so easily. But, at the end of the day, Baby was Mona's friend, and how she handled that friendship was her business. His focus should be on his daughter, and it seemed Mona was stepping up in that department. He already felt himself getting in too deep when it came to Baby, and he needed to pull back before he made a mistake that couldn't be fixed.

"Don't thank me for being a good mother, Memphis. Now bye; I have to finish getting ready," Mona shot back before hurriedly hanging up the phone. Beauty took time, and she couldn't be half-stepping because everybody who was somebody in the city would be in attendance at Dino's party tonight, and she had to represent.

Lifting her phone, she scrolled down to Sly's number and contemplated sending him a message before shaking her head, locking her phone, and placing it back down on the side of the tub. Although she was more than curious about him, she still wanted to stick to her old rule of not contacting a man first. Sly had her number, and he was free to use it if he really wanted her. With a heavy sigh, she closed her eyes and relaxed her head on the back edge of the tub, allowing the jets to massage her body.

In this moment, everything was absolutely perfect.

CHAPTER EIGHT

"*I* can't believe this shit!" Mona spat with her lip twisted in disgust. She nearly had smoke coming out of her ears as she watched Bambi and Laz strut into the party wearing matching mink coats, with their arms linked, waving to the crowd around them like they were the Beyoncé and Jay-Z of the hood.

Instead of making the same type of grand entrance, Memphis had refused to walk in through the front and chose to be more discreet, entering through the building from the back. That was not at all Mona's style. She was never one to bow out of the spotlight, and the fact that Memphis was trying to be behind the scenes rather than *making* a scene, as she preferred, had her pissed to the max. Baby watched as Mona stomped over to where Memphis was babysitting a glass of Hennessy he hadn't yet touched.

"This the shit I'm talking about, Memphis! *You're* the boss... not Laz. Why he always actin' like he run shit all of a sudden?"

"He *will* be runnin' shit in a minute when I step down. And how my niggas make moves isn't your concern," Memphis reminded her, an icy glare in his eye that told her to calm down before she took things to a level she didn't want them to go to. Mona caught his threat and simply huffed out a breath before walking back over to Baby and plopping down in the chair next to her.

Feeling awkward, Baby stirred a little but continued to sway to the music without saying anything to Mona. When pouting, she knew it was best to give her a moment until she was ready to speak.

There was a fire burning slow in the pit of Mona's stomach as she looked down the bridge of her nose at everyone fawning over Bambi in the same way that they normally did her. Bambi didn't even deserve it... showing up in an ugly ass mink coat that was probably pulled from the clearance rack of some department store Mona wouldn't ever step foot in. It was sickening to say the least. She couldn't understand why Memphis would want to hand over his power to someone else. It made no sense! Isn't that what everyone worked their whole lives for? Success, money, and power? Just when Memphis had it all, he wanted to give it away, but she wasn't having that.

Under hooded brows, Mona watched as Bambi finished up her conversations as if she was speaking to her adoring fans before walking up the stairs to where they were sitting. Memphis's crew circled Laz and followed him up as well before finding seats on the other end where Memphis had been sitting alone.

"Hey! You must be Baby." Bambi smiled brightly and pulled off her mink before walking over to Baby and bending down to give her a hug. When she leaned over, the hem of her dress pulled up and showed off the bend of her ass. Seeing it, Mona sniffed with disgust and rolled her eyes. *This* was the woman slated to take her place? Please...

This bitch could never, she thought, still seething.

"I am," Baby replied, liking Bambi instantly. She was beautiful but seemed humble and personable, as if all the glitz and glamour in the world didn't mean a thing to her.

"Mona's told me a lot about you, but she never told me how gorgeous you are!" Bambi gushed, looking Baby up and down. "Baby, girl, you are stunning!"

Baby beamed at the compliment, but her smile dimmed a bit when she heard Mona snort. Both women glanced in her direction and caught the sour look on her face.

"Girl, what's wrong with you? It's not like you to be all bitchy at a party!" Bambi said and took a seat on the other side of Mona.

Looking down at her dress, she smoothed it down and quickly inspected it to make sure she hadn't messed it up already. Laz had told her that he was taking over Memphis's place and that meant that she would be under a lot of scrutiny... something she wasn't ready for and didn't want. While Mona seemed to blossom in the position, Bambi couldn't help feeling inadequate, but she knew if she wanted to be with Laz, she would have to rise to the occasion because this was part of his lifestyle.

"Where did you get that dress from?" Mona's voice was snarky, but Bambi didn't catch it. She smiled and straightened her back, hoping that she would get Mona's approval on her outfit, knowing the latest fashions was more Mona's department than hers, but she'd try her hardest to dress accordingly.

"It's Prada," Bambi enthused. "You like it?"

"It looks like something that I wore last year sometime. Back when it was still in style."

Baby's mouth nearly dropped open at Mona's rudeness, and she immediately felt compelled to fix it when she saw Bambi's eyes fill up with tears.

"I think you look beautiful," she told Bambi with sincerity. "And those heels... You're killin' it! I could never walk in those things and look as graceful as you do." Not one to let things bother her for too long, Bambi smiled and took the compliment with a slight nod of her head.

"This is my *song*!" Bambi started dancing in her seat, and Baby did the same, both of them ignoring the dark cloud hanging over Mona who was quietly pouting in the middle. Maybe it was all the wine that she'd had before arriving, or maybe it was her need to get away from Mona's negativity so that she could have a good time, but Baby felt the urge to dance.

"Let's go out to the dance floor! You wanna go, Mona?"

Mona turned up her nose like it was the craziest thing she'd ever heard. In her position, she never mixed and mingled with the crowd below. She always held her spot in the V.I.P. section that was reserved for her and had her fun with the other elites. And if Bambi knew any better, she would do the same.

"Um, no. I'll pass."

"I'll go!" Bambi hurriedly agreed, eager to have some real fun. Sure, it was all good hanging out in the V.I.P. with Mona, but there was nothing like being able to blend in and have fun for once without feeling like you were on display. Grabbing Baby's hand, she walked with her to the middle of the dance floor, and they began to work their bodies and have fun while Mona sulked by herself.

"Memph, nigga, I can't believe you really wanna step out of this shit so soon," Chris, one of Memphis's closest friends, said. "I mean, you're at your prime, my nigga! This street shit is all we've ever done since we were boys. What you gon' get into with all that free time you about to have on your hands?"

"He ain't gon' have no free time!" Laz butt in, which was usual for him. He was forever taking up for the man he saw as a brother. "You know that nigga can't just sit around and not do shit. Just like he dominated the streets, he gon' dominate the entire city. Restaurants and clubs on every corner... He swappin' one hustle for another."

Laz was right, but Memphis didn't confirm nor deny the statement. It wasn't in him to let anyone know his next moves, but Laz was close enough to guess what was on his mind and to know that he wouldn't step out the streets unless it meant he would be making at least twice as much money as he was making in them.

It was something Memphis hadn't even confided in Mona about. She seemed so concerned that he was walking them straight into the poor house, and part of him wanted her to believe that so she'd find a reason to leave. But poor was never an option for him. He'd started from the dirt and hustled up, but he would never hustle backwards.

To be real, she could continue spending money like it was going out of style, and it wouldn't do shit to dent his accounts.

Memphis listened to his niggas shoot the breeze, discussing money, women, and cars—a street nigga's delight—as he sat quietly, thinking to himself. It wasn't until their topic of choice turned to the woman on his mind, that his attention returned to the conversation.

"Aye, who is Ms. Fine Brown that's over there dancing with yo' girl, Laz? I might just have to make her baby mama number four," Rick, another one of Memphis's top hustlers, said.

"Baby mama number four? Nigga, don't you think you need to slow your ass down?" Dino laughed as he puffed on a cigar.

Laz chuckled a little before shrugging. "I don't think I seen her before, but shawty's body is bangin' under that long ass dress."

"That's Baby," Memphis found himself saying to no one in particular as he watched her do her thing. She was perfection in the flesh as she danced happily with Bambi like she didn't have a care in the world. Her smile was bright and easy, like she was simply happy to be alive even if she had nothing else working in her favor. Seeing her warmed his dark soul.

"Baby?" Laz quipped, thinking for a minute. "Mona's friend, right? Damn, she look different from the last time I seen her."

Laz, along with Chris, Rick, and Dino, turned to watch her, all of them momentarily hypnotized as thoughts circulated through their minds... the normal things that came to mind when niggas saw such a beauty. Baby was a rarity in the hood... a chick that hadn't lost out on the innocence and good spirit that the street life stole from them a long time ago. She was a gem to street niggas who grew tired of the doom and gloom of their days and wished to come home to a woman who could be their peace and show them a more positive outlook than what they'd become used to.

"I'm about to go and shoot my shot," Rick informed them before suddenly standing up and buttoning up his Gucci jacket as if it would soften his thug appeal.

"Naw," Memphis replied simply but with a matter-of-fact tone that made every man turn to look at him. He kept his eyes on Baby, watching her and also understanding that a shift was taking place in his mind. If he thought that he was getting dangerously close to crossing a line that shouldn't have been crossed before, he knew for sure that he was about to cross it now.

The atmosphere became tense and Laz chuckled a little, his attempt to put everyone at ease. "Bruh, you cock-blockin' now, nigga? Rick ain't good enough to holla?"

"She's off limits," Memphis said, and it became law. All of his men shot curious glances at each other as Rick sat back down in his chair, each of them recognizing what was going on but none having the courage to question him about it. None but Laz who made a mental note to bring the subject up later once they were alone.

"You heard back from Taraj?" Memphis questioned, switching gears.

"Yeah, he hit me back and said he was on his way over there before I walked in," Laz replied, although he could tell that his boy's focus was split between him and what was happening on the dance floor.

"Yeah?" Memphis replied, not really paying attention; his thoughts were elsewhere. He watched someone bump into Baby on the dance floor and felt his body jerk to attention, but he stopped himself before he leapt out of his seat to go and check the dude, knowing it wouldn't be a good look. But when the nigga bumped into her again, Memphis realized he was on some playing games type shit... a lame nigga's way of trying to get some conversation.

"I guess that's our cue to talk business—"

"Hold that thought," Memphis told him, standing up so quickly that Laz's hand instantly went to his side for his banger.

"Somethin' up?"

Memphis heard Laz's question, but by that time, he was already walking down the stairs, heading to where Baby was mean-mugging the goofy ass nigga who had ran into her once more.

"You can't fuckin' see, nigga?" Memphis sneered at the man, his fingers situated close to the banger on his waist just in case things took a turn in a direction that he knew they wouldn't.

The man gawked at the street god, perplexed by his fury but still struggling to provide an answer. "No, I can see just fine… I mean, last time I checked my shit was 20/20 but…"

"Fuck all that," Memphis shot back, automatically pegging dude as the clown he was. "Run into her one mo' fuckin' time and I'll be handin' you yo' fuckin' eyes, a'ight?"

The man swallowed hard and nodded his head. Memphis felt a presence beside him, but he continued his vicious stare down, not once flinching or moving a muscle. If he could set something on fire with his eyes, dude would be burned to a crisp.

"Aye, there a problem, Memph? This my cousin, Bruno, but if this nigga needs to be checked, I can take care of his ass," Dino said with all seriousness, walking up from behind Memphis with his upper lip curled maliciously. In the *Murda Mob*, gang trumped even blood.

Eyes never leaving Bruno's, Memphis kept the intensity high for a few seconds longer before addressing his man.

"Naw, we good, fam."

Dino cut his eyes at his cousin, giving him a silent warning to get his shit together, before he walked away. With her eyes wide, Baby watched the exchange between Memphis and the man she now knew was called Bruno, hoping their altercation wouldn't escalate further.

"My bad, man," Bruno apologized, holding his hand out to Memphis. "I was just tryin' to have a good time."

Memphis never acknowledged Bruno's outstretched hand, so he sheepishly pushed it back into his pocket.

"How about you go have a good time somewhere else?" The steel in Memphis's tone made his words sound more like a command than a request. Bruno obeyed eagerly and turned to leave without giving Baby a second glance.

"I'm sorry if that was my fault," Baby cut in as Bambi stood by watching. "I wasn't looking. I might have bumped into him."

"Just watch out for these dumb ass niggas out here… before you make me body a muthafucka."

Baby thought she heard Memphis add the last part under his breath, but she couldn't be sure. However, nothing was wrong with Bambi's hearing, and she was positive that she heard exactly the same thing. Her eyes bugged slightly as she looked from him to Baby, easily picking up on the chemistry between the two of them and the body language coming from him. The way he stood next to her, shielding her body with his like he was protecting her... the unspoken intimacy in his stance was definitely something that alarmed her.

Mona is stupid as fuck for letting Baby be anywhere near him, she thought to herself before glancing up to the V.I.P. to see if Mona was seeing what she was.

However, Mona was no longer sitting where she had been and had missed it all. Her attention was elsewhere. She had no idea at all that half of the people in the club now knew there was another woman in her husband's heart, threatening the throne she'd worked so hard to obtain.

CHAPTER NINE

*T*oo focused on her own misery to give even the slightest attention to anything or anyone else, Mona had been brooding about what she was considering a terrible night, when the screen of the phone sitting in her lap illuminated.

Damn, you're fine as fuck, were the words on the screen, and when Mona saw who the message had come from, her lips melted into a smile.

Looking up, she scanned the room for only a few seconds until her eyes narrowed on the object of her search. Standing in the shadows, looking tasty enough to appeal to both of her sets of lips, was Sly. Tonight, he'd traded the all-white ensemble for something a little more casual, although he still stood out like a sore thumb in comparison to the group of men around him. They just couldn't match his swag.

Mona took a deep breath and tried to keep her expression nonchalant under his stare. With her phone in hand, she ran her fingers over the screen to send him a quick reply.

You're not looking too bad yourself.

As soon as she sent the text, she raised her head to watch him, curious about his reaction. He read the message, and a slow smirk tugged at the edge of his lips. The sight of it sent tingles down her spine.

Let me talk to you for a minute... alone.

Mona took a deep breath when she read the message, feeling her panties grow moist just over the thought of what could possibly go down if Sly caught her alone. She barely even knew him, but his sex appeal had her caught up in ways she'd never experienced before. Not even with Memphis. Although she fought hard to get her position as Memphis's official woman, she always felt that he was holding back when it came to their relationship. As if he wasn't fully invested. This was not at all the impression she got from Sly, and as a woman who craved a man's attention more than most, she couldn't resist the opportunity to be wooed by a boss.

She watched Sly slip away from his crew and begin walking down the hall. Biting at the corners of her lips, she glanced in Memphis's direction just as he stood up and started walking out to the dance-floor, his full attention on some man standing near Baby who she had never seen.

Now is my chance! she thought and stood up quickly. As soon as Memphis passed in front of her, she took off behind him but made a sharp turn to head in the same direction as Sly.

Running her fingers along the wall as she walked slowly down the hall, Mona felt herself nearly tremble with excitement from whatever was about to happen. There was something about living dangerously that gave her the type of enjoyment that she craved on a daily basis. Life in the fast lane was what she was addicted to, and it was the main reason why she just couldn't deal with Memphis's goals of slowing it all down. Nothing got her wetter than a man who was feared, respected, and honored because of the shit that he did in the streets, and if Memphis was deciding that wasn't who he wanted to be any longer, he was leaving a spot open for another man to take his place— in the streets as well as in her heart.

Pausing, Mona took a second to think about where Sly was waiting for her. The supply closet was locked to anyone who didn't have the code, which left the bathrooms and Memphis's office, a place he definitely did not have access to enter. She was just about to check the men's restroom for him when she felt her phone vibrate in her hand.

Walk out the back door.

Her stomach filled with nervous energy, and she did as he instructed. Cold air blew onto her cheeks as she peered through the night, looking for Sly. When her eyes finally landed on him, her whole body went warm in spite of the disrespectful harsh winter wind. Posted up on the hood of a black Rolls Royce, Sly was as sexy as he wanted to be. Without saying a single word, he walked to the back of the car and opened the door, his eyes never leaving hers. Complete with a sexy strut, Mona twisted her hips seductively the entire way to him, knowing that she was giving him more than an eyeful of her bodacious body. She had left very little to the imagination, wearing a short dress that hugged every one of her sexy curves as if it had been painted on.

"After you," Sly whispered, moistening his lips with his tongue while he watched her.

Mona smirked and then took her seat, allowing the dress to roll up her thick thighs. Sly's eyes trailed down her body as he fought the urge to palm her ass the second she booted it out toward him before sitting it on his cream leather seats. Although he didn't care about her on any level, he couldn't say he wasn't looking forward to having his way with her body. She was sexy as hell, and he knew the pussy had to be good. She had the body of a goddess with a bum bitch's mentality. She was poison to the game and he knew it, but his dick had no objections.

Sly ran his hand over his face to get his mind together before following behind her and closing the door, giving them complete privacy thanks to his double-tinted windows.

"I just wanted to talk to you for a minute. If you don't mind." His tone was gentle and kind enough for Mona to not see the snake lying beneath. A coy smile spread across her face, and she tilted her head to the side. She had a lot of things on her mind to do now that they were alone, and none of those things required talking, but she was willing to play the game.

"What do you want to talk to me about? And what's that in your hands?" she added after seeing him continuously fumbling with something.

Sly licked his lips. "My lucky dice," he said, opening his hand to reveal two black dice. "And I wanna talk to you about being mine."

His bluntness made her laugh. "I thought we already talked about this. I'm married to Memphis. What makes you think I'll just leave my husband?"

Chuckling, he rolled the die in his hand and then lowered it for her to see. "I just rolled a lucky seven. That means luck is on my side. Plus, I already told you what type of nigga I am. I don't dwell on the past. So what's it gonna be, because in my line of business, a nigga can't afford to move too slow."

Cocking her neck, Mona had her own assumptions about what 'line of business' Sly was in but decided to play dumb.

With wide, bright eyes, she replied, "And what line of business is that?"

Sly wasn't prepared for her question and couldn't help but chuckle. "I do a few things. Let's leave it at that."

Smiling, she rolled her eyes. "Well, whatever you do must pay pretty well if you can afford all of this." She motioned around the car.

He picked up on her meaning and played right into it, letting his brows shoot to the sky. "This? This ain't shit."

"I don't think I've ever heard anyone say that a Rolls Royce ain't shit." She smirked at Sly's straight face.

"Oh yeah?"

Before she could reply, he reached into his pocket and pulled out a set of keys. Looping one off the ring, he grabbed her hand and placed it gently into her palm.

"Then it's yours," he told her like it was nothing.

Mona's eyes bugged from the keys to his face. "What?"

Sly simply shrugged. "It's yours, if you want it. But I prefer to cop you one brand new. When something is mine, I decorate it in luxury. Ain't no limit to what I won't do, and you deserve the finest."

And just that quickly, Mona was as good as his. Still, she couldn't let him know that just yet, and she definitely didn't want to appear too thirsty.

"I can afford my own nice things," Mona told him, pushing the key back into his hand. "I'm not sure what type of women you're used to, but money doesn't impress me."

She was lying her ass off, and both of them knew it. She would sell her soul for the right price and a little bit of attention. From watching her and Memphis for only a few minutes before texting her, he picked up on things she didn't even know. It was obvious that she was being neglected at home because Memphis barely paid her any attention in public. It was also obvious to him that her so-called husband was more interested in her best friend than his wife. He was willing to bet that if he could convince her that she had a chance at real love as well as a life of luxury that she would play right into his hands.

"I'm not tryin' to impress you. I'm just letting you know that I want you, and I'm ready to take care of you," Sly explained, and Mona felt like she could see the truth in his crystal-clear eyes. "This ain't really my style, but I knew I wanted you when I first saw you. You're rare... Ain't no chick out here like you, ma." He was laying the game on thick.

"You wouldn't be the first," she countered with a slight scoff.

Sly laughed and then shook his head. "Your mouth slick as fuck. But I like that shit. You're irresistible, ma."

Before Mona could come up with another smart-ass reply, Sly reached over and grabbed her, scooping her up easily into his arms. He pulled her onto his lap so that she was facing him and pushed her thighs apart so that she was straddling him. It was hard to conceal her desire for him when she felt the bulge in his pants nestled between her thighs, and before she knew it, she found herself grinding into him.

Sly palmed her ass and squeezed hard, pulling her further into him. He lifted his head and she lowered hers until their lips found each other. They kissed each other greedily, like long-time lovers who had been separated for years and finally found their way back into each other's arms. Sly slipped a finger into the warmth between her thighs, and Mona trembled when he began expertly running his finger back and forth over her nub, not breaking their kiss. His tongue danced circles around the confines of her mouth, and she found herself spellbound, completely at his mercy.

Reaching down, Mona grabbed at the lump in his pants, eager to wrap her fingers around his manhood to fully see what he was working with. Sly knew exactly what she wanted, and within seconds, he'd unzipped his pants and pulled it out, laying it across the top of her thigh. Mona couldn't resist taking a peek. She broke their kiss and glanced down, licking her lips when she saw how thick and long he was. He was working with an anaconda in his pants, and she couldn't wait to feel it inside of her.

"I want it," she whispered, grinding into him, and Sly replied with a chuckle.

"I thought you said you had a man," he teased, and Mona shot him a look. Memphis was the furthest thing from her mind at the moment.

"I thought you said you don't dwell on the past," she reminded him with sass. Sly nodded and then let his head fall back, closing his eyes. The hint of a smile remained on his face. He had her exactly where he wanted her, and they both knew it.

"I don't. But until you let me know what you got in mind for the future, I can't let you sample this." Sly pushed himself back into his pants and began to zip them up as she watched him, ready to snap.

"Excuse me?"

He lifted up and looked at her, his seriousness showing in his eyes. "When you make it known that you wanna be mine, I'll give it to you. My dick ain't for everybody, and I won't have another nigga following up behind where I choose to stick it. Ya dig?"

Not believing what she was hearing, Mona rolled her eyes. "Oh, so now you got a special dick, huh?"

"You fuckin' right," Sly told her, his eyes on her hard nipples that were poking through the thin material of her dress. "I need your loyalty before I can give you my heart. So take it or leave it, mama."

He reached out and flicked one of Mona's nipples with his thumb, and she felt her clit thump.

She smirked and gave him a sideways look. "Let me roll the dice."

Sly grinned as he placed the black dice in her hands. She twisted her lips to the side, gave the dice a roll, and then opened her hands. One was a five and the other was a two. She quickly nudged the second die and it rolled to a six.

"Eleven! What does that mean?"

"Eleven means somebody is about to die. Lucky you didn't really roll that, right?" Sly chuckled and changed the six back to a two. "Think you're slick, but I'm the slickest. Seven means it's your lucky day, so what's it gonna be? Take it or leave it?"

"I'll take it," she whispered to her surprise, but though shocked, she was certain she meant it. This was the closest to a fairytale romance that she could think of, and she was eager to see how it would play out. She couldn't pass it up. Just when she thought that she was headed for a downward spiral that she wouldn't be able to find her way out of, here came Sly to save the day, promising her a life of luxury, real love, and good sex to boot. She couldn't say no.

"Prove it," Sly tested her.

"How?" she asked, her eagerness showing through her expression.

"I'll let you know. But you better not give what's mine to that nigga you living with until I do. I wanna treat you like my queen, but you gotta act like one. So that shit you got going... dead it. And when I roll up out of here to D.C., you need to be ready to leave with me."

Mona's mouth went dry and she faltered. Talk about going after what you wanted! Sly came on full-force, but Mona recognized it as the boss move it was. He was used to getting what he wanted *when* he wanted it. Niggas like him didn't follow rules because they made the rules.

"I—I can't... I mean, I—I have to think about it, I can't just—"

"I'm feelin' you, ma," Sly said and sucked in his bottom lip while staring into her eyes. "I know it sounds like bullshit, but I feel like I am in love. I don't wanna leave here without you, but I know you need time to get shit right. So, I'll give you some time, but I can't wait forever."

Mona was shocked into silence for once in her life. It was absolutely insane how fast her life had taken a turn. Last week, she was putting up with Memphis's demands to be legit and push them into a life of poverty. But today, she was being offered a chance at true love. She could get everything that she should have been getting with Memphis but also be with someone who made it crystal clear that he wanted no one other than her. Whereas she had to chase Memphis down before he gave her the time of day, a fact that always had her second-guessing where she really stood with him, Sly was stepping to her properly... making it known that he wanted to love her better.

"I can deal with that," Mona told him, nodding her head slowly as she began to contemplate leaving her current life for another. The thought of leaving her daughter behind as well didn't even weigh in on her decision.

She'll be fine with Memphis. She reasoned away any traces of guilt. *She likes him better anyways.*

Pressing his lips against hers, Sly gave her the sweetest kiss, but she was too caught up to know it was the kiss of death. When he pulled away, Mona still felt like she was floating on clouds. She barely knew anything about this man, didn't even know his last name, but she was prepared to give it all up for him. It seemed crazy, but living on the edge wasn't something she was afraid to do. You couldn't be afraid of a little spontaneity when you enjoyed living life in the fast lane.

Mona snuck back through the back door of the club, making sure that she wasn't spotted getting out of Sly's car. Even if she decided to leave Memphis for Sly, she still had to make sure she survived long enough to toss out the old and pursue the new. She didn't need anything getting back to him about what she was up to before she made a move.

"It's a dangerous thing to be walkin' around alone in a building packed full of this many goons. Don't want the wolves to get ya."

Jumping slightly at the sound of a voice behind her, Mona turned and looked at Laz just as he walked out of the restroom, still zipping up his jeans. Even though Laz was Memphis's right-hand man, there was nothing subservient about him. He was just as much as a boss as Memphis, being that he'd been by his side helping him commit every single one of his crimes since they were eight years old.

In the looks department, Laz was much more rugged with his long dreadlocks that he kept in a crinkly-curly style and cascading down his back with perfectly cropped sideburns that ran directly into his perfectly manicured goatee. He had diamond-studded golds covering his four canine teeth, and a sexy ass piercing in his nose and under his bottom lip. It was easy to see why bitches everywhere were falling over their feet to get his attention. Hell, even Mona had her sights on him at one time.

When she thought that Memphis wasn't paying her any attention, she'd tried to get at Laz, and he took the bait. They'd fucked around more than a few times behind Bambi's back, but Laz was a dog, and she couldn't get with a nigga like him. He was more loyal to his niggas than he was to his girl, and Mona wouldn't stand to be played for a fool. Laz hadn't even known that she was dealing with Memphis on any level, but when he found out, he never said a word about the things they'd done. Mona was grateful for that, but many times she'd asked herself why.

"I'm a grown woman and perfectly capable of taking care of myself. You should know that," was Mona's snappy reply. On the outside, she appeared calm and collected, but on the inside, her nerves were jumping. The look of suspicion in his eyes made her feel like she'd been caught with her hand in the cookie jar. Had he seen something? Did he know she'd been with Sly?

Laz's gaze narrowed, and he looked over her, thinking to himself as Mona eyed the unreadable expression on his face. She saw a hint of something cross through his eyes and she recognized it immediately. Mona licked her lips and played the game that she was born to play, parting her thighs a bit and pushing her breasts up in the air.

Laz grinned and licked his lips. "You tryin' to get a nigga killed, huh?" He meant her and not him, but she had no idea.

Playing it coy, Mona shook her head. "Not at all. But you're the boss now, right? Doesn't that give you the right to do whatever you want to do?"

Laz pretended to let the words ruminate through his mind for a few seconds. "That's true."

He didn't let Mona wonder too long about whether they were on the same page. Reaching down, he loosened his jeans and pulled his manhood out, letting it dangle in the space between them. From the very beginning when he first met Mona, he'd picked up on the type of chick she was and figured that Memphis had also. The day he heard that Memphis had put a ring on her finger and decided to make shit official, there wasn't a nigga on Earth more surprised than he'd been, but he didn't say shit because he knew better than to question Memphis's decisions. Plus, he knew Memphis would come to his senses on his own.

Mona was a slut, someone only worthy of being mutted and nutted in. Never in life was she supposed to get to the position of wifey, and her current willingness to be disloyal to her husband was his proof. She deserved all the bullshit that he knew was coming her way.

Eyeing Laz's beefy body part, Mona felt her mouth begin to water. He wasn't holding the way that Memphis was, but what he had wasn't shit to sneeze at. Waltzing toward him, she pushed him back through the door he'd just walked out of and locked it behind them before dropping to her knees. Before she could pop his stiffening pole between her jaws, his phone rang, and Laz shoved her eager hands away before taking the call.

"Hello?" he answered while Mona frowned at him, put off by the fact that he was making her wait. Laz wasn't as refined as Memphis, and it was an instant turn off. But he was only treating her for who she was instead of how she saw herself.

"FUCK! You got any idea who is behind it?" she heard him say and tried to hide her annoyance when he began fixing up his clothes, paying her no attention.

"Um, excuse me? I know you not 'bout to try me like you do Bambi." Mona began to pop off at the mouth on Laz for being so rude. Before she could get another word out, he looked down at her, a malicious snarl on his face that was so evil, it nearly took her breath away. Grabbing her around the mouth, he snatched her up roughly and lowered the phone from his ear so that he could whisper his poison into hers.

"Don't get it twisted and think I give a shit about you just because I was gon' let you suck my dick, bitch," he growled into her ear. "If it wasn't for my goddaughter, I would have been unloaded this clip into ya stankin' ass."

He released her, and Mona fell back down to her knees, frozen into a state of shock as the blood went cold in her veins. Never had Laz spoken to her in that way, regardless to whatever his true feelings were about her. Without giving a second glance or saying a single word to her, Laz quickly finished up his call while fixing his clothes and then darted out the bathroom, leaving her devastated and alone.

CHAPTER TEN

"You ain't gon' be able to get out now, Memph. Not in the middle of a war."

Memphis didn't say anything, even though he was thinking the exact same thing that Laz had said. There standing in Johnny's mama's house, they were witnesses to a crime so horrific that Chris and Rick couldn't even stomach it and were outside spewing their guts into the front lawn. Johnny, along with his entire family, had been murdered, their blood covering every single wall of the small home. Johnny's body was strapped to a chair in the living room, his severed head lying in his lap. His mother, sister, and cousin's bullet-ridden bodies were laid out in the rooms they'd last been in before their untimely demise.

"Send word that we need anybody who knows anything about this to come forward," Memphis ordered, and Laz got to work on carrying out his order. Although his voice was flat, his heart was bleeding, and Laz knew it. Johnny wasn't the best when it came to being in the streets, but he was someone Memphis could count on, and he proved his worth to them many times. It wasn't just Memphis who was grieving over the loss of a friend; the entire crew was fucked up about it.

"From what I hear, this is a revenge kill," Laz said once he walked back into the room after about fifteen minutes of being on the phone. "Remember that nigga we got at for planning that hit on 8-Ball? He was Reese's cousin."

As soon as Laz said it, everything became clear. Reese was a hustler from North Carolina that Memphis had decided to partner with rather than erase off the map, as he normally did. The reason he opted for a partnership was because Reese was running a decent organization from what he heard, so he figured he would simply let them do what they did, just change up the chain of command so that they would answer to him. A few weeks back, he'd sent Johnny to meet with Reese to set things in motion, but now he saw that all he'd done was walk him right into the Lion's Den.

"How da fuck we miss that shit?"

Laz shrugged. "His cousin ain't someone he mess with all that much. Nigga lives here and don't even fuck with Reese on no business level, but that's still fam, so when he heard that the nigga got bodied and we were the ones responsible, he went after the one nigga he knew he could touch: Johnny. It's bullshit... How the hell was we supposed to know that nigga was his cousin?"

"It don't fuckin' matter," Memphis replied because he knew how niggas like Reese thought. It was the same way he thought. He knew if anyone laid a hand on his blood, he'd have zero understanding. 'If you didn't know, you should've known' was his thought process, because not a single soul could stop him from getting his revenge.

Memphis pressed his lips together and leaned down over Johnny's mother's body to close her eyes and hide the look of sheer terror that still resided in them. At one point in the game, the rules were that families were off limits, but niggas these days didn't operate that way. It was the reason Memphis had always wanted to get out before he brought on a wife and kids, because he knew for sure if anyone touched one of his, he wouldn't sleep until he wiped out that nigga's entire bloodline. He would singlehandedly bring down hell on Earth without giving it a second thought.

"We got a location for 'em?" Memphis asked, and Laz nodded his head.

"Yeah. These niggas are either cocky or sloppy as shit. They left breadcrumbs the size of muthafuckin' Texas that got every nigga on the street talkin'."

"Let's ride out," was all Memphis said, and Laz simply nodded his head, ready to go. He had other things he needed to talk to Memphis about, but he knew now wasn't the time. When business matters came about, the personal shit had to be pushed to the side.

"MOMMY, YOU WANT TO WATCH A MOVIE WITH ME AND GOTTY?"

Curious, Baby's head lifted as Mona walked into the room. Since she'd been there, she hadn't seen Mona interact with Genie much at all, and from the scowl on Mona's face, this wouldn't be the day she'd start.

"No, I have other things to do," she replied hastily while pecking on her phone.

Genie tried to hide the disappointment in her face with a forced smile, but Baby saw through it anyways.

"Want me to make some popcorn?" she offered, hoping that it would help ease Genie's displeasure, and it did exactly that.

"Yes!" she squealed, clapping her thanks.

About an hour into the movie, her phone chirped.

How's Genie? were the words on her screen. The number wasn't one she had saved, but only one person would be asking about her goddaughter.

She's fine, she replied back to Memphis. After a few seconds of thinking, she followed up with, *You could have asked Mona. She's here too.*

But I knew you would be the one spending time with my daughter, was his reply. The bitter truth in his statement stung her insides. She bit her bottom lip, and her eyes rolled around in her skull as she tried to think of something to say, but Memphis didn't give her time to respond.

Take care, he texted, letting her off the hook. She quickly pecked out an equally platonic reply and dropped the phone into her lap. Trying to focus on the movie was now a chore because her thoughts were elsewhere.

By the time the movie had ended, Genie was fast asleep in her lap. She cradled her small body in her arms and put her to bed, placing a gentle kiss on her cheek before she pulled the covers up under her chin.

"Goodnight, Mommy. I love you," Genie whispered in her sleep. Baby looked at her, and a wave of sadness covered her soul. Not once had she ever seen Mona come in to tuck her daughter in or kiss her goodnight. But in Genie's dreams, her mother was present, even though in reality, she was not.

"I love you too, Genie," Baby whispered back, and her heart squeezed tight in her chest when she saw the small smile on Genie's lips.

With her lips pressed into a thin line, Baby turned and took off toward Mona's room. She couldn't continue to sit around and allow her goddaughter to be treated wrong, and she wouldn't be a friend if she didn't give Mona the reality check she needed. She was no replacement for her in Genie's life, neither was the nurse, and neither was Memphis. Genie needed her mother.

"What? You can't come here!"

Furrowing her brows, Baby paused before pushing through the door into Mona's room.

"I know... and I am certain about my decision, but I can't..." She listened to the person on the other line for a few seconds. "He's not here but I'm not alone. You can't just—"

The doorbell rang, cutting off Mona's words, and Baby scurried away so that her eavesdropping wouldn't be discovered. As soon as her ass hit the sofa and she had the remote in hand, Mona stormed out of her bedroom with red cheeks standing out against her pale skin. She looked panicked, stressed, and frantic all in one.

"Is everything okay?" Baby asked, hoping that whoever was at the door wasn't there to cause trouble. It was then that Mona noticed her, and she fixed her face enough to give her an easy grin.

"Yeah... just one of Memphis's men stopping by to discuss business."

"With you?" Baby asked doubtfully.

"Yes, with me!" Mona snapped. "Can you go downstairs to give us a little privacy?"

Nothing about what Mona was saying made sense, and it was definitely full of lies, but Baby was a guest in her home and wouldn't argue. With a sigh, she stood and walked to the basement door, but her curiosity plagued her. Instead of going down the stairs and into her room, she lingered on the first step and left the door slightly ajar so she could peek out of the small opening.

"I can't believe you're here!" Mona hissed out in a whisper.

"Why not? You gave me the address," a man replied. Baby frowned, thinking that his voice sounded familiar.

"Yeah, but I didn't think you'd actually be crazy enough to come!"

"Well, I'm here now, so why don't you show me around?"

Heavy steps sounded off on the custom hardwood floors, and within seconds, Baby saw who the visitor was. She recognized him immediately as the man who had tried to speak to her at the club; Sly. But what was he doing here?

Biting down on the inside corner of her mouth, Baby carefully closed the door and crept down the stairs to the basement. Mona was up to something, and it was obvious that she didn't want anyone, not even her best friend to know about it.

"WE CAN'T DO THIS IN HERE. PLEASE..."

Mona pled breathlessly as Sly began to kiss her from head-to-toe. She was nearly naked, lying in the bed that she shared with her husband as his replacement provided her with the utmost pleasure. Sly's boldness was like an aphrodisiac. His lack of regard or fear of Memphis was alarming to her, but it set her sex on fire.

"You said you were mine, so I'll have you where the fuck I want," Sly mumbled as he teased one of her nipples between his teeth. He pushed his hand between her thighs and pressed his thumb right against her nub. She thrashed against him, mistaking his mannish aggression for passion. In Sly's mind, she was nothing but a quick fuck, but Mona romanticized his behavior and told herself that he craved her and couldn't wait to get a taste.

"Whose pussy is this?" Sly asked, blowing cold air on her love button. She spread her legs wide in anticipation.

"It's yours…" she cooed with her eyes closed, opening her thighs even wider.

Looking down on her, Sly snickered to himself. He knew that she was waiting for him to get on all fours and lap at her juicy pussy like a starving dog, but he had no intentions of tasting her sex. She wasn't worth it.

Reaching down, he released himself from his jeans and was about to push up into her when he thought twice. If she was letting him hit this easily, he couldn't take any chances. Leaning down, he reached into his pocket and grabbed a magnum. The sound of him tearing at the wrapper with his teeth made her snatch her eyes open.

"What are you doing? I'm clean," she said, and her ignorance almost made him go soft. She may have been clean, but she didn't know shit about him and was copping an attitude because he wouldn't fuck her raw.

"Your pussy so good, I don't know if I'll be able to pull right out. And I ain't tryin' to have no kids right now, ma."

That she couldn't argue with because she didn't want any more either. She barely wanted the one she had, but Genie was the only thing ensuring that Memphis would always allow her to bask in the good life. Well, that was until Sly came into the picture.

"Oh!" she gasped when Sly pushed right into her folds. She was wet, so he cruised right in and began rocking into her without mercy, smashing her like he was trying to crush her spine. Gripping the sides of her hips, he tore through her, slamming his dick in a circle and then jabbing hard, right to her center with the precision of a heavyweight

129

champ. Pulling the pillow from under her head, she covered her face with it to mute her cries of pleasure.

Sly was so close to getting a nut, but he slowed the pace, knowing that if he played his cards right, his dick could do all the work for him. The right moves in this moment could make his job fairly easy.

"Aye, I wanna make you cum first, ma. I need to see that love in your eyes."

Pulling out, he began to massage her nub with precision, like he'd studied Clitology and graduated with honors. He was just as self-absorbed as she was, so seeing her pleasure did absolutely nothing for him. Watching her with dead eyes, he brushed his thumb back and forth over her clit while impaling her with his middle fingers as she squirmed and bucked on the bed. When she arched her back and released her milky cream, she stared up at him with lazy, lust-filled eyes, and he smirked, knowing he had her where he wanted her.

DISGUSTED, BABY LAY IN HER BED AND LISTENED TO THE RHYTHMIC thumps above. In the time that she'd known her, Mona had done many things that she felt were wrong or distasteful, but she had never judged her as much as she did now.

She sighed and turned up the volume on the television, trying to drown out the noise, but the thumping continued. Tossing the remote on the nightstand, she grumbled out her discontent and grabbed her phone into her hands as the demon on her shoulder began to speak into her ear.

Baby was almost raw with anger, and there was no mistaking it; the only reason she felt as intensely as she did was because of *who* Mona was married to... *who* she was cheating on. Memphis was the man that Baby had obsessed over for nearly a year after the day she'd met him. He was the man she thought of at night before she closed her eyes and, once he'd married Mona, he was the man that she prayed to God that she could get over.

Mona was the lucky woman who had snagged the heart of the man that Baby could barely find the willpower to resist, and she was ruining it for some lame she'd just met. Sly was nothing close to the man that Memphis was, and as naïve as Mona claimed Baby to be, she had easily picked up on it. He was a slickster… a snake, probably the reason he'd been given his name. He wasn't who he claimed to be, and it was easily seen. He paraded around like he was a boss, but the leather on his Giuseppe boots was cracked and worn, the Rolex he wore on his wrist didn't tick, his edge was crooked on the sides, and his fade was uneven, a telling sign that he'd cut it himself. He wasn't a boss; he was a pretender. But Mona was too engrossed in the lies that he was feeding her and all the fake-adoration to see it for herself.

Baby held her phone in her hands, wanting so badly to text Memphis… just to ask if he was okay since it was obvious his own wife wasn't thinking about him. He had been gone three days already after running out of the club the last time she'd seen him. She was well aware that he was chasing danger and wanted to be assured that he would return.

Is everything okay… with you?

Her thumb hovered over the 'send' button, and she considered erasing the message. It wasn't her place to check on his wellbeing. Even telling herself that she was only a friend checking on a friend didn't make it better, because she knew her true feelings. She could tell herself all day that Memphis was nothing more to her than a friend, but the truth was she wanted so much more.

Just as she was about to erase the message and power off her phone to get rid of the temptation, the thumping above her became even louder. Gritting her teeth, she covered her ears and squeezed her eyes closed. Her fury was just as intense as if she were the one being betrayed. With her phone in her hands, she pressed hard on the 'send' button and then slammed the phone down on the nightstand. She bit on her thumbnail as she waited for his reply. Nervous jitters flooded her belly, and she prayed that he wouldn't think she'd overstepped.

"I know it ain't Mona that got you grinning like that, nigga,"

Laz teased as he cut his eyes at the smirk on Memphis's face. "What woman you got hittin' up the main line?"

Dressed in clothes that they'd picked up from a cheap corner store, he and Memphis were cruising through the streets, still dishing out punishment to the niggas who had killed their friend. Memphis was the judge, and Laz was the executioner. Days like this, they didn't eat, didn't sleep... didn't even fuckin' bathe. Any moment spent on anything other than retribution was a moment they could be caught slipping, and that wasn't an option.

"Why the hell it gotta be a woman makin' a nigga smile? A mutha-fucka like me can't just be happy?" Memphis joked, still smirking, and Laz shook his head.

"Don't nothing make a nigga grin like that but pussy... unless you like the chick attached to it. Then I guess she'd make you smile, too." Laz shrugged. When Memphis didn't reply, he glanced over at him, jerking the wheel slightly when he took his eyes off the road.

"That wouldn't happen to be Baby you textin'?"

"Why you ask that?" Memphis inquired, peering at Laz from under hooded brows.

"I've been noticin' some shit," was all Laz said. He left it at that and waited to see whether Memphis would respond or not. If he didn't, Laz would leave it alone. They were friends, but he knew better than to question Memphis on some personal shit unless he was welcomed into it.

"If it ain't about my wife, ain't shit worth noticin'," he said, and silence filled the air around them. Memphis ran his thumb along the thickness of his bottom lip as he mentally struggled between the things he knew were wrong and what he knew was right. Glancing at Laz from the side of his eyes, he sniffed and flicked the side of his nostril with his thumb, knowing he was about to do something he'd never done.

"What you think about her?" he asked, barely believing the question had left his lips. "About Baby."

The word 'shocked' couldn't even properly explain how Laz felt. Never in the decades of years that he'd known Memphis had he once asked him about a woman. Cutting his eyes to him, he could see, that even now, Memphis was uncomfortable with the conversation, but the fact that he was still waiting on Laz to answer told him everything he needed to know. His boy was whipped, and though he'd never fix his mouth to say it, Laz could see it clearly.

"I mean... I don't know much about her except that she's a good girl. The type I would've picked for you. Never thought you'd go after Mona." He deliberately said that last line to get a reaction, but Memphis was too poised for that. The sting of Laz's statement did burn in his chest, but he wouldn't admit it.

"She's the mother of my child, and it was the right thing to do."

The part of Memphis's genetic makeup that made him stubborn was also the side that made him deadly. This was why Laz never contested him, never disagreed, and always allowed him to lead. But, in this instance, he felt there was something that needed to be said. And even though he wasn't positive, he felt like Memphis needed to hear him say it.

"The only right thing a father has to do when it comes to his child is provide, protect, and give love. God ain't put you on this Earth to be miserable. My moms says children are a blessin'... Why the hell would God bless you right into a life of misery?"

There was no visual indication that Memphis had heard what Laz said, but he did. Even though he knew it to be true and it made perfect sense, he was a strong believer of lying in the bed he'd made. He had taken charge of his future when he married Mona, knowing that he loved her best friend, and now there was nothing he could do. Looking down at the text message on the screen of his phone, he ran a weary hand over his face and replied.

I'm good. Just missin' the woman I love.

It was the truth, but he knew that she would take it the wrong way. Whereas Mona always mistook everything he said for flattery, Baby didn't know how tight the grip was that she had on his heart.

I'm sure Mona misses you, too.

Reading her reply fucked with his mind. He needed to remain focused for the mission he and Laz were on, but here was Baby, holding his every thought hostage in the way that she always had once she entered the picture. She had reacted exactly as he'd intended her to, but he couldn't force himself to leave things that way.

I didn't mean Mona.

He sent the text before he had a chance to have a second thought. Noticing his man was unsettled by his constant movement, Laz raised a brow and glanced his way.

"Aye, you good, bruh?"

"Peachy," Memphis replied tensely, and Laz chuckled.

"Now I know somethin' up. 'Peachy' ain't never been part of the street nigga vocabulary," he joked, but Memphis didn't join in with his laughter because Baby had texted him back.

Genie?

She was reaching, and he could tell. If ever there was a sign that Baby might care for him in the way that he did her, it was this. If she didn't think of him in any way, she wouldn't be searching for clarity.

"We're here," Laz said as he began creeping through a desolate and dilapidated neighborhood. "One of the niggas involved lives with his baby moms out here. You ready?" His hand gripped his banger as he surveyed the area.

"Always ready," Memphis replied, tossing the phone into the glove compartment. His mind was on his mission, and there was no time for slip ups. Baby wanted something from him, but she wouldn't get it today.

CHAPTER ELEVEN

"*D*id you and Memphis's friend get to the business you needed to discuss?" Baby asked with a pointed stare. She'd been waiting all day to ask about Mona's late-night escapade and finally had the chance.

Flinching, Mona's shame was easily seen when her cheeks flushed ruby red.

"Don't judge me, Baby," she said with pleading eyes. "You don't know my situation."

Baby's brows shot up. "Oh, I don't? Why don't you tell me then?"

After having a long awkward dinner together, Genie was in her room reading, giving the two of them a chance to talk. All day at work, Baby couldn't get the night before off her mind. Standing, she grabbed her empty plate as well as Mona's, even though she'd barely touched her food, and tossed them into the sink. With her back to Mona, she began washing dishes as she waited for her to speak.

"Memphis and I have been having issues for a while..."

"So you just have sex with someone you just met?" Baby snapped, whipping around to look at her. "You know if you're wrong, I'm going to tell you that you're wrong. And that was *very* wrong, Mona. You were with another man, in your husband's bed, while your child was sleeping right down the hall!"

"Shh!" Mona hissed with her finger to her lips. She pointed her eyes toward Genie's room. Baby scoffed and rolled her eyes.

"You should have worried about her hearing something last night. Y'all almost came through the damn roof."

Mona couldn't bite back the dreamy smile on her face as she thought back to what she'd done with Sly. The things he'd done to her body... she couldn't wait to get more.

"Do you even love Memphis?" Baby asked and turned back to the dishes so that Mona couldn't see the hurt in her face.

"Of course I love him! I just—" She searched for something to say but came up blank. "Do you really think he's always been faithful to me?"

Thankful that her back was to Mona, Baby swallowed hard before she answered. If she'd been asked this question days ago, she wouldn't have hesitated to say that Memphis would never cheat because it wasn't who he was. But the chemistry they shared made her question that. If it came to it... if the opportunity was there, would he make a move?

"Only Memphis can answer that," Baby said. "But no, I don't think he's ever cheated on you. But this is a dangerous game you're playing. You need to get yourself together and fix this before he comes back home."

She turned to Mona and saw the distressed look on her face. "I know. I didn't mean for this thing to go this far with Sly. But the conversations felt good and..." Her words faded off.

There was nothing else that Mona needed to say because Baby understood her completely. It had been the same way with Memphis, and if she hadn't been strong enough to leave, who knows what would have happened? She could have easily been in the same position, only it would have been worse because she'd have slept with her best friend's man.

"I can't judge you," Baby admitted. "I'm in no position to. But just be careful... and figure out what you want. I don't trust Sly. Something about him is creepy and—"

"No need for you to mention him anymore," Mona said with her hand raised. "I'm done. I made a stupid mistake, but I'm going to work through my issues, and it won't happen again."

The weak smile on her face told Baby that Mona wasn't even sure if that was the truth, but she didn't argue with her.

"I hope not," Baby said. "At least for Genie's sake."

Regardless to her personal feelings, Mona was a married woman, and Baby was her friend. She would never encourage her to destroy her family.

"I'm going to get it together," Mona repeated, and then her eyes lit up. "You know what, I'm glad you're here. I can trust you, and it's good to have someone to talk to."

Baby's guilt built up in her throat, and she swallowed hard to push it down.

"I'll always be someone you can trust," she told Mona as well as herself. It would be hard, but she had to get herself together too. And she would... All she had to do was keep her distance from Memphis.

ᔥ

ANOTHER TWO DAYS PASSED BEFORE MEMPHIS WAS FINALLY ON HIS WAY back home. He'd been putting in work for nearly the entire forty-eight hours, only taking breaks to call Genie and let her know he loved her each day. Living the street life was glamorous to everyone but the ones who actually had to deal with it. To Memphis, there was nothing desirable about running up on niggas and stealing souls on the daily, all the while watching your back to make sure nobody was about to pull a sneak attack on you. It was a way of life that he'd adopted, and he was good at it, but he was also smart enough to know it wasn't the only way of life. Even still, no matter how many times he tried to get out the game, something always popped up to pull him back in.

"So, plans have changed, right? I mean, I know you wanna go legit, and I can definitely deal with what's jumpin' off on my own, but—"

"I ain't gon' leave you hangin', bruh," Memphis replied, cutting Laz off. "I know you can handle this shit on your own, but you won't have to."

Laz nodded his head and continued to drive, not saying anything, although he was truly happy that Memphis was staying in the game a little longer before making his exit. Whereas there were plenty of niggas on the streets who would jump at the opportunity to be a boss and take Memphis's place, Laz was completely content with being second in command. He felt like they could take over any hood they set their sights on if they worked together, but he also respected the fact that Memphis wanted out. Going legit wasn't in the cards for him, but if Memphis could get there, Laz would be happy for him.

"I need to talk to you about somethin'. Some personal shit," Laz began, licking his lips as he waited for Memphis to respond. When Memphis said nothing, he continued anyways.

"Ya girl, Mona... she rotten. You know I ain't never spoke much on you bein' with her because it ain't my business, but you need to let her go. Trust me on this."

To Memphis, Laz was the closest thing he had to a brother, so his warning didn't fall on deaf ears. In all the time they'd been together, not once had Laz ever opened his mouth to speak on his choice in women, so the fact that he was saying something now meant that he had a good reason for speaking up.

"Tell me what happened."

Nearly a full minute of silence passed between them before Laz even opened his mouth to say a word. He knew that Memphis was normally calm and collected when it came to most things, but he wasn't sure how he would react in this instance.

"I caught her chillin' with some nigga. And by chillin', I mean that she was damn near ridin' his dick in the back seat of his whip while you were handling that lil' situation with Baby the other night. I confronted her, and before I could even tell her that I saw her lil' stankin' ass, she dropped to her knees to suck my dick."

Memphis's jaw clenched tight. "You let her?"

"Thought about it because I knew her days with you were over, but I got the call about Johnny and dipped," he admitted. There was very little that Laz kept from Memphis, and he never lied to him.

"Who was the nigga she was with?"

"He left before I could see his face." Laz only told a half-lie because Sly *had* made off before he could see his face. He knew that he was the nigga Mona had been with, but for his own reasons, he withheld that bit of knowledge.

A sharp pain settled in the middle of Memphis's chest. Flicking the bridge of his nose, he looked out the window as he fought to regain control of himself. He wasn't hurt by what Mona had done because, emotionally, he didn't love her. However, he wasn't the type of nigga who dealt well with disrespect. He'd never once disrespected her, and he demanded the same in return. He knew she was the type to throw pussy to any nigga with fat pockets, but once he'd given in, he thought that she'd changed her ways.

On top of everything, his seething anger came from the fact that he knew that the family life he'd tried to give his daughter was ruined. There was no way he could stay with a woman who was comfortable throwing shit in his face for the world to see. He'd tried to elevate her to the status of a queen, but she wasn't worthy of the throne he had tried to give her. He could do a lot of things, but he couldn't turn dirt into diamonds.

"I knew she wasn't worth shit when I met her," Memphis replied with his honest thoughts, admitting to Laz how he felt for the very first time.

Laz's eyes nearly bugged out of his skull. "And you still married the broad?"

"I did it for Genie. She deserved to have a family, and Mona promised she would do anything to be a good mother if I married her."

Laz nodded quietly. If nothing else, he knew how much Memphis loved his daughter. She was the center of his life, and there wasn't a thing he wouldn't do for her.

"Well, that's a stand-up thing to do, but I think we all knew that she wasn't the one you *really* wanted."

Before Memphis could stop them, his thoughts had drifted off to Baby. It was hard as hell for a man like him to admit to doing some stupid shit, but he had. From the very beginning, he knew that Baby was who he should've been with and that he'd only paid Mona the slightest attention as his own stupid way to get over being rejected.

"The other day, I found out some bullshit about how she lied to make me even look her way. Her days are numbered."

"Damn, that's fucked up." Laz spoke with a flat tone because he wasn't at all surprised. If anyone did, he knew what Mona was capable of.

"She's a sorry ass friend. Baby is the only one who doesn't see that shit." Memphis let out a pressed snort before turning to look out the window. He felt himself getting angry, but he was trying to bridle it, which was becoming harder and harder the more he thought things through.

"So what you gon' do about Mona?" Laz asked, genuinely interested in the situation that Memphis was in. Never before had he known him to have issues with women, but this shit right here that he was dealing with... it was something that not even he had experience with.

"It's a wrap. But I'm patient. I'll get rid of her when the time is right," he added. If he made Mona leave, Baby would follow, and he couldn't let that happen just yet.

"I know I ain't really gotta say this shit to you, but I wouldn't be your boy if I held it in," Laz began. "Just make sure you hide your cheese. When it comes to these bird ass females out here, soon as they get in their feelings, the first thing they do is fly away with your bread."

"I know it. She ain't got access to shit but what I got in the safe... and I don't keep much in there anyways."

"So what you gonna do about Baby?" Laz asked, trying his luck for the sake of his curiosity.

Make her mine, was the immediate thought that came to Memphis's mind, but he didn't say a word. After waiting in vain for him to respond, Laz knew he wouldn't and put his attention back on the road. He really didn't need a response to know that Memphis was going to make his move on Baby, and he would be the first in line to congratulate him once he succeeded in getting the woman he should have been with all along.

CHAPTER TWELVE

*A*fter speaking with Baby, Mona tried her hardest to stay away from Sly. She erased their messages from her phone, blocked his number, and even made her Facebook page private to anyone who wasn't a friend so that she wouldn't have to deal with him there either. At one point in her marriage with Memphis, she had felt loved, and if she could get that back, she might be able to be happy in her relationship again.

When Genie was first born, Memphis was so happy to have a child, and the fact that she'd given him one elevated her in his eyes. Even though they both knew their daughter was the only thing that brought them together, it felt like they had a chance at a real love because of the bond they now shared.

But then Genie became sick, and it was nothing but stress, doctors, surgeries, and arguments from there. They couldn't agree on how to care for her or compromise on the medical decisions that needed to be made. Memphis spent all his time at Genie's bedside when she was awake, and when she was asleep, he left to command the streets. Mona was neglected. She felt like the weird uncle that nobody really liked but dealt with because they had to. While Memphis and Genie's relationships bloomed into something beautiful and sacred, his relationship with Mona dwindled into nothing.

"I can get him back," Mona said.

She glanced at her watch. Memphis had told Genie earlier that he was about thirty minutes away, so he should've been walking through the door any minute. When he did, she would be ready for him. New sheets were on the bed, a fruit platter lay on the table beside it, candles were lit, champagne was on ice, and the fireplace was lit. Underneath her gold robe she wore an expensive lace negligee that she loved but hoped wouldn't stay on very long. It was time to remind Memphis why she was the only one who deserved the spot as his queen.

The front door opened, and she sucked in a breath and then let it out slow. It was showtime.

"Dadddyyyy!" Genie shrieked. She was sitting on the sofa playing Connect Four with Baby when she saw Memphis walk through the door. Mona leaned against the wall across from them and watched him bend down to kiss her on the forehead. Then he looked at Baby and they exchanged glances before Baby dropped her head and looked away. Mona's breath stalled in her lungs, and she prayed that Baby would be able to keep her secret like she promised.

"Hey, my love," Mona cooed, strolling over to Memphis. She wrapped her arms around his neck and hugged him tight, but he made no movements to hug her back. It wasn't until Genie glanced in their direction that he lifted one hand and pressed it to her back, but he used that same hand to tug her away.

"Hey," he replied. He finally brought his eyes to her face, but they were cold as ice. Mona could feel all of her courage fleeing. It hadn't even been five minutes and she was losing her nerve.

"I have a surprise for you..." she began, talking to Memphis's back as he stomped away toward the basement. This was normal for him. He always said that whatever he did in the streets changed him. Before coming home, he always took time to diffuse and then he would retreat to his private space to further collect himself. Mona knew it, but she had hoped she could be part of his relaxation process this time.

"I'm not interested," he said. Sensing something was wrong, Genie lifted her head and cut her eyes between her parents. Memphis saw her watching and sighed before turning back to Mona.

"Maybe later."

Although that was enough for Genie, Mona knew better.

"You don't have to lie, Memphis. I'm a big girl; you can tell me the truth."

Knowing the conversation wasn't heading anywhere good, Baby was quick on her feet.

"Genie, how about we go play dolls in your room? And then will you help me grade papers for tomorrow?"

As she'd suspected, Genie's face lit up, and she nodded eagerly. She grabbed Genie in her arms and gave Mona a sympathetic look as they left down the hall. Her mind was full of conflicting emotions. She wanted the best for Mona, but her feelings for Memphis made things difficult. She was already too involved.

"That's some foul shit for you to try and pick a fight in front of Genie," Memphis said once he and Mona were alone.

She cocked her head back. "Oh? You don't think she needs to see what real life is? Or do you prefer that we keep doing this make believe shit in front of her? Married people fight, and she needs to know that!"

"We don't argue in front of Genie, period. So kill that shit." He wasn't willing to back down. "She already has enough shit to deal with, and I don't want her worrying about—"

"How her daddy doesn't give a shit about her mommy?" Mona butted in. With her arms crossed in front of her chest, she took a few steps forward and stood in front of Memphis as if to challenge him. He ran his hand over his face and tried to suppress his anger from flaring. She was testing his patience.

"Or how her mommy tricked and gamed her daddy into even looking her way to begin with," he added. "What about that? Don't pretend like you don't know what this is, Mo. What we got going on has never been about love. You wanted a paid nigga to buy you shit, and I wanted a home with my daughter living in it. I ain't want my kid calling another nigga daddy. That's it."

"That's it?" Mona repeated. Her bottom lip trembled slightly, and her eyes filled with tears, but she sniffed them away. She had made her bed, and now she had to lie in it. She couldn't get Memphis to love her when he never did, and having his baby may have given her access to his lifestyle but not to his heart.

"That's how you made it," he told her. "This is what you asked for, isn't it?"

With that last question floating in the air, Memphis retreated to the basement, leaving her standing there. This may have been what she asked for, but it wasn't what she wanted. All the money in the world was no replacement for affection or passion.

With tears in her eyes, she ran back to her bedroom, blew out all the candles, tossed the fruit tray in the fireplace, and flushed the champagne down the toilet. It was a $300 bottle of Ace of Spades, but she didn't care. She craved affection, and she wasn't getting it from her husband... The one man who should love her never would.

She stared into the fireplace as she cried. People judged her for clubbing all the time, spending money like it was going out of style, and staying out late instead of tending to her husband's needs, but who could really blame her? Memphis wasn't interested in being anything to her other than a baby daddy. The rings they wore on their fingers didn't mean a thing.

By the time the last tear fell from her eyes, she had made her decision. She was tired of mourning her marriage and regretting her mistakes. If she knew then what she knew now, she wouldn't have done what she did in order to get Memphis. She didn't know that it would lead her into a life of misery. There was nothing that she could do about the past, but she could change her future. With her phone in hand, she unblocked Sly's number and sent him a quick text.

Can we meet? Tonight?

She took shallow breaths as she waited for him to reply. When he did, the message was only a short 'yes', but the fact that he even wanted to spend time with her, when all Memphis offered was rejection, gave her comfort. She shot him a text with a time and location and then went into her closet to get dressed.

Memphis didn't want her, but someone else did.

"I'M GOING OUT... YOU'LL PROBABLY BE GONE TO BED BY THE TIME I GET back, so I guess I'll see you in the morning," Mona said, sashaying into the living room.

Baby pulled her attention away from the mound of papers she had left to grade and ran her eyes over Mona. In a short, blazing red sequence dress with strap-up heels and a matching clutch, she was dressed to kill.

"Memphis going with you?" Baby asked with a lifted brow, and Mona shook her head. Walking into the living room, she sat down and sighed.

"No, he's not. We have an understanding now. The only reason we are together is to be parents to Genie, and that's it. There is no marriage."

Baby placed her hands on her thighs and gave Mona her full attention.

"Is that what you want?"

"No," she whispered, looking down. "In the beginning, I was cool with that. But now... I want to be loved."

It was a rare moment when Mona showed her vulnerability. But just as quickly as it came, it went away when she stood and sighed deeply.

"So anyways, I'll be back. I'm just going to hang with Bambi for a while."

Baby didn't believe that for one minute.

"Just Bambi, or someone else too?"

Placing her hand on her hip, Mona sucked her teeth.

"Yes, *just* Bambi," she lied. "Regardless to what is going on, I'm done with Sly. If I get caught fuckin' with another nigga, ain't no tellin' what Memphis would do. He don't play 'bout that shit."

Baby wasn't fully convinced, but she dropped it and wished Mona a good night. Once she was alone again, she went back to grading the papers that were left over after Genie had gone to bed. Truthfully, she was exhausted and would have pushed them off until later, but Memphis was still in the basement, and she wanted to keep her distance. However, only a few minutes after Mona had left, the basement door opened and out walked the very man she'd been trying to avoid.

"Working late?" he asked.

The fine hairs on the back of her neck stood on end as she listened to him walk into the kitchen. She refused to look his way, thinking if she never met his eyes and kept the conversation short, it would be easier on her.

"Yeah, just for a little while."

"Want company?" he asked.

No, her mind said.

"Sure," her lips replied.

Her heart beat faster with each step she heard him take in her direction. By the time he was standing right in front of her, it felt like it would jump out of her chest.

"Drink?" she heard Memphis ask, and it was then that she realized she'd have to look up. She had to look at him.

Taking a deep breath, she placed her papers to the side and lifted her head. Her entire body went warm under his gentle gaze, and she hurried to grab the glass from his hand before looking away. Memphis, on the other hand, couldn't stop staring.

"Thanks," she mumbled and took a sip from the glass. "This is good... what is it?"

"Just something I made... no name for it."

He sat down, and Baby couldn't help but think about Mona. There was something she had to ask, and it needed to come out now.

"Why are you so mean to her? To Mona?" she began. "She loves you and—"

"Mona doesn't love me," he cut in. "She loves what comes with being with me."

Frowning, Baby shook her head at him. "That's not true. She had

147

planned a surprise for you... You should've seen how disappointed she was when you weren't interested."

His brows rose. "And you think that was mean of me?"

Sipping from her glass, Baby nodded her head. "Of course! You told her you weren't interested... You should've seen how it crushed her. She's your wife and—"

"But what about all the slick shit she did to become my wife?" Memphis narrowed his eyes as he spoke. "I messed around with her after she told me you had a boyfriend that you did *not* have. Never spoke to her again after that until she hit me up about being pregnant. We used a condom, and she said she was on the pill, so I didn't believe the baby was mine.

Once she had Genie, I took a paternity test and realized that I was a father. I don't fault her for that because it takes two to make a baby. I married her thinking that one day I would fall in love—I did my best to be a good husband, but she never turned into a wife. She sits around, and she doesn't do shit but spend money. After a while, I just gave up and accepted that this was my life. I made a stupid ass decision, placed my faith in the wrong woman, and I deal with that shit every day. We both gotta boss up and deal with the consequences of our actions."

"But now she's just trying to make the best of the situation. I'm sure if she could go back, she would change everything," Baby defended. Memphis nodded his head and then looked up, gazing deeply into her eyes.

"Yeah... and I would, too."

Before she could stop him, he leaned in and kissed her sweetly on the lips. The touch was so gentle, she would have thought she'd imagined it if she hadn't seen it coming. He pressed his forehead to hers for a second, both of them knowing that they were on the brink of passion. And then he raised his hand and gently caressed her cheek, instantly setting things in motion.

Memphis crushed his lips into hers while wrapping her in his arms. He sucked on her lips and then pushed his tongue inside, tasting the fruity flavor of the liquor on her tongue. She opened her mind, body, and soul to him as he ravished her. He was wild, almost feral in his attempt to consume her. Her scent was intoxicating, a mixture of honey and cocoa butter that was as sweet as her taste. They had to stop this... He knew it and so did she, but neither was able to.

She felt his fingertips teasing the clasp of her bra, and it was then that she began to panic.

"Wait... stop." She pressed her hands against his chest.

Memphis looked down at her, knowing that if he ignored her, she would most likely give in, but he didn't want any part of their relationship to be forced. He was used to forcing niggas to abide by his wishes on the daily, but with her, he wanted to operate differently.

"We can't do this," she said more to herself than to him. "This isn't right."

She felt the need to remind herself that what they were doing was wrong. *Very* wrong. Not just because she was with Semaj... In the grand scheme of things, she knew that any normal person would understand her need for the touch of a man being that hers was locked down. But the fact that Memphis was her best friend's husband —that was taboo behavior. Under no circumstances should a woman ever involve herself with him. It was one of those things that never even had to be said because every woman knew it. It was just something you didn't do.

Memphis watched as his love backed away, reminding him of the type of rejection he never wanted to experience ever again when it came to her. He knew having her heart wouldn't come without putting in work, but he was prepared to do just that.

"What's wrong is ignoring your feelings... which might be something that you're able to do, but I can't do that shit anymore. I want to make love to you, but it's deeper than that. This feeling isn't going anywhere, and I'm done fighting it."

All the fight left in her was gone. Baby's eyes fluttered under the weight of her desire, and he pulled her back into his arms. She grabbed his hand and forced it under her shirt. Without delay, he expertly freed her breasts with one simple motion and allowed his hands to roam as they kissed passionately.

After all the years of waiting, he finally had the chance he'd been waiting for. This wasn't quite how he'd imagined it, and he would have loved for their first time to be on some exotic island somewhere, overlooking the water, or some cheesy shit like that. But there was no telling when he'd get that chance, and he was too far gone to care. She was giving herself to him, and he was going to take her right there.

"FUCK!" MONA CURSED, SEARCHING THROUGH HER SMALL CLUTCH.

She had been in such a rush to get the hell out of the house that somehow, she'd left her phone. She considered leaving it, but she couldn't. Memphis wasn't the type to go snooping through her things, but with the way things were going between them, she didn't want to take the chance. Especially since Sly would be calling once he arrived at their destination.

Turning back now would make her late, but she was worth the wait. Sly wouldn't go anywhere. Making an illegal U-turn, she pressed hard on the gas and raced back home, hoping that she could slide in and out without Memphis noticing. She didn't feel like arguing about what she was wearing, where she was going, or who she would be with. When it came to him, it was better to ask for forgiveness than permission. The same argument would be waiting for her when she came home from being with Sly, but at least then, she would have already had her fun.

THE MOMENT HAD NEARLY ARRIVED.

With her head falling back, Baby enjoyed the feel of Memphis's tongue as he licked from her navel down to the edge of her black lace panties. He teased her a little longer, nudging slightly under them with the tip of his tongue before using his teeth to peel them off. She let out a slow breath as he tugged them down her thighs, lifting her bare ass with his hands so that he could pull them all the way off.

Oh god...

She was completely naked, and the nervous energy in her stomach made her anxious. With open eyes, she watched as Memphis pulled his shirt over his head, and the sight of his rock-hard body made her want to lick her lips. But then she thought she heard something in the distance and she froze.

"What?" Memphis asked breathlessly. Leaning down, he hovered over her mound and she felt cool air brush over her clit when he pushed her thighs open. Closing her eyes, she told herself that she was paranoid and prepared herself to enjoy the moment. But then they both froze when they each heard the unmistakable sound of a car door shutting.

"Mona's back!" Panicked, she pulled herself from under Memphis and grabbed at her clothing while he watched her with a frown.

"Get dressed!" she hissed, throwing his shirt at him, but he didn't move a muscle.

The moment Baby willingly crossed the line with him, Mona was a done deal. It wasn't ideal for her to catch them in the middle of what had gotten started, but he wasn't the type of nigga to duck and hide from anyone either.

"Give me my panties," Baby whispered, but he shook his head and stuck them into his pocket. She looked mortified but quickly decided to just get dressed without them.

They both heard Mona's key twist in the lock before Baby could find her bra, so she simply pulled her shirt over her head. Wearing only half of the clothing she should have been, she scurried off to the kitchen at the same moment that Mona entered the room.

"I forgot my damn phone," she mumbled, rushing so fast down the hall that she hadn't even noticed Memphis sitting on the couch with his shirt still off. She disappeared down the hall, and Baby took the opportunity to run in the living room and search for her bra.

"At least put your shirt on!" she whispered, and he clenched his jaw before giving into her request. "And can you give me my panties, please?"

With a playful gleam in his eyes, he pulled Baby's panties out of his pocket, pressed them against his nose and inhaled deeply, and then hung them from his teeth. She cursed him under her breath as she snatched them away. Here she was, absolutely humiliated, but he was amused.

"Got it!" Mona announced, coming back down the hall. "Bye, Baby, I'll see—Oh!"

She stepped into the living room and her eyes focused on Memphis for the first time.

"I'm just going out with Bambi," she offered. "I'll be back around—"

"You'll be back late. Yeah, I know," he said without looking her way.

Satisfied with her decision to go hang with Sly, Mona rolled her eyes and waved her hand at Baby before storming back out the door. As soon as she was gone, Baby glared at Memphis before stomping down to the basement. It was bad enough they'd almost done something they both knew was wrong, but for him to be so bold about it... it angered her.

Memphis sat on the couch alone for a few minutes, wondering if he should follow behind her. She was upset, and he knew it. Although he didn't give a shit about Mona finding out about them, Baby still did. He warred with his thoughts for a short while until he realized that there was no way he'd be able to let this night pass without setting things right.

"Can I come in?" he asked, knocking on her door.

"You have to wait. I'm about to get in the shower."

He didn't hesitate a second before opening the door. Baby had one leg suspended in the air, about to step in the shower, when she heard the door open, and shouted in surprise.

"What are you doing in here? I told you to wait!"

She snatched up a bath towel to cover herself as if he hadn't seen all of her already. As if he hadn't *licked* all of her already. Or almost all of her.

"Damn, we do a little something, and you rush down here to wash a nigga off? That's fucked up," he said, frowning.

Once she secured the towel, she crossed her arms in front of her chest and narrowed her eyes into him.

"No, what's fucked up is that we were just about to have sex... in the living room! This has gone way too far. Much farther than it ever should have, and you act like we're not doing anything wrong!"

"Did it feel wrong to you?" he asked and leaned back against the wall. The steam from the shower was thick, making it hard for Baby to breathe. Or maybe it was the sight of Memphis standing there and the memory of what they'd almost done that did it.

"It doesn't matter what it felt like. We can't do that again. Mona is your wife and… I'm with Semaj," she explained, putting words to her worries and hoping that hearing them from her lips would push her emotions back in line.

Unfortunately, her body still throbbed and longed for Memphis's touch. She took a few steps backward to increase the distance between them, thinking maybe that would help. No… it didn't. She still wanted him, and from the expression on his face, he wanted her even more.

"You shouldn't give a fuck about either one of them," he replied brashly, turning up his nose.

"But *I* do!" Baby countered, placing her hands at each side of her head. "I was going to marry Semaj. And Mona—she is my best friend."

"She is *not* your best friend," Memphis shot back, letting out a pressed snort. "Never once has she gone out on a limb for you. She barely supports you. If it don't concern her, she's not interested. Haven't you noticed that? She barely looks at her fuckin' child! Do you really think she gives a damn about you or anyone else?"

Baby's bottom lip trembled as she listened to his words, wanting to reject them, but the bottom line was that they were true. In her heart of hearts, she knew that Mona was selfish and only really cared about herself, but it had never bothered her all that much. Everyone had their vices, and that was Mona's. Over time, she'd learned to deal with it and not take the things that Mona did to her too seriously.

"Even now… every night she leaves you alone for her own selfish ass reasons. You're going through some real shit right now, and you came here because you needed her help. Well, where the hell is she, and how has she really helped you through it?"

"You need to leave!" Baby cried.

Frustrated to the max after he'd hit her with some hard truths, her eyes were brimming with tears. Memphis ran his thumb over his lips pensively but didn't say another word. He wanted to bring her joy and fill her heart with love... not see her cry. Weighing his thoughts in his head, he eventually decided that he'd said enough for the moment and turned to leave. Being a man who knew women, especially *this* woman, he didn't bother speaking on Semaj because he already considered that nigga a nonfactor.

The only thing standing between him and the woman he loved was Mona, but he also knew that Baby would soon see that being loyal to her was a wasted cause. Never had Mona shown loyalty to her, and the truth was in all the things he'd learned about the woman he'd once called his wife. She wasn't built to be a real friend to anyone other than herself, and the sooner Baby understood that, the sooner he could have her. Forever.

§

"DAMN, YOU WEARIN' THAT FUCKIN' DRESS," SLY SAID. TAKING IN A generous eyeful, he licked his chops hungrily as Mona walked up to him. She giggled shyly and rolled her eyes.

"Whatever... Of course I gotta represent on our date," she replied.

Sly's lips spread wide. "Oh? So this is a date?"

She shrugged. "I guess so."

Not speaking, he looked around them. They were standing in the parking lot of Phipps Plaza, cars were honking and racing by, teenagers were skateboarding along the sidewalk, and somewhere in the distance, a dog was barking relentlessly. Nothing about this said 'date'.

"This your idea of a date?" he asked with a lifted brow, and Mona fell into him as she laughed.

"Well, no, but I figured we could just meet here and then we can go somewhere. It just has to be out of the city," she added. Sly didn't like the sound of that, but she knew he wouldn't when she'd said it.

"Out of the city? Why?"

She rolled her eyes and let out a heavy breath. "Because everyone here knows Memphis, and I don't want any troubles from him. If he found out—"

Sly recoiled as if he'd been hit and glared down at her. "What? That nigga ain't gon' do shit to you because I ain't gon' let him!" He lifted the side of his shirt to show that he had his piece on him. "A nigga stay strapped, so if that nigga want some, he can get some."

The way that Sly easily made it his business to protect her made her swoon. She grinned and rose up on the tip of her toes to give him a kiss. He deepened it and cuffed her ass to stop her from pulling away. Things got heated fast, and before long, he'd reached his hand under her dress to tickle her kitty.

"Damn... can you feed a bitch first?" Mona joked, pulling away. She glanced around quickly to make sure no one was watching as she fixed her clothes. Sly picked up on her paranoia but let it go because he would be addressing it later.

"Hop in," he told her, holding open the passenger door of his whip. "I got a spot in mind that I want to take you to."

She jumped in happily and waited for him to get in. Sly walked to the driver's side with a smile on his face because he knew that tonight, he was about to mess up her life.

ॐ

As soon as Sly pulled into the parking lot of their next destination, Mona took one glance and folded her arms in front of her chest.

"Hell naw, I'm not going in there."

"Why not?" Sly was playing dumb. He had deliberately taken her to a restaurant that was a known favorite of members of the *Murda Mob*.

"Because..." She let her words fade, not wanting to bring Memphis up for a second time that night.

"Yo, listen," Sly began. He reached out and tugged her lightly by the chin until she met his eyes. "I know it's too soon to say, but I feel like you the type of woman that a nigga could fall in love with. I won't ever harm you, and I won't let anyone else do shit to you either. On God."

They strolled into the restaurant hand-in-hand, Sly's doing, and when they had to wait for the hostess to seat them, Mona was reminded how privileged her life with Memphis really was. Never once had she ever had to wait to be seated at any restaurant when she was with him, but that was because this was his city. Once Sly took her to D.C. where he reigned, things would be different. The food was delicious, the wine wasn't exactly what she was used to, but she was ready to try new things with this new man.

Sly was the perfect conversationalist. Whereas Memphis rarely uttered more than a few words at a time her way, Sly couldn't stop asking questions to know her better. It was like he wanted to know everything about her, and he never got bored with listening. She felt comfortable with him, and eventually, all of her defenses fell by the wayside.

What Mona didn't know was that there was another couple walking into the same restaurant, and outside of Memphis, they were the very last people she wanted to see.

"Is that Mona?" Bambi asked, squinting as she and Laz were shown to their table. "And that's definitely not Memphis she's with."

Lifting his head, Laz only took a lazy glance in the direction Bambi was staring, but he immediately recognized Mona sitting at a table with Sly.

"That is definitely Mona," he replied with a satisfied grin.

"Oh hell no! I'm about to snatch that bitch—"

"Yo, chill," Laz said, grabbing her by the hand before she stormed away. "Maybe that's just her friend."

The entire time she and Laz sat at their table, drinking and eating, she could not stop herself from stealing glances across the room. She wanted to give her the benefit of the doubt, but Mona just looked way too chummy with the man she was sitting with. When she saw Sly lean over and kiss her softly on the lips, Bambi knew for certain that this was more than a platonic dinner with a friend, and she was prepared to throw hands.

The thing about the *Murda Mob* was if you were in an official relationship with one of the crew, you were in it, too. Bambi wasn't too much involved in the street shit that Laz was into, but she'd pledged her loyalty to Memphis all the same. The moment that Mona married him, the same loyalty was extended to her, but Bambi's devotion was to Laz first and Memphis second. She refused to sit back and let Mona play him for a fool in the very restaurant his crew frequented. She was tossing up a very direct message that she didn't give a fuck about Memphis, and Bambi had caught it.

Standing suddenly, she glared at Mona who must have sensed it, because she looked up right into her eyes. Her face went white as a ghost, and she began looking around for the nearest exit, but it was too late. Bambi was already heading her way with Laz on her heels.

"Bambi, don't—"

Before Mona could finish, Bambi reared back and slapped her so hard that her neck swiveled. When she turned back, Mona's eyes were blazing, and her teeth were bared. She leapt forward and pounced right on top of Bambi, who began pummeling her with punches, left and right. Although cute, Bambi was born and raised in the gutter, and she was quick with her hands. Even though Mona held her own, she was no match.

"Aye!" Sly yelled, jumping to defend her, but Laz was on him quick.

With a pistol aimed at his back, partially hidden by Laz's jacket, Sly maintained his cool and let the women handle their issue. They bumped into tables, knocked over chairs, and destroyed property as they tousled in the middle of the main room. Guests laughed, 'oohed' and 'ahhed', hooted and hollered as the women fought, but when Laz saw phones pop up, he moved to end the fight. He had been waiting for the day that Mona would get her ass beat for a while now, but he wouldn't let Memphis be clowned by niggas watching his wife getting pummeled. Even if it was his soon to be ex-wife.

He snatched Bambi into a bear hug, but while he was pulling her away, Mona decided to play it dirty and reached out, raking her nails against Bambi's face. Her skin split into four bloody lines across her cheek.

"You dirty bitch!" Bambi shouted as Laz dragged her out of the entrance of the restaurant. "I can't wait to tell Memphis about your hoe ass, and when I do, I hope he kills you!"

Fixing her hair and her clothes, Mona tried to pretend like Bambi's words didn't rattle her, but they did. She didn't know where she was going to go tonight, but she knew that she couldn't go home. Not until it was safe.

"Damn, we gotta get you some boxing lessons or some shit," Sly joked, and Mona cut her eyes at him. "Too soon?" he asked, and she groaned before storming away.

With a pleased smirk, Sly followed behind her knowing that he had her right where he wanted her. She was an enemy of the city. He was the only one she could run to.

CHAPTER THIRTEEN

aby was in a deep sleep when her phone rang. Moaning, she opened her eyes, peered at the clock, and then groaned again before answering it.

"Mona?"

"Baby! I need your help."

The urgency in her voice put Baby on alert, and she bolted straight up in the bed.

"What is it?"

Before she could even speak, Mona burst into tears. It took another five minutes before she could get her to calm down enough to speak.

"I—I was with Sly... Baby, I messed up, and it was bad."

She let out a puff of hot air and then encouraged Mona to calm down and tell her what happened. Once everything was out, it took everything to stop Baby from telling her how stupid, reckless, and ignorant she'd been.

"What do you need me to do?" Baby sighed.

"I just need you to tell me when he leaves," she asked.

"He's already left," Baby informed her with a yawn. "About an hour ago, I heard him when he walked out the door."

PORSCHA STERLING

She didn't add that the reason she'd still been up was because she had been in the bed, listening to his every movement as he walked around above. She spent every moment telling herself that she couldn't go to him because it wouldn't be right. It wasn't until the moment she heard him storm out the front door that she was able to relax enough to go to sleep.

"Okay, I'm on my way home now."

The second she ran through the front door, Mona was a nervous wreck. She almost wore a hole in the floor pacing back and forth through the kitchen, muttering about how stupid she was. The night hadn't gone anything close to how she'd wanted it to, but she couldn't blame anyone but herself for being so sloppy with her moves.

"What are you going to do?" Baby asked as she sat on a barstool watching her.

Her voice pierced through Mona's thoughts, alarming her to the point that she nearly jumped straight up in the air. With tears in her eyes, she looked at Baby and shook her head.

"I don't know... I—I did something stupid, and I don't know how to fix it. I'm so scared..."

Frowning, Baby walked over to Mona, grabbing her hand in an effort to calm her down.

"You need to calm down," she began. "Just relax, and when Memphis comes back, I'll help you talk to him—"

"You don't understand!" Mona started to cry as she spoke. "Talking is not going to fix this! You don't know Memphis like I do. I have to leave; there is no other way."

Baby shook her head at Mona's dramatics. She was panicking over a simple dinner! It wasn't like she'd been caught with her skirt up over her head.

"You're not thinking straight. This isn't that big of a deal that you'd actually need to leave. What about Genie?"

With her eyes squeezed shut, Mona shook her head. "She'll be better off without me. She prefers Memphis anyways."

Baby simply shook her head with disappointment. Everyone knew that Mona was selfish, but even Baby had no idea that it was to this

160

degree. How could she leave her daughter, who needed her mother more than anyone in the entire world?

There was no way that Baby would understand where she was coming from, and Mona knew it. They just saw the world differently, and they always had.

"This may be a good thing," Mona said with a dry chuckle, shrugging. "I never wanted to be a mother. And I don't want to sit around and be Memphis's housewife. I want to *be* somebody special, Baby. I wasn't put on this Earth to be regular. I wasn't put here to live a regular life. It's not me. And I'm not going to be that way for anyone. I have to leave… tonight."

"You're being dramatic. It's not as bad as you're making it. Just talk to him."

"I can't," Mona replied. Baby was naïve. She was an idealist, but Mona was a realist. Once Bambi told Memphis what she knew, she'd be out on her ass anyways.

"And even if he does forgive me, what's the point of me sticking around and being unhappy when nothing is going to change? Then there is Genie…" Tears came to Mona's eyes as she prepared to admit the feelings that she'd never voiced to anyone. "I can't deal with her… I can barely look at her. She needs something all the time, and it's a constant reminder that I never wanted to be a mother."

Hearing those words nearly broke Baby's heart. When she looked at Genie, she never saw anything other than perfection. She had such a beautiful spirit. She was a fighter, and that was something she'd gotten from her mother. How could Mona not feel prideful about giving birth to a child who had been through so much and triumphed through it all? In that moment, it was a struggle to be a friend to Mona because she sincerely felt like she couldn't stand her.

The second Baby cast her judgment on her, Mona could see it by the coldness of her eyes.

"I actually think you're right," Baby said. "You need to go."

Mona swallowed the lump in her throat and stood. She knew that no one would understand how she felt, and that's why she never confided in anyone. Although cruel, she couldn't help feeling the way she did. She'd never connected with Genie on any level because she'd never wanted her. Had she not thought a baby would join her to Memphis, she would have gotten rid of Genie as soon as she found out she was pregnant. Instead, she kept her and then told herself that she would get used to the idea of being a mother as long as she was able to get her man. But then Genie's sickness robbed her of the willingness to mother her own child.

Standing in the doorway of Mona's room, Baby watched as she packed a duffle bag of clothes. She walked to a portrait on the wall and pulled it down, revealing the door to what appeared to be a safe that was behind it. The lock made a clicking sound once she keyed in the code, and Mona opened the safe, making Baby's eyes widen when she saw all of the neat bands of money situated inside. She grabbed a hefty amount for herself and tossed it into the duffle bag before placing a stack of hundreds into Baby's hand.

"I'm not taking this money," she said, snatching her hand back. "You're stealing."

"I wouldn't steal," Mona replied. "This is money Memphis gives me to shop. I know you'll have to move when I'm gone, so I just want to help you out."

She tried to force the money back into Baby's hand, but she refused it again, so Mona shrugged before placing it on the dresser.

"In case you change your mind," she said.

Before leaving, Mona turned around and looked at her bedroom one last time, wondering if she was making the right decision by leaving. There was a possibility that she could lie her way out of this and use Genie as a reason for Memphis not putting her out. But the more she thought about it, the more she knew leaving was the right move. Although her parents weren't the best and they neglected her at every chance they got, tossing money at her in order to keep her busy while they lived their lives, there was one lesson that they drilled into her brain. And that lesson was 'if something doesn't make you happy, go find the thing that does.'

This was the rule they'd followed all throughout her childhood, dodging their responsibilities of raising her to indulge in grandiose parties with their friends; diving headfirst in piles of white powder, which Mona's mother affectionately referred to as her 'nose candy', mounted atop their living room table. As much as Mona hated the fact that they couldn't control themselves enough to make her feel loved and cared for when she most needed it, she unknowingly absorbed their selfishness and found herself placing her wants and needs above the people who cared for her the most.

"Mommy?"

The sound of Genie's voice calling out to her made Mona freeze in place. She glanced up at Baby with wide, terrified eyes.

"Your daughter is calling you," Baby said with her hurt showing up in her tone. There was a period of silence before Mona shook her head.

"I can't go in there."

Baby narrowed her eyes. "You can't tell your own daughter goodbye?"

"Mommy, where are you?" Genie called again, and Baby stood still, facing Mona as she waited to see what she was going to do. Tears welled up in her eyes and began to stream down her cheeks, but she still didn't make a move toward Genie's room.

Dropping the duffle bag, Mona grabbed Baby and hugged her tight as tears continued to run down her cheeks. Regardless to what anyone thought about the way that she may have acted toward Baby, Mona sincerely felt like she did the best job she could at being her friend. She truly thought of her as a sister and treated her in the only way she knew to treat anyone. Mona wasn't capable of doing more because it wasn't in her to be anyone other than the person she was. She could only give to Baby what it was in her to give, and while Baby was the type of friend who gave her all and sacrificed herself for the sake of friendship, Mona wasn't conditioned or raised to think that way.

"I'll always be here for you, Baby. Please don't judge me for my mistakes. I'm not the person that you are. I wish I had your heart, but I don't. Please don't hate me."

Baby didn't return the hug and really didn't want to say anything else to Mona, but for Genie's sake, she made one final plea.

"Please, just give her a kiss goodbye before you go. Regardless to how you feel, that little girl in there loves you, and you're the only mother she has. Don't do this to her."

For a brief moment, Mona felt a tugging in her heart to go speak to her only child. She truly loved Genie in her own way, but she knew she couldn't be the mother that she needed. Part of her felt like being around Genie may cause more harm than anything else.

It's better for her that I leave, she told herself.

"She's young enough to forget me, so she'll be fine. Just... tell her I love her," was all she said before walking past Baby and out the front door.

Rubbing the tears from her eyes, Baby tried to collect herself as much as possible before rushing into Genie's room. With a broken heart, she looked down at her goddaughter and forced a smile on her face.

"Where's Mommy? I thought I heard her," Genie asked, and a tear slipped from Baby's eye. She swiped it away before sighing heavily and sitting on the edge of the bed.

"Mommy had to go away for a little while. But she wanted me to tell you that she loves you more than anything in the world."

Frowning, Genie thought for a second and then looked at Baby. "When will she be back?"

The aching in Baby's heart intensified, and she swallowed hard to force her tears down before she could reply.

"I don't know," she said honestly. "Sometimes adults have issues that they have to deal with. And those issues may keep them away from the people they love, but they have to work them out."

Genie nodded her head and looked away as she thought quietly to herself. Baby watched her, seeing her strength in her eyes. She reached out and ran her hands through Genie's curly brownish-blonde hair. How Mona could do wrong to this child, she could never understand. Genie had her mother's beauty but had none of her shortcomings. She was like an angel.

"Do you think she loves me?" Genie finally asked, her bottom lip quivering with her question. A tear cascaded down her caramel cheeks, and Baby wiped it away.

"I know she loves you. She—she just doesn't love herself very much right now, and that has to happen before she can be here with you."

"Okay," Genie replied and wiped the tears from her eyes. She sniffed a few times, and Baby could only admire her strength as she watched her put on her big girl face.

"Please don't leave me, Gotty." She wrapped her small hands around one of Baby's with her plea.

"I'll never leave you. You never have to worry about that," she promised before lying down beside her and telling her made up fairy-tale stories until she fell asleep.

CHAPTER FOURTEEN

The next morning came, and neither Mona nor Memphis had returned.

Even though Trina came over in time for Baby to go to work, she called in anyways. Her anxiety was at an all-time high, and she could barely handle it. After speaking with her mother, she decided that she had to move out and figure out how to live life on her own, but since she didn't want to leave Genie with Trina until Memphis returned, she waited.

"After you're done cooking, can we watch movies?" Genie asked as she rolled into the kitchen where her godmother was hard at work cooking dinner.

"Of course. What do you want to watch?"

"You can pick this time!" The smile on Genie's face calmed Baby's spirits. At least someone in the house wasn't having a panic attack like she was.

"Did you speak to your daddy this morning?" Baby asked, and Genie nodded her head.

"Yes, he called and woke me up. If he calls again, I won't tell him about Mommy, just like you asked. I'll keep our secret," she added, dropping her voice to a hushed whisper.

"It's not a secret," Baby told her with a reprimanding gaze. "Remember, you should never keep secrets from your daddy. We just aren't saying anything until he gets back. Okay?"

Smiling, Genie nodded her head, and Baby went back to fussing with the pots on the stove.

The moment she heard the door open, she knew who it was before she even saw him, and her body responded automatically, putting her on notice about her true feelings. Her cheeks pricked warm with shame as she kept her eyes on the stove, mixing the gumbo she'd prepared. Even though Mona had left and claimed that she was done with her marriage, to want Memphis for herself was still taboo. He was still married to her best friend, which meant that he was off limits to Baby. For life.

"Dadddyyyyyy!" Genie exclaimed as soon as Memphis walked into the room. He came straight to her and kissed her on the forehead before plucking her right up from her seat and into his arms. She giggled like she had not a single worry in the world as he tickled her and peppered her cheeks with kisses.

"I missed you, Daddy."

"I missed you more," he said as he placed her back in her seat. It was then that his eyes left her face and landed on Baby.

"Hey, Baby."

"Hi," was all she could get out. She felt her heart skip a beat and had to look away, turning back to the stove.

"Damn, it smells good as hell in here."

Closing her eyes, Baby exhaled slowly and counted to ten to calm her nerves before turning back around. Even with all of that, her stomach still twisted in knots when she settled her attention on his looming, muscular frame.

"Genie, can you give us a minute to talk?" she asked, and Genie nodded before making her exit, leaving the two of them alone.

Memphis watched Baby with hooded eyes, low from exhaustion as well as his shameless desire, following the rise of her chest as her breathing quickened. He could see that she was antsy about some-thing—he didn't know what, but he could pick up on her emotions just as easily as he could if they were his own. She took a few even breaths, shifting back and forth between her feet as she squirmed under his stare before she cleared her throat, squared her shoulders, and began to speak.

"Mona... Mona's gone. She said she wasn't happy. But she did say she loved you," Baby quickly added. She deliberately didn't mention anything about the restaurant, Sly, Bambi, or Laz because she assumed he already knew.

"She just said that she loved herself and needed to move on," she finished with a sigh.

Although after speaking with Laz, he was prepared to let Mona know that their marriage was over, this came as a surprise to him. He'd never expected her to leave. Not when they had a daughter to care for. His head turned toward Genie's room, and Baby could read his thoughts as if they were written on the walls. The pain that he felt in his heart for his daughter was too much, and he couldn't utter a single word. His mind automatically went into 'fix it' mode.

"Does she know?"

Baby nodded her head sadly before wiping a tear from her eye.

"I told her myself."

Memphis's eyes narrowed, and he took a step closer to Baby. Heat radiated from his stare, and she nearly felt suffocated by it.

"You mean to tell me she didn't even say goodbye to her daughter?"

Unable to lie, but not wanting to admit the sad truth, Baby didn't answer, but Memphis could pick up on the truth in her eyes. In that instance, his heart turned stone-cold, and Mona was dead to him.

"She can never come back," he muttered more to himself than to Baby. "If she does, I'll kill her myself."

Baby's neck snapped up and her eyes widened as she wondered whether or not she'd heard him correctly. But she could see the hate in his eyes and knew he'd made a promise that he had no intentions of breaking.

"I'm not going to be at your mercy for much longer," Baby continued. "With Mona no longer here, I can't stay. I'll come whenever you need me so that I can help with Genie, and that's it. If you'll just give me a week or so to find my own place, I'll—"

"You don't want to stay with me?" Memphis asked, making Baby's mouth go dry. Something about how he said the words and the way his entire expression had changed hit her right in the center of her gut, making her lose her words. His eyes were soft as he looked at her, almost pleading with her to take back the last thing she'd said.

"I—I just mean..."

Memphis saw her cheeks flush red from shame, and he hated that he'd made her feel that way.

"I don't mean to be rude," he started. "But I can't let you leave."

Her eyes fluttered at the last part of his statement, but she quickly collected herself enough to respond.

"But I can't just—"

His face turned to steel, letting her know that it wasn't up for discussion. Her words were muted in her throat, and she stood stoically silent as she watched him walk away to Genie's room. By the time he emerged from the hall, it was over an hour later, and he'd put Genie to bed. Baby padded over to him and handed him the drink that she'd made.

"It's your favorite. Henny and coke," she said with a smile. "Or at least I think it's your favorite."

"It is now."

Sitting at the bar, he leaned on it and sipped from his drink while watching Baby intensely. She squirmed under his gaze before dropping her eyes to her hands.

"Do I make you uncomfortable?" He asked the question with sincerity. He really wanted to know if he did so he could make moves to change whatever he needed to so that she would be totally at ease around him.

"*You* don't make me feel uncomfortable," Baby began to clarify, still looking at her palms so she didn't have to peer into his eyes. "It's just that you are married to Mona and—"

She was so beautiful to him, and it was taking all of his willpower to stop from touching her in some way. But the sudden mention of

Mona put a sour taste in his mouth. Memphis's brows furrowed tight and he shook his head.

"Don't ever mention her name in front of me again."

An awkwardness lingered in the air between them, and Baby began to make herself a drink to ease her mind. Memphis rolled his harsh liquor around in his mouth, knowing that it was time to come out with the truth.

"From the very first time I saw you, I wanted you."

Baby's eyes widened before she glanced away, feeling her heart thump to life in her chest.

"I waited a year for you before I made the mistake of giving in to Mona. And I only did it after she told me to forget about you because you had a boyfriend," he added to her utter shock and surprise.

"A year?" Her eyes narrowed into him. The fire he saw inside of her beautiful browns only added to her allure. "Mona told me that you and her started talking the same night after I first met you."

Releasing another pressed chuckle, though he didn't find a damn thing funny, Memphis poured himself another drink and shook his head incredulously. Mona's lies just got deeper and deeper to the point that he wondered if she even knew the difference between her make-believe stories and the truth.

"Naw, that's not how that shit played out at all."

They stood in silence, staring at each other with their own thoughts circulating through their mind. Baby felt like she was stuck inside a bad movie. Had Mona really done this to her—lie and create her own reality in order to keep her away from Memphis so that she could have him for herself?

"I—I think I need to go lay down," Baby said, placing her hand on the counter to steady herself. Everything was happening so quickly that it had her head spinning. Her emotions were in an uproar. Memphis watched her carefully and decided he wouldn't say anything more about Mona's betrayals against her. She needed to know, but he couldn't bring himself to cause her more pain.

"Wait, Baby, let me talk to you for a min—"

Before he could finish, Baby's phone started to ring, and she jumped slightly before grabbing it. It was a private number, and she knew exactly who it was. After two days of not hearing from him, Semaj was calling while she was having a conversation with Memphis that had her questioning everything. His timing was impeccable.

"I have to answer this," Baby said before rushing off to answer the call.

Memphis watched her, knowing why she was hurrying away and not liking that there was another man stealing her time. He squeezed the bridge of his nose and then ran his hand over his mouth, trying to suppress his distress. Pacing back and forth in the kitchen, he clenched his jaw tight and told himself that it wouldn't be right to just burst into her room, snatch the phone out of her hand, and tell Semaj that Baby was no longer his. She didn't even like the nigga and was only dealing with him because of Mona's lies. Now that Mona was no longer in the picture, his determination to make his move on the woman his heart craved was at an all-time high.

"Fuck it," he muttered and then stalked toward the basement door.

In his mind, Baby now belonged to him. God had granted him another chance to claim the woman that should have been his from the beginning, and who was he to go against God's will? She was everything that he was promised. If God took the rib of man in order to create his perfect match, Memphis knew that the piece missing from him could be found inside of her. There was no way he could just sit back and let her go.

Baby could hear his heavy steps coming down the basement stairs even before he appeared, and she felt her heart begin to thump like a drum within her chest. Licking her dry lips with an even dryer tongue, she glanced toward her bedroom door while clutching the phone in her hand, trying to focus on what Semaj was saying.

"Sorry I ain't been able to call you lately, lil' mama. Had a lil' disagreement with a nigga in here and lost some privileges. But all is good right now." She was about to respond, but Memphis appeared in her doorway and stole her thoughts along with her voice.

"Aye, I need to talk to you," he said, not at all worrying about whether or not he would be heard by Semaj. The man on the other line was the least of his worries.

"Yo, who that nigga I hear in the background!" Semaj yelled loud enough for his voice to meet Memphis's ears.

Speaking with all of the authority that the streets had given him and that he commanded, Memphis answered without giving Baby a chance to come up with an excuse or a lie.

"This is Memphis. She gon' have to holla at you later, bruh. We was in the middle of something."

Baby's lips parted in shock and surprise as Semaj went silent on the other line, both of them unbelieving of Memphis's audacity.

"Yo, let me holla at dude," Semaj said finally, his voice low in tone. He knew that he was in no position to make demands on Baby or go toe-to-toe with another nigga who might have been vying for her affection. Being locked up meant to him that one day he'd lose her. Although he hadn't banked on the day coming so soon, he was prepared.

With her brows furrowed and her mind at a loss for what it was that she should do, Baby handed the phone over to Memphis slowly, her eyes begging him to not start any problems between her and Semaj. He took the phone from her fingers gently and then pressed the button to end the call. It wasn't in his nature to negotiate with another nigga when it came to the things he wanted. To him, Baby wasn't up for discussion. She was his, and that's all it was. There was no need for him to go back and forth with Semaj about it, because he didn't give a damn what he had to say.

"You hung up?" She stood, settling her eyes on the screen of her cell phone before lifting them up to Memphis's face. "Why would you do that?"

"Why would you sit on the phone with a nigga you know you don't love?"

She paused, her mouth falling open in shock that he would throw something like that in her face. The audacity of him to take her truth and shove it back at her at the worst moment. She was enraged.

"Why don't you mind your own fuckin' business? I'm not your concern!"

Memphis saw through her anger to the frustration that lay beneath. She wasn't mad at him; she only thought she was. She was frustrated about the situation they were in. He knew it because he'd felt that same frustration a few times, and it made him want to push her away. But these days, he just didn't give a shit.

The weight of her emotions finally broke her down, and she dropped her head in her hand as she began to cry. Memphis watched her sob, feeling her turmoil as if they were one flesh. He could understand the position she must have found herself in, feeling as though she were losing the people closest to her all at one time, but he had to make her understand that he would be the only one she needed. If she trusted in him, he would spend every day of his life figuring out new ways to make her smile. It was something that he'd never done for any woman before, and he had no idea where to start, but she was worth the challenge.

"I don't know how to do anything else but be concerned when it comes to you, Baby," he told her and then stopped speaking.

She was pushing him into a position he'd never been in before. He'd never had to convince a woman to let him love her... simply because he'd never once loved one. But here he was, nearly at the point of pleading Baby not to turn him away, and even though the thought of begging seemed so ridiculous to him, he knew if it were necessary, he would do it anyways.

"You didn't choose me, you chose Mona," she continued to cry. "You need to deal with that. Take ownership of your decisions, no matter how fucked up they—"

Before he could listen to her utter another word about the bad choices he'd made in the past, about how he didn't choose her, he decided to make his true choice clear. Strolling forward, he gripped her face in his and pressed his forehead against hers. In that moment, he paused, thinking and knowing for sure that he was about to cross a line that he'd never thought. He was about to cheat on his wife, the mother of his child, with her best friend. He would never again hesitate when it came to Baby. He no longer would consider the disastrous consequences that would follow if he took her as his.

She sucked in a soft breath and it broke into his consciousness, reminding him of just how much he craved her. Pressing forward, his lips found hers, and he kissed her the way that a man kissed a woman that he'd truly given his heart to and she accepted him. Once she opened up to him, he could no longer quench his hunger for her. He ripped at her clothing, tearing it off without conviction or condemnation about their taboo deed. Once she was naked, he couldn't control himself. There was so much of her to grope, taste, cherish, and love... in all his eagerness to give her pleasure, he barely knew where to start.

He palmed her ass and pulled her up in the air, holding her up as he flipped over on his back. His strength surprised her as he moved her body around effortlessly, controlling their movements to place her in the positions that he desired. Twisting her around with ease, he sat her right on top of his face, opening her folds right over his mouth. She screamed out her bliss when he slurped from her, licked, suckled, kissed, and nibbled on her pearl with precision and expertise as if he'd been given the roadmap to her body. Her thighs began to quake as he lapped from her, taking her nub in between his lips, teasing it with his tongue as she muttered incoherently for him to stop, miserable in her pleasure.

She glazed his face with her love, and he took her to a level no one ever had before. Her eyes moistened with tears because she never knew it could feel this good. He wasn't her first, but the emotions he was stirring inside of her made it seem like the first time. Her head fell back, and her mouth opened as her thighs began to tremble. The sensation was overwhelming. She tried to run, but he gripped her hips and held her in place.

"Fuck..." she whispered as her body tensed up. She rode his face, driving his tongue deeper into her, and he loved it. He was enveloped in her and she filled all of his five senses, but he still wanted more. Even still it wasn't enough. He opened her even further and pushed even deeper down her love canal, curving his long tongue so that he was massaging her clit and simultaneously penetrating her at the same time. Her body began to jump. He was driving her absolutely insane.

"I'm about to cu—"

She was overcome with pleasure before she could even finish, and she tried to move away from him, but he kept her in place, sucking her honey as she let it flow. She was so sweet... utterly delicious to him. He couldn't get enough. He would fuck her forever if it were possible, never once stopping for nourishment other than what he got from her. She could be all he needed to survive.

Laying her down gently on the bed, he stared at her as he undressed, watching the drunken way her eyes fluttered. The rise and fall of her chest, the way her nipples pebbled as she waited anxiously for his next move, the slight tremble still in her legs as she recovered from her orgasm... she was exquisite, absolute perfection in his eyes. He wanted to have her, but it seemed almost wrong to experience her on the bed, in the most regular of ways. She was exotic, unique, and exceptional; she deserved so much more than that.

Leaning down, he scooped her into his arms and cradled her, holding her body close to his chest as he walked out of her room and down the winding hall until they got to his secret chambers. She'd been there before, but she hadn't seen everything. There was a room down there that only he knew about it, and after tonight, she would too.

Baby was in a haze after the loving he'd just put on her, but her body ached for more. She watched from under low lids as he walked through his private area and then peered curiously as he went to a bookshelf and tugged it away, exposing a door she'd never known was there before.

It was his oasis, the true place he went to when he needed peace and needed to clear his mind. It was a place he'd created for himself so that he could rest. Sure, he had a bedroom upstairs that he'd shared with Mona, but that woman brought him anything but peace. Sleeping next to her could never be mistaken for rest. This was where he went when he needed that.

He laid her down in the middle of his custom-made bed that

nearly took up the entire room. It was circular in shape, massive, and covered with custom-made black silk sheets. She nearly sunk into it as she marveled at the room. Candles of various heights circled the entire bed and covered most of the floor. Speakers hung on the deep burgundy walls, and the scent of lavender permeated through the air. It was the perfect intimate hideaway.

Grabbing a remote, Memphis hit a button that illuminated the candles and then another that turned on the music. Her ears prickled at the sound of Jhene Aiko's beautiful, melodic voice, and she brought her knees together, squeezing her thighs tight when she finally took a glimpse at Memphis's body.

Under her watchful stare, he slipped out of his boxers, and her eyes almost bulged when she saw his length. He wasn't even completely hard, but he was dangling nearly to his mid-thigh. Nervous energy flooded into her. She wasn't sure she could handle a man like this. Even though many of her dreams had involved this moment, now that it was here, she was hesitant. Would she be enough? Would he enjoy her? Could she satisfy him? She wasn't sure.

Memphis saw the fear in her eyes and could read her thoughts clearly. His muscle throbbed, and he felt himself begin to harden to his full length. He couldn't wait any longer. Grabbing one of her legs, he tugged her until she was at the edge of the bed and then tugged even more so that her lower body was suspended in the air with only the strength of his arms for support, and her back was lifted in an arch on the bed. She raked at the sheets with her nails, fighting not to fall, but she couldn't get a good grip on the silk.

"Calm down. I won't let you fall," he whispered, leaning down to kiss her gently on her belly. It was the last bit of gentility he offered her before his assault.

Ripping open her legs with his hands, he stretched her knees from east to west and pushed into her. Watching her facial expressions shift, he offered her inch-by-inch until he was buried in her warmth. Then he switched gears. The savage in him came forth as he thrust into her, beating down her walls like an untamed beast. He was a man who had craved something so much that it hurt... something that he wasn't sure he would ever get, and now that he had the chance to have it, he feared that he'd never be able to let go.

Baby cried out as he continued his assault into her. The pain felt so good that her emotions were scattered and her brain was frazzled. She didn't know what to do, what to think, or even what was happening, but she could feel everything and it felt oh so good. Wrapping her legs around his middle, she gritted her teeth as his girth pushed into her, thrashing against untapped parts of her... parts that she didn't even know she had. Semaj had been big, but he was nothing like *this*. And Memphis worked his dick with magnificence, filling her to the brim, to the point that she couldn't even speak. All she could do was feel and experience all that he was. He was more than enough.

He gripped hard on her hips, working into her like he was digging a home for himself inside of her body. Everything she had was his, and he made it that way without even demanding for it to be done. She knew right then that if he'd have her, she would never give herself to another. She winded her hips into him, and he started to lose his mind. They weren't using a condom, he never asked her if she was on the pill, they hadn't taken any precautions whatsoever, and he knew he had to pull out, but it felt so good that she was making him weak. He couldn't let go.

"Fuck me, Memphis. Pleeeaaase," she whispered.

The way she begged for the dick gripped his soul, and he knew then that she was a dangerous woman. There was nothing that she could ask for that he wouldn't give to her. He gritted his teeth and plowed down into her, delivering thrust after thrust, and she rode the waves of his body like a skilled surfer. Her body convulsed and she came hard, holding him tight in her arms as the sensation overpowered her. Memphis looked at her, never once letting his eyes leave off her face as he let go and spilled his seeds into her. She moaned as he filled her. It was cool and sent chills riveting all over her body. Her body went limp in his arms as her energy left her. She couldn't move a muscle, and truthfully, she didn't want to.

"We can't do this again," she whispered so softly that it was barely audible. Memphis heard it... and ignored it. They would do this again.

And again and again and again… but if it made her feel better to make an attempt to resist him, then he'd let her have that.

He kissed her sweetly against her hairline and then moved to kiss her once again on her soft lips. His body ached for more, but he could see that she'd given her all. She was tired, completely spent, and still enjoying her share of ecstasy, so he decided to let her rest. She wasn't going anywhere because he wouldn't let her. They had the rest of their lives to spend together.

CHAPTER FIFTEEN

"How long have you known Mona?"

"Since high school," Baby replied, taking a second to turn toward Bambi.

Laz had come over to speak to Memphis about a few things concerning business, and Bambi took the opportunity to come with him, her curiosity about how things were going with Mona gone getting to her. Although she hadn't said a word of it to Laz, Bambi had strong suspicions that there was something going on between Baby and Memphis, and she was nearly having a panic attack trying to get to the bottom of it.

"And y'all have been best friends ever since?" she continued to pry, lifting one brow as she waited for Baby to respond.

Baby shrugged a little and then grabbed the remote to turn down the volume on the show they'd been watching before Bambi's inquisition began.

"Not really. When I first met her, Mona didn't seem to like me. We were made to work together on a project and it kinda went from there. Her parents weren't the best, so my family took her in. We became friends that way."

"Oh," Bambi replied, but her mind was working overtime trying to come up with a way to bring up the topic that she really wanted to talk about. How did Baby meet Memphis, and what was the nature of their friendship? And with Mona gone, was Baby going to leave as well, or was she planning to stay?

"Well, I've only known Mona since she's been with Memphis, but I've realized a few things about her. One is that she's very selfish, but… I guess you know that, huh?" Bambi looked at her with pointed eyes, making sure her point of Mona's abandonment of her family and home as evidence of her selfishness was caught.

"Mona is…" Baby started, carefully choosing her words. "She's the type that has always been sure about what she wanted and what she didn't want. And she moves quickly once she figures that out, not always thinking about the people left behind to clean up her mess. I think she's just doing like the rest of us… searching for happiness and love."

"Is that what you're doing with Memphis?"

Baby's eyes bugged, and Bambi could do nothing but shrug. Keeping in her true thoughts had never been a strength of hers, and it was too mentally grueling for her to try and continue parsing her words with Baby, so she just decided to get right to it.

"What do you mean?"

Bambi rolled her eyes and then settled them on Baby's face.

"Listen, let's be honest. Mona may have not been paying attention, but I saw the way he defended you that one night in the club. He was territorial… like how a man does for *his* woman, not just a friend. I've never seen Memphis that way with Mona, and I was surprised. And I see the way the two of you look at each other. You speak with your eyes, the way that lovers do."

She paused, and an uneasy expression crossed Baby's face. Her stomach flipped around with nervous energy, and the back of her neck stung with guilt. If Bambi had been able to pick up on that, who else had? Was it that obvious what they were up to? And what did people think of her knowing that she'd possibly fallen for her best friend's husband?

"I—I'm not a bad person," Baby said with a small voice. She had initially wanted to deny what Bambi was suggesting, but there was no use. The things that she'd picked up on told their own truth. There was something very real growing between Baby and Memphis, and Bambi was exactly right. No point in denying it.

"I didn't say you were. I know you're not a bad person," Bambi soothed. "And even if I did, who the hell am I to judge? If you knew the things I've dealt with concerning Laz, you'd think so low of me..."

Her words faded off as she thought about a few secrets in her past that she prayed would never come to the light. She shook the thoughts away, but the embarrassment she felt thinking on them, even in that brief moment, showed in her eyes. Baby saw it and gave her a kind smile.

"I wouldn't think low of you. I'm in no position to judge. I can't even judge Mona, no matter how I feel about what she's done."

Bambi's neck snapped back, and she narrowed her eyes into slits. "Oh, hell nah! We can judge her ass. Matter of fact, you know I beat her ass the other night when I saw her in the restaurant with some basic ass nigga. Did she tell you about that?"

Baby shook her head, her eyes stretched wide. Being able to tell her the story lifted Bambi's spirits. Jumping up from the sofa, she got animated, walking back and forth, and punching her fist in the palm of her hand as she told Baby the complete story in detail of what had occurred the night that Mona decided to leave.

"I don't know what just happened—it was like I totally blanked on that bitch! And if I see her anytime soon, I'm gon' light that ass up again."

Baby couldn't help but giggle at Mona's expense, watching the light in Bambi's eyes as she recounted punch after punch. She knew she shouldn't laugh, but deep down, she felt Mona deserved it. Even though she defended Mona by saying that she was the type of person to go full throttle after what she wanted and didn't always think of the consequences, it was a cowardly move to leave her daughter behind, and Baby was happy that she'd not been able to leave without getting some form of payback; in this case, by way of Bambi's quick fists.

"I think you're crazy," Baby said, laughing incredulously at the details of Mona's beat down.

"Crazy over Memphis," Bambi corrected her, winking one eye. "He's like a brother to me, and Genie is like a niece. I don't take too kindly to muthafuckas hurting my peoples, which is why I made it a point to see where your mind was at too."

Now Baby understood Bambi a little better than she had before. She was loyal through and through. The type of friend that you could call at the drop of a hat when shit hit the fan and you knew she would show up with her hair in a ponytail, sneakers on her feet, and Vaseline on her face, ready to fight it out for you—no questions asked. She was the type you wanted in your corner.

"You can believe that I feel the same way. I would never do anything to hurt Memphis or Genie. Not if I can help it."

Hearing that did nothing for Bambi, because she'd already known it before the words had even been said. The few moments she'd spent with Baby showed her that she was a good person inside and out. And everything that Laz had told her backed that up too.

She's the perfect woman for Memphis, Bambi thought.

It was a thought she'd never had about Mona, even though she'd been cordial to her for Memphis and Genie's sake. In fact, never had she thought any woman was a good choice for Memphis in all the time she'd known him; but Baby... she was the real deal. She was the one that he needed.

"When the last time you spoke to Mama?" Baby's sister Gala asked her. Of all her siblings, she was closest to Gala, and they spoke on a regular basis. Although she knew that she could call on any of her brothers and sisters if she needed them, Gala was the one that she'd bonded with the most being that they were closest in age.

"She called me some days back, but it was a quick conversation." She sighed and sat back in her recliner as she thumbed through some papers that needed to be graded.

Wearing sweats with her legs kicked up and a glass of red wine nearby, this was easily her favorite part of the day. Working with kids was fulfilling to her, but she could never lie and say it was easy. She was a teacher and the only adult in a classroom of over twenty students, the majority of them being little rambunctious boys who seemed to spend all night thinking of ways they could make her day difficult the following morning.

"Quick conversation, hmm? Sounds to me like what you're saying is that you rushed her off the phone again." Her voice was dripping with sarcasm, and Baby could just about hear Gala's eye roll through the phone.

"She wants to talk to me about Semaj. She wants to know if I knew about his illegal activities and ask all these questions that I'm not ready to answer…"

"Of course she does, Baby! She's your mother, and that's what mothers do when they are at their child's wedding and their son-in-law-to-be is arrested and drug out the church by the Feds with drug charges!"

Well, saying it that way makes perfect sense, Baby admitted in her thoughts but still pursed her lips.

"I'll speak to her in person. I have to go home some time soon, and we will talk then."

In the distance, she thought that she heard a door slam shut, and her heart fluttered. It had to be Memphis. After falling asleep beside him, she woke up the next morning in her own bed and wondered if it had all been a dream. But every part of her body remembered how it felt to be wrapped in his arms and to feel his lips pressed against hers, so it had to have been real. She squeezed her eyes closed to push away the thoughts of that moment, but the images then flooded her mind's eye. She couldn't escape the effect he had on her. It was the sweetest type of torture. She wanted to rid herself of it, but then again, she didn't.

"Um, I need to tell you something," she started, running her tongue over her bottom lip as she wondered whether or not she should keep her thoughts to herself. She needed someone to vent to, and Gala was the next closest person to her outside of Mona.

"A couple days ago, Mona moved out. She said she wasn't happy with Memphis and wanted to find herself... or something." She was intentionally vague because Gala didn't like Mona at all and had always been very vocal about it.

"Find herself, huh? More like find a new dick to ride on."

"Gala!" Baby shouted, but she couldn't resist falling into a fit of giggles at her sister's cold honesty.

"What?" She sucked her teeth. "Baby, be real about this, please. Since when have you ever known Mona to leave any man just to be alone? Especially the one she had, who is highly paid and giving her everything that her little selfish ass heart desires. Don't tell me you actually fell for that lie she tossed you."

Gala had a way of saying things that made her look at situations differently from how she had initially, and now Baby couldn't help thinking that her sister was definitely right. Not once in life had Mona *ever* left one man unless it was for another. She craved the attention of men in a way that Baby had never understood, and would endure being mistreated by one rather than to leave him and be alone.

"Well, you may be right because I haven't heard from her since she left..." She allowed that thought to linger in her mind for a moment before continuing. "But anyways, she left, but I'm still here... with Memphis."

There was silence on the other line, and Baby could only imagine the thoughts that were cycling through Gala's mind. Not once had she ever spoken to Gala about Memphis other than telling her about the first day they'd met and then following up that conversation by letting her know that he'd started a relationship with Mona a short while later. Something that she now knew was a lie.

"So you're in a house alone with Mona's husband," Gala said slowly as if she were trying to make sure that the meaning lying under her words wasn't lost to Baby. "Just you and him..."

"Yeah, but I'm in the basement, and he's in the main part of the house, so it's not like we're ever really together. I barely see him," she quickly added. "I plan to leave, but I want to help him with Genie. With Mona gone, he needs it."

184

"Please! We both know that Mona didn't take care of her child. Her leaving hasn't affected much at all. All her ass is good for is spending money. Everyone in that house may be better off with her gone."

Baby didn't say anything, but she had to admit that Gala was right. She was sure that Genie missed her mother, but for the most part, she seemed pretty unaffected by her being gone. Her daily routine hadn't been changed at all because Mona never really did anything with her.

"So it's you and Memphis in the house. And he's a man... one who you were attracted to—"

"I wasn't attracted to—"

"Baby, I know you well enough to hear what you are saying and also to hear what you're *not* saying. When you first told me about meeting Memphis, you didn't have to tell me you liked him. I could tell by the way that you spoke about him. And I also could tell that Mona's bitch ass blocked whatever y'all was about to get into and you just let her!" Gala blew out a breath and then sighed heavily. "And that's why I have absolutely nothing bad to say about you getting with her *ex* man."

How the hell did—What made her think that—Could Gala read her mind? Baby sat straight up in her seat, causing the papers in her lap to go cascading down to the floor.

"I didn't say anything about getting with him. I was just telling you that—"

"Like I said, I know you well enough to hear what you're saying but also what you're not saying," her sister replied with a matter-of-fact tone.

Opening her mouth, she was going to protest further, but then she heard the door to the basement open, and her mind and body froze. Until Gala's voice boomed loudly from the speakerphone.

"If it hadn't been for that fake ass friend of yours, Memphis would be your nigga anyways, so I say fuck that nigga the long way all day and night until—"

For an award-winning physician, Gala had such a dirty mouth.

"Gala, lemme call you back!" she shouted, cutting off her words about a few seconds too late. Without waiting for her to respond, she ended the call at the exact moment that Memphis appeared before her eyes.

She looked at him without speaking, allowing her eyes to fully delight in his visual appeal. And *got damn* was he fine. Standing before her dressed simply in a pair of black sweats and a white wife-beater that showed off his muscular arms and flat abs, he was every bit as sexy as she *didn't* want him to be. Resisting him would be so much easier if he was ugly. If he'd heard what Gala had been saying, it didn't show in his eyes. He stared at her with an unspoken desire that made her feel self-conscious about her appearance.

"You eat yet?"

Baby shook her head at his inquiry, simultaneously answering his question as well as telling herself that it would be wrong to respond with 'No, but I'm ready to if you're on the menu,' which was the reply that had instantly come to mind. It was a sin for a man to be this appealing when it was wrong to want him. She had to wonder if this was how Eve felt in the Garden of Eden, knowing that she could have her fill of all the fruits on all the other trees but unable to take her attention off the one apple that would bring her entire life crashing down around her. She knew he was poison, but like a cancer patient still happily sucking away on a cigarette, she found pleasure in her inability to resist him.

"Get some shoes on and let's go," he said.

And then he walked away. Just like that... not at all leaving room for her to protest. It was obvious to her that he was used to his word being obeyed and expected her to fall in line, which was exactly what she was going to do. So against the warning bells ringing in her mind, Baby stood up and walked into her closet to do just as he demanded.

&·

"WHERE IS EVERYONE?" BABY ASKED, COMING UP BEHIND MEMPHIS WHO had led her into a beautiful but empty restaurant.

"I like my privacy, so the owner closed it for a couple hours for us to eat." He explained like it was as normal to him as waking up every morning. Her eyes scanned the empty restaurant as she marveled at his power. To be able to shut down a place such as this with just a simple word… She could barely grasp how it must feel to have that type of status in the game.

"I've always wanted to come here… heard about it, but never had the chance. Semaj's favorite restaurant is The Cheesecake Factory, so that's where we always went. I've probably tried everything on the menu," Baby said after they sat down at a round table right in the middle of the restaurant, near a glass wall that gave them a magnificent view of the river running behind the building.

Memphis didn't reply to her statement, but in his mind, he was thinking about how much of a lame ass nigga Semaj was to only take his woman to the place that he enjoyed without letting her experience the finer things. He didn't know much about Semaj and didn't care to. He was Baby's present, and Semaj was the past. His goal was to make her present so amazing that she wouldn't even have a moment to think about her past because she'd be so focused on her future. The future she would share with him.

"We don't have menus."

Smirking slightly, he watched as she searched the tabletop with her brows crumpled before spinning her neck around, looking for a waiter or someone who could help.

"There is a reason for that," Memphis stated, and she brought her eyes to his, contemplating his meaning. She got the subtle hint that the reason was a surprise, but before she could press further, three waiters appeared pushing trays of food toward them.

"Memphis! It's been a while since I've had a visit from you, champ!"

A man, obviously the chef from his uniform, walked over to Memphis, and he stood to shake the man's hand. They embraced with a half-hug, the way that homies in the hood do, and then Memphis took his seat. It was at that moment that the chef's eyes traveled over to Baby. His approval of her was easily seen from the sparkle in his eyes, but he didn't say anything. Giving her nothing more than a simple nod of a greeting, he swooped his hand over the tables of food that had been brought out.

"As you requested, I've prepared the entire menu, but I also added a special surprise of some items that I've yet to add to our list of options. They are new recipes, and I can't think of anyone who I would be more than honored to try them out. Please let me know what you think of everything once you finish."

By the time the chef walked away, Baby's eyes were so big that Memphis could almost see his reflection in them. Never once had she ever imagined she would be in a position to get this type of treatment. It was almost like being with a celebrity.

No... it was like being with a *boss*.

"Go on and dig in," he told her, and Baby didn't miss the twinkle in his eyes. She knew that he was showing off—giving her a glimpse of how life would be as his woman. This was more than a simple dinner. It was his way of letting her know that he was *that nigga*, and if she accepted him, he would make her *that woman* who could have access to all of this. The problem was... as impressive as this all was, Baby just wasn't this high maintenance.

"You didn't have to do all of this. I mean... it's nice, but I'm really just a burger and fries type of girl," she let him know. He accepted her words with a nod but said nothing. With a sigh, she stood and grabbed a plate. There was enough food laid out for them to feed an entire neighborhood.

"This really is just so... *wasteful*. We aren't going to eat all this."

"What?" Memphis's brows lifted nearly to his hairline.

"There are so many people who have nothing to eat, and here we are about to waste all of this food, just so you can prove a point. I have students who come to class hungry... The only good meal they get is what we give them during lunch. I just feel guilty about wasting all of this just because you want to impress me."

"Who says I wanna impress you?" he teased, and Baby cut her eyes at him to let him know she wasn't stupid. He had to chuckle at her subtle fire. To him, she was everything that perfection was made of, and he couldn't get enough.

"I'm being serious, Memph," she continued, and he bit down on the corner of his mouth, loving the way she'd given him a nickname. "It's just wrong. We could bless so many people with this food. You don't even know."

"No, I don't know," Memphis admitted. "The thought never occurred to me that I was doing something wrong. I wanted to eat, had a taste for my favorite spot, but couldn't decide what I wanted most, so I ordered the menu. When I want something, I go after it full throttle without thinking about the next muthafucka." He added that last part, but the both of them knew the last thing he was talking about was food.

Baby gave him a pointed look. "Maybe that's your problem... that you go after what you want without thinking about what's right and wrong."

"Maybe your problem is that you're too concerned with what's right and wrong instead of going after what you want."

Her thoughts merged, and she was at a loss on how to respond. He'd shot back his reply with so much ease, she wondered if he'd deliberately walked her into it. Sitting back down, Baby poked at her plate and pushed a forkful of food into her mouth—the food being what she would use as her excuse for not having anything to say.

Although Memphis would have been just as comfortable sitting there and watching her eat, admiring the many expressions of delight that crossed her face as she sampled each bite for the first time, he didn't want to seem like a creep, so he made a plate of his own. But who could eat while sitting in front of a woman like this? Baby was beautiful to him, and it was beyond the physical. Her spirit connected with his on a level that none had ever done before. He didn't want to just take up space in her presence... he wanted to *know* her. He wanted to learn everything there was to know about her. There wasn't a doubt in his mind that he loved her already. She was the type of woman who was easy to love and hard to hate. But he craved her in a way that he'd never craved anything or anyone ever before.

"Tell me about these kids," he started, knowing the way to her heart was to appeal to the things already in it. "The ones who don't have food to eat. What's up with that?"

Her eyes brightened on the spot, and the light only grew from there as she spoke on something that pertained to her passion.

"There are two in my class… both boys. They come from low-income families. I've tried to contact their parents on multiple occasions, but they aren't very responsive." An annoyed expression crossed her face. "I don't want to say that they don't care about their children's education because what parent wouldn't? But I just can't get in contact with them."

Memphis nodded his head and then looked away, thinking about how much there was about life that Baby obviously didn't know. Growing up in the hood, he knew firsthand that there were plenty of people with kids who didn't give a damn about whatever it was they did at school. They were just happy they didn't have to deal with them for at least eight hours for five days out of the week. Hell, her own best friend was one of those types of parents.

"Not everyone has the heart you have," Memphis said, making her blush at his compliment. But he didn't say it to flatter her—he meant it. In his life, it was rare that he'd stumble upon a woman even half as compassionate and giving as Baby. In fact, he'd be comfortable saying that he never had met a person as caring. He'd definitely not ever found anyone who could compare to her.

"What about you?" she asked, surprising him by turning the tables. "Do you ever feel like you should be helping out your community? I mean, you have so much to give…"

A pressed chuckle escaped his lips, and he ran his hand over his beard. Many would say that Memphis and his crew were everything that was *wrong* with his community. Never had anyone suggested he do anything to help, and the thought had never occurred to him. He'd gotten so used to hearing that he was destroying the Black community that he accepted it as the one blemish on his character that he just had to deal with until he could make a change.

"How about I'll make the money and let you be the one to figure out a way to spend it helping others," was his cheeky reply.

Baby was taken aback by his cockiness but didn't say anything against his statement. He had a way of speaking things as though they were, even though they weren't just yet. Almost like he knew that he was definitely going to be a permanent figure in her future. It intrigued her to say the least.

"How do you do that?" she asked, finally.

"Do what?"

"You make statements… as though they are fact. It's like you don't even consider any other options."

"Because when it comes to the things I say, there *are* no other options."

She couldn't argue with that, so she didn't even try. Sitting back in his chair, Memphis looked her square in her eyes, cradling hers with his so that she couldn't look away.

"If I'd had this way of thinking when I first saw you, you would already be mine."

"Oh?" Baby questioned with lifted brows. "Well, why didn't you?"

The answer came easy to him because it was something he'd considered more than a few times. "Because I was young and dumb."

Giggling, she rolled her eyes at him. Something about the way she did it made Memphis brick up in his sweatpants.

"But that was only some years ago."

He replied with wide eyes, "It was five. That's nearly a lifetime on the streets. You're working with the same mindset you had five years ago?"

She shook her head and then cleared her throat before clarifying her statement.

"No… I just mean, how much more can you have grown in that amount of time?"

His stare steeled. "You want a reminder?"

Baby almost died. Thankfully, the chef returned to save her from further embarrassing herself.

"How's everything?" he asked and then looked down at Memphis's untouched plate before frowning deeply. "You haven't eaten a thing. You don't like it?"

Memphis shook his head, his eyes still pinned on Baby's face.

"I'm sure it's good. Just not what I have a taste for at the moment."

Her already red-tinged face blushed a deeper shade of crimson, and the chef smiled hard as his eyes ran back and forth between the two of them. He picked up on the double meaning behind Memphis's statement but was smart enough to pretend that he hadn't.

"Well, take your time and enjoy!" he replied simply before removing himself from the conversation.

"Why did you say that?" Baby asked, laughing a little, something she did when she was embarrassed.

"Because it's true," Memphis replied and then decided to tease her further. "You wanna know what I have a taste for?"

"I can guess your meaning," she replied and then bit at the corner of her mouth. "But we agreed that we can't do that anymore. I told you… I'm with Semaj and—"

Memphis flicked the bridge of his nose and looked away before muttering, "Soon you ain't even gon' want that nigga no more."

She was about to ask him what he meant by that statement, but his phone rang before she got the chance.

"Yo?" Memphis answered. He listened for a while and then his eyes went to her before he continued speaking. "I'm having dinner with the future Mrs. Luciano right now, but I'll give you two minutes to tell me what's up."

He excused himself from the table and walked away to have his call. She watched him as he paced back and forth, speaking on the phone. Although she couldn't hear what he was saying, she watched the expressions on his face. It was almost like seeing him in a different element. The softness in his eyes, the mild smirk on his lips… all of that was gone once he became Memphis, the leader of the *Murda Mob*. He spoke with an authority and coldness that was felt to her even though she couldn't even hear his words. It was appealing in the sexiest way, and she pressed her thighs tightly together when she felt her sex began to gush.

What am I gonna do about this man? she asked herself, but there was no immediate answer.

Even still, she knew something had to be done. Memphis had made it clear that as long as it was up to him, he wouldn't stop until she was his for good. And as long as she stayed under his roof, it *was* up to him. She was at his mercy and available to him whenever he wanted her.

I have to move, was the conclusion she came to. But the more she watched this man, this king of a thug who was used to speaking words through his lips that became law the moment they left them, the more she knew that there was no way Memphis would let her go, and the more she had to admit that, there was no way she would ever choose to leave.

CHAPTER SIXTEEN

"Carlos! It is not time to pack up yet. We still have three minutes of class left which means that I still have time to teach!"

Carlos snapped to attention, dropping the backpack he'd been stuffing his belongings in onto the floor before folding his hands on top of his desk and focusing on his teacher. Principal Fletcher gave Baby a look of approval, loving the way that she'd been able to take command of her overfull classroom in such a short time. It was obvious that she was the perfect person to hold the job as a teacher. She was wonderful with children, and they loved her.

Riiiiiiiiinnnnnngggg!

As soon as the bell sounded off, her students jumped up to get their things together and Principal Fletcher stood to leave. At first glance, Baby looked completely in her element, cool as a fan. But in reality, she was nearing a nervous breakdown, wondering what her boss thought about her skills as a teacher. It was the first time anyone had ever sat in her class since she became a professional instructor, and she couldn't wait for feedback.

Looking down at her desk, she began to fidget with her own

belongings as she waited for Principal Fletcher to walk over to her. It was then that she noticed her glowing cell phone screen.

Calm down. I know you're nervous but you got this... Boss swag, remember?

Her body tingled, and she bit down on the smile that was easing up the corners of her lips. During dinner, she'd confided in Memphis about this day and how nervous she was about her skills as a teacher and whether they were up to par. He'd told her that he would lend her some of his 'boss swag' so that she'd kill it. It was the perfect thing to say to calm her nerves, and she didn't know how in the world he knew it. They talked for hours like old friends. Looking into his eyes, Baby felt like she'd known him her whole life.

"Ms. Taylor... I know you have to walk your class out, so I will meet with you once you're back in your classroom," Principal Fletcher said with a monotone, neither that nor her expression giving Baby an inkling of a hint about her thoughts.

"Okay. Yes, Principal Fletcher," Baby said hurriedly, her nerves showing all over her face although she was trying to play it cool. Maria Fletcher began to feel sorry for the woman she'd started to consider her favorite employee and decided to ease her worries.

"But..." she began with a smile. "...I will tell you that I only have good things to say."

Baby's infectious smile appeared instantly, and she bowed her head, whispering a quick 'Thank you' before turning back to her class.

"Okay, everyone! Get in line so that I can walk you out to the—"

A knock on her door interrupted her, and she paused to see who it was. When she saw Memphis's handsome face staring back at her through the small glass square on the door, she nearly fell into a cold sweat.

"Oh my... who is that cutie over there?" Maria asked, grinning hard as she looked from Memphis to Baby. "Is this the fiancé?" Her eyes went down to the diamond ring on Baby's finger, causing her cheeks to tinge red.

"Um, no. He's... just a friend."

"Mm hmm," Maria mused, but she knew better.

Baby squirmed under Maria's stare as the door opened, and Memphis walked in.

"Hey... just give me a couple minutes. I have to walk the kids out and then—"

"I'll walk with you. I got you a surprise," he stated with a smile. Perfect teeth, perfect face, perfect body... he was perfection personified. Baby was about to lose her cool, so she shifted her focus and simply nodded her head.

"Ms. Taylor, is that your *booooyyyyfriend?*" Carlos, the most outspoken of her students, asked. Baby nearly died from shock as she looked at her class, each student staring at her intently with slick smiles on their face as they waited for their teacher to answer their question.

"Um—"

"Yes, I am," Memphis answered with a smug grin that only grew wider when he saw the look of shock on Baby's face. "Hey... I'm a boy and I'm your friend, right?"

She twisted up her lips at his attempt at somewhat fixing the situation. "Riiiight." She gave Memphis a look that said he would hear more about this later, and he shrugged. The opportunity to have a conversation with her, whether she was chewing him out or not, would be his pleasure.

"Okay, class. Let's go. We don't want to be late!"

Baby took off, leading her class out of the classroom, and Memphis followed to her side. Not bothering to wait around for an invite, Maria followed in step behind them, noting the way that Memphis claimed Baby as his by his presence alone. He didn't have to hold her hand or even touch her in any way. It was just *felt*. Regardless to what Baby said, Maria's experience taught her more than a few things about men. She knew that Memphis had every intention of making his position in Baby's life much more permanent than even she probably knew.

"What in the world!" Baby exclaimed, throwing her hands to her mouth as she stared in front of her with wide eyes. "What is all this?"

She turned to Memphis and the gloating grin on his face. "*You did this?*"

He didn't answer and didn't need to. Who else but Memphis had the gut, nerve, and authority to bring an entourage of food trucks to the elementary school where she worked and line them up in the parking lot without a second thought?

"I thought about what you said, and you were right. There is a lot that I can do." Baby stared at him with eyes that oozed adoration and utter admiration as he turned to her class. "Aye... y'all go over there and get all the food you can eat. It's on me."

"For real?" one of Baby's students asked, and it warmed her soul. Tyler was one of the boys that she suspected rarely got a decent meal at home. He was always the first one rushing into the cafeteria for his free breakfast and free lunch and was still hungry the second he'd gobbled it all up. A few times, Baby had snuck away food for him to eat and take home for later, but she knew it wasn't nearly enough to meet his need.

"Have at it, lil' man," Memphis answered, chuckling a little at the expression of sheer shock plastered on Tyler's face. Before he could barely get the last word out, the kids were already running at top speed to the food truck of their choice. Thinking twice, Tyler doubled back and ran straight to Memphis, wrapping his arms around his legs.

"Thank you!" he said graciously, and Memphis shifted, feeling somewhat awkward. He wasn't used to this and could barely believe he was even doing it. If he told Laz, his boy would probably fall out laughing and snatch his 'thug card' away.

"Damn, nigga, you friendly," Memphis muttered with a half-smile as he gently pulled Tyler's arms from around his legs. He bent down and looked the boy square in the eyes. "You gotta learn to trust no one." He paused and shifted his eyes to the sky for just a second. "Stranger danger... you heard of that?" Tyler wagged his head happily. "It's just like that, a'ight? Now go eat."

Baby and Maria stood back in silence for a few moments as they watched the children happily order food and play amongst themselves as if they didn't have a care in the world.

"Okay, hurry so you won't miss your bus!" Baby finally called out when she was able to get over the overwhelming feeling of gratitude of what Memphis had done. To be honest, it choked her up and elevated him to another position in her eyes. To know that of all the things they'd spoken about at dinner, he'd been able to pick up on the one topic closest to her heart and then put effort in place to remedy it for her... It was the most powerful love potion in the world.

"I'm going to go ask the drivers to wait for a few minutes so the kids can make it," Maria said before scurrying away to do just as she said. When she passed by Memphis, she paused for a second to pat him on the back and give him a genuine smile of thanks. Of all her years teaching, Baby and Memphis were the youngest couple she'd crossed paths with, but they were making the biggest difference she'd ever seen.

"This—this is just amazing." Baby gushed, still in awe while looking at the kids who didn't have buses to catch double back in the lines for more food.

"Well, shit... don't just stand here watching. Let's go get some food."

Memphis wrapped his arm over her shoulders, and she found herself leaning into him as they walked over.

"Pick your poison," he said as they stood in front of the trucks, and Baby looked at each one, thinking about what she was in the mood for.

"Let's try that one," she replied, pointing at a truck painted green, yellow, and black. "I'm in the mood for some jerk chicken and rice and peas."

"A woman after my own heart." Memphis patted his chest, and they moved forward to place their order.

❧

LATER THAT NIGHT, BABY HAD HER EYES PLANTED BETWEEN THE PAGES of a book when she heard the basement door open and then slam closed. Memphis's heavy footsteps echoed in her ears, and her heart rate seemed to slow as she heard him nearing her door, wondering if he was coming to pay her a visit. Once she heard him pass by her room and then continue down the hall and into his personal cave, she let out a sigh and relaxed although she couldn't help feeling somewhat disappointed that he hadn't come down to see her.

He had stayed at the school with her for hours, speaking to her colleagues as they all enjoyed the free food and drinks at his expense. The way that everyone seemed to love him instantly had Baby feeling some type of way. But the ease at which he conducted himself with these college-educated professionals was so intriguing to her. To be a man of the streets, the deadliest thug in the city, but still be able to maneuver and network with people on the total opposite ends of the tracks… it was the reason that Memphis was the supreme leader that he was.

Laying the book down on the bed beside her, she stared up at the ceiling and allowed her thoughts to move to the man who was taking up more of her mental space than she cared to admit. She hadn't even thought about Semaj a single time that entire day, which she shamefully realized as soon as she laid down in her bed.

UNKNOWN TO HER, MEMPHIS WAS ALREADY AWARE OF WHAT WAS happening because he planned it that way. His objective was to first make love to Baby's mind because he knew her heart and body would follow. He was a patient man… not *too* patient, but with her, he wanted to take his time to make sure that he did it right. He had already messed up once and wouldn't let it happen again.

Sitting inside of his private room, he took a sip of D'USSE as he puffed on a blunt. The smoke filled his lungs, and he let it out slow, the single thought in his mind being how much he wanted to be in there chilling with Baby. His reason for even walking down to the basement was to see her, but when he saw her door was closed, he figured that she was asleep. Against the urgings of his mind, he walked by her door without knocking and closed himself up in his room.

His phone rang, and he answered it quickly, eager for something else to distract his mind.

"What is it?"

"Yo... ain't nothing really happenin'. I just ain't heard from you in a min, nigga," Laz said on the other line. "Wanted to make sure you're not too tore up over what happened with Mona."

A chuckle escaped his lips, and Laz also began to laugh. Both of them knew damn well that Memphis couldn't possibly care less about Mona leaving now that she was finally gone.

"Mona who, nigga?"

"Damn, bruh, that's some savage shit." Laz laughed even harder. "You got jokes."

"Naw, never that." He mused before putting out the lit blunt.

"Aye, you hear from her?"

"Not a word, and she knows better than to hit up my line after that bullshit she pulled. Why, you hear somethin'?"

The pause that followed let Memphis know that Laz definitely knew a lot more than he did, and whatever it was he'd found out couldn't be good.

"Spill it, nigga."

"You remember that D.C. nigga you ain't wanna meet up with?"

Memphis paused to rack his mind before he nodded. "How can I forget that whack ass nigga? Came at us like he was makin' shit happen but really wanted us to front him some product."

Annoyed, Laz sucked the skin of his teeth. "Yeah, that's the one. The rat."

He was still mad as hell about even trying to coordinate the meet up between Memphis and Sly. He hadn't looked into Sly's background properly, and it could have caused a lot of bullshit for him. Luckily, Memphis was a little more trained than Laz when it came to sizing niggas up for flaws, and he knew that Sly wasn't all he said he was as soon as he laid eyes on him. Based off what he learned about Sly from Memphis, Laz was able to put his own plan into motion.

"Anyways, I heard from a friend of a friend that Mona's been spotted with the nigga. In D.C."

Memphis's brows shot to the sky. He didn't know what Mona was up to once she'd left him, but hearing this was not at all what he'd been expecting. What could a fake thug have that she'd want?

"Word?"

"Word," Laz confirmed. "I'm sending the pic that I was sent to your phone right now."

Sitting up, Memphis waited for his phone to beep, indicating the message had arrived, and then checked his phone out of sheer curiosity. Sure enough, there was Mona walking hand-in-hand with that lame ass nigga Sly. He stared at the photo for something less than a second, not feeling an ounce of emotion one way or the other. He wasn't jealous; he wasn't angry. To be frank, he really didn't give a shit.

"Once she finds out that nigga ain't worth shit, she'll be back," Laz spoke, saying the words that were on Memphis's mind. He had to make a move with Baby faster than he'd planned because he knew that if Mona resurfaced and got in her head, he'd lose out on another opportunity to be with her. He couldn't let that happen. *Wouldn't* let that happen.

"Aye, lemme call you back."

"Yeah."

Placing the phone down, he stood up and ran his tongue over his top row of teeth before taking off toward his door, prepared to do whatever it took to get Baby in front of him at that very moment. But when he opened the door, he was shocked to see her already there. Wearing nothing but a flimsy, thin pajama shirt that left very little to his imagination, she stood before him with a 'deer caught in headlights' expression. Her thick, long hair was messy, loose, and hanging down her back, her perfectly pouted lips were slightly tinted by her cherry Chapstick, and on her feet, she wore fuzzy slippers. Nothing was more stunning to him than how she looked right then.

"I—I heard you come down and I was—" She looked down and frowned as she struggled to put together her words. "I—I just wanted to thank you for…"

"You already thanked me... a lot," he teased, and she blushed. "I mean... unless you wanted to thank me another way."

She cut her eyes to him and narrowed them in on his face. "Another way? What kind of woman do you think I am?"

Not at all bothered by her seething glare, Memphis shrugged. "I don't know. Maybe the type that wouldn't mind chilling with a nigga for a little bit instead of saying 'thank you' for the hundredth time today. I already told you that I don't need you to thank me for anything. You got me to see things another way, and I admire you for that."

Her feelings for him seemed to blossom inside of her to the point that she felt like she would explode.

"Oh... thanks," she whispered bashfully.

"What I just told you about that 'thank you' shit?" Memphis caught her gaze, and she couldn't resist smiling before she rolled her eyes.

"Whatever!"

Whisking by him, Baby enveloped him in her sweet scent as she fluttered into the room, turning up her nose at the smell of weed. She turned sharply and gave him a disapproving look to which he simply shrugged as if to say 'my bad'.

"Drugs kill," she admonished.

"Lies. Weed ain't never killed nobody."

He watched her move about the room, studying everything as if he'd opened a door into his soul and was letting her in. As she approached the chessboard situated on a table in the middle of the room, he watched while she ran her pretty fingertips along the top of the board before plucking up one of the pieces. He didn't know whether she knew it or not, but every time she moved, the long shirt she wore would shift slightly, giving him a glimpse of the roundness of her ass. She was dick-teasing him like a motherfucker and probably had no idea.

"You play?" she asked, a mischievous and challenging look on her face.

Memphis gave her a slight nod before running his hand down to adjust himself when she looked away. He was on brick status just off a simple glance at her body. He knew that once he really got to sample her love, she would easily drive him insane.

"You're dangerous as fuck," he said so low that she couldn't make out his words.

"What's that?" Baby asked, and he simply shook his head.

"Nothing." He walked over to the opposite side of the table. "Let's play."

"YOU MIND IF I ROLL UP?" MEMPHIS ASKED, LIFTING HIS UNLIT BLUNT up, and Baby shook her head. The game was nearly over, and she was beating his ass... or so she thought.

"Check! And I got your queen!" she yelled after making her move and then stuck her tongue out at him to rub it in. Memphis chuckled and then puffed a few times on the blunt, giving her a little time to celebrate before he stole her joy.

"Checkmate." Her jaw dropped as she watched him move in on her king, whisking him away with his rook, a move she hadn't even seen coming. She had been so focused on her move that she hadn't even noticed that she was playing right into his plan.

"I've never lost!" She brought her eyes up to him in amazement. "I've still got my trophies to prove it!"

He shrugged as if it were no big deal. Which it really wasn't for him.

"A nigga in the hood with six toes showed me how to play."

"Six toes?" Baby echoed.

"Yeah, his name was Six Toes."

She scoffed and rolled her eyes. "Six Toes. How fitting."

He didn't say anything but took another long pull of his blunt. She watched the smoke as he blew it out, making perfect O-shapes to entertain her. She scrunched up her nose and narrowed her eyes. The sight was adorably amusing to him.

"I—I think I wanna try it."

He lifted one brow, thinking he couldn't have heard her right. "This? You wanna take a pull?"

She hesitated slightly before nodding her head. Memphis stifled the chuckle that was coming up his throat and screwed up his nose instead, imitating a face she'd made earlier.

"But drugs kill."

Baby reached out and playfully punched him in his shoulder, making him laugh. She watched him as she pretended to sulk, admiring the way that his whole face lit up with pleasure when he was in her presence. Never had she seen a man seem as happy as he did with her. Especially since Mona had left.

"Here."

Memphis offered Baby the blunt, and she held it in her hand, rolling it around as she scrutinized it.

"I've never smoked anything in my life," she confessed.

"Nothing?"

"Nothing. Not even a piece of meat."

It took him about a second, but his lips cracked into a smile.

"Yo, you corny. You know that, right?"

Instead of replying, Baby thought about the motions Memphis had gone through when she watched him smoke.

Easy enough, she thought.

Raising it to her lips, she took a long pull and held it in for about two good seconds before the burn in her chest made her fall into a fit of coughs.

"Ugh!" She gagged as she held her chest. Memphis jumped up to get her a glass of water and took a sip of it before handing it over to her.

"Why you sip it first?" she asked, looking at him suspiciously before grabbing the glass.

"Because this your first time, and you might get paranoid. Don't want you thinking I slipped you a mickey or some shit if you end up with your legs over my shoulders."

She shuddered at the image in her mind but recovered easily.

"I wouldn't think you would do something like that."

He bit down on his bottom lip briefly before responding. "So you think you know me, huh?"

She shrugged her shoulders timidly. "I at least know that much about you."

"There is so much more you'll learn," he said without looking at her, and she felt her lady lips tingle. Grabbing the blunt from her fingers, he locked his steely eyes into hers while taking a long pull. Baby watched in fascination of the man he was and also of how he made her feel, not saying a word. Her heart thumped in her chest in anticipation. She just knew something was about to happen.

His eyes not leaving hers, Memphis held the smoke in his mouth and leaned into her. She battled a million different emotions the closer he got to her face. His lips touched hers, and she gushed honey when he teased her lips with his tongue, forcing them to part. As soon as she relented to his wishes, he pushed the smoke into her mouth, and she sucked it up as if he were giving her the air her survival demanded.

"Wow," she whispered against his lips.

He'd backed away slightly, but his face was so close to hers that if she puckered her lips, she'd be giving him a kiss. A light-headed feeling came over her, and she knew it was the effects of the drug she'd inhaled, already taking hold. Whatever paranoia she was supposed to have never came; instead, it seemed like every sense in her body was building up between her thighs. She felt her love box throbbing for him, and though normally she would have pushed her needs to the side, reminding herself that she wasn't the type of woman to betray her best friend by coming on to her ex, what she was feeling right now was anything but normal. She felt all of her inhibitions float to the wayside. She wanted Memphis in ways that she'd been scared to admit to herself until this moment, but now that the truth of how powerful her feelings were for him was uncovered, she wasn't equipped with what it took to control them.

Dropping to her knees, Baby slid between his legs and pushed his thighs gently apart. She looked up at him and felt her sex stir when she saw the intense way he stared at her with his jaw clenched. He was fascinated by her sexuality, the way that she walked the line between innocent and vixen. It was mind blowing.

Reaching down, she pulled him free and was momentarily unnerved when she was reminded of just how blessed Memphis was. She swallowed hard as her mouth moistened in anticipation. She wanted to taste him, and it was something that she'd never experienced before. Never once had she wanted to taste anything—any*one* so badly before. Opening her mouth, she sucked him in, and her clit throbbed when she heard him suck in a breath. He moaned, and her inhibitions fell away. She went to work on his dick like a porn star, pulling tricks out the bag that she didn't even know she had. He groaned and let his head fall back as he fisted her hair with one fist, not forcing her but pulling her close.

"Fuck... You don't even know how good that shit is," he whispered.

You don't even know how good you taste, she thought. She licked a droplet of precum when it bubbled up on the head and was surprised at the sweetness of it. Everything about him was everything she thought it would be. Pushing deeper down onto him, she became a little more aggressive in her hunger of him, and Memphis was nearly caught up, but he had to make her stop. With a firm touch on her shoulder, he nudged her softly away, but she pushed back against him, sucking him in past her tonsils.

"Shit!" he cursed, feeling his toes curl.

He was on the brink of release, but he couldn't let go into her mouth. It was something he didn't hesitate to do with any woman in his past, but Baby was different. She was like a queen to him, and he just couldn't see himself doing that.

"Move!" he ordered her, but she didn't listen. Instead, she clamped her lips down harder around him, creating a vacuum that he was nearly powerless against.

"Baby... Fuck!"

Reaching down, he grabbed her off him, just in a nick of time, and lifted her up. He noticed she wasn't wearing any panties once he pushed her shorts to the side and then slid her right on top of him. She winced as she took him in, winding her hips on his lap until he filled her completely as she tried to find her groove. Her ass spread over his lap, and he palmed it, rocking her hips back and forth as he continued to ease in his length. Her scent was intoxicating, like warm honey. She was so sweet, so perfect... she felt so good. God, she was driving him insane.

"I love you," she whispered, and it was like time stalled.

Leaning down, he bit into her shoulder and guided her hips, working her into him as he pushed up into her. Their bodies made beautiful music, a beatbox of love as they enjoyed each other. This was the sweetest taboo.

"Cum for me," he told her.

Still stroking up as she winded down, he pushed two fingers onto her clit and massaged it as they drove into each other. She bucked against him, feeling her love stir and sparks fly through her body. She was about to explode. It was like dynamite. He'd sparked the flame, and it was slowly getting closer and closer to the point where she'd detonate. This feeling was almost too much to bear.

Eyes closed, she jerked, and her mouth fell open. He wound her hair around his fist, rearing her neck back to lay kisses against the front of it. Fireworks erupted inside of her as she came, and she screamed while tearing her nails into him. Before she could totally gather what was occurring, he jumped up and twisted around so that the arm of the chair was against her back, and he started to plow into her mannishly. His hands squeezed at her breasts, and he pinched her nipples hard before leaning back to admire the way that his hardness bobbed in and out of her body. It glistened with her nectar. He felt himself about to let go, and he couldn't pull out. She had him in a trance that he was powerless to break out of. He released right into her warmth, spilling his seeds liberally, emptying his love right into her, and she gasped at the feeling.

"We can't do this again," she said breathlessly. "We have to find a way to stop."

"I won't," he told her, and she knew there was no point in arguing it. He said it with certainty, like a matter of fact. And if he wouldn't stop, neither would she.

CHAPTER SEVENTEEN

"How long will we be here?" Mona asked while taking a long look at her fresh manicure. The D.C. shop she went to couldn't come close to her girl that usually hooked her up in Atlanta, but it was decent enough.

"It's going to take another week or so until they're done with construction on my new crib. Why, this place ain't good enough for you?" Sly held out his arms and glanced around the luxurious suite that he and Mona had been taking residence in for the past few weeks since they landed in D.C.

Scrunching up her nose, she shrugged. "It's alright."

"Alright?" he parroted with his eyes bugged. "This shit is nearly a grand a night!"

Without saying anything, Mona simply shrugged again and rolled over to grab the remote. She started flipping through the channels while Sly stood watching her with an incredulous look on his face. Maybe to another woman, the room would have been something to gush about, but she wasn't impressed.

"I have a massage scheduled for later on, and then I'll probably hit the mall or something. I don't like being stuffed in here all day."

She rotated over on her stomach, making the curve of her ass peek out from under her tiny shorts. When she saw Sly's eyes fall to her body, she had to bite down on her smile, but then he quickly glanced away, and she began to pout on the inside. Even though things had been so hot and heavy before leaving Atlanta, Sly hadn't made any real moves to have sex with her since she'd been with him. That definitely wasn't what she'd expected. Other than Memphis and now Sly, no man had ever been able to control himself while around her. Especially when she was offering up her body so eagerly.

What she didn't know was that Sly was an expert on women, and he knew that the more he pushed Mona's offerings of sex away, the more that she'd want to give herself to him. She was the type that was used to a nigga falling over his own feet to win her over, and he wanted her to understand that he was the one in control. He gave her enough of the things she wanted to keep her happy, money to blow, and the attention she'd desired but never got from Memphis, but he consistently refused her advances without giving her a reason. He was playing mind games. For someone like Mona, who had gotten ahead in life by use of her body and good looks, he knew that refusing her, now that she'd made the choice to be with him, only made her more determined to prove herself worthy of him.

"Nothing on TV," Mona scoffed before cutting it off and tossing the remote to the side. "I still have a little time before my massage... Is there anything you wanna get into?"

She did nothing to hide the sexual undertones in her statement as she pushed her ass up in the air and wiggled it slightly. Sly watched her, not at all denying that she was sexy. He let his eyes roam over her slowly, eating up everything she was giving him. A smirk teased the edge of her lips, and she rolled over on her back, giving him another eyeful of her body, when she pushed her breasts up in the air and allowed her thighs to part, showing off her mound. Sly snickered and shook his head at her.

"You tryin' to get a nigga in trouble, I see."

"This is the kind of trouble you'll like."

Smiling, she teased him by using her finger to make circles around her hardened nipples. She could see the lust in his eyes as he watched her. Since he was enjoying the show, she decided to give him more. Parting her thighs, she allowed her knees to drop to the bed in opposite directions and pushed her fingers slowly under the waistband of her shorts, watching him the entire time. Sly leaned back on the wall behind him and folded his arms in front of his chest as he stared at her. She closed her eyes and started to moan while working her middle, pulling her fingers out a few times to lick at her own juices. He felt himself rock up in his sweatpants and knew that this would be the moment he'd make his move.

"Take all that shit off," he demanded her with a gruff tone, and she obeyed quickly.

He pulled his t-shirt up, exposing his rock-hard abs before pulling his hardness out of his pants. Mona's love juice ran down her thighs as she looked at him. He was sexy as hell with the body of a god. His rod was thick, long, and hooked to the right. She'd already had a sample before and knew what he was capable of. She was ready for another dose.

Once she was completely naked, Sly slid on a rubber, letting her know that she was finally about to get what she'd been waiting for. As soon as it was in place, Mona opened her legs wide and waited in anticipation for what would come next, but Sly grabbed her by one leg and flipped her over quickly. When her belly hit the bed, he pushed in from behind, impaling her quickly and easily, thanks to fact that she was about as wet as the ocean.

"Damn," Mona cursed when he began rocking into her.

He fucked her like a savage, using her ass like handles, pulling her back after each powerful thrust. The kinky side of her loved this rough shit, and she could barely contain her excitement. She started bucking against him, intensifying the sensation that he was giving her, and it only seemed to make Sly go even harder. He smacked her hard on her ass and started jabbing her pussy even harder than before, filling her completely. Her eyes started to water, and she bit down on her bottom lip as she felt the orgasm creeping up from her toes. Never in life had she been fucked like this before.

Sly lifted one of her legs in the air, forcing her into a position where she was nearly doing a split, while he bucked into her so hard that her upper body fell off the edge of the bed and her back half was hanging in the air. She felt lightheaded, like he was about to fuck her into a coma, but it was too good for her to tell him to stop. He continued to plow forward until both of them were off of the bed, and she was damn near doing a handstand. She screamed as she came, and his climax followed shortly after, breathing hard like he'd just finished running a marathon.

Mona was lying in the bed, reliving the last few moments, when Sly sat up and grabbed a few things out of the drawer next to the bed. She peeked over to see what he was doing and noticed that he was rolling up a blunt. But when he sprinkled a little white dust on top of the green, her brow rose.

"What's that?"

"Nothing. I'm just rolling up," he told her without looking in her direction. "You smoke?"

"Yeah, but… not like that. I don't fuck with coke."

"You should," he replied in between licking it closed. "It intensifies the high. Ain't shit like it. I'll show you."

Mona was hesitant. Memphis had always made it clear that he didn't fuck with chicks who did anything more than a little weed here and there, so she'd never tried it. At the same time, she was curious about what Sly was saying, and she wasn't Memphis's wife anymore. That meant she could do whatever the hell she wanted.

"I'll try it," she told him as she watched him take a few puffs. The scent wasn't like anything she'd ever smelled before, making her scrunch up her nose. Sly handed it over to her, and she looked at it for a second before putting it to her lips and taking a long, hard pull.

"Daaaaamn." She smiled coyly. "That shit is good. Strong, too."

He nodded his head and didn't say anything as he watched her take a few more pulls. Sly knew that he should have stopped her right then before she got too carried away, but he pulled back and let her do her thing. He had a mission in mind, and it would be that much easier if she was able to release her inhibitions.

"What you think about going on a lil' shopping spree later? I know you ain't pack all that much, so we can get you a few things. Not too much though since we ain't in my permanent spot yet."

Just as he suspected, Mona's eyes instantly lit up at the prospect of spending money. What she didn't know is that it wasn't his money that they'd be spending, but hers—the money she'd taken from Memphis. Sly had stumbled upon it a few days after they'd left and started pinching off a little at a time whenever he needed it.

She closed her eyes as her high set in and Sly was silent for a few moments before he decided it was time to make his move.

"So... how you feel about being a thug's wifey? You know I'm a street nigga, and I need to know that you got what it takes to ride."

Snorting, Mona handed him the blunt before she replied. "I've been unofficially playing that position with Memphis for nearly five years already. Believe me, I know what it takes to be a thug's wifey."

"Oh yeah?" Sly asked as he put out the blunt. "So you helped him with his lil' operation?"

Her eyes twisted up to the ceiling for a second before she replied. The truth was that Memphis kept her as far away from his business as he could. Not only did Mona know nothing about how he made his moves, but she barely knew anyone on his team outside of the few that he dealt with on the regular. However, she didn't want to let Sly know that. It was obvious that he wanted a woman who could be an asset to him in the game. He wanted a partner whereas Memphis seemed to only want a trophy. She wanted to let Sly know that she could be the one to help him run his empire if that's what he desired.

"I did. I kept his books, made runs when he needed it... things like that," she lied. She didn't know a thing about the drug game, but she hoped what she was saying made sense to Sly. He was trying to elevate her to a position that she'd only dreamed of when it came to Memphis, and she didn't want to mess it up.

"I like the sound of that," he told her. "What about his connect? You know who that is?"

The room got precariously quiet. Sly looked at her, thinking that she was still holding on to some bit of loyalty for Memphis that he hadn't yet fucked out of her. It didn't make sense… any other oppor-tunistic bitch would have had diarrhea of the mouth by now.

Unless she's still been talkin' to that nigga, Sly thought.

"He contact you since you been gone?" he asked nonchalantly as to not alarm her. He watched her body language for dishonesty as she replied.

Mona frowned. "No, he hasn't." She seemed upset by the admis-sion, so he knew it was true.

"Damn." Sly was shocked by that. What nigga lost his wife and didn't even bother contacting her once she left. And then a thought occurred to him.

A nigga who ain't want the bitch anyways because he got his eye on something else.

He thought back to the night at the club when he'd seen Memphis staring at Baby. He'd been so caught up in what she was doing that he hadn't even noticed when Mona left out the back door to meet with him. Mona had told him that she'd left her daughter with Memphis but wasn't worried about her because her friend Baby was there to help with her. Sly was sure that Baby was probably helping out with more than just Mona's daughter by now.

"That nigga on some foul shit, I bet. No muthafucka in the world just gon' be cool with his wife leaving," Sly started, planting a seed in Mona's mind that he would continue to water as time went by. "I bet he fuckin' with that chick. What's her name? Baby, right? That's why he ain't hit you up."

As soon as the words hit Mona's ears, she burst out laughing. "Not happening. There is no way that he would fuck around with Baby. And even if he would, she would never. You don't know Baby. She's not that type."

"Oh?" Sly lit the blunt again and took a long pull. "You left that nigga, and he probably all hurt and shit. Who you think was around to make him feel better?"

Pressing her lips together into a firm line, Mona thought about what he was saying. She hadn't quite thought about all of that when she left because she'd been so focused on her own desires and saving her own ass. The thought never came to mind that she was setting Memphis up to be with another woman. But now that Sly had mentioned it, it seemed possible. Baby's caring nature wouldn't let her not try to comfort Memphis if he was in distress.

"No way," she said, shaking the thought from her mind. "Like I said, you don't know Baby. She would never do no shit like that because she knows I'd never forgive her."

"Yeah, okay," Sly replied, a cruel smirk on his lips as he sent a quick text message to one of his Atlanta homeboys.

Track Memphis and send me any pics you see of him with that fine ass bitch from the club. The friend.

After sending the message off and getting confirmation from his boy that he was on the job, Sly stretched out his lean body across the bed before standing up to get himself together to leave. He glanced at Mona and could tell from the faraway look on her face that her mind was still ruminating over his words just as he'd planned it. She was so easily manipulated. In no time, he was going to get exactly what he needed from her to get back on top of the game and become the king of the streets he was supposed to be.

CHAPTER EIGHTEEN

Caught ya bitch ass!

An evil smirk rose up on Sly's face as he looked at the present he'd been sent via text, courtesy of his Atlanta homeboy. He finally felt like he had exactly what he needed to get Mona to get rid of whatever loyalty she still had for Memphis and begin to run her mouth.

"Aye," he said, walking into the hotel room from the balcony with a lit blunt in the corner of his mouth.

He'd been hiding outside, getting his smoke on, because ever since he let Mona get a few puffs of the laced blunt he'd rolled, she'd been smoking his shit up like a chimney. His funds weren't what they used to be, so he couldn't let her continue flying through his stash the same way she was trying to fly through his pockets.

"What?" Mona replied dryly as she flipped through a stack of menus trying to find something to eat.

Sly couldn't hide the disgust on his face as he watched her. She was lazy as hell and didn't do a damn thing that he expected of any woman he was with. She didn't cook, didn't clean… she just *didn't do shit*. She was a waste of a woman, and he didn't know how Memphis had been able to put up with her for all these years.

"Look what we have here," he said with a smile. "I told you that nigga was flaw."

With eyes glossed with indifference, Mona glanced up into his face and he handed his phone over to her. She sighed heavily before looking at the screen, but once she saw the picture on it, her eyes narrowed, and her entire body went rigid.

"Scroll to the right... there's more."

She flipped through the photos on the phone and got an eyeful of what Memphis and Baby had been up to while she was gone. There was a picture of her husband, her daughter, and her best friend riding in a drop-top Bentley, laughing and smiling as if they were having the time of their life. Then another one of them walking in the park, with Baby pushing Genie's wheelchair as Memphis felt her up from behind. The next picture was just about the same except Memphis was squeezing Baby's ass. That one set off a volcanic eruption in Mona's head. She clenched her jaw so tight that her teeth nearly crushed into dust.

"I told you that nigga had moved on. Shit... by the looks of it, they all have. It's almost like they are happier without you," Sly said, adding fuel to the flame. "And she still livin' with his ass, too."

"I can't believe this shit. She told me she was moving out. I gave her money to!"

Mona went through the pictures a few more times, and each time she felt the hate in her heart grow to another level. But it wasn't Memphis that was the focus of this new emotion. It was Baby.

From the first day that she'd met Baby, she'd been jealous of her. It wasn't something that she would ever admit, but it was true. There was never a person who met Baby and wasn't instantly drawn to her. With her gentle spirit and caring heart, she was just the type of person you instantly loved. When Mona was introduced to her family, the first thing she noticed was how much they loved each other, but they all doted on the youngest child most of all.

No, Baby didn't have even half of the material things that Mona did, but she never envied them no matter how much they were flaunted in her face. Baby was always content with whatever she was given and was also genuinely happy for Mona for the things she was able to obtain. She was selfless to a fault, and Mona hated it. Truthfully, she felt like she loved Baby like a sister, but through the years, she was never able to get over her deep-seated feelings about how everyone always seemed to love on Baby and not her. People always thought Mona was pretty, but they never admired her the way they did her best friend. She couldn't help always wanting whatever it was that Baby had, and stealing it away was Mona's way of proving to herself, as well as to Baby, that she was the superior one.

Still, the things that Mona did to her never deterred Baby from being a kind and gentle person which frustrated Mona to the max. Baby's spirit couldn't be broken no matter what she went through.

"I told you," Sly repeated for good measure. "I mean, they might've been messing around behind your back the entire time, because it ain't take long for them to move on. Shit, you ain't been gone long."

Mona's face balled up into a frown that gave her a look only a mother could love. Reaching up, she snatched the lit blunt from Sly's fingers and pulled hard on it. She had been fiending for it before he'd walked in, but now she really needed it to work its magic and put her at ease.

"That bitch stole my man *and* my baby," she grumbled as she continued to think on Baby's betrayal.

"She ain't do that shit alone. Memphis is right there with her." Sly wanted to make sure that she stayed on point, wanting her to remember that Baby wasn't the only one at fault. He needed her to hate Memphis just as much as she did her friend. But like so many women who had been put in a position similar to hers, Mona's focus was on the woman and not the man. She easily gave Memphis a pass, telling herself that he was just doing what men did. But Baby couldn't be forgiven.

"We need to get back at them for this shit." Sly began feeding her the thoughts he needed to circulate through her mind. "That nigga is goin' to give that bitch everything that he gave to you and more! He gon' have your daughter callin' her 'mommy' and all types of shit."

"He wouldn't do that," Mona spat with a snort. "I'd kill his ass first."

She didn't even like it when Genie called her mommy, but she'd be damned if her daughter used that name for anyone else.

"I bet you he would. Just some days ago, you was saying the nigga wouldn't fuck your best friend. But now look!" He pointed at his phone. "He probably deep in that sweet pussy right now."

Unable to cope with the image that came in her mind of Baby and Memphis together, enjoying the throws of passion, Mona closed her eyes and pressed her fingers against her temple.

"Look… I feel like the two of us together can take him down. The sweetest revenge that you can get on muthafuckas who have betrayed you is to take they asses down and let them see you on top. All you need to do is tell me who Memphis gets his supply from. Who is his connect?"

Taking another long pull, Mona sat back and let the smoke fill up her lungs. She didn't have a single clue who supplied Memphis. There was nothing she could tell Sly to get him any closer to being on top of the game than he had been before he met her. Truthfully, he'd been better off had he just left her alone. At least before he met her, he was desperate but had a little money to his name. Now, he was just desperate.

"I don't know," she said honestly, but he eyed her with suspicion.

"You don't know what? You have to know something if you was handlin' all that shit for the nigga that you claim you was. That nigga ain't bein' loyal to you anymore, so he don't deserve yours. Speak!"

Sly's patience was running thin, and he felt himself about to lose it if she didn't tell him anything he could use. His back was against the wall, and it was a dangerous place for a man in his position to be in. He had nothing left to lose and would do anything in order to get a foot up in the game.

"I don't *know*. How many times I gotta say the shit? Damn!"

Whap!

Sly hit Mona so hard that she flew out of the chair that she'd been sitting in and landed on the floor with a loud *thud*. Her pale cheek was marred by a red mark that stung so badly it thumped like it had its own heartbeat.

"I've given you every fuckin' thing you could want, and you disrespect me by bein' loyal to another nigga right in my fuckin' face?" Sly roared with seething anger.

Mona's eyes darted from left to right as she tried to collect her thoughts and figure out what had just happened. No one had ever laid a hand on her in her life. Not even her parents had disciplined her physically.

"I'm not being loyal to him!" she cried out as tears started to run down her cheeks. "I really don't know anything!"

Sly's anger multiplied as the possibility that she didn't know anything started to set in. With a shake of his head, he told himself it couldn't be true. There was no way Mona had been with Memphis for so long and didn't know a single thing he could use. She was his wife, not his side bitch, so she had to know *something*. But what Sly didn't know was that Memphis had never loved Mona and barely trusted her. She had been his wife but only because he felt it was what his daughter needed. He had never let his guard down enough to let her in the way a man would normally do for the woman he'd given his last name. Their marriage was anything but typical.

"Since you wanna play dumb, I'mma get dumb right with you," Sly snarled.

He grabbed her by the hair and pulled her up until she was on her feet. She opened her mouth to scream, but her howl was muted when he lifted his beefy hand up yet again, prepared to wallop the very sound from her lungs.

"Don't. Please! I can remember something. I just need a minute. Please!"

Those words were like music to his ears. Sly released her hair, and she took a deep breath then reached up to massage her throbbing roots. He'd nearly pulled strands from her scalp. She opened her mouth to speak, but before she could, she collapsed into tears. The shock of the new situation she was finding herself in was so overwhelming. Her little selfish heart could barely take it.

"I just can't believe he would do this to me!" Mona sobbed, crying her eyes out as Sly watched. She got hysterical, tossing her body from left to right as she rolled around on the floor, holding her face like a spoiled child.

Letting her have her moment, Sly ran his hand over his face and exhaled. It wasn't in his nature to put his hands on a woman, and he'd never done it before, but Mona took him there. He was frantic. There was nothing worse than a street nigga who had fallen from grace and couldn't figure out a way to get a leg up. No matter what he did, he was met with a closed door to the face. She was his only hope.

"I'm sorry for puttin' my hands on you, ma," he apologized with sincerity. "You just made me so fuckin' angry bein' loyal to that nigga still. Don't I mean anything to you?"

Sobbing, Mona nodded her head, but the tears didn't stop. Sly massaged his beard and turned away, knowing that he needed a minute to collect himself. He had to be careful with how he came at Mona, because she was the key to his entire plan. Once she fessed up with anything she knew, he could begin to make moves to change his situation.

"Aye, I'll be back," he told her before walking out the front door.

Once she heard it shut behind him, Mona sucked up her tears and ran into the bedroom. She reached under the bed and pulled out a shoebox that Sly didn't think she knew about. Inside were small baggies filled with a powdery substance that she saw as the answer to all her problems. Taking a pinch in her hands, she spread it out right on the tile floor and hastily sucked it through one nostril. The high came quickly, but it wasn't as powerful as the time before.

Unknown to Sly, she'd been hitting up his secret stash for a minute. The dirties he rolled were no longer enough for her. She had a craving for something more potent. Reaching back inside the box, Mona took a bigger pinch, lined it up, and then snorted it down like a seasoned pro. A lazy grin tickled her lips as she let her neck fall back so that she could enjoy the feeling. Then she hurried and packed everything back up and pushed the shoebox back under the bed before Sly returned.

By the time he crept into the room later on that night, she was fast asleep. She'd sucked an entire bag up through her nose and filled it with baby powder to cover up her sins.

CHAPTER NINETEEN

"*A*hem!"

Baby's eyes fluttered as she slowly stirred awake, stretching her lean, slim body out to its full extent on her king-sized bed.

"AHEM!"

"Oh God!" She gasped and nearly jumped straight out of the bed, grabbing the covers up to her chin as if it would actually provide some protection against a real intruder.

As soon as her eyes were able to focus in on the source of the uninvited sounds in her room, she recognized the face but did everything but relax. Sitting in a chair beside her bed with her arms folded in front of her chest and an expression that easily showed her disapproval of something that Baby had obviously done, was Janine Taylor —her mother. Like Baby, she was blessed to look much younger than she was and stood at only about five feet four, but her temper was quick and intimidating enough to take down grown men twice her size.

"Mama! What are you doing here?"

"The better question is why are *you* here when Mona isn't?" She gave Baby a disapproving look while taking a quick pause to allow her words to sink in. With accusing eyes, she watched her daughter scramble for a response.

"Sh—she left," was all Baby could come up with. And it sounded just as sorry to Janine's ears as it did to hers. "I told you on the phone. She said she wasn't happy."

Janine sat back in her seat, tight-lipped. "Yes, I remember. And even if I didn't, Memphis seemed happy to inform me that Mona no longer lived here once I asked. What I'm trying to figure out is... if Mona isn't here anymore, what are you doing here with her husband?"

Baby hadn't forgotten that Memphis was still Mona's husband, but for some reason, hearing it now singed her soul.

"I plan on leaving soon."

"Is that true?" Janine asked rhetorically as she scrutinized her daughter.

One person she knew better than anyone else was her youngest child. Being that she'd given birth to her around the time that her other children were just about on their way out the house, she spent a lot of time one-on-one with Baby and could read her as easily as the back of her hand. And right now, as she looked into her face and saw the hint of shame that lie in her eyes, she had a suspicion about what was going on in Baby's life.

"Yes. As soon as I find a new place, I'll go," Baby explained, sitting up on the bed.

She could barely meet her mother's prying eyes because she felt like all of her inner thoughts would be easily exposed.

"This isn't like you, Baby. You've never before mentioned Mona's husband to me, so how could you know him well enough to be comfortable in his home without Mona? There is something you aren't telling me."

Taking a deep breath, Baby struggled to put the most convincing smile on her face as she let out her lie.

"Mama, you're just being extra suspicious right now, but there is nothing else to it. I know Memphis enough to call him a friend, and that's why he's letting me stay here. It's just until I get on my feet."

Janine didn't reply, but her eyes spoke volumes as she stared into her daughter's eyes. The wisdom that came with her years let her know that Baby was creating her own version of the truth. Still, she said nothing and instead decided to table that topic for later. There was a more pressing issue that she needed to address.

"What is going on with Semaj? You've avoided this topic for too long, and I'm not going to let it go anymore. I'm your mother, and I deserve an explanation! Did you know what he was involved in?"

"No!" Baby said much louder than she'd wanted to. "I—I know it sounds crazy, but I really didn't. I mean—I suspected that he was doing something that wasn't entirely legal, but I never asked, and he never explained."

"You never asked? You were going to marry a man without having an inkling of a clue about how he earned his money?"

Baby's cheeks burned, and she dropped her neck to look down at her lap. She didn't want to admit the truth which was that she deliberately never breached the topic because she didn't want to know how Semaj made his money. In her mind, she constructed her own reality regarding how he got it so that she never had to deal with the fact that she was the dope man's girl. Her mother had bust her ass to give her and her siblings a better life so they wouldn't be affected by the consequences of living in the hood, and here Baby was, deciding to be a gangster's wife.

"I don't know where I went wrong with you. Did I shelter you too much? Not expose you to enough? You can't be this naïve. And then you're here with this man..." Janine sighed, her heart hurting because she already knew the path her child was on. This situation was familiar to her in ways her daughter didn't even know.

"You're dealing with the loss of your own fiancé... you're fresh out of a relationship, and now you're here with this man. How long do you think it's going to be before you and him cross the line?"

With tears teasing the corner of her eyes, Baby kept her eyes low and shook her head stubbornly. She'd already crossed the line many times. She felt like she could die in her shame.

"We're just friends, Mama. That's all."

Janine's lips formed a straight line before a gloomy expression crossed her face. She wanted to tell Baby about her own father. A man who was now happily married to Janine's own friend, a woman she had once trusted with her life. The memory of how she'd lost the man of her dreams still burned her heart whenever she thought about it. There were so many signs she'd ignored because she never wanted to believe that her friend would ever betray her in that way. But eventually she had, and it devastated Janine to the point that she nearly lost herself. The only reason she was able to pull herself together was the fact that she was pregnant with Baby and had seven other children who needed her.

Diving into work and mothering her babies, Janine was able to push the hurt that she felt to the back of her mind, but she'd never properly dealt with the pain. This was evidenced by the fact that, to this day, Baby thought her father was the same as her other brothers and sisters—a man who had died when she was barely able to walk. Janine had never told her the truth, and Baby's siblings kept the secret as their way of protecting their mother. Sometimes Janine thought about telling Baby the truth, but her father was clear that he wanted nothing to do with her or their child, so she figured it was best to leave it alone rather than open up a world of hurt.

"Get up and get yourself together to come upstairs. I'm going to make us breakfast."

Before Baby was able to object, Janine stood up and walked away, disappearing in a whoosh and leaving her to listen as she ambled up the basement stairs. Lying back on her fluffy pillows, she tried to collect her thoughts before gathering the nerve to go face her new reality.

"I TOLD SEMAJ THAT I WOULD VISIT HIM TODAY," BABY INFORMED JANINE as she stuffed a piece of egg into her mouth.

She was sitting at the table with Janine and Genie with a plate in front of her full of all her breakfast favorites: grits, eggs, turkey bacon, toast, and a small stack of pancakes. The problem was that she didn't have even the smallest appetite and was forcing down every bite.

"Well, you will just have to miss today," Janine replied, giving her a pointed look while cutting up the pancake on her plate. "Mama's in town, and I need to spend time with my Baby."

"Oh, that's funny, because her name is Baby *and* she's your baby," Genie chimed in and then began to giggle loudly when Janine smiled at her.

"That's right. You're such a smart girl," she complimented her, making Genie grin.

Baby's mood was too sour to be moved by their pleasantries.

"But I promised I would see him today," she fussed. "I have to get on the bus in about an hour if I want to make it there and back in time."

Keeping her eyes on Baby, Janine continued to eat without saying a word. She knew there was something going on, and she wasn't going to stop until she got to the bottom of it. It didn't matter whose business she had to poke her nose in either.

Just as she was about to lay down the final word and tell Baby that she didn't care what plans she had made with her so-called man, Memphis walked into the dining room, and she decided to take another route.

"You really did your thing, Ms. Taylor," he said with a polite smile in Janine's direction.

Even though Janine knew there was something going on that she didn't approve of between Memphis and her daughter, she was still no match for his charm and found herself blushing at his compliment.

"Thank you," she replied. "Would you like me to make you a plate?"

"Oh no, enjoy your breakfast. You've done enough today. I'll make it," he told her.

It was a bold move to ogle Memphis with her mother right in front of her, but Baby couldn't resist. Donned in a cream sweater with the sleeves pulled up to his elbows, showing off his chiseled, tattooed arms and a simple pair of creased jeans that perfectly adorned his physique, he was breathtaking.

"Baby was just saying that she had to go see Semaj today," Janine spoke to Memphis, deliberately starting a fire. "But I want to spend a little time with her, so she won't be able to make the bus. You don't mind her taking one of your cars to see him, do you? I mean, you have so many of them."

A lump formed in Baby's throat, and she dropped her fork to her plate with a loud *clang*. Padding her eyes to Memphis's face, she knew immediately that this conversation wasn't going to end well. She watched with bated breath as his eyes narrowed into her, and his tongue trailed over his top row of teeth.

"No," was all he said.

Janine's brows shot up in surprise. "Oh? So she can use your car to see him?"

"No," Memphis said once again, his eyes still on Baby as he took a sip of orange juice. "She can't."

Silence fell over all of them. Baby's eyes went to her plate, and Janine's traveled back and forth between her daughter and Memphis while Memphis began eating his breakfast as if there was nothing wrong. Noting that something was off but not knowing exactly what, Genie lifted her head, surveyed the adults around her and then scrunched up her nose.

"But *why* can't she take your car to see Uncle Maj, Daddy?" she asked her father. "You got lots of 'em."

Memphis lifted his head and spoke to her with a tone so smooth.

"That ain't your uncle no more."

Genie cocked her head quizzically to the side but didn't question her father's statement. Janine, on the other hand, was too intrigued to let it slide.

"So you have a problem with my daughter seeing her fiancé?" she asked, putting extra emphasis on the word 'fiancé'. She cradled her chin in her open palm as she waited for Memphis to reply.

"I don't have anything to say about how she chooses to spend her day," he replied with ease. "She just won't be using nothing of mine to do it."

And with that, Memphis stood, grabbed his empty plate, and carried it with him out of the room. Baby couldn't even lift her head as he walked behind her with so much force that the wind trailing him knocked her napkin to the floor.

"Well!" Janine said, happily clasping her hands together in front of her. "Since you can't use his car, how about I drive you there? I feel like we have lots to talk about."

&

THE DRIVE TO THE PRISON WAS QUICKER THAN NORMAL, BUT FOR BABY, it seemed to drag on twice as long. After the way that everything ended up at the house, she couldn't deny Janine's suspicions any longer and was forced to come clean with the truth. Or at least *some* of the truth. She couldn't bring herself to admit that her relationship with Memphis had not only moved beyond simple interest but had taken the forbidden plunge into intimacy.

About an hour into Janine's constant reprimands about how stupid Baby was for being emotionally involved with a married man, her phone chimed, and she glanced at her mother before checking it. Janine was so caught up in disciplining Baby for everything that she done and everything she warned her was coming that she didn't even notice her checking her phone.

I'm sorry if I fucked up anything with you and your moms... but I couldn't agree to that.

Baby sucked in a long breath before she replied.

I know.

She wasn't mad at Memphis. Although he was a gentle beast when he was with her, he was still a beast. And part of being who he was meant that he was unmoving when it came to his beliefs. He believed that Baby's place was with him, and even though he couldn't force her to go along with that, he refused to aid her journey into the arms of another.

228

"Who are you coming to see?"

With a blank face, Baby looked at the security guard without saying a word. As many times as she'd been there to see Semaj, everyone should have known who it was that she wanted to visit. The female guard stared back at her with a dull expression that said she hadn't a single thing to do and would wait all day for a response if Baby wanted her to.

"Semaj Daniels," Baby answered after realizing she really was going to pretend like she was clueless.

"Daniels," the woman repeated and used her finger to scroll down a list of names in front of her. "Ah, here we go." Turning to the ancient computer next to her, courtesy of the department's meager budget, she pecked a few keys and then furrowed her brows as she read something on the screen.

"Daniels has no visitation time left for today," she stated with a monotone.

Baby's mouth dropped open.

"What?"

"He has no visitation time left for—"

"I heard what you said," Baby interrupted. "But that can't be possible because I'm the only one who comes here to visit him. Can you look again?"

The woman pursed her lips and cocked her head to the side, giving Baby the same dull look that she had before. She'd seen this situation many times since she'd been working in the prison system, and it never ended well. A dog on the streets always found a way to be a dog in prison, cycling women through visitations while telling each one they were the only one holding him down.

"I checked again. He still has no visitation time left. Sorry."

The woman twirled around in her chair, putting her back to Baby to let her know their exchange was over. With her lips parted in shock and a deep frown creasing her forehead, Baby turned to Janine who appeared to be just as puzzled as she.

"Maybe he has some family that showed up?" she offered with a shrug, but Baby was clueless. Semaj had grown up in the foster care system and had no family to speak of.

"I guess this was a wasted trip," she said as they walked out of the building. "He never mentioned any family. He told me that no one was visiting him here. No one but me."

"Well, there's obviously a few more things about your fiancé that you need to learn," Janine told her as she rubbed her back reassuringly. "Ask him about it when he calls."

SITTING ON THE FLOOR WITH HER LEGS FOLDED INDIAN-STYLE, BABY held her phone in her hands, texting Gala. One thing about her older sister is that Gala had strong opinions and was never one to hold her tongue. In this instance, it was exactly what Baby needed. Her mind was reeling; she felt unsettled with all the changes going on around her. In the midst of this thing she had going on with Memphis—whatever this thing was—now she had another situation going on with Semaj.

Staring at the last message that had come through from Gala, she took a deep breath and pursed her lips slightly before she began to answer.

You have to do something about this situation with Semaj and Memphis and then decide what you want to do. You can't run from making a decision.

Gala was right. In her heart, Baby knew exactly what needed to be done. The problem was that it was just *so* hard. For someone who had always put others before herself, it was so hard to think outside of what was needed of her and make decisions based on solely what she wanted. The answer was clear—she wanted Memphis. But what would that mean for Semaj? She had almost married him until she was caught up in the whirlwind of events that changed her life forever. Shouldn't that count for something?

"Baby?"

The sound of her mother's voice calling her name made her heart jump in her chest. The edge in Janine's voice set off alarms in her mind. Turning around, she looked into her mother's sad and distressed face, the corners of her eyes drooped down in grief, and she was wringing her hands in front of her as if she were worried about something. Baby placed her phone face down on the floor beside her and gave her mother her full attention.

"Yes, Mama?"

Janine sighed and sat down on the couch next to her daughter, closing her eyes as she urged her heart to stop beating wildly in her chest. Ever since the moment that Memphis had left along with Genie to give she and Baby some time alone, Janine had been preparing herself for the conversation that she knew she would have to have with her daughter. It was a conversation that she always knew at some point she would have to have, but that didn't make her any more prepared.

"I need to talk to you about something," she began, licking her lips.

Baby felt the hairs on her arm raise on end, and she swiveled around so that she could sit facing her mother. Like a small child, she sat at Janine's feet, looking up with expectant eyes, somewhat worried about what she would hear. Picking up on the non-verbal cues coming from her, it was obvious that whatever Janine had to say was hard for her to get out, and although it caused Baby to feel slightly on edge, she forced herself to stay calm in order to send her mother positive energy.

"You can tell me anything, Mama. You know that," she encouraged, but Janine shook her head.

She knew that what Baby was saying had always been true, but in this instance, she wasn't quite so sure. Telling a child that the man they always thought was their father wasn't, was one thing... but to also tell that child that their father was actually alive and living his best life, while knowing that she existed but still not wanting anything to do with her—that was another thing.

"I need to talk to you about your father," Janine started. Baby's eyes narrowed in confusion, but she said nothing, and Janine continued.

"Before you were born, your daddy—the man you know as your father—he and I had separated. As you know, he was a musician, and even though he tried to be a family man and raise our children together, the pull to be on the road, traveling with his band was too much. So he left, and I had to deal with that pain on my own." Tears came to her eyes, and she paused, pinching her lips together to force them away.

"Eventually, I was able to pull myself together, and I recovered from that heartbreak. I met another man, and he was everything I thought I wanted. A businessman, but he hadn't achieved much just yet... He was on the way up from the bottom, but it was obvious that he had so much potential. I knew that he would achieve every one of his dreams. I believed in him, and he romanced me." Janine smiled to herself as she went down memory lane. Her eyes stared at some space behind Baby, but it was clear that her mind was elsewhere. She was reliving some of her best moments. But there was more heartbreak to follow.

"It was a quick romance. We were so in love with each other and wanted to do nothing but be in each other's arms. Then I became pregnant, and things got hard. I was so emotional, and this pregnancy was much harder on me. I was older, but I was also trying to run a household and help Kevin get his business off the ground. I worked around the clock, to make him comfortable, take care of my babies, and take care of myself... I was so busy, stressed, and depressed that I didn't have time for anything. My best friend, Renee, volunteered to help me out, and I was so grateful, but it was the worst mistake I ever made.

Kevin started changing, and I didn't even notice. First, our intimacy changed. He didn't seem as interested in me as he had been. On the other hand, his relationship with Renee seemed to blossom. I would come home from work to find that she was already at my house... making dinner for my husband and taking care of my babies. I was so tired that I didn't think anything of it. I was just happy to be getting some help. I didn't think about the fact that Kevin was now looking at Renee in the way that he'd once done me. I didn't think about how I would walk into the room and find them whispering, giggling amongst each other... My focus wasn't there. I never thought the two people I loved most would betray me. Until they did."

By this time, Baby had tears in her own eyes as she watched Janine's stream down her face. This had all happened decades ago, before Baby had even been born, but the hurt was still there. Her heart bled for her mother... Baby's unselfish nature made it so that she couldn't even deal with the fact that she was learning that the man she thought was her father really wasn't. She was too concerned about her mother's pain; pain that she'd never reconciled because she had been too busy trying to cover it up for the sake of her children. For the sake of Baby.

"One day I came home to discover that Kevin was gone. I was devastated, but the one person I wanted to call to cry out to, I couldn't, because she was gone too. That day, I lost the man I thought was my soul mate, and I lost my best friend, too. There was no way for me to contact either of them, and they made sure of that. It was like they disappeared without a trace, leaving me alone to pick up the pieces. I was so scared... I wanted to be angry and depressed and grieve for all that I'd lost, but I couldn't. I was pregnant, and I didn't want my child to be affected by my emotional state... I never got a chance to heal."

Standing up, Baby sat next to her mother and wrapped her arms around her shoulders. The embrace was just enough to tear through the walls of Janine's emotional block, and she released years of hurt into her daughter's arms, crying out all the tears that she'd kept inside for so long. Like so many other Black women, Janine had been severely hurt but never received closure or took time to deal with her pain. She had children depending on her, and for them as well as her unborn child, she had to do what needed to be done.

"Seth and I were no longer together, but in visiting with your brothers and sisters, he was able to bond with you, and everything just fell in line. You thought of him as your father, and he never told you differently. We just moved through life, putting the pieces together along the way."

Now that her story had ended, Janine pulled back and brought her teary eyes to Baby's face. Her daughter was a grown woman and would make her own choices in life as well as her own mistakes, but

Janine felt it was her duty as her mother to at least guide her along the way.

"I know you and Memphis have something going on—it's obvious. And I'm not going to say your situation is the complete same as mine, but I want you to understand what you're doing to your friendship with Mona and what you may be doing to Genie. Some things you can never come back from, and you need to understand that."

"This isn't exactly the same, Mama," Baby started. "I'm so sorry about what happened to you. You didn't deserve it, and no one does. But Mona left her family and... there are a few things about Memphis and I that you still don't know. It's hard to explain, but I promise you that I'm nothing like the woman who betrayed you, and Memphis is nothing like Kevin. I need you to trust me that I wouldn't do anything to hurt the people I love."

A few moments passed between them as they looked into each other's eyes, and Janine thought about all the things she knew about her daughter. Baby was kind, selfless, thoughtful, and loving. She was nothing like Renee. The more that Janine actually took time to think about her past, all of the things that she tried to forget and cover up, she realized that Renee was more like Mona than anything. She was friendly to Janine, but she wasn't a *real* friend. Like Baby, Janine had always seen the underhanded ways that Mona moved, but she believed that with age, Mona would mature to be a better person. Maybe they'd both been wrong.

"I trust you, Baby," Janine told her finally. "And I know one day, when it all sinks in, you'll want me to tell you about your father. When that day comes, I'm here."

Shaking her head, Baby spoke with all honesty. "I don't need to know anything about Kevin. My father... my real dad is the one who loved me every day of my life until God took the breath from his body. That's all I know, and that's how it will remain."

Baby's response warmed Janine's heart. No matter how she came into the world and the circumstances surrounding it, Baby had grown to be a beautiful woman with a beautiful heart. Janine hugged her tightly, pressing her lips against her daughter's forehead as she let all of the guilt, pain, and devastation of her past melt away.

"I love you, and I'll support whatever decision you make," she told her.

The words were so sweet to Baby's ears.

"Thank you, Mama. I love you too."

CHAPTER TWENTY

"Yo, ain't you had enough of them fuckin' purses already?" Sly barked rendering nothing more than a sassy eye-roll from Mona.

Reaching into her brand-new Hermes bag, she pulled out her fire engine red lipstick, puckered her lips, and spread it on while he watched, nearly busting at the seams with anger. It had barely been three weeks that she had been with him, and she was already driving him insane. Not only was she mouthy as hell with an attitude to match, but in less than thirty days, she'd blown through most of the money he had saved, and he was no closer to getting a new connect than he had been the day he'd met her.

The more time that passed, the more he was beginning to think that Mona was a waste of his damn time. Initially, he'd thought that she would have valuable information for him that could assist him with taking down the infamous Memphis, but from the looks of it, Memphis had never told her shit. At first Sly had figured that Mona was just loyal and lying to him to make it seem like she didn't know anything about how he made moves. The more time that passed, it was becoming obvious that she didn't know a damn thing unless it involved spending money.

"Stop shouting. This bag is worth every penny that I paid for it."

"Then maybe you should start using your own fuckin' pennies!" he snarled, getting angrier by the second as he watched Mona pull more expensive things out of her new purse; a wallet, new iPhone complete with a Louis Vuitton case, and a brand-new iPad were among the many things she had inside. She had only been in the car for about three minutes and was already dancing on his last nerve.

"And what the hell you got that tablet thing for?"

Cocking her neck back, Mona frowned, giving him a look that told him to 'chill out'.

"Um… this is an iPad. People get these to work on—"

"Bitch! You ain't got no damn job!" he snapped, making her flinch so hard that she nearly pelted it out the window. "Only fuckin' thing you work is my gotdamn patience!"

"Calm down!" She held up her hands as a signal for him to relax before she ended up with another black eye. Since the first time he'd put his hands on her, he'd done it a few times more, but she got over it by using her newfound method of therapy to ease the pain. Sooner or later, Sly would figure out that she was replacing his dope with baby powder, but she prayed she would be long gone by then.

"I really don't get why niggas act like this once they get used to a bitch," Mona continued, smacking her jaws. "You knew I wasn't fuckin' with a broke ass nigga when you approached me. You promised me a certain lifestyle, so why are you gettin' pissy just because I'm buying shit? You got the money!"

Sly's frustration began to build up to levels that he wasn't mentally prepared for. He'd played his position for long enough. He couldn't stand Mona, and it was eating him alive to keep dealing with her when he wouldn't be giving her the time of day otherwise. The women Sly liked were not the pampered type. He preferred a 'queen of the ghetto'—the type of woman that smelled like Pink Oil Moisturizer and Cocoa Butter when she floated by, wearing knockers in her ears, with tattoos decorating her thick thighs. He liked the type that had the pain of the struggle in her eyes with the will to 'make a way out of no way' in her mind. She had a heart bruised by loves of the past but still enough room in her heart to love yet again.

That was the type of woman who did it for him, and to be honest, he was ready to find her. But after things didn't go as planned with Memphis, he had to put that pursuit to the side in order to deal with Mona. Now it was becoming clear that the only thing he'd been doing was wasting his time, which angered him to the fullest. Time was money, and he was short on both.

"Listen, I don't have a damn thing to my name," Sly admitted, tossing his hands in the air. "I just got out of prison not too long ago, and I'm in the process of building up from the bottom. Memphis was supposed to help me with that, but he turned me down. I'm broke as fuck."

You could've shoved an entire bus through Mona's open mouth.

"Broke? You're lying! What about this car? And your house!"

She watched the grim expression on Sly's face in absolute horror as he shook his head.

"This car and the other one I got at the hotel... all this shit is old. I got locked up and my moms made sure that my whips were straight until I was able to hit the bricks again."

With her jaw nearly in her lap, Mona's eyes darted back and forth as she thought through what he was telling her. This couldn't possibly be true! There was no way that she had actually been tricked into leaving Memphis for a man she just knew was better, only for it all to be a joke. Tears began to run down her face, and in no time, she looked like she'd been splashed with a bucket of water. This was probably the lowest place she'd ever been in life.

"What about your new house you're building? You said that we would be moving into it within a week!"

Sly didn't say a word, but she could tell from the look in his eyes that the house—everything he told her—it was all a lie. He wasn't even paying for the hotel room they were in. His homeboy worked at the front desk and was letting them stay for free. But even that was over now because he could no longer hold the room. The luxurious life was over.

"Oh my God, what am I going to do now?" she whined, and Sly wanted nothing more than to take a sock and stuff it down her throat to seal off the noise. "I left a man who loved me—a man who *married* me and ended up with this broke fool!"

Gritting his teeth, Sly was a second away from wrapping his fingers around her neck and choking her to death, when something occurred to him. Memphis did marry Mona, and she was the mother of his child, so he obviously cared for her and wouldn't want her harmed. Maybe there was still a way that he could get back on his feet. Sly had never been low enough to hold a bitch ransom, but there was a first time for everything.

"Aye, stop all the damn crying! It's gonna be alright."

The little bit of hope that Mona had left quieted her enough to stop what was quickly about to become a full-on tantrum to listen to what Sly had to say.

"Listen..." he began, throwing on the charm he used in order to get her in the first place. "I am on the verge of making the deal of a lifetime that will bless me with exactly what I need in order to make more money than you could ever spend. I just need to know you'll be down with me until I get there before I can truly trust you to be my one."

Mona suppressed an eye roll. She didn't like it one bit and made a mental note to hop on the next thing smoking out of D.C. and fly home so she could at least beg her parents to take care of her until she found someone new.

Or I could always go back to Memphis, she thought. Although he hadn't tried once to contact her at all since she'd left—and she had most definitely checked—she was convinced that he still cared for her and would welcome her back into his good graces if she played her cards right. Her ace in the hole being their daughter.

"So what's it gonna be? You gon' ride it out with a nigga until we come up? I'mma make you the happiest woman on Earth."

Sly sold the dream, giving her the sweetest smile to go along with the bitter lie. Still, even as he saw Mona nod her vow to him, he knew that she wouldn't really fall for the charm enough to look past the lint he had in his pockets. He would have to take things up a notch.

"Good. Let's go home then," he told her before turning on the engine.

Pursing her lips, Mona crossed her arms and looked out the window, watching the city pass her by. This was definitely her lowest hour—she'd cut off everybody to be with a man who turned out to be a fraud. Eagerly waiting for the life of luxury she was promised, she hadn't even bothered to send anything but a couple texts to tell her parents that she was alive. She hadn't spoken to anyone.

But that means they'll miss me, be happy to hear from me and, in no time, I'll have my old life back, she thought, already laying out her plan.

❧

SLY KNEW THAT MONA WASN'T ABOUT SHIT, AND SINCE SHE NOW KNEW the truth about his nonexistent wealth, he could no longer bring himself to trust her. She had no information that he could use to better his situation, but his dick was in the dirt, and she was all he had left to work with. He couldn't let her go.

With one hand still on the steering wheel, he reached in the back seat, and to Mona's horror, pulled out the shoebox that she recognized as the one he normally kept under the bed. Opening it, he pulled out a baggie and took a pinch of one before dropping the white substance on the tip of his tongue. After smacking his lips a bit, his face balled up into a frown, and he began spitting and scraping his tongue raw with his nails.

"What da fuck!" He looked back into the bag and took a sniff. "Is this fuckin' baby powder?"

His glare fell on Mona who was sitting silently next to him, and she lifted her hands in the air.

"What? I don't know anything about that."

"Bitch—" he started but caught himself when he saw a sheriff pass them by.

With his eyes narrowed and his blood boiling, he dropped the bag of baby powder into the shoebox, closed it, and placed it down near his feet. Mona crossed her arms in front of her chest and looked out the window as her thoughts ran rampant. Sly had now found out that she'd been dipping in his stash, and she knew that an ass beating would soon follow. She wasn't as concerned about that as she was about the fact that once it was over, she'd have nothing available to help her recover from it.

"Get out," he told her roughly after pulling in front of a small, dingy house that was right smack in the middle of an equally dingy neighborhood.

With her nose turned up, Mona sucked her teeth and shook her head stubbornly.

"Oh hell naw, I'm not going in there! It don't look safe and—"
Whap! Whap! Whap!

Before she could get out another word, Sly was on her like a heavyweight champ, knocking her with hard enough blows to put her to sleep. But for some reason, she fought to stay conscious.

"I should kill you for what you did! You used up all my shit. Do you have any idea how much this shit cost?"

She didn't, so instead of trying to answer him, Mona wearily drooped her forehead against the window. She swallowed down the bitter taste of her own blood and touched her busted lip. The pain shot through her, and she winced hard, knowing that her lip was only the beginning of it. She could already feel both of her eyes beginning to swell.

Sly went through the bags in his shoebox, furiously tossing the ones filled with baby powder out the window. Once he was sure he'd gotten rid of all the fake product, he counted up what he had left and came up with another evil plan.

"Get the fuck out," he told Mona, and this time, she quickly obeyed. Seeing her willingness to jump at his command made his heart smile. He felt that he was finally getting a breakthrough.

"Since you wanna get high, I'mma give you exactly what you need."

Mona's face hurt so bad that she couldn't even make an expression to indicate how she felt inside, but she definitely had no idea what Sly was plotting for her. Grabbing her hand, he pulled her forward, leading her since he knew she probably couldn't see much with blood in her eyes. Once they walked into the house, Mona picked up on the stale smell inside and shrunk into herself. She was afraid, and for once in her life, at a loss of what to do next.

"Sit in that chair and hold your hands out," he ordered her, and she did.

Sly tied her arms around the back of the chair and then left the room. It felt like hours later when he finally returned. The blood on Mona's face had crusted to the point that she could barely see out of her eyes.

"Since you wanna get high all day and shit, let's see how you deal with this."

"Ah!" Mona yelped out in fear when she felt a needle go through her skin.

Sly injected her with pure cocaine. The drug went straight into her bloodstream and she became so high that she didn't know up from down. Her face was numb, her worries were gone. It was pure bliss. In fact, she looked so at peace that Sly turned the needle on himself and tried a little bit.

"Fuck," he moaned as the feeling set in.

"Mmmm," Mona hummed, and he looked at her.

She was wiggling in her seat as if she was trying to get away, but the motion was making her short dress rise up her round hips. Sly licked his lips lustfully and grabbed his crotch. The drug had his man below rock hard, and he knew Mona had just what he needed to satisfy him. If nothing else, she had good pussy. It was tight, stayed wet, and her head game wasn't bad either. When she was high, she'd deepthroat him without gagging, expanding her neck to swallow him down with ease like a python did its prey. Just thinking about it had precum oozing from the tip of his dick.

He released her from the chair and dropped his pants before twisting her around so that she was booted over. Her hands were still tied, even though he knew she was too high to resist. She didn't even flinch when he pushed his thick rod straight into her and started humping her with no mercy. She was completely still, even when he forced himself into her tight ass and then began alternating between her two holes, pleasuring himself to the max.

Days merged into nights and nights merged into days with Sly repeating this cycle over and over with her. Drugs filled her veins, and he filled her in other areas. At one point, he cut the drug with some of the baby powder, aspirin, Boric acid, and a few other choice ingredients, then watched her trip to the max once it settled in her veins. The concoction made her frantic... She howled to the heavens, pacing while screaming about how she could say her name backward but not frontward. Once he and his boys had their fill of laughter, they all fucked her until she calmed down. Hours after, she couldn't recall a thing and was begging for more.

Sly was determined to get her so addicted to the drug and so dependent on him as her supplier that there wouldn't be a single thing she wouldn't do. When his supply ran low, he borrowed more on credit, promising that he would get the money to pay his debt with added interest.

It was taking longer than he'd planned, but he was unwavering and almost obsessed with the idea of getting back on top. Being patient until his plan unfolded properly was a small price to pay.

CHAPTER TWENTY-ONE

"Gotty, I feel hot."

Looking up from her book, Baby dropped her eyes to Genie who had been playing quietly on the floor near where she lay on the sofa. She was so engrossed in her new novel that she didn't even realize Genie was no longer playing but lying back against a pillow. There was a sheen of sweat on her forehead.

"Oh my God, Genie!" Baby gasped, jumping up. She kneeled down and pressed her hand against Genie's forehead. She didn't need a thermometer to know that the young child was running a fever. Cradling her in her arms, Baby carried Genie to her room and laid her down on the bed. She then ran cold water on a washcloth and rubbed it over her face.

"Other than hot, how do you feel?" she asked, and Genie frowned thoughtfully before replying. She looked up at the worried expression on her gotty's face and forced a smile. She didn't want to worry her any more than she already had.

"I'm a little tired, but that's it." Genie thought for a second and then her eyes lit up. "Maybe you can give me the medicine Mommy gives me all the time. The Benamil."

"Benamil?" Baby repeated, thinking. "You mean Benadryl?"

Genie nodded her head. "Yes. She says it keeps me healthy."

"How often does she give you the Benadryl?" Baby asked, feeling a cold shiver run down her spine.

Tell me Mona was not drugging this baby to sleep, she prayed.

"She gives it to me every time Trina leaves and we have our special alone time together!" Genie informed her with a smile, not even knowing just how heartbreaking her words were to Baby's ears. "Mommy always wanted me to be really healthy, so she gave me a lot."

Then, sensing from Baby's expression that something wasn't quite right, she bunched her brows together and frowned.

"Was that not good?" she asked, and Baby quickly pushed her thoughts away so that she could focus on the present.

"Sometimes we need Benadryl to help us feel better, but you don't need it right now. Close your eyes and rest... I'll stay until you're asleep."

She could see the fatigue in Genie's face and knew there was more that she was not telling her about how she currently felt, but Baby didn't press her for more. Sitting there, she said a quick prayer, rubbed the side of Genie's face, and sang to her until she drifted off to sleep. Once she was sure that Genie was out cold, she ran to grab her cell phone and called her mother.

"Mama?"

"Yes, Baby?" Janine could hear the urgency in her child's voice. "Did something happen? Do I need to drive back to Atlanta?"

Baby closed her eyes and pressed her fingers to her temple in frustration. Truthfully, she wanted nothing more than her mother to come back to help her. Being that Janine was a registered nurse, she would be the perfect person to assist.

"No, Mama. I know you have work and other commitments. I can handle this. Genie is running a fever... and I don't know what to do."

"How high is it?" Janine asked, and Baby cursed herself for not even thinking to actually take her temperature before calling.

"Hold on!"

She ran to the cabinet in the kitchen where Memphis kept all the medicine and searched for a thermometer. As soon as she found one, she ran into Genie's room and carefully inserted it into her mouth and under her tongue as she slept.

"It says her temperature is 101.2," Baby said once she was back on the phone.

"Okay…" Janine began slowly. "That's definitely higher than normal. Try giving her some Tylenol and keep monitoring it. Make sure she drinks lots of fluid. If it doesn't go down, you'll need to call her doctor or take her to the emergency room."

Baby spent the rest of the day doing exactly as her mother instructed. She nearly ran herself crazy checking Genie's temperature every half hour and taking notes. She woke her only to make her drink and give her more medicine when it was time. Within about four hours, Genie's temperature was still mildly high, but it was in the healthy range for a child her age, so Baby was able to relax enough to pick back up her book. But before going back to reading, she decided to send a quick text to Memphis. Not wanting to worry him unless things were urgent, she'd avoided messaging him until she was able to get everything under control.

Genie's not feeling well. She had a fever but it's fine now. I called my mom and she told me what to do.

As Memphis's eyes swept over the screen of his phone, he felt his heart squeeze tight in his chest. For the average child, a fever was a normal occurrence, but Genie wasn't the average child. When it came to any ailment that she had, he took it seriously because he knew not doing so could be the difference between life and death for her.

Placing the phone down, he thought back to the moment he held his baby girl in his hands for the first time. She was so small, so fragile, and so helpless that he immediately made it his one goal in life to forever keep her safe. The doctors had told him that she wouldn't make it past three-years-old, but like the champ she was, she'd proved them all wrong. They'd told him that his daughter would never be able to speak to him—would never be able to say the word 'daddy'. But here she was, and she could say 'daddy' in at least five different languages; six, if you counted sign.

Genie was a soldier, but he was her protector. And he took that responsibility very seriously. So even though Baby was telling him that everything was 'fine,' that wasn't enough for him.

"Yo, Laz… I gotta hang this shit up early tonight. Like right now," Memphis said just as Laz pulled up to their destination. They'd gotten in a new product from their connect, and even though Memphis stood to nearly triple his revenue once it hit the streets, his baby girl was more important, and this meet up could be pushed to later.

On the other end, Laz's eyes bugged out of his skull. Not only had they been trying to work this deal for weeks, there was no telling when they would get the opportunity to meet with Xu and his crew again to make a purchase. Xu was Japanese, and the muthafucka was extremely serious about how he spent his time. He would see it as the utmost disrespect if Memphis cancelled on him this late in the game.

"This nigga gon' think we ain't got our funds straight if we pull out now, bruh. It took a lot to get his ass here. You know them Japanese muthafuckas already don't like fuckin' with niggas on any level anyways," Laz informed him carefully. He knew that Memphis wasn't the one to tolerate being challenged, but he felt like he wouldn't be playing his position as a true friend in the game if he didn't at least let his man know the consequences of his actions.

"My baby girl needs me," was all Memphis said. Laz heard it, and even though he had no children that he knew of, he understood how much Memphis loved his daughter. Still, he had to try and break through to him one last time.

"I understand, bruh. This meeting won't take too long. And the whole reason for this deal is so that we can set shit in place so that you can step out of the game for good. When we get this done, you're one step closer to being with your family 24/7 if you want it that way."

Running his finger over his top lip, Memphis had to take a second to think on Laz's words. He was right. The purpose behind even making this connection was to give him the boost he needed to be comfortable making his exit and leaving Laz in charge. He clenched his jaw tight as he waged the competing thoughts in his mind.

"A'ight. Let me make a call right quick."

With a nod of his head, Laz stepped out of the car to give Memphis privacy as he made his call. Memphis sighed heavily and looked down at the message from Baby once more before going to his contacts and pressing on the name of the only other woman, besides Baby and Genie, who held a special place in his heart.

"Hey, son!"

The sound of her voice brought a smile to his lips.

"Ma, what's good?" Memphis replied. Although he hadn't seen his biological mother since the day he was old enough to leave, there was another woman who had taken her place. Over the years, Cleo Donaldson had become more than just the teacher who saved him. She was part of his family.

"It's about time I've heard from you. When you gon' bring my grandbaby by to see me? It's been much too long, and you know I can't count on that raggedy mama of hers to bring her by," Cleo said, making her hatred of Mona obvious in her tone. She didn't like the girl the second she laid eyes on her, and her dislike of Mona only grew from there the more that she saw her interaction—or lack of interaction—with Genie.

"Actually, Genie is the reason for the call," Memphis began, and his distressed tenor set off alarms in Cleo's soul.

"What? What is wrong with my baby?"

"Calm down, Ma, she's fine. Her godmother is over there. She just texted me and said Genie had a fever. It's good now, but I wanted to know if you can go and check on her for me. I'm in the middle of something and can't leave right now."

There was silence on the other end, and Memphis knew that Cleo was biting her tongue. It was no secret to her what Memphis did in the streets, and she had constantly voiced her opinion on his lifestyle every chance she got. She felt that a man like him was much too smart

248

for the drug game, telling him that he had what it took to be a doctor, stockbroker, lawyer… anything that he wanted to be. Memphis knew she was right. He tested at a genius level and was even offered a full ride into a prestigious, ivy league college once he graduated high school, but he was a king in the streets by then and felt a responsibility to fulfill a destiny that Cleo would never understand.

"I'm on my way over there," Cleo said, and Memphis was grateful that she was making the call easy for him. "I remember Baby, but she may not remember me, so make sure she knows I'm on my way and she can let me in."

Memphis ended the call and sent a text to Baby before turning off his phone and placing it in his pocket. Laz tapped lightly on the hood of the car, letting him know that Xu and his team were ready to make a move, and he nodded before stepping out. When he was younger, he lived for the moments he could make deals like this, but now, he lived for Genie. He couldn't wait for the moment he could let this all go so that he could spend his nights watching movies for hours with his baby girl at home.

MY MOMS IS ON THE WAY TO CHECK ON GENIE. I'LL BE BACK SOON.

The moment Baby read the message, she pressed her lips together into a thin line. Did Memphis think that she wasn't capable of watching his daughter?

No, that's not it, she told herself. Anyone with eyes could see how much Memphis loved Genie. He was just being overly cautious, which was his right as a father.

With a restless sigh, Baby started to place her phone down but then it rang. It was an unknown number, and her heart skipped a beat. She'd been waiting for Semaj to call ever since her visit to the prison that ended with her being turned away

"Yes, I accept the charges," Baby said hastily to the computerized voice and waited for Semaj to come on the line.

"Hey, Babycakes," he began, using the nickname that he'd given her in their former life. "What's poppin'?"

"I came to see you last Sunday, but they said you had no visitation time left because someone had already been there."

Semaj paused for only a second, but something about it made the hairs on Baby's arm stand on end.

"Yeah... one of my homies swung through to see me. I wasn't expectin' it. You know, everybody done dropped a nigga since I got in the joint. You the only one who has been by my side, holdin' a nigga down."

"Oh," Baby said softly, her guilt nearly eating her alive.

"I got caught up in some bullshit in here, so I lost my phone privileges all last week. That's why I ain't been calling. I just got them back," he told her, and Baby's shame intensified when she realized that he was right. He hadn't called her the entire week, and not once had she noticed. Looking at her hand, she stared at the diamond ring that she still wore on her finger. She still looked like an engaged woman, but circumstances had changed.

"That's crazy. Are you okay?"

"Yeah, wasn't nothing but some bitch shit that I had to handle. Muthafucka tried me like a chump, and I had to show him what it was." Semaj explained further, telling her about how another inmate tried to rob him of his sneakers.

Baby heard what he was saying, but she had no connection at all to it. What he dealt with in prison was so different from anything she had going on in her life. There was a disconnect between the two of them. Time had stopped for Semaj, whereas Baby was still living her life. Other than the past, they had nothing in common.

"Gottyyy?"

Baby had started thumbing through her book as Semaj talked on about all the things happening around him in prison, when she heard Genie call out to her.

"Semaj, hold on," she said and placed the phone down without giving him a chance to reply. She ran into the room and looked down at Genie, who was holding the covers up under her chin, shivering severely. Her bottom lip was trembling, and her pale skin appeared even paler than normal. Something was wrong, and Baby's anxiety gripped her racing heart.

"What's going on, sweetie? How are you feeling?" She touched Genie's forehead, but it wasn't hot at all. Her fever was gone, and Baby was at a loss for what she should do next.

"I'm just so cold." Genie's teeth began to chatter.

"I'm going to get you another blanket." She turned to leave, but then another idea came to her. "Actually... why don't I bring you out to the living room with me? We can sit by the fireplace."

Genie gave her a weak smile and nodded her head. Before moving her, Baby paused and thought about whether this would be the right thing to do. Genie looked so weak, and even though she'd been sleeping for hours, there were dark circles around her eyes.

"Ohhh, it's so cold," she whined, poking out her trembling bottom lip. A single tear fell down her cheek, and that was all the sign that Baby needed. Genie was a fighter and rarely cried or complained about anything, so this was serious.

Leaning down, she tenderly scooped Genie's small body into her arms, making sure to keep the comforter wrapped snug around her as she carried her into the living room. She sat her on the sofa and pressed the button to fire up the gas fireplace before nestling up against her goddaughter. They sat there enjoying each other's company in a comfortable silence until there was a knock on the door.

"Is that Daddy?" Genie asked, and Baby shook her head.

"No, I don't think so, but I think you're going to be happy when you see who it is!" she told her with a smile. Genie's eyes lit up, and she smiled brightly.

"Is it Mommy?" The question nearly broke Baby's heart, but she was able to keep her composure.

"How about I open the door and let you see who has come to see you?"

Turning on her heels, Baby went to the front door and opened it.

"So nice to see you again, Ms. Donaldson," she greeted the woman with a smile before pulling her into a hug. "I don't know if you remember me, but I'm Baby... Genie's—"

"Godmother," Cleo finished for her. "Oh, I remember you. A face so beautiful, I could never forget."

Baby blushed underneath her caramel cheeks and stepped to the side to let Cleo in. Although Baby's beauty wasn't easily forgotten, it wasn't the only reason Cleo remembered her so well. The one and only time she'd seen Baby was at a cookout that Memphis had thrown to celebrate the birth of his daughter and subsequent marriage. Cleo spent the entire time watching the way her son looked at the woman who had been introduced to her as Mona's best friend, noticing that there was a stark difference in comparison to how he looked at Mona, his brand-new wife. She knew then that Memphis had married the wrong woman.

"Mama!" Genie exclaimed when she saw her grandmother enter the room. "You came to see me?"

"Yes, I came to see you," Cleo answered, giving her a kiss on the forehead. "How are you feeling?"

She sat down next to Genie as Baby watched from a short distance.

"I—I..." Genie started, her eyes darting around the room as she began to collect her words. Cleo touched Genie lightly on the chin and turned her face so that she was looking her right in the eyes.

"I want you to tell me the truth, Genie. You don't lie to mama."

Genie's eyes dropped, and her bottom lip began to tremble. "But I don't want to worry you. Every time I get sick, everybody gets so sad."

Baby's eyes filled with tears, and she had to look away. Even Cleo had to pause and take a deep breath before she could speak again.

"I understand." She ran her fingers through Genie's soft curls. "But you have to tell me and Gotty the truth. How do you feel, baby?"

Dropping her head, Genie started to cry. "I don't feel good. I'm cold and... it hurts so bad."

With furrowed brows, Cleo crowded in closer to her grand-daughter.

"Where does it hurt? Can you tell me?"

Genie paused for a short while and then lifted her teary eyes. "All over."

Baby saw Cleo's entire body tense up, and she knew something was very wrong. Cleo patted Genie on the back and told her to lay down in her lap to rest.

"Call 911," she mouthed to Baby, and with a short nod, Baby ran to do exactly as she was told.

CHAPTER TWENTY-TWO

*S*ly was on top of the world. He barely had a dollar to his name, but he was confident that his luck was about to change. Mona was easily broken, and he'd successfully made her into a true fiend. After giving her a healthy dose of her desired drug back-to-back, he had begun pulling back a little at a time, even though he knew her body craved the high. She got to the point that she couldn't think of anything but getting her next fix and started begging him for a hit.

"Please… say you got something for me, Sly. All I need is a little bit… you ain't got that?"

He'd barely been able to close the front door before Mona was on his heels. In a short while, she was a far cry from the woman she'd been when he first laid eyes on her. Her hair used to be her pride and joy. She'd gone to the most luxurious salons to get it shampooed, and they used products that only celebrities could buy. Now it was so stringy and dirty that there was no telling when she'd washed it last. The Givenchy and Prada gowns she'd once wore were now a thing of the past; they'd been traded out for soiled and dirty corner store fashions instead. While in her former life she used hot exotic oils to keep the skin on her pretty feet soft and smelling sweet, her soles were now black and crusted with dirt.

With a sigh, Sly turned to look at her, his forehead wrinkled into a frown.

"I got bad news, ma. I don't got shit... money is low, and I can't buy no more."

Mona licked her dry lips and scratched her scalp hard, causing flakes to fly. "You can't get none on credit?"

Sly shook his head sadly. "Naw, I did that the last time, remember?"

He watched as Mona's shoulders slumped and her bottom lip pushed out into a mild pout. Sticking his hand in his pocket, he fingered the small baggie that he had in there while he worked through the details of his plan.

After putting a word out in the streets that he was holding Mona hostage and would release her for a fee, it became obvious that Memphis didn't give a shit. Sly knew for a fact that he'd gotten word of it, but the street king made no moves to save his child's mother. At his wits end, Sly pulled out his last bit of coke and decided to have one last round of fun before he let Mona go. But in the midst of their high, Mona let it slip that her parents were rich, and his antennas went up. Sly worked her from there, getting her to admit that they had all kinds of expensive jewelry and shit in the house to go along with the mountains of cash in their bank accounts.

"Why don't you call your folks and get them to loan you some money?" he suggested. "They're rich, right? And you're their only child. I'm sure they'd give you whatever you ask for."

Mona thought about it for a second and then shook her head. She hadn't spoken to her parents in years because they'd cut her off financially the second she dropped out of college. It wasn't nothing that she spent time crying about, because once she had Memphis, she didn't need them anymore. In fact, they hadn't even met their granddaughter because she'd erased them from her mind and never looked back.

"They cut me off when I dropped out of college. My dad won't give me a thing."

Sly already knew that because she'd mentioned it the night before, but he continued to play along, running his finger over his chin as he pretended to think.

"I think I got a plan… If it works out how I think it should, your folks will still be rich, but you and I will have enough money to keep your nose candy supply from runnin' dry, and I can get back in the game. In less than a couple weeks, you'll be sportin' all that fly shit your sexy ass should be in."

Mona's eyes lit up and she smiled, giving Sly a glimpse of the woman she used to be before he'd fucked her over. His chest tinged with guilt as he thought about how he'd destroyed her, but he quickly pushed that away. In the game, there was no room for sympathy. For him, Mona was a means to an end, and he was almost where he needed to be. There was no turning back now.

"What's your plan?" Mona asked, and Sly wasted no time unfolding it to her. By the time he got to the end, her eyes were wide with fright, and she was wagging her head back and forth.

"I can't do that… What if they get hurt?"

"They won't," Sly assured her. "Me and my niggas do this type of shit all the time. It's as easy as takin' candy from a baby. You just do your part and we'll do ours, okay? We are only gonna get just what we need, and once we are done, I have a little celebratory gift for you."

He pulled the bag of dope from his pocket and waved it in front of Mona's face. Her eyes lit up like the sky on the Fourth of July, and she licked her lips hungrily. She winced and scratched at her skin, feeling itchy all over as if she'd been bitten by a swarm of mosquitoes.

"You promise they won't get hurt?" she asked Sly once again, although her mind was already made up to fall in line with his evil plan.

"I promise," he vowed with a nod. "We won't harm a hair on their head."

❧

TERRY AND HIS WIFE, VON, HAD NEVER BEEN THE BEST OF PARENTS, AND they attributed this to the fact that they'd married so young. When Von became pregnant at only sixteen from the spoiled, rich son of her father's boss, her father demanded that Terry marry his daughter and make an honest woman of her. Although he was young, Terry went ahead and married Von because he truly loved her and wanted to be with her forever. They both knew that their love would last, and they couldn't imagine life without each other. What they hadn't considered was that they weren't ready to be parents, but it was too late... their first child was on the way.

The same month that Mona was born, Terry's father died, and his company, as well as his wealth, went to his only son. Overnight, Terry and Von became multi-millionaires. But being so young, they weren't equipped with what it took to handle their newfound wealth, and it nearly destroyed them.

Most of Mona's childhood was spent with her being shipped away to private boarding schools so that her parents could travel and live their lives without her. With parents that were uninterested in anything she had going on, Mona's behavior was terrible, and she was kicked out of every school they sent her to. Instead of dealing with her behavior and realizing that she was acting out to get their attention, Terry and Von would simply ship her to another school once she was expelled from the one before.

By the time Mona hit high school, they had no more options of boarding schools to send her to because she'd gotten expelled from every single one. They reluctantly decided to bring her back home and send her to a school in Atlanta, which is where she met Baby. Having their daughter home didn't throw a wrench in their party plans. Terry and Von continued to throw lavish parties for all of their elite friends, snort mountains of cocaine, and cruise through life as Mona took care of herself.

Now it was years later, and there wasn't a day that Terry didn't regret the lack of positive influence that he'd had in his child's life. Being much older and much more mature, he wanted nothing other than to reach out to his only child and set things right so that he could be part of her life. The only problem was, he didn't know how. He had never developed a relationship with Mona as her father and didn't really know anything about her. He had no idea what he would even say to her to fix what he'd broken.

The exact moment that his doorbell rang, Terry was sitting in his favorite chair looking at a collection of photos that he hadn't even shown to his wife. Months ago, he'd hired a private investigator to track down Mona and was delighted to find out that not only was she married and living a wonderful, luxurious life, but she'd given birth to a child—his granddaughter. His heart wanted nothing more than to meet this beautiful child that looked so much like his baby did when she was little. He felt like he could have a chance to right his wrongs by being the best grandfather she could ever have, but the problem was... he didn't know where to start.

Pushing the photos back into the manila envelope, Terry sighed and stood up to see who it was at his door.

"You need me to get it?" Von called out from upstairs.

"No, I'm already—" he began, but when he saw the outline of a familiar figure through the French doors leading into their home, his words were snatched away, and his heart began to race. Wasting not a single second more, Terry raced to the door and pulled it open.

"Mona?" he gasped as he looked down into the eyes of his daughter.

She didn't look like herself... not even like the woman she appeared to be in the investigator's photos, but she was his daughter still. Her golden complexion seemed duller than usual, her hair a bit dry and messy, her eyes much dimmer than before, but she was his child, and he loved her. It seemed like a gift from God that she would show up at the exact moment he'd been thinking about her most.

"Daddy..." Mona began as she shifted back and forth in the Chanel heels that Sly had boosted from the mall the day before. "I—I know I haven't talked to you in a while but—"

Before she could say another word, Terry scooped her into his arms and held her tightly against his chest. Tears welled up in both of their eyes as they embraced. Neither one could remember the last time they'd ever hugged.

"Who is that at the—Mona!"

Once Von's eyes landed on the woman wrapped in her husband's arms, she immediately recognized her daughter and ran down the stairs. Tears of joy were already falling down her cheeks before she made it to them, and Terry opened his arms to accept his wife into their three-way embrace. The next few moments were spent with kisses and hugs circulating around as they all celebrated being joined together once again. Mona was shocked at how they'd greeted her because it was such a change from what she was used to. She'd never grown up in a house full of love, but that was exactly what she got once she returned home.

"Now tell us what has been happening in your life," Terry began, eager to hear about his granddaughter. He didn't want to mention that he already knew of her existence because he'd have to come clean to both Mona and Von about how he'd hired an investigator to track her down.

"Um..." Mona's eyes searched the ceiling. "Well, I'm married and—I have a daughter. Her name is Genie, which is short for Ginger. We came up with that name because she came out with a head full of red hair. It's not red anymore but..." Guilt flooded into her, and she squirmed in her seat as she thought about the daughter she'd abandoned. "She looks just like me."

"I have a grandbaby!" Von exclaimed, graciously clasping her hands together. "When can I meet her?"

Straightening his posture, Terry sat up to the edge of his seat, and both he and his wife planted their eyes on Mona's face as they waited anxiously for her to answer.

"Um..." Mona scratched with agitation at her neck. She felt uncomfortable and was fiending for a hit to get her nerves together. Closing her eyes, she took a deep breath and reminded herself that once all this was over, she would have everything she wanted right at her fingertips.

"You can meet her tomorrow," she effortlessly lied. "I can bring her by then. I just wanted to come first and make sure that everything is alright between us before I bring her by."

"Well, of course it is!" Terry replied before reaching out to grab his daughter's hand. "I know I hurt you… We didn't always make the best decisions when it came to you. But I'm sorry for all of that. I want nothing more than to make things right, Mona."

Nodding her head quietly, Mona felt her cheeks grow hot, and she squirmed even more. She was on edge. Although she didn't initially want to go along with Sly's plan, she did because she thought it would be easy. She had never really connected with her parents on any level and had always harbored a grudge against them for the way they dealt with her as a child. They had been strangers to her for the most part… strangers who simply shoved money at her so that she could buy everything she wanted. But now she was seeing that the love she'd always wanted from them was available.

I can't do this.

She couldn't go through with the plan, and she had to tell Sly to call off his goons. There was no way she could be part of what he was about to do. As she looked into Terry and Von's eyes, she felt safe enough to come clean and tell them all of her mistakes. She didn't feel like they'd judge her for them. They could help her get her life together and right her wrongs.

"I have to… I think I need to use the bathroom," Mona said and then rushed away with her cell phone in hand.

Locking the bathroom door behind her, she dialed Sly's number and waited until he picked up on the other line.

"Hey, Sugarlips, you made it in?"

She squeezed her eyes closed and sunk down to the floor, pressing her forehead against the top of her knees.

"I can't do this, Sly… You gotta call off the plan."

"What!" he shot back with so much force that she almost fumbled the phone. "Da fuck you mean 'call off the plan'? I stole all that shit for you to wear, spent all my muthafuckin' money to fly you all the way the hell out to Bubblefuck Land—I got my goons waitin' and ready to hit a lick after promisin' them niggas that I'll make it worth their time, and you askin' me to pull out? Hell *fuck* naw!"

Mona's bottom lip began to tremble. She could barely think

straight. If only she had something to mellow her mood, she could come up with something else they could do to get the money. Something that didn't involve anything Sly had told her that he wanted to do.

"I—I don't know if I can do it. They... they were happy to see me and—I don't want them hurt!"

Sensing that Mona was flipping out which was bad for business, Sly calmed down and changed his approach. He knew that it was stupid to trust a junkie in the first place, but there had been no other way.

"Aye, baby, calm down. I told you that I wasn't gonna hurt them, and I meant that shit, aight?" he started, pacifying her with the gentleness of his tone. "I would never hurt your folks because I know how much they mean to you. Just do what we came out here to do, and I'll handle the rest. By the end of the night, you'll have your reward, and we'll be sleepin' in a fuckin' five-star hotel with a smile on our face."

"Okay," Mona agreed quietly.

"I just need you to play it cool, okay? You'll have the rest of your life to fix shit with mommy and daddy. Actually... after this bullshit is over, it might bring you all closer. They'll never want to let you out of their sight again."

The final nails were hammered into the coffin. Mona's deepest desire at one time was for a family that truly loved her, and she was so close to getting it, along with everything else she ever wanted.

"I'll be ready," was the last thing she said before she hung up the phone.

§

IT WAS THREE IN THE MORNING WHEN TERRY AND VON WERE EACH snatched up out of their beds by masked intruders holding loaded guns.

"You say one fuckin' word and I'll kill you, bitch!" Sly whispered harshly into Von's ear as he pushed a .44 caliber pistol against her temple.

"Don't be on no brave shit, old man," his partner said to Terry whose face was contorted with fear and anger as he looked at his wife being held at gunpoint.

As Sly and his homeboy held their weapons to the couple's heads, his other three boys got to work tying them up to chairs that they'd pulled up from the dining room. Once they were strapped into place, Sly signaled one of his men to grab Mona and bring her in. A few minutes later, the man reappeared holding Mona in his arms with the barrel of his gun pressed against her head.

"No! Don't hurt her, please!" Von yelled. She began to get frantic and started twisting and squirming with all her might, attempting to loosen the rope on her arms so that she could help save her child. Terry was less emotional than Von and more of a thinker, so his response was more calculated. These were robbers, and he felt like he knew exactly what they wanted. Maybe if he gave it to them, they would let them all go.

"Please... I know you want money, and we have lots of it. Please, just don't hurt my daughter," he said with a calm voice, trying to appeal to their desire.

An evil grin rose up on Sly's lips as he realized his plan was working out perfectly. It was even easier than he'd thought it would be. With Terry's help, his man worked the room, collecting all of Terry and Von's jewelry as well as anything else of value. With wide, horrified eyes, Von bit down on her bottom lip when she felt one of the men tugging at her wedding ring. It slipped off her finger, and she hung her head in despair, sobbing silently as the intruders took everything.

"I know you got a safe in here with some money in it," Sly pressed, leaning on the information that Mona had given him. "Tell me where it's at and the combination. And it better be some money inside, or I'mma blow this bitch's brains out."

He shoved the barrel of his gun so hard against Mona's skull that he broke the skin, and a droplet of blood trickled down her face. When she winced in pain, he knocked the butt of his weapon against the top of her head, and she nearly fell unconscious.

"Stop! I'll give you everything you want. But you have to untie me... The safe has a thumbprint scanner. It's the only way it'll open."

"So why don't I just cut off your fuckin' thumb?" one of Sly's men suggested, immediately waking Mona from her dazed and confused state.

"No!" she screamed. She snatched her neck up and stared at Sly with eyes stretched wide with panic. "You can't hurt them! You said you wouldn't hur—"

Before she could finish her statement, he slammed the butt of his gun against her head once more to silence her, and her body went limp as she fell unconscious.

"Stupid bitch," he muttered under his breath. She'd almost fucked up his plan that quickly, but he was a man of his word, if nothing else. He wouldn't hurt her parents.

"Untie him and let him open the safe," he commanded one of his men.

Von watched in horror as they grabbed her husband, untied him, and roughly snatched him up from his seat. Terry told them where the safe was and they waited with guns aimed at him, Von, and also at Mona, for him to unlock it so they could see what was inside.

"Damn," was all Sly could say when he feasted his eyes upon the stacks and stacks of green neatly strapped up inside. His lips melted into a grin. It was more money than he'd ever seen at one time in his life. Definitely much more than he needed to buy a few bricks to get his empire back on track. Everybody who had ever counted him out would bow before him.

That muthafucka Memphis will be first in line, he thought to himself. In the midst of his greed, he'd apparently lost some of his marbles because everyone knew Memphis bowed to no one.

"Get it all," Sly said, and his man went to work stuffing all of the cash inside of bags.

As they stacked all the money into bags, Terry's mind went to work for something he could do. He was the man of the house, and his family was in danger. The money, he couldn't care less about, but he couldn't live another day if something were to happen to either his daughter or his wife. There was a possibility that the robbers would simply take what he had to give and leave, but there was an even greater chance that they would rob them blind and kill them still. He couldn't sit back and risk losing two of the women most important to him.

And so he waited for the perfect opportunity to reach into the drawer of the small desk next to where he stood, watching the men stack his hard-earned cash into their bags and grabbed the small gun inside. The moment his fingers touched the cold metal, a surge of courage and strength entered his body, and he knew then he was ready to do what he had to do. Gritting his teeth, he snatched the weapon into his hands and held it up at the exact moment that Mona regained consciousness. The first thing she saw was the look of determination on her father's face as he bit down on his bottom lip and bravely held the gun with both of his hands.

"Daddy, no!" she screamed, making Sly turn to see what was happening around him.

"Fuck! He's got a gun!" a man yelled, and everyone's weapons went up in the air.

Shots were fired!

Pow! Pow! Pow! Pow!

The entire room filled with the sound and sulfuric scent of gunfire, and Mona hugged the ground, wailing to the top of her lungs for it to stop. She screamed continuously until her throat felt raw, but even still, she didn't stop. With her face pressed into the ground, she continued to howl out her sorrows. She was too afraid to look up because she didn't know what sight would be waiting for her once she did.

"Get up. We gotta get out of here *now*."

The voice belonged to Sly, and before she could fully process what he was saying, he was grabbing her by the arm and pulling her up to her feet. He tried to tug her out of the door before she got a chance to see anything around her, but she fought against him. The second she saw the carnage surrounding them, she felt her soul rip to pieces. She let out an agonizing scream that was so emotion-filled it nearly brought a man as evil as Sly to his knees.

"You said you wouldn't hurt them!" she cried, fighting against him as he pulled her away. Her father's bullet-ridden body lay only a few feet away from her mother's. The positioning of their lifeless figures making it seem as if Terry had spent his last breath attempting to reach out to his wife.

"It was an accident," Sly gritted through his teeth as he fought with Mona, holding her tight so that he could get her out the house before the police arrived. There wasn't a single doubt in his mind that someone had called the police by now. They didn't have a lot of time; in neighborhoods like these, the police came faster than a young nigga going balls deep in some pussy for the first time. Too much time had already been wasted as it was.

"It wasn't a fuckin' accident!" Mona shouted.

Rage flooded into her as if it had been injected through her veins. Turning to Sly, she began to kick and punch him with all her might, hitting him wherever she could. She was hysterical, gnashing her teeth at him and nearly foaming at the mouth like a rabid animal as she tossed punch after punch. She wanted to kill him and then turn the gun on herself to escape from the misery of what she'd done.

Sly fought with Mona and dodged her hits as much as he could while he carried her down the stairs. He could have just killed her, but he couldn't bring himself to do it. Although he'd committed many callous acts, he wasn't as heartless as he seemed, or she thought. Never once had he planned on Mona's family getting hurt; he'd simply saw an easy lick, and he went for it. If the old man hadn't grabbed a gun and tried to fire on his crew, everything would have gone according to plan. It wasn't his fault.

"I hate you! I fuckin' hate you!" Mona cursed as she continued to fight while he struggled to control her. In the far distance, he heard sirens and knew his time was running thin.

"Sly... them folks are on the way. We gotta get da fuck outta here," one of his men said, and he nodded his head.

Raising his gun, he slammed his weapon next to the first knot he'd planted on Mona's skull and made a twin. The force of his blow knocked her out cold. Her body went limp, and he adjusted her in his arms, cradling her before he made his quick escape out of the house.

"Shit!" he cursed, punching the back of the passenger seat as they drove away.

During the gun battle, he'd lost a soldier, so Mona wasn't the only one grieving. He closed his eyes and pressed his fingers hard against his eyelids, forcing his emotions at bay. The niggas he'd called to run up in Mona's parents' crib with him were the same niggas he'd grown up with. They were the only ones still loyal to him after he fell off. Losing one was like losing a brother. His heart was bleeding.

"You should've killed that broad," his homeboy who was driving said. "She might talk."

"She won't."

Although he wasn't sure of that, Sly wouldn't hear anything of killing Mona. Even though she might never forgive him for what had happened that evening, she'd done what he'd needed, and she was the reason that he was finally able to get back in the game. He'd taken everything from her, and he felt compelled to at least give her a little bit of her old life back once he got on his feet again.

"I'm sorry," he whispered as he stroked her hair.

Lying in his lap, he figured that Mona was still unconscious, but he was wrong. She was sitting still, crying quietly as her heart bled inside of her chest. She heard his apology, but it was not enough. As soon as they made it back to D.C., she planned to leave.

CHAPTER TWENTY-THREE

For the first time, Baby held Memphis's hand without worrying whether or not it was the right or the wrong thing to do. She didn't care who saw them, who knew about their history, or who would pass judgment on the nature of their relationship. She just knew that she loved the man next to her, and he needed her right then more than he'd ever needed anyone before.

They sat in a cold room, enveloped in a painful silence. The pungent odor of antiseptic and bleach burned Baby's nostrils, and the bright, fluorescent lights stung her weary eyes, but she didn't complain. These were the least of her worries.

A door ahead of them opened, and Memphis was the first one to shoot to his feet. Lifting her head, Baby stood as well, so quickly that her sneakers squeaked against the shiny linoleum floors. Genie's physician walked over to them with his head lifted but with down-turned eyes that revealed more than he meant for them to.

For all of Genie's life, Carl had been her doctor, and throughout the years, he'd been consistently and pleasantly surprised at the fight in the young child. Every single limitation that his research told him she should have, she'd pushed through, miraculously beating the odds. It pained his soul to see her in the current state that she was in, and it was even more gut-wrenching to have to explain to her father that there was nothing he could do.

"It seems that Genie has pneumonia," he said with sad eyes. "We are giving her fluids and some pain medication to keep her comfortable."

"Comfortable?" Cleo repeated, stepping from behind Memphis as she took a step closer to the doctor. "What about something to make her better?"

Carl pulled his lips into his mouth for a minute as he thought about the best way to deliver bad news to a family he knew had experienced more than their share of trauma over the years. Taking a deep breath, he lifted his head and looked directly into Memphis's eyes but had to pause once more when he saw the hopelessness in them. Being a man, Memphis understood before Carl even said a word that his little girl was in grave danger... the kind of danger that he was powerless to protect her from.

"It's bacterial pneumonia which can be deadly to anyone, especially children Genie's age," he said, sighing again. "But the thing is... the medication that Genie takes for her cancer has her immune system severely compromised which puts her at a disadvantage to fight the bacteria in her body. This is why the sickness is taking hold so rapidly. Her health is declining at a rate much quicker than normal. Her lungs are—"

"That's enough," Memphis said, stopping him.

Carl's mouth snapped closed, and Cleo let out a loud sob before walking to the far corner behind them to cry in peace. Baby tried to keep her composure as much as she could, but the way that Memphis was grasping her hand for dear life told her that, although his expression was blank, and his demeanor seemed calm, his heart was breaking inside. Using her other hand, she brushed away the tears streaming down her cheeks and tried to stay strong.

"What can you do?" Memphis asked the question with an even tone.

Anyone who didn't know him would be asking themselves what kind of man was this who could stand strong as a soldier while hearing that the one person he loved more than life was suffering. But to the ones who knew him, it was understood that this was all an act. Memphis was broken inside; he was just strong enough to not let it show.

"I—I..." Under intense pressure, Carl began to stutter. "I gave her antibiotics to treat the bacteria, but there's been no improvement. If we had caught it when she was first brought in, we could have—"

Realizing that he was putting his foot in his mouth, Carl stopped talking abruptly. He felt Memphis's eyes on him, and his cheeks went warm. His eyes searched the ground, and he found himself wishing that there was a hole in the ground big enough for him to jump into.

"If you would've caught it, then what?" Memphis snapped. Releasing Baby's hand, he walked closer so that he stood toe-to-toe with Carl, glaring right into his face. Baby's lips parted as she looked back and forth between the two men, on edge while she waited for what would happen next. Even Cleo had stopped crying and was watching them intently.

"Um..." Carl eyes shifted as he cleared his throat. "Well, you brought Genie to us late Friday night. The physician on call read her chart and went through normal protocols based on her past medical history. He thought her symptoms were related to her cancer... He didn't think to check for pneumonia."

The entire room went silent as everyone processed what it was that Carl was saying. The tension in the room was so strong that the man could barely breathe. Carl was no dummy. He knew exactly who Memphis was. In fact, he knew about Memphis the first time he met him, when Genie was only a small child, because his reputation preceded him. However, in none of their interactions had Memphis ever behaved like the hardened, merciless criminal that Carl had heard him to be, so there'd never been a reason for fear.

This was the day that all that changed. It was all he could do not to shrink under Memphis's hardened glare. Lifting his hand, he grasped the cross on the end of the thin, gold chain he wore around his neck and said a simple prayer that he would make it home that night.

"Why didn't they call you as soon as she was brought here? You're her doctor, and we established a long time ago that nobody was supposed to touch my daughter without your approval."

Carl pressed his lips together, forming a straight line, and then nodded. "That's true. But that's not the normal protocol; that's simply what we've done. The weekend staff didn't know that—"

"So because the muthafuckas you got workin' in here don't know shit, my daughter might die. Is that what you're tellin' me?"

Memphis took a step closer so that he and Carl were now nearly standing nose-to-nose and glared into him with a stare so vicious, Carl was convinced he had daggers going through his skull. The heat of Memphis's wrath was swirling around them, silencing both Cleo and Baby to the point that all they could do was watch everything unfolding before them with wide eyes.

"N—no, I'm saying that... I mean, I didn't think that—"

A hollow but malicious chuckle pushed through Memphis's lips, and looking away, he flicked the bridge of his nose before turning back to Carl.

"I already know you don't fuckin' think," he spat savagely without ever raising his voice. "Listen, I'mma need that muthafucka's information tonight. The one who fucked over my daughter."

"Memphis..." Baby started, placing her hand on his shoulder to comfort him, but he simply batted it away without even turning in her direction. She took a few steps back, realizing that at the moment, the man she knew and loved had left the building. She was getting a front row seat to witness the menace that stood at the helm of a team of street savages known as the Murda Mob.

"I—I can't give you... Dr. Franklin is a good doctor, he just..." Carl's mouth gaped open like a fish out of water as he lost his words. He was being pushed into a place that no doctor ever wanted to be in.

"I ain't ask you to shoot me that muthafucka's credentials. It's all too late for that," Memphis told him coolly, the tense smile on his face about as congenial to Carl as it would be if it were on the face of a hungry lion.

"But I—"

"Listen, if you make me ask again, I'mma have matching toe-tags made for you and that nigga. Choice is yours."

After laying down the law, Memphis sat down quietly, and Carl knew that was his signal to leave and do as told. In less than five minutes, he was back with his colleague's full biographical sheet, complete with addresses, phone numbers, and information for next of kin. He didn't need any evidence of Memphis's past crimes to know of his power and understand that every threat that passed through his lips was more like a sincere promise.

"This is everything you requested," Carl said, pushing the papers into Memphis's hands once he returned to the room. Memphis rolled them up and stuffed them in his pocket.

"Now show me to my daughter."

❧

BABY PRESSED HER FINGERTIPS AGAINST HER LIPS AS SHE FOUGHT HER emotions. She wiped away her own tears while Cleo sobbed quietly beside her. In front of them, Memphis was standing at Genie's bedside, holding her hand as she slept peacefully. She looked so frail, her body so small. Her skin was an ashen gray, and her beautiful curls were far less vibrant than they'd been before.

Looking down at his baby girl, Memphis felt like he'd lost his soul. His tired eyes were red from stress, heartbreak, and grief. He was broken, and only God could keep him from falling apart.

The door to Genie's room opened, but he didn't flinch nor did he look away from his daughter's face; something not typical at all of him. Paranoia was a symptom of being raised in the streets the way he had, which meant that your head stayed on swivel, making sure that you scoped out everything happening around you so that a nigga never caught you slipping. But in this moment, Memphis wasn't worried about all that. If someone wanted to gun him down, this moment would be the ideal time because he didn't care about whether or not he'd make it another day. His heart was leaving him, and the body couldn't survive without the heart.

"Aye, Mama, good to see you," Laz said, greeting Cleo as he walked into the room.

"Good to see you too, son," she said with tears in her eyes and gave him a hug. "I just wish the circumstances were different."

Laz knew there was nothing comforting that he could say, so he simply gave her hand a firm squeeze and kissed her on her cheek. Turning to Baby, he gave her a curt nod of a greeting and then walked slowly up to stand next to Memphis, the man he beheld as a brother.

"You handle that?" Memphis asked, his eyes never leaving Genie's face.

"Yezzur," Laz replied.

Nodding his head, Memphis fell silent, retreating back into his thoughts. Even though he now knew the man responsible for his daughter's sickness had met his end, he still found no peace. He would never find peace.

The door opened once again, and Carl walked in. Unknown to them, he'd been pacing back and forth in his office for nearly a half hour, mentally preparing himself for what he now had to tell Memphis. Clearing his throat, he squared his shoulders and began to speak.

"I got back the test results that I needed. Unfortunately, I—"

"How long?" Memphis cut in, already knowing what was coming next.

Every heart in the room stopped, and every eye turned to look at Memphis once they realized what it was that he was asking. With her mouth open and fresh tears in her eyes, Baby covered her mouth with her hand to stifle her sobs.

Carl took a deep breath and started wringing his hands together.

"Three days," he replied. "Maybe four... but no more than that. Her organs have already begun to shut down. We can try to slow it down, but that's all we can do. I'm so—so very sorry."

Even though he knew that it might put him in the line of his wrath, Carl placed his hand on Memphis's shoulder to give him some consolation. He didn't push him away or fight against the embrace because he had no fight left in him. He was nothing more than an empty shell.

Carl left, and time seemed to slow as Memphis stood unmoving, holding his daughter's hand with his head down and his eyes closed. He knew that sometime soon, the warmth in them would no longer be there, and he wanted to remember this moment for the rest of his days.

"Get out," he whispered after about an hour.

Crumpling his brows, Laz stood up, knowing he'd heard Memphis say something but unsure of what it was he'd said.

"What was that, boss?"

"Get out!" Memphis shouted, making them all jump.

Turning to the two women in the room, Laz waved his hand toward the door.

"Okay, Mama and Baby, y'all come with me. I'll get y'all something to eat right quick."

Nodding quietly, Cleo walked out of the room, but Baby paused and glanced in Memphis's direction. She could see that her man was hurting, and she had no idea what she could do to make it better for him.

There isn't anything you can do.

With a sigh, Baby turned to leave but stopped as she passed him by. Reaching out, she grabbed his hand and gave it a gentle squeeze… just enough to let him know that she was there. There wasn't a thing she could do, but she wanted him to know that she was here for him and would always be.

"Wait," he said just as she released his hand and began to walk away. She halted mid-step and turned back around.

"Yes?"

"You stay," he replied without looking away from Genie. She mired, looked at Laz to make sure that he'd heard the same thing she did, but then Memphis turned to look at her. The distress in his eyes almost broke her down to her knees.

"You stay," he repeated once more. "I need you."

She nodded, and Laz did as well. Giving Baby a light pat on the back, Laz walked out the door feeling slightly more content knowing that his boy had someone to help him through this dark time.

CHAPTER TWENTY-FOUR

Once they landed in D.C., Sly checked into the same hotel he'd first put Mona in, hoping that a little bit of luxury and nice things would make her feel at least a little better about the terrible night they'd had. He opened the door and said nothing as she walked slowly inside, her head hanging nearly between her shoulders, and darted straight to the bed. She lay down and covered her head with the white silk sheets, then tugged her aching body into fetal position.

"I know I can't do shit to bring ya folks back, but I can give you this," Sly said, tossing the small bag of coke on the bed next to her. "I'll have more when I come back."

With a duffle bag full of blood money hanging over his shoulder, he started to walk to the door but stopped before he left out. Even though he felt guilty for how things had turned out, he had to play it smart. No matter how he felt about the situation, he still didn't really know Mona well enough to really trust her. Before leaving, he spewed poison from his lips.

"If you're thinking about turning rat, just know that you will go down, too. Shit didn't turn out how we wanted it to, but you played your part just like everyone else did."

The reminder renewed Mona's pain. She squeezed her eyes shut and bit down hard on her tongue until she tasted her own blood. Raw with guilt, she wanted to come clean to rid herself of the burden of her mistakes, but she would never. She would die with this secret before she let anyone know that she was the reason for her parents' demise. But even knowing that, she was still certain she had to leave Sly for good. There was no place for her in D.C. with the man who would be a constant reminder of the blood on her hands.

After counting to one hundred twice, she jumped up and ran to the door to leave. Thinking again, she ran back, stuffed the baggie of cocaine in her pocket, and then sprinted out the door. She vowed to kick her habit eventually, but until then, she would resort to her usual remedies for easing her pain.

Without looking at her surroundings, Mona ran full speed ahead through the lobby of the hotel, thankful that it was nearly empty since it was so early in the morning. She pelted straight out the front double doors, squinting when harsh, frigid air blew over her face. Her feet hit the pavement, and she attempted to speed up her pace, but her foot caught on something and she tumbled forward, smacking headfirst into the concrete sidewalk.

"Ugh!" she groaned. A sticky substance was leaking from her nose, and she knew it was blood. Pain radiated through her skull as her nose continued to gush. It had to be broken.

"I knew you couldn't fuckin' be trusted!" Sly spat before pulling her up by her hair. "I tried to give you a little treat, but you've proven once again that you ain't worth shit."

As Mona grimaced and whimpered quietly, Sly dragged her to his car by her hair. He had no mercy, gripping her tresses firmly and nearly yanking them free from her head until he opened the passenger door and carelessly flung her in. Everything about how he was acting made it seem like he hated Mona, but it wasn't true. The fact that she'd been so instrumental in him getting back on top earned her a bit of his loyalty, but when she'd tried to run off on him, that devotion flitted away.

"You shitted on everyone who could help you! All you got is me, and now you wanna shit on me, too?" Sly roared as he sped through the streets heading back to his home. "Should've known you would take the first chance you got to go and run your mouth."

"I wasn't going to tell anyone anything!" Mona yelled out. "I just wanted to leave. I wanna go hoooome."

"Bitch, that's where I'm about to take yo' stankin' ass right now!"

Dragging her into the house that had been her prison for weeks before, Sly cursed the entire way, telling her how much she wasn't worth shit and how he would've looked out for her if she could just prove she'd stay down. She tried to fight back when he started to put the rope around her wrists, and it only angered him anymore. What Mona didn't know was that Sly had been using drugs right along with her, in order to escape his own misery. In the weeks that he'd succeeded in making her dependent on drugs, he'd developed an addiction of his own. His erratic behavior and fiery temper was due to more than just her own actions; he was fiending for a hit, and dealing with her was holding him up.

Whap! Whap! Whap!

Reaching back, Sly bitch-slapped the saliva from her tongue before pummeling her with punch after punch, beating her into submission. The interesting thing was that Mona was at the lowest point in her life; she seemingly had nothing to lose, but she was fighting harder than she ever had in all her years. Still, she was no match for Sly's strength, especially once he began to beat her in the same way he would another man.

"Oomph!" She grunted when he lifted his foot and started stomping her out. Her insides seemed to split in half. There wasn't a single part of her body that didn't burn like it was on fire. She dropped her fists and curled her body into a ball, but he still attacked her, stomping and kicking until she was nothing but a bloody mess on the old, cracked tile floor.

"Look what da fuck you made me do!"

Hovering over the top of Mona's body, Sly felt himself begin to panic. In his anger, he'd gone overboard, but it was never his intent to truly hurt her. He had gotten carried away, and from the looks of it, she'd need more than time to heal her wounds. If he didn't get her medical attention, he wasn't sure she'd make it.

"Fuck," he cursed, running his hand over the top of his head. This wasn't the way he'd wanted the day to go, but there was nothing he could do. Taking her to the hospital was out of the question.

"I'll—I'll be back later," Sly told her before turning and walking out the front door.

He felt bad about what he'd done, but there was no going back now, and he still had business to conduct. In the duffle bag over his shoulder, he had more than enough money to buy all the keys of coke that he needed to take over every block in his city.

❧

EVERY SQUARE INCH OF MONA'S BODY WAS RADIATING FROM PAIN. Never in life had she gotten beaten in the way Sly had abused her. Nothing about her was weak—she'd never been the type of woman who was comfortable taking shit from anybody. But in this moment, she felt her mind start to play tricks on her, telling her that she would be better off if she stayed with Sly for fear that he would end up killing her if she tried to leave.

Thinking about her parents, she felt her face get wet with tears. She truly felt like she had no one she could depend on.

Memphis, she thought, thinking back to the man who had cared for her enough to marry her.

Fresh tears came to her eyes when she thought about the life of privilege that she'd abandoned only to wind up where she was now, in her state of utter despair.

The crazy thing about life was that when you had something, it was easy to take it for granted, but as soon as you lost it, you realized how much it really meant to you. That was exactly how she felt about Memphis and her family. Even though Baby had betrayed her, she knew that Memphis would never turn away the mother of his only child. He would welcome her back with open arms if it was best for

Genie. He did anything for that little girl, and Mona banked on that love being what would free her from this situation.

"Ugh!"

Groaning, she took her time and was eventually able to stand. Her entire body felt like she had shards of glass pushing through it. Every step that she took seemed like it would be her last, but she fueled herself with strength by thinking on how happy she would be once she got her life back on track. All of the complaints she had about Memphis's treatment of her and wanting to get out of the game to live a regular life, no longer seemed valid. It was just the whining of a woman who didn't know how good she had it.

By the time that Sly made it back in, Mona had bathed, changed her clothes, and cleaned the blood off of her face. She was bruised and swollen in so many places that she barely recognized herself when she stared at her reflection in the mirror. Tears ran down her cheeks, and as she swatted them away, she tried to push all of her regrets from her mind. In such a short time, so much had changed, and she felt like she had grown so much.

"Damn," Sly said as soon as he saw her. Walking up, he touched her gently on the side of the face, and she flinched.

"I didn't mean to do all this. You just made me so fuckin' mad. I know I've done a lot of shit that was wrong, but I was down bad and lookin' for a come up. You're the reason I was able to come up, and I owe you for that. But I can't let you just leave though… not right now. You feel me?"

His eyes pried into her face, but Mona couldn't bring herself to lift her head to look at him. There was so much hate in her heart for Sly that she could barely stand to even be so close to him. With every second that she thought about the things wrong in her life, she hated him more for being the reason it all had gone so sour so fast. If she'd never met him, her parents would be alive, and she would still be happily married to Memphis and living the good life.

"Let me try to make it better," Sly offered, and his fingertips dropped down to her round breasts.

Mona bit the inside of her cheek as he touched her, fondling her nipples, before running his hand down her side and under her shirt. The second his hand grazed her skin, she felt a bitter, sickly taste in the back of her throat and thought she would vomit. He dropped to his knees and pulled down her shorts, exposing her lower lips and she winced. When he pushed his face forward and slipped his tongue between her thighs, she had to cover her mouth to stop from retching. She hated him to the point that every second she had to endure was torture.

"Let's go to the bedroom," Sly mumbled, his breath heating her thighs.

She didn't say a word, but he seemed satisfied with that as he got up and grabbed her hand to lead her down the hall. Mona followed quietly, feeling like nothing but a shell of her former self. A tear escaped her eye and ran down her cheek, but she couldn't even find the strength to brush it away. The man that she detested more than anyone in the world was about to violate her body in the worst way, and there was nothing she could do about it.

"Don't cry, mama," Sly whispered once he faced her and saw the tears in her eyes. "I just want to make you feel good. Let daddy take care of you."

The mention of 'daddy' was like a dagger through Mona's heart, and she gasped in pain as if she'd really felt the blade. Starting with her neck, Sly began kissing her body and running his fingers between her thighs as Mona's mind ran rampant. There was no way she could let him do this to her. She had to stop this sick man from touching her ever again.

"Let me do you." Mona forced the words out through her teeth. Sly was so eager for the blessing, he totally missed the curse in the delivery. It had been a minute since he'd been able to experience Mona's superb head game, and he was definitely in the mood for some sloppy toppy.

"Hold on. Let me get on the bed so you can give it to me good," he enthused, kicking off his jeans in a hurry.

Oh, I'm going to give it to you good alright, Mona thought as she helped him out of his jeans and eyed the handle of the Glock sticking

279

out his back pocket. He was so transfixed by his lusty thoughts that he didn't even see her reaching for it. Grabbing his pole with one hand, Mona swallowed down the bile in her throat as she massaged his tool, further igniting his thirst to be between her jaws.

"Go on and kiss it, baby," he coaxed her.

"Okay. Get ready," Mona breathed out just as her fingers circled around the handle of the gun. She snatched it up, and before Sly could even open his eyes to see what the delay was, she had the barrel pointed directly at his chest.

"I'm about to give you exactly what you deserve," she hissed as she stood slowly, keeping the gun pointed. Confused, Sly frowned slightly before opening his eyes. When he saw the gun aimed at him, the blood drained from his face, and his eyes widened with panic.

"Aye, you don't wanna do this, Mona," he started, holding his hand up. "Give me that gun. You're no killer."

Taking a few steps back, Mona shook her head as tears fell down her cheeks. She was finally getting the breakthrough that she'd been praying for. This was the moment that she would set things right.

"You destroyed my entire life! I'm giving you what you deserve," she told him. Sly gave her a blank look before a malicious sneer crossed his lips. He bared his teeth and narrowed his eyes into slits before speaking.

"As usual, you're so fuckin' stupid. You wanna blame everybody but yourself for the shit that's happened to you, but the truth is that you've brought all this shit on yourself. When I first saw you, I knew you'd be an easy one to fool because you were so full of your damn self and was so jealous of your friend. You had everything but still wanted more... you're never satisfied! You even set up your own fuckin' parents. You're rotten just like me, Mona. No one else will want you. You left your own daughter to be with a nigga who ain't even give a shit about you. Shit... you was *married* to a nigga who ain't give a shit about you. They'll be disgusted by you."

Mona's bottom lip trembled, but her heart wasn't in the right place in order to accept the truth he was spitting to her. In her self-absorbed, narcissistic mind, she still reasoned that she'd done nothing wrong. Outside of fighting for her own happiness, she'd committed no crimes. Wanting to be happy couldn't possibly be wrong, right?

Sly saw the turmoil in her eyes and knew that his words had affected her. He decided it was the perfect time to make a move. Lurching forward, he snatched for the gun but startled Mona, whose finger was already on the trigger. With a surprised squawk, she panicked and pressed down.

Pow!

The bullet went through Sly's chest, searing his skin and inflicting more pain than his brain could fully process.

"Arrrgh!" he yelled, pressing his hand to his bloody wound.

Falling back on the bed, his wide eyes focused on the ceiling as his entire upper body was covered with blood. Mona dropped the gun and pressed her hands to the side of her head in anguish as she watched him stare at something that seemed faraway in the distance while his lifeline left him. He was dying and she'd killed him. She was a murderer.

"Oh God," she whispered as her eyes darted frantically around the room.

There was no way she could leave him like this. She'd been in the house alone with him for weeks; her DNA was all over. Once the police investigated, it would be all too easy to pin her as the killer.

Running into the kitchen with her thoughts swirling like a spinning top, she searched for something—anything—that could help her. It wasn't until she opened the pantry that she was hit with an idea. There in front of her were a couple cans of fuel amongst some grilling materials. She scooped them all within her arms and began sprinkling the liquid all over the house, ending with the room that Sly's body was in.

Once she was finished, she looked at him and could barely contain the excitement she felt at seeing his lifeless body on the bed with his eyes closed. After being at his mercy for so long, she was finally victorious. She rummaged through his jeans and found a knot of cash as well as a lighter and a box of matches. It was exactly what she needed, and she acknowledged it like a gift from God. He was telling her that she was doing exactly what He wanted her to.

"Right plan, wrong bitch," she spat as she held the lit match in her hands, regarding Sly for the very last time.

With a smile on her face, she dropped it to her feet, and the room erupted into flames. It was like a weight lifted from off her back when she saw the sheets of the bed ignite around Sly's body. Everything in her wanted to stay and watch his body burn, giving him hell on Earth before he spent the rest of eternity rubbing shoulders with satan, but she had to make it out before it took her too.

"See you in hell," she whispered and blew him a sweet kiss before turning on her heels. Precariously, she shielded herself from the smoke and fled from the room, then out of the house with his keys in hand.

By the time the house burned to the ground, she was on the highway driving with the windows down and the music high, singing happily to the top of her lungs. She was finally free.

CHAPTER TWENTY-FIVE

"*M*emphis, all tests say that Genie is doing even better than can be expected... Why don't you go home to shower, change, and get something to eat?" Carl suggested as he walked into Genie's room.

The sorrow in his eyes was too much to hide as he looked at Memphis, who was sitting by his daughter's bedside, his sad eyes rimmed red with distress and grief.

"I'm not going anywhere," Memphis reputed and shook his head. "She's going to wake up... I know it, and I want to be here when she does."

Carl pressed his lips together and thought carefully about his next words. His trained eyes easily surmised that the more Memphis pushed away sleep, food, and taking care of himself, the worst off he would be until he would be the one in a hospital bed being cared for. But how could he tell a father to leave his dying daughter's bedside? Thankfully, Baby saw the concern that Carl had for Memphis's well-being because she was the only one who could get through to the mourning street king.

"Memphis... I'm worried about you. It's been days and you haven't left here. You've had nothing to eat and nothing to drink. I need you to come with me and let me take care of you. We can come right back after, okay?"

When he didn't say anything in response, she pressed her hand against his back and began to rub gently. Something about her touch gave him peace even in the most devastating of situations. He didn't want to leave Genie's side for a single second, but he also knew that his strength was fading, and fatigue was setting in. If she came to —*when* she came to—he didn't want Genie to see him in anguish. He wanted to be the father that she knew, because he didn't need his baby girl to worry.

"Okay," was the only word that he could get out, but it was enough to send a jolt of relief through Baby's heart.

"Okay," she repeated with a nod of her head. "Let me call Ms. Donaldson to see if she can stay with Genie while we are gone."

Growing up in the hood and seeing the devastation that plagued his family as well as his neighborhood had hardened Memphis's heart to the point that he didn't experience emotions the way most would consider 'normal.' He had little to no regard for the lives of people who he felt deserved to feel his wrath and felt no guilt about extinguishing them and their family members without a blink of an eye. He was used to pushing his own needs and desires to the side in order to fulfill his responsibility to the streets, and he suppressed his own emotions with ease after years of training himself to feel nothing. But now he was experiencing a situation that he wasn't equipped to deal with. He was at the brink of losing his mind. His heart was torn, and the immense pressure of appearing strong for everyone around him was destroying him.

Baby could see that Memphis's soul was crumbling right before her very eyes, and although she was also hurting, she knew that her own pain couldn't measure up to his. In this moment, he needed her strength because his was nearly gone. When a man was at his lowest, the only person who could lift him high is the woman that is by his side. She was that woman for him.

"Let me bathe you," she said, grabbing Memphis's hand. He didn't say a word, but he allowed her to lead him into the master bathroom.

His mind was so full of thoughts regarding his child that he had no room to consider anything else. Luckily, Baby would think for him and tend to his every need so that he didn't need to.

She ran the water in the shower until it was the perfect temperature and undressed Memphis carefully, running her hands over his body as she did it to provide him with some comfort. He didn't speak, but he closed his eyes and enjoyed the love that oozed from her fingertips. Her tenderness enveloped him and was a small form of reprieve from his sorrow. Grabbing his hand, she led him to the shower and watched as he stepped in. The water beat down on his body, trailing every muscular curve of his perfectly crafted physique, and Baby had to fight to not let her eyes linger. Biting down on her bottom lip, she peeled off her own clothes and then grabbed a washcloth before stepping in behind him.

Memphis lowered his head and watched the water flow down the drain as Baby lathered up the washcloth with soap. She cleaned him, making him new, and then washed everything down the drain to never be seen again. He imagined that he could wash away Genie's ailments just as easily, but he couldn't. It was hard for him to comprehend that of all the things in his life that he had control over, the one thing he needed to control, he couldn't. He was supposed to protect his baby girl, but he had failed at that. Now he was powerless.

"Turn around," Baby requested of him softly, and he did as he was told.

She ran the soapy cloth over his body, taking care of him in a way that he'd never experienced before, and he admired her. Never had anyone been this gentle and compassionate with him. Never had anyone loved him this much. His eyes raked over her face and then her body. The emotions within him intensified to depths that he never knew possible. This was the woman of his dreams, the woman he felt that God had created for him. She was his everything and would always be.

The moment Baby looked up and met Memphis's eyes, she sensed that something between them had shifted. It was the moment they went from lovers to soulmates. His eyes were narrowed... so full of heated passion and tenderness that a lump formed in her throat, and her knees seemed to go weak. He cupped her in his arms and pulled her close to him, embracing her the way a man is supposed to do a woman the moment he understands that she completes him. Baby was overwhelmed by so many emotions that she dropped the washcloth to their feet.

With a subtle motion, Memphis lifted her up and cradled her in his arms while pressing her back against the back wall of the shower. She wrapped her legs around his torso at the exact moment that he pressed his lips against hers. He ravished her, sucking and biting on her lips, exploring her mouth with his tongue, squeezing and pulling on her skin with hunger that only she could satisfy. When he pushed himself between her, she gasped and let her head fall back as he tore through her heat, sending fireworks up her spine. He made love to her like he knew it could be his last time. More than ever, he understood that the present was a gift because another second of life wasn't promised to either of them. Just in case God saw fit to take one of them away from the other, he wanted his love to be etched into her soul.

Still holding her in his arms and with their intimate connection still in place, Memphis stepped out of the shower and sucked on Baby's hardened nipples before laying her carefully on the heated tile floor. He pulled away only for a few seconds to take a look at her body and write the image in his mind's eye. She was perfect and so beautiful to him. She was the woman that he should have always been with... He'd lost out on so much time that could have been spent making every second of her every day the happiest she'd ever experienced. Thinking of the moments he had left, he vowed to do just that as long as God continued to blow breath into his body.

"I love you," he whispered, pushing in and out with gentle thrusts —just enough to drive her crazy. "I'll never leave you.... never mistreat you. Just say you'll never leave me."

"I won't," Baby could barely utter. She lifted her legs up and wrapped them around his back, nudging him deeper into her. "I won't leave you. Ever."

"I need to hear you promise," he said, and his voice cracked with emotion, filling her eyes with tears.

"I promise I won't leave you," she swore as she cried silently.

Memphis lifted her hips up and went deeper—so deep that it almost hurt when he filled her, but she took the pain with ease, knowing that he needed her close. But Memphis was attempting to be more than just close to Baby. He wanted to become one with her... to fuse her soul into his so that he would never have to fear losing someone he loved so much ever again.

"Oh God," she whispered in pleasure as Memphis sped up the pace.

His movements became more forceful and jagged as he worked out his frustrations. His fingers ripped at her skin, kneading and grabbing, clutching and pulling as he plowed forward, delivering powerful jabs straight toward her spine. Her love gushed as he buried his head into her neck and continued his assault. Knowing that he was working through his pain, she gritted her teeth and took everything he was giving while wrapping her arms around him and holding him close. He pierced her neck with his teeth as he came, and she winced slightly but not much because she was too caught up in the feeling of her own climax. With her lips parted and her pupils panning to the back of her head, she enjoyed the result of their sexual union. It was almost supernatural.

When Memphis pulled away, she felt moisture there but saw no tears in his eyes. And although the sorrow was still present, she could also see his acceptance of the hand that had been dealt to him. He didn't want anything to happen to his baby, and if it were possible, he would take her place without a single thought. His hope was still strong; Memphis was prepared to fight until the end, but he wouldn't let any outcome destroy him. Genie wouldn't want to see her father broken beyond repair.

Leaning down, he kissed Baby first on her forehead and then on her lips before rolling on his back. In a single motion, he slid her onto his chest without pulling himself out of her body. It didn't take long before they were overcome with exhaustion from going days without sleep, and they rested right there in each other's arms, still joined as one.

AFTER A SHORT NAP, BABY AWOKE AND CAREFULLY PULLED AWAY FROM Memphis. She grabbed a blanket off the bed, covered him with it, and then snuck out of the room. It hadn't been long, but she wanted to call Cleo to see how everything was going with Genie. Creeping through the quiet house on her tiptoes, she dialed the number and waited until the other line picked up.

"Hello?"

"Hi, Ms. Donaldson, I—"

"Baby," she interrupted. "We have passed the 'Ms. Donaldson' stage. You can feel free to call me mama or ma, the same as Memphis, because I know one day you will be my daughter. I've seen the way that he looks at you, the way you care for him... We are family now."

In spite of the circumstances they were facing, Baby felt herself give up a small smile.

"Thank you, Mama," she started. "I wanted to check on Genie... Memphis is sleeping, but if there is any change with her, I have to get him there."

"Genie is the same," Cleo said, her tone filled with hurt. "She's gotten no worst nor any better. My son can continue to rest. I'll make sure to update you as soon as anything changes."

"Thank you," Baby said and ended the call.

Before she knew it, she had walked into Genie's room and was standing at the door looking at what was the perfect getaway for a princess. Everything was in the same exact place she'd left it. Baby's eyes clouded with tears as she stepped back to close the door. It was at that moment that she heard a knock coming from the front.

With a sigh, she walked to answer it quickly so that Memphis would not be disturbed. On the front stoop stood a woman she'd seen before. With her hands on the curve of her wide hips, she balanced her weight on one leg while she tapped impatiently. Her very presence along with the irritated scowl on her face told Baby that, although she wasn't sure what it was, things were about to change.

"Um, can I help you?" Baby asked as she looked at the familiar face. It was the same woman she'd seen staring at her in the mall and the one she'd also seen when she went to visit Semaj. They said lightning didn't strike in the same place twice, and she had a constant nagging that it was too much of a coincidence to run into this woman more than once. She'd been right.

"Yeah," she started, squinting her eyes as she crossed her arms in front of her chest. "Is Mona around?"

Baby's head jerked back, her posture stiffened. "You know Mona?"

"Yes, I know her, and I need to see her right now." Her gaze bounced from place to place as she took in the large, magnificent entry of the home as well as the foreign cars in the driveway. "Damn, that bitch livin' it up but gon' default on givin' me my shit."

Her meaning was lost to Baby who was still trying to figure out how Mona knew this woman as well as why she lied about it that one day at the mall.

"Mona no longer lives here... She left, and I haven't heard from her since."

"Left!" the woman barked. "Oh, I know the hell she didn't! You need to tell me where that bitch is right now. She owes me money and I need it."

Owes her money? Baby thought, definitely curious about what was going on between Mona and the woman that she'd claimed not to know.

"Yes. And if I don't get it within the next hour, you can let her know that I'm telling Memphis about all the shit that she's done. I need my money right now, and I don't care what she's got going on because I have shit happening too!"

With that said, the woman flipped her long weave behind her back and crossed her arms in front of her chest. Baby started to speak but then stopped, taking a glance behind her back before she stepped forward and closed the door behind her.

"Listen... I don't know what is going on between you and Mona, but you won't be getting paid because we have no idea where she is. But you need to tell me whatever it is that you want Memphis to know."

The woman screwed up her nose and peered at Baby for a few seconds before shaking her head. "No... I need to speak to him directly."

"His daughter is in the hospital," Baby revealed, hoping that it would help. "He's not in any condition to deal with anything right now, so you need to tell me whatever it is you're holding back for Mona."

When the woman made no movement to spill the news, Baby knew exactly what she needed to do in order to get her to talk. Placing her finger up to signal her not to move, she ran back into the house and grabbed the wad of money Mona had given her when she left. It had finally come in handy. She cut it in half and then ran back out the door.

"Here," she said, forcing the money into the woman's hand. "I'm paying you now, so I need you to speak."

A few beats of silence passed between them as each woman scrutinized the other, thinking their own separate thoughts. The wind stirred around them.

"First off, I'll say that you don't know me, but I know you."

"How?" Baby asked, cocking her head to the side.

The woman looked away, forced out a chuckle, and then ran her hand through her hair before looking back to Baby.

"My name is Felicity. We have a mutual friend... Semaj."

It was a blow that Baby wasn't expecting, but she didn't say anything because she needed answers and wanted them quick. What did this woman, Memphis, Mona, and Semaj all have in common?

"A while back, Semaj and I fucked around, and I got pregnant. I ended up losing the baby, went to Semaj's spot to tell him, and found him and Mona in the bed fucking. Since I knew he was with you and that Mona was your best friend, he gave me money for my silence, and I was good with that."

If a gust of wind had blown their way, it would have knocked Baby to her knees. She couldn't believe what it was that she was hearing. There was no way that what this woman was saying was true. Mona couldn't possibly have been sleeping with Semaj!

"I don't believe you," Baby countered, feeling her anger rise. "Mona wouldn't do that to me."

Felicity's head cocked back like she'd been hit and then she began to laugh incredulously. It was obvious to her that Baby had no idea about the type of person that Mona was. This was only the tip of the iceberg... She hadn't even gotten to her great reveal yet.

"Believe it, honey. Your friend Mona is an evil bitch. I never loved Semaj... I saw him as a come up, and people look down on that, but it's nothing in comparison to what your girl has done."

Felicity paused, feeling somewhat sorry about being the bearer of bad news. It was easy to do terrible things against Baby when she was nothing more than a beautiful picture on the wall in Semaj's home. But now that she was standing in front of her, Felicity could see what Semaj saw in her to make him want to cover up his mistakes.

A cool breeze blew across Baby's face at the same moment that she swiped at the layer of sweat on her forehead. The basic fibers of her mind shifted, and a panic attack threatened to take hold. She swallowed hard to force down the bile at the back of her throat. Her lungs constricted, and she gasped, barely able to get out another breath. It was all she could do to give a simple nod for Felicity to continue.

"A few months after paying me to keep his secret, I contacted Semaj because my money was low, and he hit me with another opportunity to get some money. Mona was pregnant, and he thought the baby was his. Being that I worked at a diagnostics center that performs paternity tests, he paid me to fake a test to say that the nigga she was with was the father. So I took the money, but when the baby was born and I saw that Memphis was the man she was tricking, I demanded more, and Mona promised me that in exchange for my secrecy, she would pay me each month. She missed her last payment, and now we're coming up on another one. It's been almost two months, and I got bills to fuckin' pay, so unless you wanna take up her payments, I will be letting Memphis know that the little girl he thinks is his really belongs to Semaj."

"But what do you have to earn by telling him?" Baby countered, forced to look beyond her pain to save Memphis from the same grief. "You still won't get your money each month."

Felicity shrugged. "I will if you don't want me to tell him."

Covering her face with her hands, Baby muffled her cries so that Memphis wouldn't hear and wake up to discover that his world was nothing like what he knew it to be. She couldn't understand how someone could be so evil, so cruel as to intervene in someone's life in the way that Mona had. For the first time in her life, she knew that she'd been wrong by dismissing Mona's ugly ways over the years and chucking it up to her immaturity and privileged upbringing. There was no excuse for this kind of wickedness. Mona was the devil.

"Fine, I'll get you the money somehow," Baby heard herself saying. "I can't let you tell him this... It would break him."

Unknown to Baby, Memphis was on the other end of the door listening to everything that was being said. Even in a deep sleep, he felt the exact moment Baby had separated her body from his and forced himself awake. When he heard her answer the door and begin to speak in a hushed tone, he had been too curious to stay put and wait for her to return. Now he was glad for that.

There was nothing more devastating to him than hearing that his daughter was dying, so nothing else had the power to break him. When Genie was born, he held her in his arms and looked for any sign of himself. The baby was angelic, born with wide, alert brown eyes, a beautiful caramel complexion just a smidge darker than her mother's, and the most peculiar red hair... but she looked nothing like him. Over the years, Genie's features came in even more; her hair turned from red to a golden brown, and her eyes curved like almonds, but she was her mother's twin.

When Genie turned three, he'd found out that she had a cell abnormality that complicated her cancer. It was hereditary and had to be passed down from both parents. Mona had been a fit of nerves throughout the testing, and Memphis knew then that something was up. He'd told Carl to get back to him with the results first, and when he did, Memphis found out then that Genie wasn't biologically his. That was his chance to be free, but Genie was fighting for her life, and he couldn't leave.

Whether or not Genie had his DNA inside of her, she was Memphis's daughter because there was no way he could have loved her more than he already did. The emotional connection they shared had been formed, and it didn't matter to him how she'd came into the world. The only person he confided in was Laz, who went with him to the diagnostic center that confirmed his paternity. But their records showed that his DNA was a 99.9% match to Genie's, so he figured they'd just made a mistake.

But now he knew Mona was involved. His need for vengeance burned in his chest, and he wouldn't rest until he paid back everyone who had a hand in this deception. When Baby returned, he was lying on the sofa in the living room with his eyes closed and his arms pulled up behind his head. His calm exterior gave no indication that anything was wrong. Lazily opening his eyes, he squinted when he saw the pleased expression on Baby's face.

"I just spoke with your mom," she said, holding her cell phone up in the air. Her eyes were shining with tears which caused some alarm, but her smile kept him from panicking.

"We need to get to the hospital now. She said that Genie is awake."

CHAPTER TWENTY-SIX

$\mathcal{M}$ona was watching from around the corner with a scowl on her face as Felicity spoke to Baby. She didn't have to hear a single word to pick up on the exact moment that she spilled the beans. When Memphis took away her credit cards, she never thought he'd actually cut them off. But he had, and the one bill that she made sure never to forget hadn't been getting paid.

"Fuckin' greedy bitch!"

"Excuse me?" the taxi driver quipped, narrowing his eyes at her through the rearview mirror.

"Not you," Mona scoffed and batted her hand at him. "Circle around the corner and stop when you get there. I have a call to make."

She was seething. Baby was answering doors and walking about like she was the woman of the house, fucking *her* husband like she was his wife, and playing mommy to *her* child! What kind of best friend was she to betray her in this way?

So focused on her own hatred and jealousy, Mona never once thought about all of the ways she'd betrayed her own best friend. Her selfish opinion was that Baby deserved everything she'd done to her. In Mona's eyes, Baby was always flaunting how happy she was and how perfect her life was. She was always so loved by everyone without putting in any effort to even deserve it. She needed to be taken down a few pegs, and Mona did just that, as if it were a favor.

Her survival depended on getting ahead of this situation, so she had to take matters into her own hands before they spiraled out of control. With the leftover blood money she'd taken from Sly, she was able to turn back on her phone service and buy a replacement phone. It was far cheaper than the one she'd had before but just enough for what she needed at the moment. Pulling it out, she scrolled through her contacts and pressed the green button. Time seemed to slow as she waited for someone to answer. Her anxiety made her nibble on the inside of her busted bottom lip. A wound reopened, and she tasted fresh blood.

"Hello?"

"Hi, Trina. This is Mona. Are you at the park with Genie? I need to pick her up."

She admired her fresh manicure as she spoke. She wasted no time getting a full makeover as soon as she landed in Atlanta. She still didn't look like herself, but after a few more pampering sessions, she'd be back to normal.

"The park?" Trina nearly yelled like Mona had lost her mind.

In all her years of working with Genie, Trina always hated Mona and felt that she was a terrible mother, but this right here took the cake. She couldn't believe that Mona had no idea about her own daughter's wellbeing.

"What the hell are you talking about, Mona? Your daughter is in the hospital... she's fighting to survive! Are you telling me you don't even know?"

"What!" Mona shouted so loudly that her driver almost swerved off the road. "What the hell are you talking about?"

"Exactly what the hell I said," Trina snapped. "You know what? I hate to say this—naw, that's a lie because I've been *waiting* to say this. You are a sorry excuse for a mother. Consider yourself lucky that your daughter doesn't fuckin' hate you."

Trina's words were lost to Mona because her mind was elsewhere. With her eyes positioned ahead of her, aimless and unfocused as thoughts sped through her mind, her jaw dropped. She hung up the phone and placed her hand over her racing heart. The air grew thick and suffocating. She smashed her finger on the button to let down the window and gasped in a gust of cold air.

"I—I gotta get to the hospital," she whispered.

"Huh?" the driver asked, frowning deeply.

"The hospital," she repeated as a tear slid down her cheek. "Please... I need you to drive me, and you need to be fast."

She rattled off the address to the driver, and he took off, all too eager to get rid of her for once and for all. But when he looked into the back seat and saw her sobbing quietly to herself and wiping at her eyes, he found himself pitying her. She wasn't a good person, from what he'd gathered, but something was destroying her.

"We're here," he told her as he pulled up to the front of the Emory Hospital. Mona wasted no time tossing a few bills his way and jumping out of the car. Before he pulled off, he said a quick prayer that she'd be able to get to whoever she was trying to see in time and would be able to find peace.

"I NEED TO SEE GENIE LUCIANO, PLEASE!" MONA SHOUTED AT THE woman sitting at the front desk of the main floor of the hospital. "Can you tell me which room she is in?"

As soon as the woman heard Genie's name, she felt a bolt of sadness go through her heart. She knew exactly who Genie was, had heard her story, and was deeply affected by what was happening to the young girl.

"Yes... are you family?" she asked.

"I'm her mother," Mona replied with haste. The woman frowned slightly, thinking to herself that she'd thought the other young woman who had been by Genie's side was her mother but then remembered that this wasn't her business.

"Okay," she said as she scribbled down something on a piece of paper. "This is the floor and the room she's in. You can use the elevators behind you."

"Thank you."

The words had just barely left her lips before Mona was rushing away. She mashed the button to call the elevator with all her might and tapped her foot anxiously as she waited for it to arrive.

"DADDY, I'VE BEEN WAITING FOR YOU," GENIE SAID WITH A SMILE AS soon as Memphis walked in the room. Sitting up on what he'd been told was her deathbed, Genie was the perfect picture of health. The color had returned to her face, the sparkle was back in her eyes, and her curls sprung to life with every subtle motion of her head.

His heart was overcome by joy, and his lips curved into a full smile for the first time in ages. Genie didn't appear sick at all... She was his perfect child: happy, bright, and energized. Seeing her weak, fragile body lying in the hospital bed with no hint of life anywhere to be found had left a hole in his heart, but this moment was filling it up once again.

"And Gotty!" she squealed, seeing Baby enter the room behind Memphis. Her eyes dropped down, and a sneaky smile came to her lips when she saw they were holding hands. Realizing their mistake, Baby pulled away from Memphis, but it was too late because Genie had seen it all.

Baby leaned over and kissed Genie on her cheek, and the young child wrapped her tiny arms around her godmother's neck. It was the embrace that Baby had begged for in the days before, and now she was able to hug her once again.

"I saw you and Daddy," Genie whispered in her ear before Baby pulled away.

Baby's eyes bugged. She stepped back slightly so that she could determine whether it was time to dive headfirst into damage control. But the only thing she saw was pure love in her eyes. Genie was a child who 'had been here before' as the older folks said. She was wise beyond her years and was able to pick up the subtlest things that many others her age missed.

"He loves you like I do," she said and gave Baby another big hug before letting her go.

Baby quickly swiped a tear from her cheeks and moved back to give Memphis space to spend time with his daughter. He stepped forward, and she watched as he spoke to Genie about any and everything that came to mind. For the first time in days, he seemed alive and relaxed. Baby had been battling whether or not to keep the secret she'd discovered earlier that day, but this moment showed her that she'd made the right decision. She'd do everything she could to make sure that he never found out the truth.

"Let's give them a moment alone," Cleo urged, grabbing Baby's hand.

With a last glance at the two of them, she nodded her head and followed Cleo out of the room. Baby felt her hand tense up in hers before she even knew what was happening. With a frown, she followed her eyes down the hall toward whatever had caught her glare.

"Mona?" she gasped as she saw her former best friend running her way. She almost hadn't recognized her. Though she'd tried her best to cover it with makeup, Mona's face was badly bruised with purplish and bluish markings that showed up clearly on her buttery skin. There was some swelling around her eyes, and her bottom lip was busted.

Before Baby could react further, Cleo stepped in front of Genie's door, blocking Mona as soon as she reached them. With her jaw tight and her eyes spewing flames, the older woman scowled into her face.

"You have no business here!"

"Excuse me?" Mona spat the words like they burned coming out. "It's *my* daughter in that room, you old bitch! Now get the fuck out of my way."

She reached around Cleo for the doorknob and was met with a hard slap to the face. Both Baby's and Mona's mouths dropped when they realized that Cleo had been the one to attack. Mona held on to her stinging cheek with one hand and formed a fist with the other. If a fight was what Cleo wanted, it was exactly what she was going to get.

"Get. The *fuck*. Out. Of. My. Way."

Each word was forcefully pushed through her teeth. Mona's face balled up into an expression so demented that Baby had to put a hand over her open mouth. She was almost demonic in her rage.

"Don't get shit twisted," Mona snarled. "I'll fight an old bitch."

The disrespect was real. The battle between Mona and Cleo was years in the making and was now about to come to a head. But Cleo wasn't afraid, especially when it was clear that Mona had already been handed one ass whooping in the recent past. If it called for it, Cleo would freely hand out another in order to protect her grandchild.

"You need to leave. *My* son is in here speaking to *his* daughter, and I will not let you interrupt them."

An evil cackle escaped from Mona's lips, and it was then that Baby knew she had to get her out of there. Her evil intentions were clear, and there was no telling what would come out of Mona's mouth next.

"Mona, just—" She started, grabbing at Mona's arm, but she snatched away and took a step forward, right into Cleo's face.

"That isn't *your* son, and Genie isn't *his* daughter!" Mona spoke through gnashed teeth as her eyes bore into Cleo. "So I suggest you get the fuck out of my way."

Frozen in place by Mona's revelation, Cleo succumbed to her shock, giving her the perfect opportunity to pass her by. But Baby grabbed her before she could make her move.

"Mona, don't do this. Let Memphis have his moment and then—"

"Get your fuckin' hands off me!" Mona shouted as she slapped Baby away. "You have a lot of nerve even being here right now after fuckin' my husband, and if I wasn't trying to get to my daughter right now, I'd be killing you with my bare hands!"

A vicious stare down ensued, and a brave member of the hospital staff stepped up and stood between Mona and Baby, looking from one face to the other.

"Um, I need to ask you both to keep the noise to a minimum, or you'll have to leave," the woman informed them with a calm but firm tone.

"*She* needs to be escorted out of here," Mona said, jabbing her finger at Baby's chest. "She's not anything to my daughter… She's not family, and she doesn't deserve to be here. She's merely the trash that my husband is fuckin' for the moment."

The woman's jaw dropped, and she looked at the security guard who had walked up beside her for help. With a sigh, the man shook his head at Baby, hoping that she wouldn't give him any problems and would leave quietly.

"Ma'am, you're going to have to come with me," the guard said.

"Oh no she won't!" Cleo snapped before pointing at Mona. "Take this trash instead. She's no mother. She abandoned her child when she needed her the most and has treated her like a burden every day of her life! She's a coward and a snake. You're not even worthy to be in Genie's presence!"

Tears came to Mona's eyes, but she shook her head in rejection of Cleo's words. She knew what she'd said was true, but it was too painful to admit it to herself. Denial was her real best friend, and she held on to it in order to keep herself from falling apart.

"That's not true! I love my daughter, and I've always done what was right for her. You may hate me, but you are *not* her family. I am the only family she has!"

Before anyone could say another word, the door behind Cleo opened, and Memphis appeared. The stone look on his face was threatening enough, but the fiery blaze in his eyes as he raked them around everyone standing in the hall almost stole the air from their lungs.

"Memphis!" Mona shrieked and grabbed onto his arm as tears fell down her cheeks. "Trina told me our daughter was—is dying. Please, I need to see her. I need to tell her I love her."

Looking down on her with pure hate in his eyes, Memphis knew right then that if they had been alone and without witnesses, Mona would be taking her last breath. There was nothing more certain to him in that moment than the fact that he knew he would kill her the second he had a chance.

"You should leave before I fuckin' kill you."

Mona's eyes grew to three times their normal size when she heard the words fall from his lips. She snatched her hand away from his arm as if she'd been burned. He spoke as a matter of fact, not a warning. She knew him enough to know that he was not playing, not harboring a single fuck to give about how much she needed to see Genie. She was dead to him, and if he had his way, she would be dead to everyone else too. But Mona was fueled by the love she had in her heart for her child, and for the first time since Genie had been born, she was willing to sacrifice herself for her daughter.

"She's dying. Please, Memphis—I know I fucked up, but don't rob me of this moment. I need to see my baby."

She began to cry, and even while feeling that she was the vilest thing on the face of the planet, Baby couldn't help but feel sorry for her. Pulling her lips into her mouth, she forced herself to be silent as she waited for Memphis to speak. The look on his face was so petrifying, even to her, that she wondered how in the world Mona had the courage to even stand before him. He was a man protecting his child, and there was nothing he wouldn't do, even if it meant squeezing the air out of Mona's lungs while in the middle of a crowded hospital hall, if she pushed him to do so.

"If I gotta tell you this shit again, I promise—"

"Memph," Baby began, placing her hand gently on his forearm. He didn't look her way, but she felt his body respond to her touch.

"Genie needs to see her mother... at least this one time. Mona has done some terrible things, but give her the chance to make some of them right. Please, just—"

Memphis shook himself free and glared at Mona with murderous intent in his eyes. The tension around them all was so thick, you could slice it with a spoon.

"Genie doesn't need a fuckin' thing from you."

His tone was coarse—rugged. It sent a chill down Baby's spine. She trained her eyes on Mona and prayed she would leave, but Mona made no effort to move. She folded her bottom lip into her mouth as her eyes shined with tears, then lifted her head to plea yet again to any bit of mercy in Memphis's cold heart.

"I'm her mother. If she's sick...I can't let this happen without—"

Squeezing the bridge of his nose, Memphis shook his head incredulously. With a crude chuckle, he ran his eyes over the hall behind Mona before taking a step closer. He leaned down and uttered words for her ears only.

"Check this... I know all about you and Semaj. I know your secret," he told her, and the blood drained from her face. "You're living your final moments, so go and enjoy yourself."

No one else knew what Memphis said to Mona, but when he pulled back, they were able to see the haunted expression on her face. The drama was officially over. Turning quickly, Mona covered her face with her hands and ran back down the hall toward the elevators, disappearing just as suddenly as she'd come.

Once she was out of sight, Memphis turned to Baby. It took a few moments, but his love eventually returned to his eyes.

"Genie wants to speak with you," he told her. "I'll stand out here until y'all are done."

With a slight nod of her head, Baby reached out to give his hand a squeeze and then pushed through the door to speak to her.

Even with all the chaos, Genie was perfectly at peace. The television in her room was nearly blaring cartoons, most likely Memphis's doing so that she wouldn't hear anything happening outside of her room. She was sitting Indian-style in the bed, dressed in her favorite Disney princess nightgown as she sipped from a juice box. This couldn't possibly be the child that degreed medical professionals had said was dying. There had been a mistake.

"Gotty, I know that's you," Genie said without turning from the television. When she finally did and their eyes connected, a magnetic energy seemed to pass between them, making them both smile.

"Can you braid my hair?"

The request made Baby's day. Genie loved when she braided her hair, and Baby loved to do it. She always did a terrible job, and her parts were always crooked, but it was done with love, which meant everything.

"Of course I will," Baby told her and did just that.

They chatted for what felt like forever about whatever came to

Genie's mind until the little girl fell silent. Knowing that something was on her mind, Baby took a second to ask.

"What are you thinking so hard about?"

"I—I'm thinking about my daddy," Genie said quietly.

"Do you want me to get him?"

Genie shook her head and rubbed at her eyes. "Not that daddy."

Baby's heart nearly stopped, but she forced herself to continue braiding Genie's hair as if nothing had happened.

Forcing out a light chuckle, she said, "Silly girl. What are you talking about? That's the only daddy you have."

Genie fell silent once again, and Baby got the feeling that there was a lot that the young child knew... more than any of them could have ever guessed.

"My mommy took me to see Uncle Maj alone a lot when I was little. She always told me to keep it secret... She said it was something just for us, and I couldn't tell Daddy, or he would get mad. One day I heard them arguing. I heard her say that he was my real daddy."

Squeezing her eyes, Baby tried to force her tears away. She had been pushing away her emotions that entire day, trying to remain strong for the people around her, but she wasn't ready for this.

"Genie, listen to me," she started, whipping her around by the shoulders so that she was facing her. "You only have *one* daddy, and he's the one who has been with you for your entire life. Someone else may have helped to make you, but a father is more than that. Your daddy is the one who loves you, takes care of you, and never lets anyone get in the way of that. He's the one who lives here." She pointed to Genie's heart. "Your mommy made a mistake by not being honest with everyone, but in the end, you got the best daddy ever. No man could ever love you the way that he loves you."

Smiling, Genie nodded her head. She turned around and Baby began braiding her hair once again as they sat in silence.

"Gotty, can you make a video? And when you go see Uncle Maj again, can you let him see?"

Although Baby had no intentions of ever seeing Semaj again, she nodded her head, knowing she would do anything for Genie. Grabbing her phone, she positioned her camera in front of her face and pressed the red button to start the recording. As Genie spoke, she listened and marveled at the child's strength. It didn't matter whether or not she had Memphis's blood running through her veins, a child this strong couldn't possibly not be his. He'd loved her so much that she had grown to be just as fearless and resilient as he was.

"Will you make sure he sees it?" Genie asked, and Baby nodded.

"I will." She held up her hand. "Pinky promise."

CHAPTER TWENTY-SEVEN

*A*gainst all odds, Genie survived well past the four days that Carl had given her, but then her condition took a sudden turn for the worst, and she fell into a coma once again. After being able to revel in her presence for seven whole days, Genie was now unconscious, and Baby couldn't decide whether God was cursing them or whether He'd given them the greatest blessing by allowing them to be with her one last time.

It was the wee hours of the morning. Genie's room was cold and reeked of disinfectant and grief. Baby was by Memphis's side, rubbing his back gently as he held Genie's hand. His head was bent down between his shoulders, his eyes closed as if in prayer. Holding her phone in her hand, Baby began scrolling through her contacts, and she paused on Mona's name. The past couple days, she couldn't get her off her mind. Even with all the wrong she had done, being unable to say goodbye to her dying child had to hurt immensely.

"Memph... let's take a walk around the hall. I need you to take a break. Just talk to me for a minute and we'll come back, okay?"

He shook his head, but Baby wasn't going to back down, and he knew it the second she placed her hand firmly on his back. Lifting his head, he looked first at Genie and then caught her eyes.

"Just a couple minutes. Then we come back."

Baby nodded her head in agreement. "Okay."

Once they were in the hall, they took a few paces forward before Baby sent off a text.

Hurry, was all it said.

As soon as she saw the words cross her screen, Mona jolted to attention, and her heart began to race. She rounded the corner and saw Memphis and Baby walking away hand-in-hand, but she was so emotionally raw that she felt nothing. No anger. No jealousy... just nothing. Her best friend was in a full-blown relationship with the man that she'd once called her husband, but she couldn't even bring herself to care. For the past five days, her only thoughts had been of her daughter. Genie's lifeline was fading, and the only thing she wanted was to make things right.

"Oh my God," she whispered out in a single breath, placing her hand over her open mouth as she looked at her baby girl.

Genie had always seemed big for her age, but in this moment, she appeared to be so little and so vulnerable... nothing like the vibrant young lady she remembered.

"Jesus Christ... what have I done?"

Mona felt her heart breaking into pieces, and she held onto the edge of the bed to keep from falling to her knees. She was so torn by her guilt that she could barely stand.

"Genie," she began, grabbing her daughter's hand. Genie's skin was cold to her touch.

"Genie, I—I want you to know that I've always loved you. I know it didn't seem that way, but I did." She felt herself began to mentally break down, but she fought through it. "It was never your fault—you were never the reason I was so bad at being your mother. I never felt like I was good enough for you. And I was scared... The day that the doctors told me that you didn't have long to live, I was scared about the thought of losing you one day. So I tried to push you away, thinking that if I didn't get too close, I would never feel the pain once you were gone. I made so many mistakes."

Mona was so caught up in her emotional turmoil that she didn't even realize that Baby was trying to reach her on her phone. She'd tried to keep Memphis away for at least ten minutes to give Mona some privacy with her daughter, but he wasn't feeling it, and she was in a near state of panic.

"Yo, who you texting?" Memphis asked as he looked at her with suspicion. Something was off, and he knew it. His connection with Baby told him when she was hiding things from him, and he didn't like it.

"Um..." Baby began and paused. He could see the lie forming in her head.

When her eyes darted toward the room that Genie was in, he knew then what she'd done. Breaking away from her, he pulled his hand from hers and ran toward his daughter's room. Baby was hot on his heels, but she couldn't stop him because he was much faster. He grabbed the handle of the door and burst inside of Genie's room, ready to turn everything upside down. But when he heard Mona's tear-filled ramblings, something in him snapped, and he froze. Baby came up behind him a few seconds later, and they stood in the doorway listening as Mona continued speaking. She was so caught up in her feelings that she hadn't even realized she was no longer alone.

"I've always been so selfish," she continued. "I've hurt everyone around me, including you. And I know I can never make it right no matter how hard I try. I don't know what I did to deserve you, Genie. I don't know why God picked me to be your mother. You're so much better than me... I could never be good enough for you."

Mona dropped her head and began sobbing hard, and Baby slipped her hand back into Memphis's, for her own comfort. He watched Mona's breakdown with his jaw clenched, not moved by her emotions but willing to fall back so that she could continue.

"Genie, please, forgive me for the things I've done," Mona cried. "I hated Baby for so long because she was so much of a better person than I was, and you're the same. Part of me treated you so badly because you reminded me of *her*. You may look like me, but you have her heart... You're so loving, so caring, so kind... all the things I'd never be. In spite of everything I'd done, God blessed me with a child that was better than me, and I was too selfish to see it as anything but a curse. I felt like He was reminding me of what I could never be. I was so, so stupid, and I'm so sorry."

Having met the end of his patience, Memphis cleared his throat, and it was then that Mona realized she wasn't alone. Wiping the tears from her eyes, she collected herself and stood to her feet.

"I—I'm leaving now," she muttered as she wrung her hands. "Sorry."

Memphis didn't move as she darted past him toward the door, but Baby reached out and grabbed her before she made her exit. Wrapping her arms around her shoulders, she hugged her tightly as if it was the last time she'd see her. Mona sighed and fell into the embrace, appreciating for the first time in her life that Baby was a better person than she was. She'd needed this and was grateful that someone was willing to show her the kindness she craved but didn't deserve.

"I'm sorry, Baby," she whispered in her friend's ear. "Thank you for letting me speak to her."

"I'm not blameless," Baby admitted. "I'm sorry, too. I'll always be here if you need me."

They separated, and Mona left out of the door, glancing one final time at Genie before she ran down the hallway. Her feet hit the wet pavement outside, and she continued to run through the rain, not caring about how hard it was coming down, how frizzy it was making her hair, or how badly it was soiling her suede shoes. She ran like her feet were on fire, and she didn't stop until she was inside of the small motel room that she'd paid to live in for the week. It was right across from the hospital because she couldn't bear to be too far away from Genie. Even if she wasn't able to see her, she wanted to be close.

As soon as she shut the door behind her and started to lock it, her sixth sense told her that something wasn't right. The room was musty —like old cigars, and though everything seemed as she had left it, fear filled her heart. She took a timid step toward the bed and then stiffened when she saw a pair of black dice on the bedspread: one was a five and the other a six.

"Eleven! What does that mean?" she remembered asking.

"Eleven means somebody is about to die..."

A gasp escaped from her lips and her blood drained. She turned back to the door, but it was too late. Sly stepped out from where he'd been hiding behind the long, floor-to-ceiling window treatments and snatched her right off her feet like she was as light as a feather.

"You fuckin' bitch!" he snarled as she tried to fight against him. "You thought I would let you get away with *this?*"

He squeezed her neck so hard that her eyes bugged. It was then that she was able to see what *this* was. Sly's right side of his face was badly burned with blisters and boils that had not received adequate medical treatment and were a puss-green color from infection. Although he'd covered a few of his scars with some kind of ointment and bandages, it wasn't nearly enough.

"I'mma fuckin' kill you!" he roared, squeezing her neck even tighter.

Mona felt her life began to fade, and she was more than ready to let go. She'd lost everything and everyone who had ever mattered to her. She'd done so much that there was no way that she could ever find her way back to a normal life. And then she thought of the last words that Baby had said to her.

I'll always be here if you need me.

She wasn't crazy enough to think that they could ever go back to being best friends again, and she wouldn't even try to reclaim that spot in Baby's life. But she was given some hope in knowing that she possibly had someone she could count on. That hope was enough to make her fight to live. Lashing out, Mona began to rake her nails against Sly's face, scratching at his burned flesh with all her might.

"ARRRGH! You bitch!" he screamed, but she didn't stop fighting. He released his hold on her, and she fell to the floor as he yelled and rubbed at his face in pain. This was exactly the interruption that Mona needed, and she ran to the small desk next to the bed to get what she needed to get rid of Sly forever. Only this time, she would make sure he was dead.

Pow!

At the very same time that Mona was able to grab the gun from the drawer and lift it in front of her, Sly's bullet pierced straight through her middle. She felt like she'd been hit by a bolt of lightning. The force of the shot lifted her from her feet, and she flew back, hitting her head on the nightstand as her body slammed to the floor. Gritting his teeth, Sly walked up on her as she fought for her next breath. Seeing the blood seeping from her body brought him the purest joy.

"You stupid bitch," he began as he looked down at her body. "I guess you had the right plan, wrong nigga."

He lifted the gun once more and let off three more shots to her torso to seal her fate.

"See you in hell, bitch."

Pow! Pow! Pow!

As the smoke rose from the barrel of his gun, Mona's eyes closed, and a malicious grin spread across his hideous face when he saw that she'd gone still. She was a beautiful sight, even in death. Sly clicked his tongue against his teeth, somewhat disappointed that he had to get rid of her. He pulled his cell phone from his pocket to let his homeboy know that he needed help cleaning up the room. With his eyes lowered, he never saw death coming. Sly, the slickest street nigga turned street rat, had finally gotten caught slipping.

Pow! Pow! Pow!

The cell phone sailed out of Sly's hand and crashed to the ground in pieces. His eyes stretched wide as he dropped his head to look down at his bullet-ridden body. Holes poured blood from his stomach and chest… It was the end. His body crumpled like a bag of bricks and walloped to the floor before going completely still. He was gone.

"I'll meet you there," Mona muttered, sputtering blood from her lips. Her body began to go cold, and she pointed her eyes to the ceiling as she waited for her time to come.

MEMPHIS WAS HOLDING GENIE'S HAND WHEN HER BODY BEGAN JUMPING erratically. The machines attached to her began wailing like sirens, and he leaped to his feet, shouting to the top of his lungs for help. Baby ran to the door, but before she could make it out, a group of doctors and nurses rushed in with a crash cart.

"She's flatlining... I need you all to leave out the room!" one of the nurses yelled, but when no one moved a muscle, she gave up and focused on the more urgent task.

"Clear!" someone yelled. Baby let out a sob as she saw Genie's body jump when they tried to restart her heart.

"Noooo, God, please, don't do this!" Cleo wailed from behind her. Laz, who had come about an hour before with Bambi, grabbed Cleo into a bear hug and held her as she bawled in his arms. Bambi gripped Baby's hand as tears ran down both of their cheeks. Memphis was fighting his own battle, trying his hardest not to break. He felt an immensity of pressure on his neck as he watched the team of doctors work fast to bring his daughter back. He was at his wit's end. Nudging the bridge of his nose before then pinching it tight between his fingers, he squeezed his eyes closed and fought his emotions.

"Her blood pressure is dropping. We gotta work fast. CLEAR!"

He opened his eyes at the exact moment that Genie's body jumped again, and he had to look away. Walking to the window opposite his baby's bed, he looked out and tried to keep his sanity. When he saw a familiar figure running toward a small rundown motel across the street from the hospital, his eyes narrowed, and his rage magnified.

"Where are you going!" Cleo shouted when she saw him stalking to the door. He didn't say a word as he grabbed the handle to leave. The doctors were still working on his daughter, and he knew he should stay, but he couldn't handle it. He had to do something to keep himself from going crazy, and the only thing he knew to fall back on when love had failed him was his hate.

"NO! You are *not* leaving her!" Cleo roared, breaking away from Laz. She ran to Memphis and started pummeling his back with his fists.

"This is all your fault! You weren't there for her because you were always in the streets instead of by her side. If you had been there with her, she would have never gotten sick! My baby is dying because of you! You're no better than that bitch you married. You left her when you should have been a father. You did this, and you will stay here and deal with it!"

Cleo knew that her words weren't true. But during times of grief, people often demonstrated their fear by anger directed at the one they loved the most. There had never been a father in the world who loved his child more than Memphis loved Genie, and it was a fact that everyone in the room could attest to—even the hospital staff who barely knew him. He'd spent every second that he could sitting by his daughter's side. He was not to blame for this. No one was to blame but definitely not him.

"Mama Cleo... you don't mean this," Laz said as he stood behind the woman. He knew better than to put his hands on her, even though he'd never in his life stood by and let anyone attack Memphis.

"You should've been home!" Cleo wailed. Memphis turned to look at her, and the defeated look in his eyes devastated her. She could see that her son was broken... She could see that he was hurting more than she'd ever know. Dropping her fists, Cleo fell into Laz and sobbed within his open arms. The door slammed shut behind Memphis as he walked away. He wouldn't watch his daughter die.

&

GOD WAS CRYING.

Rain showered over Memphis's face as he staggered through the darkness. His body had crumpled in on itself, his steps were uneven, and his head hung low as God washed his tears away. The rage that scorched inside of him had been overwhelmed by his heartache. He'd left from Genie's side thinking that even if he'd lost her, he'd find comfort in snatching the life out of the one person on Earth who'd hurt her the most.

But he wouldn't.

As much as he'd prayed, it seemed heaven refused to wait any longer. Losing his daughter… nothing could dull that kind of pain. Never in life had Memphis not acted quickly and violently against anyone who had wronged him, but this time, he wasn't able to. Every time he looked at Mona, he couldn't help but see his little girl. Genie had always been a spitting image of her mother. He hated Mona to the core, but she would never die by his hands.

Pow! Pow! Pow!

Even in the middle of a storm, there was no mistaking a gunshot. Snapping to attention, Memphis grabbed his banger from his side and keened his ears to pick up the location of the sound.

Pow! Pow! Pow!

It was coming from the motel Mona was in and, judging from the male figure he could see through the curtain, it had come from her room. Cocking his weapon, Memphis took off in a crouched sprint toward the lower-level room and positioned himself near the window as he listened intently for any movement. Seconds passed and no sound. He slowly moved to peek through the curtains, seeing first Sly's bloody body. Alarmed by a sudden jagged motion, he cut his eyes across the room and focused on Mona. She was lying still, except for the sporadic jerking of her chest as she stole her next painful breath. Slightly swollen, her eyes were pulled tight as she stared at something distant, as if daydreaming.

Memphis darted to the door and jerked it open. With his banger still in hand, he took a knee next to Mona's body and peered into her eyes. She seemed at peace, like a woman who had accepted that death was coming for her and was ready. Without blinking, he continued to stare down into her muddy-gray pupils. He wanted to witness the very second her spirit was taken away.

After only a few seconds more, a soft, inaudible noise escaped from Mona's lips, and her body pitched forward slightly. Taking a quick glance at the faint smile on her lips before swiping his eyes back into hers, Memphis watched as she released her final breath.

At exactly 5:43 a.m., both Genie and Mona died.

CHAPTER TWENTY-EIGHT

MONTHS LATER

*W*ith death comes new life.

Baby had heard folks say it many times before, but as she sat in her backyard reading while rubbing her growing belly, she realized exactly how true it was. Through one of the hardest times in her life, she'd been given a ray of sunshine in the form of a child; a love child she and Memphis had made when he was at his lowest moment and had no one but her to help him through.

"How are you feelin'?" he asked as he came up from behind her.

Leaning down, he kissed her on her cheek before dropping his head to place a kiss on her belly. She smiled and felt the warmth in her heart ignite a fire over her entire body. She was just as in love with him today as she had been the very first moment she'd laid eyes on him.

"Tomorrow is the day," he told her as he sat in the chair in front of her. "Are you ready?"

She watched the light in his eyes for a moment before nodding her head and looking down at the beautiful diamond ring on her finger.

"I can't wait."

"No take backs... so you sure you wanna marry a nigga?" He gave her a teasing smile, and she rolled her eyes.

"I'm more than sure," she said, and she meant it.

This was nothing like the last time when she was about to marry Semaj. Her nerves had been so bad, and she chucked it up to cold feet when she knew now that it was God trying to tell her that something wasn't right.

Semaj...

Her brows bent into a frown as she thought about the man she'd almost given herself to, and she was caught up in mixed feelings. The last time she'd seen Semaj, it hadn't been a good visit, and it haunted her for a while after.

"Damn... it's good to see you," he'd said with a smile as soon as he saw Baby walking through the doors into the visitation room. With her not answering his calls and no longer visiting him on the weekends, he thought that he'd lost her, but now he was happy to be proven wrong.

"I wish I could say the same," she replied with her lip twisted up in disgust, and his face dropped. His mind began to scramble for reasons for her to be acting this way toward him, but he came up with nothing.

"Wh—what you mean by that, baby girl? What's wrong?"

"Don't ever call me that again," Baby snapped loud enough for a few of his boys sitting nearby to hear. The back of his neck stung with embarrass-ment when he heard more than a few of them snicker to themselves, but he put that off to deal with later.

"I know about you and Mona," she revealed to him, and he was left speechless. "I know you were fuckin' her. I know about Felicity, and I know all about Genie being your daughter."

The look on Semaj's face would forever be etched in her mind. He was more torn up by her revelation than he'd been when the judge banged the gavel and sentenced him to fifteen years in the pen.

"Baby... I always loved you, but—"

"But how about you tell me how you ended up fuckin' my best friend behind my back?" she barked back, letting out the anger that she'd held back for so long.

She knew that she wasn't without fault... She'd slept with her best friend's man, but that had nothing to do with Semaj's treachery. Swallowing hard, Semaj took a deep breath and wearily ran his hand over his face

PORSCHA STERLING

before he began to tell her the truth, the whole truth, and nothing but the truth.

"Mona wanted the dick from the beginning, and I knew that the second I first met her, but I never gave her any play. I knew she only wanted me because I was with you. She was jealous, and anyone could see it. I cheated on you with Felicity... It was a mistake the first time, and I tried to stop, but... Mona found out that I was fuckin' around with another chick and started using it to get money from me. I had to please her so she'd keep quiet... She wanted sex, and I gave her what she wanted in exchange for silence. We started sleeping together, and Felicity found out." He shrugged and then sighed once again. *"The day before our wedding, Mona came to me and demanded that I call off the wedding. She said if I didn't, she'd tell everyone about Genie being mine. I didn't believe her because she's greedy. Telling that would have messed up what she had going with Memphis. On God, I know she's the one who called the Feds on me."*

He paused, thinking back to that day, and Baby did the same. She remembered the moment she passed out after Semaj was arrested; she thought she'd seen a smirk on Mona's face but wasn't sure. Now she knew.

"Anyways," Semaj continued. "I guess you know the rest."

Hearing it didn't hurt as much as she'd expected, but she still wasn't through. Looking over to Officer Reynolds who had did her a huge favor, she waited until he nodded his head and then pulled out her cell phone.

"Your daughter... the one who you easily gave up in order to play along with Mona's selfish and cruel plan... she died."

Semaj's breath caught up in his body, and he clenched his teeth in utter distress. Bending his head, he didn't fight it when his eyes filled with tears. Every single day that he'd spent locked up, he thought about Genie and regretted the decision he'd made in regards to his child. He vowed that one day he would set things straight and make amends, but now he'd been robbed of that.

Seeing his emotions caused Baby to momentarily lose her words, but she recovered and moved on with what she had to do.

"Before she died, she asked me to record a video for you," she continued. "She knew you were her father. She was a very smart girl, and it's a shame you'll never meet her."

316

Without delay, Baby lifted the cell phone that Reynolds had let her sneak in and pressed play. He didn't move a muscle; it was almost like he was frozen in place as he watched his daughter speaking to him with all the eloquence of a child twice her age.

She sat with perfect poise, her back straight, her bright, brown eyes full of life. Her childlike innocence gave her a glow that sent a sharp jolt through his chest. She was beautiful, but all he had to remember her by was the few memories they'd shared and this video she'd made.

"Uncle Maj... I know it's been a long time, but I think you remember me. I—I just wanted to say that I'm not mad that you went away. The last time me and my mommy came to see you, I heard her say that you are my daddy... I love you, but I'm glad that you didn't love me back. Because then I would have never met my real daddy, Memphis... He loves me most, and he needs me with him. And I—I need him too."

Although she'd heard the video plenty of times, it still brought tears to Baby's eyes. Swallowing hard, she locked her phone and pushed it back into her pocket.

"I did love her..." Semaj said with tears streaming down his cheeks. He was no longer concerned with saving face in front of the other men in his unit. He'd lost his daughter, and she didn't even think he loved her... He'd never felt this much pain.

"I loved her but..." His eyes went to Baby's face. "I loved you more, and I couldn't lose you."

Baby wasn't moved at all by his declarations.

"No, you loved yourself more."

Mona always hated the selfishness of her own parents but ended up giving her only child the same thing: parents who loved themselves more than their daughter. However, Mona's evil intentions worked for good when Memphis entered Genie's life. His love was so much that Genie didn't miss what Mona and Semaj never provided.

Opening a folder that she'd brought in with her, Baby pulled out a piece of paper and a pen. She laid them both on the table in front of Semaj, and then sat back, staring him in his eyes.

"Sign that so I can go."

His brow furrowed with confusion before he dropped his head to read the paper she'd put in front of him.

"Wait, this is... I thought you said that—"

"Sign the paper now so I can leave."

Without protest, Semaj grabbed the pen and signed each space where his name was required as Baby sat with a satisfied smirk on her lips. What she didn't know is that there was no need for him to sign anything because Memphis had already sealed Semaj's fate.

That night, when everything was dark and everyone had been locked in their cells, Semaj's new roommate sat up in his top bunk and whispered 'Showtime.' Biting down on his bottom lip with determination, he grabbed a piece of chipped brick from the wall and stuck his fingers into the small opening where he'd stashed his shank. Jacob 'Chill' Richards was a loyal member of the Murda Mob and had been a major runner on Memphis's team from the time he was only twelve years old. Memphis only had to say the word, and Chill did everything required to make sure that Memphis's word was followed to the letter.

So when Memphis said he needed Chill to take care of somebody that he was locked up with, naturally, Chill didn't hesitate for a single second.

Dropping down to the lower bunk, Chill smirked as he watched Semaj sleeping like a baby. It almost seemed too easy to kill him in this way, and he knew he wouldn't be satisfied. He reached out and shook him awake before rearing his hand back and coming forward with the shank, thrusting it right through the jugular.

"It's the Murda Mob for life, nigga," he whispered in Semaj's ear as he clutched at his throat and gargled up blood.

With a click of his teeth, Chill jumped up to his top bunk, put his arms up under his head, and closed his eyes while Semaj died slowly below. Chill had life without parole and would never see the light of day. Adding another body to the list of souls he'd taken over the years didn't affect him in any way.

"What's that look about?" Memphis asked. "Something wrong?"

"No," Baby answered, shaking her head as she emerged from her thoughts. "I was just thinking about our life and how everything is just as it should be." She paused for a beat and then added, "Did you write your vows yet? And don't lie!"

"Hold that thought." Memphis smirked with mischief. "I think I heard someone at the door."

Baby had been nagging him about writing his vows since the day they'd settled on a date for the wedding. He told her that he hadn't written them, but it was a lie. Even before he asked her to marry him, he knew what he would say. She was his lifeline. The only woman who could give him the type of peace that a man needed. In fact, she didn't *give* him peace—she *was* his peace. Without her, he was nothing. He couldn't be the person he was meant to be until he was able to call her his wife. All this and more he planned to tell her in his vows.

"Memphis, you can't avoid this!" Baby yelled, giggling as he walked back inside the house.

When he emerged, he had company. Baby's reading time was officially over, but she wouldn't miss it.

"Gotty! I missed you!" Genie squealed out her delight as Laz rolled her in. Bambi followed behind him, smiling hard when she saw Baby sitting up ahead.

"You missed me?" Baby sucked her teeth and rolled her eyes as she teased her goddaughter. "You weren't even gone that long! Only one night."

"It felt like forever…"

"Well, thanks for telling your Gotty and Daddy that Aunty Bambi ain't no fun." Bambi pretended to be offended. Baby shot Bambi a smile before reaching out to grab Genie right from her wheelchair and position her in her lap.

"I done told you about lifting that heavy ass girl up like that, Baby," Memphis said with a smile as Baby peppered Genie's face with kisses. He knew his woman enough to know that she wasn't paying him the slightest bit of attention, but it was alright.

The night Genie died, a miracle happened. And even though Carl had seen plenty of miracles since the day he became her doctor, he was still in awe to see yet another one. She was gone… totally flat-lined. He'd already called her time of death. There was nothing he could do, and he knew that he would have to explain that to Memphis once he returned, but he just couldn't accept his failure and decided to try again.

"I want to keep going," he'd said as his peers around him gawked at him like he'd lost his mind. "I want to keep trying to bring her back."

"But Doctor, she's—"

"I'm in charge here, and you'll do what I say!" he ordered with grit, and they jumped to his command.

"Clear!"

Genie's muscles went rigid as her body bolted in the air. Hopeful, Carl looked for any trace of a heartbeat but saw none. With hooded brows, he bit down on his bottom lip as the others around him exchanged awkward glances amongst each other. They thought he needed to be stopped, but none of them was brave enough to do the honors.

"Once more... Clear!"

His breathing stalled as he gaped at the heart monitor once more, waiting for even a small change in her condition. Perspiration covered his upper lip, and the others focused their hard stares on the nurse standing next to him, electing her as the one to intervene.

"Dr.—" she started, sympathetically placing her hand on his arm, but he shot his hand up to stop her. There was a tiny wave, followed by a beep. Then more and more, falling into a rhythmic sequence that was music to his ears.

"She's alive," he said.

He brought her back. Things were fragile, and she was barely hanging on, but the fact that she'd come back was all the hope that Carl had needed. He continued to push on.

"She's stable," one of the nurses said with amazement.

With a tacit nod, Carl continued to work, consulting experts that he knew from all around the country, diving head first into research, looking for anything he could use to bring Genie back to her normal self. He nursed her around the clock as if she were his child. If she wanted to fight to live, he would fight for her to survive. In the end, he'd succeeded.

This was the part of the story that Baby had held back from Semaj the day that she showed him Genie's video. She wanted him to feel the horror of losing his child before she pushed the papers in his face and demanded he sign them to relinquish his parental rights. She wanted him to know what it felt like for Genie to be gone forever because once he signed on the dotted line, that's exactly how it would be.

"Memphis, I need to kidnap your wife for a night of fun before she becomes Mrs. Luciano," Bambi said, and Memphis chuckled to himself.

"I'm cool with it... Just don't have her pregnant ass hanging from no stripper poles," he joked, and Genie covered her ears.

Before leaving, Memphis pulled Baby to her feet and wrapped her up in his arms. He pressed his lips against hers and kissed her the way he always did: as if it were the last time he'd have the privilege. Nearly losing Genie showed him that he had to cherish every moment, and he made sure that his family felt his love every single day. Beside them, Bambi and Laz embraced as well. Oblivious to the young eyes watching him, Laz stuck his tongue nearly halfway down her throat and squeezed her plump ass while Genie pretended to gag.

"Ew, Uncle Laz!"

"Don't act like that," he replied. "You need to witness true love so that when these knucklehead niggas out here try to pop game, you'll know better."

"She already do," Memphis replied, looking at his daughter. "Ain't nothing a knucklehead can say to my baby. She know to shoot that shit down as soon as it starts."

Genie beamed at the compliment, but Baby only twisted up her lips and shook her head. She gave Genie a knowing smile and then kissed her on the forehead before letting Bambi lead her away.

"I guess I'll see you at the altar," Baby said to Memphis as she strutted off.

"Ain't no 'guess' about it," he said and then looked at Bambi to deliver a sincere message. "You got my heart walking beside you. Take care of it."

"Awww!" both women sang.

Amused but somewhat in shock, Laz shook his head to himself. When he'd paid one of his homies to do him a favor, it worked out better than he could have wished for. Laz indirectly fed Sly the lie that if he got with Mona, he could access Memphis's connect, knowing that he was down on his luck and desperate for a come up. As he'd suspected, Mona was an easy target for Sly's slick ass ways, and it gave Memphis the perfect opportunity to scoop up the woman he really wanted. When it came to his loyalty to Memphis, Laz was true with it, and it went beyond the shit they did in the streets. He would never stand by and let his man be harmed.

"Enough of this cheesy shit, nigga," Laz said as soon as the women had disappeared into the house to gather all of Baby's things for the next day. "You gettin' fuckin' married tomorrow, bruh! I got all the niggas at the club ready to party."

"Naw," Memphis replied with his eyes still on the last place Baby had been. "I'm good on that shit. I'mma spend the night with my baby girl." He looked at Genie who was reaching out to catch a butterfly. The sun shined on her golden hair, giving her an angelic look that fit her spirit perfectly.

"It's the last night that she'll have me all to herself. Y'all enjoy."

Laz didn't argue with that. Since he was now officially engaged to Bambi, he decided there was no time better than the present to go ahead and have his first of many bachelor parties as he prepared for his own big day. If Memphis had no need for the strippers that Laz had gathered in order to give his boy a good time, he would have to deal with them himself… a sacrifice that he was more than willing to make.

"What you wanna do, baby girl? You got me all to yourself for the whole night," Memphis said as he scooped Genie into his arms. She giggled and began to squirm when he started to tickle her. She gave him the purest joy. There was a time when he thought he'd never hear her laughter again, but she was here, and between her, Baby, and their unborn child, he was happier than he ever thought he could be.

"How about we work on your vows?" Genie asked, and it was Memphis's turn to fall out laughing.

"Your Gotty told you to say that?"

She bunched her lips into her mouth and didn't say a word, but he already knew the truth.

"I'll tell you a secret, but you can't tell Gotty," he said and then dropped his voice. "I've already written them."

Genie's eyes lit up, and her mouth formed an 'o.' "Ooohhh! You can keep a secret!"

"Loose lips sink ships," Memphis told her. "And snitches—"

"Get stitches!" Genie excitedly finished for him. "Can I tell you a secret?"

Memphis nodded his head and kissed her forehead before she began to speak.

"Sometimes when I'm sleeping, I dream that Gotty is my mommy." Seeing the surprise in her father's eyes, Genie started to retract her statement. "I mean, I know I have a mommy and she's in heaven now but—"

He stopped her with a lifted hand. "There is no reason to explain this to me, Genie. If it's how you feel, it's how you feel. You don't owe anyone an explanation."

"Do you think she'll be okay if I call her mommy?" Genie asked, and Memphis took a second to think before he responded. He knew that Baby would have no problems with that at all, but he also knew that Genie was in a vulnerable state. She'd lost her mother without having the chance to say goodbye, something a child should never have to experience.

But it wasn't just that. Regardless of his personal feelings about Mona, he couldn't do anything to make Genie feel that he'd not loved her. Genie was a product of her mother, and he couldn't talk shit about her without Genie feeling as though he didn't like part of her, too. Wise beyond her years, she most likely had her own opinions and feelings about Mona and the type of mother she was when she was alive. But, as was usually the case, once a loved one dies, all memories of their wrongdoings were erased. Genie chose to hold on to her good memories about Mona, and Memphis would never go against it.

"I know she wouldn't mind it. But are you sure that's what you want?" he asked and felt his body tense up as he waited for her to reply.

Genie cast her eyes down before slowly twisting her head to the side and giving him a sideways look.

"Is that what *you* want?" she posed back, and he laughed.

"It's not about me."

"I spoke to Mommy in my prayers," Genie continued, her eyes wide. "She told me that I should do whatever makes me happy." Memphis smiled. "She told me that I always reminded her of my Gotty anyways, so I may be more Gotty's child than hers. I don't know what that means!"

Memphis was at a loss for words as he looked into his daughter's eyes. The fine hair on his arms prickled as he ran what she'd said over and over through his mind. There was no way that she'd actually *spoken* to Mona, but her words were so close to what her mother had told her the night she'd nearly died. Carl had said that Genie wasn't able to hear anything or respond in any way... Had he been wrong, or did Mona really speak to Genie through her prayers?

"...And, she also said to thank you for waiting with her before she left. She said she didn't want to be alone."

Shocked, he forced a short burst of air through his nose and then ran his hand over his mouth. After a short while of thinking and wondering, he ended up pushing the question from his mind. There was no rational answer to that because when it came to Genie, *nothing* was what it was supposed to be. She was his miracle child.

He felt he was being watched and turned to look behind him, discovering Baby standing a short distance behind. The tears in her eyes let him know that she'd heard a good amount of what Genie had said and was touched by it. She was much more spiritual than he was and had easily accepted it for the supernatural phenomenon it was.

"I love you," he mouthed to her, and she blew him a kiss before sashaying away.

Something about the way that her hips churned as she padded off reminded him of the first time he'd laid eyes on her. So much had happened since then, but it had been written in the stars that she was the one for him, and neither one could run from what had been predetermined.

It was fated for him to love her for the remainder of his life, and he always would.

EPILOGUE

*C*olt, Jacob, Travis, and Lewis Taylor rode up to the chapel like Black mobsters. Screw-face intact, they jumped out of Colt's black-on-black Cadillac Escalade like men on a mission. In fact, they *were* men on a mission... a mission to meet the knucklehead ass nigga their baby sister called herself getting married to.

Being so much older than her, Baby's brothers rarely knew the details of her everyday life, and they didn't talk much, but one thing was for certain: they refused to stand by and allow their sister to be hurt once more. After finding out that she was not only pregnant but getting married to a man who had been married once before to her own best friend, they all got together and decided that it was time for them to show their face and get some answers before allowing her down the road to marriage once again.

Colt, the oldest, walked into the doors of the church first, taking a moment to look around as his brothers filed in behind him. He'd taken it particularly hard after finding out about what went on with Semaj because he felt that if he had been on top of his role as the oldest, a flaw ass nigga like Semaj would have never been able to get into his sister's good graces from the beginning. He couldn't do anything about the past, but he was set on making sure that he was around for the present. Baby wouldn't make the same mistake again on his watch.

"What are y'all doing here?" Gala whispered, coming around the corner. "You're nearly an hour early than the time you're supposed to be here."

"We came to see this Memphis nigga. Where he at?" Colt affirmed, with Jacob, Travis, and Lewis lined up behind him, arms folded across their chests.

Gala's eyes bugged as she looked at them, her mind running with options as to how to blow away the smoke before the real fire got started. One look at the expressions on her brothers' faces let her know that they were up to no good, and that was the last thing she needed. Hormones raging, Baby was an emotional wreck as is. The last thing she needed was her brothers showing up hours before her wedding to rough up her fiancé.

"Oh no, y'all are *not* about to do this here! And definitely not now," Gala hissed.

Walking forward, she began pushing them back out the door, but they held their ground. She exhaled loudly and took a good look at the stubborn look on each of their faces. There was no way they would be persuaded to leave. They were set in their ways.

"Fine. I'll show you to him," she gave in. "But please remember that your sister is pregnant, and she is already having a hard time."

"She gon' have an even harder time if I find out this nigga on some bullshit," Colt added with his brothers humming in agreement behind him. "I'm not letting her almost make the same mistake again, and that's all there is to it."

With lips pressed tightly together, Gala simply shook her head and continued to lead the way to Memphis's wing in the chapel so that he could meet his future brothers-in-law. It wasn't the best time for this 'meet and greet' to occur, but thanks to Colt, she had no choice.

STANDING AT THE WINDOW, MEMPHIS LOOKED OUT, ADMIRING HOW beautiful of a day it was. He'd been standing there for longer than he knew, thanking God for the gift of a sunny, cloud-free day so that he could fully enjoy marrying the only woman he'd ever loved. Baby was his lifeline, and it brought him the greatest joy to give her his last name.

He wasn't surprised when there was a light knock on the door behind him, followed by Gala's strained voice asking him if she could enter. He'd seen the group of men jump out of the SUV below, their faces marked with their intent on being a problem—*his* problem. But he wasn't moved by it because he knew exactly who they were. Although only Baby's half-brothers, the resemblance was strong. They had her same bold and audacious eyes and walked with the same strength and confidence that she did. It was obviously a trait they all shared and inherited from their mother.

"Come in," he replied to Gala without turning.

The door opened, and he heard a stampede of feet entering in. It wasn't until the movements stopped that he finally decided to face his confronters. Pivoting, he looked into the face of Baby's brothers, thinking of something he'd said to her the first time he'd seen her.

"So I got four niggas I'mma have to step to in order to take you out, huh?"

Tongue-in-cheek, he suppressed the smile that teased his lips as he thought back to that moment. Who knew back then that he'd been talking to his future wife?

"I guess you're Memphis," one of them said, obviously the oldest and the leader of the crew.

Colt was taller than Memphis was and muscular like a body-builder. It was easy to pick up on the fact that Colt had probably never met a nigga he thought he couldn't handle, but then again, he'd never before come face to face with Memphis. There were few things that scared Memphis, and they all had to do with the safety of the ones he loved. Never had he ever been afraid of a man, and now wasn't the day he'd start.

"I am," was his simple response.

"Listen, I wanna know where you get off wantin' to marry our sister without askin' us first. That's how shit gets done these days?"

Snickering a little to himself, Memphis shook his head. He was

327

going to tolerate this because he knew he had to. Baby had brothers, and he knew that, at some point, they would give him a hard time once they felt the pressure to protect their sister. Even still, he wasn't in the business of allowing anyone to punk him, so if they thought that was how this was going to go down, they couldn't be more wrong.

"I don't know how shit normally gets done, but I know how I make my moves, and there was only one person that I was concerned about getting approval from. And I got that."

The air became thick between Colt and Memphis as they stared unwaveringly into each other's eyes, neither one willing to back down. Gala shifted nervously, cutting her eyes to the door. She wanted to leave and check on Baby, maybe tend to her latest melt-down, but she didn't want to make any sudden movements and get caught up in whatever was coming next.

Her brothers were all knuckleheads and prone to fighting, Colt the most aggressive of them all. Though they were now professionals and college-educated businessmen, certain things just became a part of you after growing up in the hood. The willingness to fight at the drop of a dime when disrespected being one of them.

Colt had a hard head and was always tight-roping across the line between being free or in prison being that he had the mind of a street nigga, although he placed himself into the corporate world where self-control was mandatory. He was a live wire, and Memphis wasn't one to back down from a confrontation. There was no telling what would happen here.

"God help us," Gala whispered out a quick prayer. From her lips to God ears.

A twinkle of emotion passed through Colt's eyes, and then suddenly, the edges of his mouth curled... into a smile. The same came to Memphis's, and in the very next second, the two men were engaging in hearty laughter and heavy handshakes, like old friends. Bewildered, Gala, Jacob, Travis, and Lewis watched with their eyes stretched wide, totally lost on what was happening before them.

"Aye, y'all, it's all good," Colt said, speaking to his stricken brothers and sister. "Me and this nigga met some time ago. He got my number from moms and got my blessing."

"You fuckin' with us, right?" the youngest boy, Lewis, stepped up, looking at Colt with crooked brows. "Y'all niggas really already know each other?"

Memphis gave a crooked smile and bent his head slightly as he shrugged his answer. It was true. He'd called Colt many months ago and they'd had a private man-to-man conversation where he explained his feelings for Baby and how he'd loved her since the first day he had seen her. Although he was his own man, Memphis was also a father, and he knew how he wanted a nigga to come at his daughter when it was time. He wanted to give Baby and her family the same treatment that he expected from anyone with the nerve to step to Genie.

"Yeah, we good, fam," Colt told him, still laughing. "But you should've seen the look on y'all faces when I said we was about to roll up on ole boy. No questions asked, y'all was ready to roll out."

"Hell yeah. We ain't gon' let sis get caught up with a bogus ass dude again," Travis said, thinking back on how they'd dropped the ball when it came to Semaj. Without their father alive, it was their responsibility to look out for their sisters, and he'd been so caught up in his own personal life that he'd almost allowed his youngest sister to make a terrible mistake.

"Well, y'all can relax because this nigga is official, and I'm proud to call him my brother-in-law," Colt declared, looking at Memphis with pride.

Nodding his head, Memphis ran his hand over his mouth pensively. He heard everything that Colt was saying and was happy to be accepted into the family, but the only thing really on his mind was that he was finally about to marry the woman he'd been waiting his whole life for. The one he'd begged to God for. She completed him in ways that he never knew possible. Being a street nigga, he'd long ago learned to accept the negatives of his behavior and flip them to make them seem positive. But Baby forced him to look at things in a better way. She made him a better man. She brought out his full potential the way that a woman should, showing him that no matter what he'd achieved, he could always be a better man. His heart was completely full of the love that he'd only craved when he was younger. He'd always wanted a family who loved him, and now he had that. It had him feeling invincible. Who would have ever thought that it was love and not violence, terror, and pain that would make a street king feel whole?

"And I can't wait to marry your sister," Memphis replied, seeming more like he was speaking to himself than to anyone else. But they all heard it, and they all knew it to be true.

MAGNOLIAS DECORATED THE ENTIRE CHURCH. IT WAS BABY'S FAVORITE flower, so Memphis demanded they be everywhere. He wanted her at her happiest the second that she said "I do". It was his surprise to her because she'd been too busy driving herself insane to focus on the details. Thankfully, he had her back.

"Calm down," Janine told her daughter. "It's normal to be nervous."

Baby nodded and took a deep breath to ease her nerves. It wasn't the same as with Semaj... That time she had a terrible feeling that something had been wrong. This time, that feeling wasn't there; instead, she was hit with the tremendous pressure of wanting everything to be perfect. Her soul was settled in that she knew this would be her one and only time walking down the aisle. Already it wasn't going how she'd planned it, but it wasn't happening at all like she'd dreamed it to be when she was a little girl. She was pregnant—literally felt big as a house. She didn't feel at her prettiest even though it was her wedding and the one time in a woman's life when she *had* to be at her best.

"I just hope Memphis thinks I'm pretty." Before she knew it, she'd voiced her insecurities out loud.

Janine smiled as she looked at her daughter, wondering what in the world she had to be worried about. She was the perfect portrait of a dream, void of any and every imperfection.

"He's going to think you're beautiful because you are."

330

Bowing her head slightly, Baby pressed her lips together in a nervous smile, allowing the diamond tiara around her head to sparkle in the soft light. Her hair was pulled up into a simple bun, her makeup was natural but regal, and her dress was as if it had been made for an angel. She was a remarkable woman who looked nothing like what she'd been through.

"It's time," Gala said, peeking through the door. Pausing, she looked from her mother to her sister and then pried into Baby's eyes with her own.

"Are you okay?"

Taking a deep breath, Baby ran her hand over her growing belly and then nodded her head. Of course she was ready. Nervous but ready. This was the moment that she had been waiting for.

"I am."

Hearing Baby's words settled the storm in Gala's chest. More than anything, she wanted everything to go perfectly for her sister. She owed her that after the fiasco from before, and she'd been working day and night around the clock to ensure that all the details were taken care of. When the day was over, she would have her feet up as she nursed herself with an entire bottle of red wine, but until then, she had work to do.

"Oh, wait!" Gala said, stopping Baby in her steps. "There is someone who just *has* to say something to you."

Baby and Janine sat back and waited with expectant eyes as Gala walked in the room and held the door open. Seconds later, they both were smiling when they saw Genie wheel into the room. Her hair was curled into soft ringlets that framed her baby face and danced down her back. She wore a white dress, just like her Gotty's, so poufy that you could barely see her legs, and a grin on her face so wide that you could count every single one of her teeth. Her eyes jumped with excitement as she looked around the room, but when they rested on her Gotty, they filled with tears.

"Gotty, you're beautiful!" Genie gushed, covering her mouth with her hand.

Baby smiled and parted her lips to speak, but before she could get out a word, Genie covered her face with her hands and started bawling, huge teardrops streaming down her face. The three women froze as they watched the little girl and then looked into each other eyes, silently asking questions. Genie had just recently lost her mother and nearly lost her own life, but she'd coped with that pain so well.

Was this the emotional breakdown they'd been waiting for? No one ever stopped to think about the effect that a parent remarrying may have on a child. Her father was moving on… moving past her mother into a new life with a new love. Did she feel left behind? Did Genie feel like her mother was being wronged?

"Genie…" Baby started, walking over to the little girl who was still crying softly into her hands. "What's wrong, baby? Did—did Gotty do something wrong?"

She looked from her mother to her sister as she waited for Genie to answer, her heart racing. She was due to walk down the aisle moments ago, but she couldn't possibly go out there now. She had to deal with this. There was no way she could walk down the aisle toward her happiness and leave Genie behind in her misery.

Grabbing her, Baby once again ignored Memphis's demands for her to not pick Genie up while pregnant, and she held her tightly in her arms, hugging her in her love as Genie continued to cry. Hearing her granddaughter from the other side of the door, Cleo slipped into the room, and her eyes grew wide with alarm when she saw Baby cradling the crying child. Sitting back in silence, she was just as lost as the rest of them as she waited for someone to get to the bottom of what was happening.

"Genie… what's wrong? Why are you so sad?"

"I'm not sad," Genie continued to sob, using her small hands to wipe the tears from her cheeks. "I just know my daddy is going to be so happy now." Not completely understanding, Baby frowned slightly as she continued to look down at her goddaughter. Genie sniffed the rest of her tears away and collected herself.

"Before you came to live with us, my daddy was only happy when I made him happy. I would watch him, and he was sad all the time—or angry. So I would try so hard to say something or be good to make him smile. Sometimes I didn't know what to do, and it was so hard, but my mommy couldn't do it, and I just wanted everyone to smile."

By the time that Genie was done speaking, there was not a dry eye in the room. Turning around so that her back was to everyone, Cleo walked to the window and wiped the tears from her eyes. It was no help; they still continued to flow. How much pressure it had to be for a child to be plagued with the burden of making a parent happy when she had so much that she was dealing with on her own. Genie had such a giving soul—a loving spirit. It was never her job to make Memphis happy, and had he known that she felt the need to, he would have told her that.

"Mona will never know the full effect her actions had on that child," Janine said, whispering to Cleo from behind. Reaching out, she put her hand on Cleo's shoulder, giving her some comfort.

"No, she won't. It's too late for that now."

Across the room, Baby felt her heart breaking with the realization of everything that Genie had been going through during her short time on Earth. What a resilient and strong child. As an adult, she would be unstoppable.

"You are the most important person in your daddy's life, and he wants you to be happy above everything else in the world. That's what makes him happiest. Don't put so much pressure on yourself, love. We adore you just the way you are. Okay?"

Nodding, Genie looked up at her godmother and smiled. It was like a glimpse of heaven, and Baby could've sworn she heard angels singing.

THE THOUGHT OF WALKING DOWN THE AISLE HAD BABY'S STOMACH filled with butterflies, but the look in Memphis's eyes when he saw her laid every single one of them to rest. His pores oozed with love and enveloped her in the most euphoric feeling that she'd ever felt in her life. This was the real deal.

The service continued on around them; they heard people speaking, they went through the motions of what they were supposed to do, but their every thought was of one another as they stared into each other's eyes and poured out their love. The time for vows came, and the only thing that Memphis could think was that he couldn't wait to get his words out. He'd been saying his vows in his mind since the day that he'd first laid eyes on this woman. He'd spoken his love for her with his heart, and they'd been sent up to heaven. The Man above went into overtime putting into place the desires of Memphis's soul, and now, finally, he was able to tell Baby the things he'd wanted to say so long ago.

"I've loved you since the second I laid eyes on you," he began, and instantly, Baby's eyes filled with tears. "Many times I've wondered why I didn't get you then. I've asked God why he took me through the fire before I could find my peace. And... he answered me. He *finally* did. Back then, I wasn't ready for you. My heart was too hard, and even though I knew what I felt, I wasn't the man that I needed to be.

We could've been together, but it would have been hard because I wasn't ready. I was in the streets day and night, something else had my attention, and that something else would have destroyed us. You would have felt unimportant, inadequate, wondering why your man wasn't with you at night. Why I was trying to work so hard to build up wealth for a family that I never had time to be with. It took time for me to learn that all the wealth in the world can't replace the people who hold my heart. But now I get that.

God works in mysterious ways because... I used to wonder why I was put on the path that I was on. I was unhappy and angry, but then Genie happened. Through her, I learned what was important. I learned that family was everything. I learned the meaning of unconditional love. It took some time, but God made me ready for you. I went through the fire so that I could appreciate the diamond He wanted to give to me. God gave me you, and I'm forever grateful. Niggas say their vows, but they don't know what it really means to be with someone through sickness and health, wealth and poverty... Just know that when I say it, I'm saying it knowing what the other side of love looks like. I know I don't want that, Baby. I know I only want you."

Tears shined in Memphis's eyes, and Baby stared into them, letting him know that it was fine to be emotional. It was okay to let go because she would always be there to hold him up when he needed it.

People always talked about holding a nigga down, but Baby felt that couldn't be a more flawed way of thinking. A good woman holds her man up when he's at his worst, not down. When he's feeling low, he doesn't need company at the bottom. He needs a woman who can cloak him in her strength and pull him back up on his feet. She would be all that and more for Memphis every single day of her life.

NOTE FROM PORSCHA STERLING

Thank you for reading! Please join my mailing list to stay up-to-date on my next releases!

I took a different direction with my writing when it came to this story and I hope you enjoyed it. As an author, it's my duty to entertain but I like to take certain situations that I feel strongly about and challenge myself to see if I can push the envelope a little.

The question I entered this series with was "is it ever right to fall for a man who is forbidden to you?" My initial answer was NO but then I went to work thinking of instances where the lines are a little blurred. From there came this story about Memphis, Baby and Mona.

These characters lead you to question the meaning of friendship, the complications surrounding mothering as well as fathering children, forgiveness, redemption and many other things as well. I hope you loved it!

Please make sure to leave a review! I love reading them!

I would love it if you reach out to me on <u>Facebook</u>, <u>Instagram</u> or

<u>Twitter</u>! Search 'Porscha Sterling's VIP Readers' on Facebook to join my reading group!

Peace, love & blessings to everyone. I love allllll of you!

Porscha Sterling

 facebook.com/PorschaFans

twitter.com/QueenPorscha

instagram.com/queenporscha

KEEP IN TOUCH!

Join Porscha Sterling's Mailing List

To join and find out more about her, visit www.porschasterling.com

Books By Porscha Sterling

Unstoppable Love

3 Queens 1-2

3 Kings

The Wife of a Hustler 1-3

Us Against the Word 1-3

All I Want is a Thug 1-2

King of the Streets, Queen of His Heart 1-4

Didn't They Tell You That I Was a Savage 1-2

Bad Boys Do It Better 1-5

A Real Love

Collabs

Keisha & Trigga 1-4

Keisha & Trigga Reloaded 1-2

Gunplay & Letavia 1-2

JOIN OUR MAILING LIST!

Join our mailing list to get a notification when Leo Sullivan Presents has another release.

Text LEOSULLIVAN to 22828 to join!

To submit a manuscript for our review, email us at submissions@leolsullivan.com.

GET LIT WITH OUR LIT EBOOK READING APP

Download in the App Store or Google Play
Text **GETLIT** to **22828** to join our mailing list!

CPSIA information can be obtained
at www.ICGtesting.com
Printed in the USA
LVHW031424220919
631867LV00003B/469/P